"YOU ARE...WICKED!"

"I know. But you are not so virtuous yourself, are you, Carlotta?"

"Do you think my family will stand aside and allow me to be kidnapped in this way?"

"They are not going to find you, sweet Carlotta." He had taken me by the shoulders. "You are irresistible. You invite. You promise. You are meant for love...our sort of love."

"Love!" I cried. "You mean lust, do you not? I am at your mercy here, Hessenfield, but if I ever get out of this place, I shall not forget you."

"I hope not," he said. "I intend to make you remember me for the rest of your life."

Fawcett Crest Books
by Victoria Holt:

THE SPRING OF THE TIGER 24297 $2.75
MY ENEMY THE QUEEN 23979 $2.25
THE DEVIL ON HORSEBACK 23687 $2.25
THE PRIDE OF THE PEACOCK 24113 $2.25
LORD OF THE FAR ISLAND 22874 $2.25
THE CURSE OF THE KINGS 23284 $2.25
ON THE NIGHT OF THE
  SEVENTH MOON 23568 $1.95
THE SECRET WOMAN 23283 $2.25
THE SHIVERING SANDS 23282 $1.95
THE QUEEN'S CONFESSION 23213 $1.95
THE KING OF THE CASTLE 23587 $2.25
MENFREYA IN THE MORNING 23757 $1.95
THE LEGEND OF THE
  SEVENTH VIRGIN 23281 $2.25
KIRKLAND REVELS 23920 $2.25
MISTRESS OF MELLYN 23924 $2.25

This offer expires 1 October 81   8999

THE
SONG OF
THE SIREN

Philippa Carr

FAWCETT CREST • NEW YORK

THE SONG OF THE SIREN

THIS BOOK CONTAINS THE COMPLETE TEXT OF THE
ORIGINAL HARDCOVER EDITION

Published by Fawcett Crest Books, a unit of CBS Publica-
tions, the Consumer Publishing division of CBS Inc. by ar-
rangement with G.P. Putnam's Sons.

ISBN: 0-449-24371-0

Printed in the United States of America

First Fawcett Crest Printing: February 1981

10 9 8 7 6 5 4 3 2 1

CONTENTS

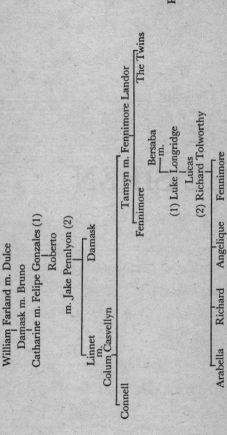

William Farland m. Dulce

Damask m. Bruno

Catharine m. Felipe Gonzales (1)

Roberto

m. Jake Pennlyon (2)

Linnet · Damask

Linnet
m.
Colum Casvellyn

Connell

Tamsyn m. Fennimore Landor

Fennimore · The Twins

Bersaba
m.
(1) Luke Longridge

Lucas

(2) Richard Tolworthy

Arabella · Richard · Angelique · Fennimore

m.
(1) Edwin Eversleigh

Edwin

(2) Carleton Eversleigh

Priscilla · Carl
m. Leigh Main

Carlotta (by Jocelyn Frinton) Damaris

Angelet
m.
Richard Tolworthy

Richard

THE
SONG OF
THE SIREN

CARLOTTA

A General Calls

Beau had come back. He was there, standing before me in all his elegance, his arrogance, his overwhelming charm. I had become alive again. I threw myself into his arms and I lifted up my face and looked at him.

I cried out "Beau! Beau! Why did you go away? Why did you leave me?"

And he answered: "All the time I have been here close . . . close. . . ." His voice went on echoing through the house saying: "Close . . . close. . . ."

Then I awoke to the realization that he was not with me. It was only a dream, and misery descended upon me, for I was alone again—even more desperately so because for a short while I had believed he had come back.

It was more than a year since he had gone away. We were to have been married. It had all been arranged. We were going to elope again—we had tried that once unsuccessfully—but this time we would plan more carefully. He had been hiding in the haunted house and I used to go there and visit him. My family had no idea of this; they thought they had separated us, but we were cleverer than they were. We had laid our plans carefully.

My family did not like Beau—particularly my mother, who became almost demented when his name was mentioned. I could see from the first that she was determined to prevent our marrying. At one time I thought that she was jealous of my love for Beau but I changed my mind later.

I had never felt I quite belonged to the Eversleighs, although Priscilla, my mother, had always made me feel I meant a great deal to her. I had always been deeply conscious of her possessiveness. She was quite unlike Harriet, who for so long I had believed to be my mother. Harriet was fond of me but not excessively so. She did not overwhelm me with her affection; and I was sure that if she knew that Beau and I had forestalled our marriage vows she would just have shrugged her shoulders and laughed, while Priscilla would have behaved as though it was a major disaster, although my very existence was evidence of her lack of conventionality in such matters.

It is known now that I am a bastard—the illegitimate daughter of Priscilla and Jocelyn Frinton, who was beheaded at the time of the Popish Plot. Of course he and my mother had intended to marry but he had been taken and executed before they could do so. Then dear Harriet had pretended to be my mother and she and Priscilla had gone to Venice, where I was born. On discovering this I had been rather pleased by my melodramatic entrance into the world. It was when my father's uncle left me his fortune that the story came out; everyone accepted it then and I came to live with my mother and her husband, Leigh, at Eversleigh, although I visited Harriet frequently.

Now Priscilla and Leigh had moved to the Dower House in the grounds of Eversleigh and lived there with my half sister, Damaris. Close by was Enderby Hall, where Beau and I used to meet. It had been left to me by my father's uncle Robert Frinton. Enderby was a house of memories. It was said to be haunted. It was for this reason, I suppose, that I had been fascinated by it ever since I was a child before it seemed possible that it could ever belong to me. Some terrible tragedy had taken place there and certainly there was an eerie atmosphere about the place. Beau liked it. He used to call out to the ghosts to come and see us. When we lay on the four-poster bed, he would draw back the curtains. "Let them join in our bliss, Carlotta," he said.

He was bold, so recklessly adventurous and he cared for no one. I was sure that if one of the ghosts appeared he would not feel a twinge of uneasiness. He would have laughed in the face of the devil himself if that awesome being had put in an appearance. He used to say he was one of the devil's own.

How I longed for him! I wanted to creep into that house and to feel his arms about me as he sprang out on me. I wanted to be lifted in those arms and carried up the stairs to the bedroom in which the ghosts had slept when they were on earth; I wanted to hear his lazy voice, so beautifully modulated, so musical, so characteristic of him—determined to get what was good out of life, no matter how—and equally determined to turn his back on what could bring him nothing.

"I'm not a saint, Carlotta," he told me, "so don't think you'll get one for your husband, dear child!"

I assured him that a saint was the last thing I wanted.

He agreed that I was wise in that. "There's a passionate woman in you, my little virgin-no-more, waiting to get out. I am giving her the key."

He had constantly reminded me that I had lost my virginity. It seemed to be a source of amusement to him. Sometimes I believed it was because he was afraid they might persuade me not to marry him. "You're committed now, my little bird," he said once. "You cannot fly away now. You belong to me."

Priscilla, when she was trying to persuade me to give him up, said that it was my fortune that he wanted. I was very rich—or I would be when I was eighteen or in the event of my marrying; and when I taxed him with this, he replied: "I'll be frank with you, my sweet child, your fortune will be useful. It will enable us to travel, to live well. You would like that, my dear heiress. We'll go to Venice, to your birthplace. I believe I was there at that auspicious time, which seems like fate, does it not? We were intended for each other, so don't let a paltry fortune come between us. We cannot with truth say we despise your fortune. Let us say we are glad of it. But do you doubt, my dearest love, after all that has happened between us that you mean more to me than a thousand such fortunes? We could live well together if you were but a little match girl, a seamstress. We are in tune, do you understand that? You were meant to love. There is such response in you. You are fiery; passion will be a part of your life; you are young yet, Carlotta. You have much to learn of yourself and the world; and fortune or not, I will be there to teach you."

I knew that he spoke the truth; that I was of a nature which matched his own. I knew that we were perfectly in harmony and that I was fortunate to have found him.

There was accord between us. I was only fifteen then and he was more than twenty years older—he would not tell me his age. He said: "I am as old as I can make the world believe I am. And you more than anyone must accept that."

So we met in the haunted house. It amused him that we should do so and it seemed a good place because so few people went there. Priscilla sent servants over once a week. They would not go singly because there was not one of them who would have entered the house alone. I knew when they would be going and could warn Beau to leave. He stayed there for three weeks; and then one day he was gone.

Why? Where? Why should he suddenly disappear? I could not understand it. At first I thought that he had been called away and there had been no means of letting me know. But when the time went on I began to be frightened.

I did not know what to do. I could not tell people that he had disappeared from the house. I could not understand it. For the first few days I was not unduly worried; but when the days went by as weeks and then the months, terror seized me and I feared some terrible doom had overtaken him.

I would go over to Enderby and stand there in the hall and listen to the silence of the house. I would whisper his name and wait for some response.

It never came. Only in dreams.

There is certain comfort in writing down my feelings. By doing so I may come to a better understanding of what has happened and of myself too.

I shall soon be seventeen. I shall go to London and there will be entertainments there and at Eversleigh, for my grandparents as well as Priscilla and Leigh will want to provide me with a husband. I shall have suitors by the score. My fortune will take care of that; but as Harriet says I have what she calls that special quality which attracts the opposite sex like bees round the honey. She should know, for she has had it all her life. "The trouble is," she once said, "that the wasps come too—and all other kinds of noisome insects. What we have can be the greatest asset a woman can have, but, like most such gifts, wrongly handled it can work against us." Harriet has never denied herself the intimate society of men and I feel sure that she would have behaved exactly as I did with Beau. She had had her first lover when she was fourteen; it had not been a passionate love affair but it had provided both her and her lover with advantages, and she added when she told me: "Made us both very happy while it lasted, which is what life is meant to do."

I think I feel closer to Harriet than to anyone—except Beau. After all I had believed Harriet to be my mother for a long time. Harriet was a perfect mother. She never smothered me with affection; she never wanted to know where I had been, how I was getting on with my lessons; she was never anxious about me. I found Priscilla's obvious anxiety exasperating. I did not want my conscience disturbed by the fears of Priscilla for my welfare—particularly after I met Beau. Harriet was a comforting presence, though. I felt that she would help me if I were in difficulties and she would understand my feelings for Beau as my real mother never could.

I was always welcome at Eyot Abbass, and Benjie was there a good deal. I was rather fond of Benjie. He was Harriet's son, and for a long time I had believed him to be my brother. I knew he was very fond of me. He was so delighted to discover that I was not his sister, and that seemed to indicate something which I might have found interesting if I had not been so completely absorbed by Beau.

Benjie is a good deal older than I—it must be about twelve years—but I know how he feels about me. I became aware of it when Beau became my lover. In fact, I became aware of a good deal then. "You grew up overnight, as they say," commented Beau, "which means, my dear innocent, that you have ceased to be a child and have become a woman." Beau laughed at everything; there was so much that he despised; I think he despised innocence so much that he wanted to destroy it. He was quite different from everyone I had ever known. There would never be anyone else to take his place. He must come back. There must be some explanation. Sometimes when I smelt somewhere the faint musk-like smell—a mixture of scent and sandalwood—it would bring back poignant memories of him. His linen had always been scented with it; he was very fastidious; once when we were at the house he made me undress and he filled a bath with water which he scented with a scent of rose and made me bathe in it; and then he anointed me with the rose-scented lotion, which he said he had made himself; and he was very amused when we made love as though it was some ritual and there was some significance in it.

Harriet talked of him now and then. She did not know of course that he had been at the house. "He's gone away," she said. "Forget him, Carlotta."

I said: "He'll come back."

She said nothing but her beautiful eyes were unusually sad.

"Why should he go away?" I demanded.

"Because he decided that it was useless to wait. There was too much opposition."

"There was no opposition from me."

"How can we know what took him?" she said. "But the fact remains that he has gone."

I knew what she was thinking. He had gone abroad. In London, where he was well known in Court circles, it was being said that that was what he had done. When Harriet went to London she had heard that he had disappeared leaving enormous debts. She hinted that he had gone off in pursuit of another heiress. I could not tell even her that we had been meeting at Enderby, that we were making plans to elope.

It was strange how at times I felt so much aware of

him. I often went to Enderby and sometimes I would shut myself in the bedroom and lie on the four-poster bed and dream it was all happening again.

I felt an irresistible urge to go there whenever I dreamed of him. That was how I felt after the dream and on the afternoon of the day which followed that night when he had seemed so real to me I rode over to Enderby. It was not very far, ten minutes' ride at the most. When I used to go to meet Beau I walked over because I didn't want anyone to see my horse and know that I was there.

On this day I tethered my horse to the post by the mounting block and taking out the key opened the door. I stood in the hall. It was a lovely old place, the vaulted roof was quite magnificent and the panelling on the walls was beautiful; at one end of the hall were the screens, beyond which were the kitchens, and at the other end was the minstrels' gallery. It was supposed to be the haunted part because one of the owners whose husband had been involved in the Rye House Plot had tried to hang herself over that gallery; the rope was too long and she injured herself and lived in lingering agony afterwards. At least that was the story I heard. I remember one occasion when I entered. Beau appeared there dressed up in a female costume he had found in the house. He liked to frighten me.

Now as I came in, my eyes immediately went to the gallery. They always did, and I thought, as I had a thousand times, how happy I would be if I could have seen him, if I could have had some indication that he was somewhere, that he would come back for me.

But there was nothing. Just silence and gloom, and that terrible oppressive atmosphere, that sense of brooding evil. I went across the hall, my footsteps ringing out on the stone pavings of the floor, and up the stairs, past the empty gallery.

I opened the door of the bedroom which we had made ours. The bed looked impressive with its velvet hangings. I began to think of the people who had died in that bed; then suddenly I flung myself down on it and buried my face in the velvet bolster.

17

"Oh, Beau. Beau, where are you?" I cried. "Why did you leave me? Where did you go?"

I started. I sat up in bed. It was as though I had been answered. I knew I was not alone. Someone was in the house. It was a movement. A footstep? Was it a footstep? I knew the sounds of this house, the creak of the old wood, the protesting groan of a floorboard. I used to be afraid when I lay on this bed with Beau that we would be discovered. How he had laughed at me. I think he rather hoped we would be. Once he said: "I should love to see Prim Priscilla's face when she saw me in bed with her daughter." Yes, I did know the sounds of the house and I now had a firm conviction that I was not alone in it.

A wild elation possessed me. My first thought was: He has come back.

"Beau!" I called. "Beau! I'm here, Beau."

The door opened. My heart leapt and I felt that it would suffocate me.

Then I felt furiously angry. It was my half sister, Damaris, who had come into the room.

"Damaris!" I stammered. "What ... what are you doing here?"

My disappointment sickened me and for the moment I hated my sister. She stood there, her lips slightly parted, her eyes round with astonishment; she was not a pretty child; she was quiet, obedient, and had a desire to please, which our mother said was "engaging." I had always found her rather dull; I ignored her in the main, but now I positively hated her. She looked so neat and clean in her pale blue gown with its sash of a slightly lighter hue and her long brown hair hanging down in loose curls. There was a certain amount of curiosity in her expression which was rapidly replacing the concern.

"I thought someone was with you, Carlotta," she said. "You were talking to someone, were you not?"

"I called out to know who was there. You startled me." I frowned at her accusingly.

Her mouth was a round O. She had no subtlety. Perhaps one should not expect it of a child of ten. What had I said? I believed I had called out Beau's name.

Had she noticed it? I felt certain she had never heard of Beau.

"I thought you said something like Bow," she said.

"You were mistaken," I told her quickly. "I said: 'Who's there?'"

"But..."

"You imagined the rest," I went on sharply. I had risen from the bed and gripped her none too gently by the shoulder so that she winced a little. I was glad. I wanted to hurt her. "You have no right to come here," I said. "This is my house and I came to see that it was all right."

"Were you testing the bed?"

I looked at her intently. No, there was no ulterior motive in the remark. No suggestions. No probing. One thing about my little sister, she was completely innocent. She was only ten years old in any case.

I pondered. Should I try to give her some explanation? No, it was best to leave things as they were.

We went out of the house together.

"How did you get here?" I asked.

"I walked."

I mounted my horse. "Then you can walk back," I said.

It was two days later and a Saturday. I was in the garden of the Dower House when a man appeared on horseback. He dismounted and bowed to me.

"Am I mistaken or is this the Dower House Eversleigh and does Captain Leigh Main live here?"

"You are right. He is not here at the moment but will be back very soon, I believe. Do come in. I'll show you where you can tether your horse."

"Thank you. You must be his daughter."

"His stepdaughter."

"I'm Gervaise Langdon. We were in the army together."

"General Langdon!" I cried. "I have heard him mention your name. General Sir Gervaise Langdon. Is that right?"

"I see you are well informed."

I took him to the post by the mounting block and as

19

I was directing him towards the house my mother appeared.

"This is General Sir Gervaise Langdon, mother," I said.

Priscilla cried: "Oh, please come in. My husband should be here very soon."

"I was passing through the district," explained Sir Gervaise, "and I remembered my old friend lived here so I thought I would pay him a visit."

"He will be delighted. He has talked of you a great deal, hasn't he, Carlotta? This is my daughter Carlotta."

Sir Gervaise bowed again to me. "It is a great pleasure," he said.

My mother led the way into the hall.

"I was about to call at the big house," said Sir Gervaise, "and one of the grooms there told me that you were now at the Dower House."

"Oh, yes," said my mother. "My parents are at the Court."

"Lord Eversleigh too, I believe. Where is Edwin now?"

"He's abroad on service," said my mother.

"Ah, yes. I had hoped to see him too."

"You know my husband has retired from the army, of course."

"Yes, indeed I do. Eversleigh stays on."

"Yes, but I think his wife would like him to do what Leigh has done."

"A pity," said the General. "We need men like them."

"I always think that their families need them too."

"Ah, the wives' complaint!" said the General with a smile.

Priscilla took him into the drawing room and sent for wine and cakes.

Damaris appeared and was introduced.

"You have two charming daughters," said the General.

He talked to us about his travels abroad and how delighted he was to be in England, and while this was going on Leigh arrived. He was delighted to see the General and after a while my mother said she was sure

20

they had a great deal to say to each other and she hoped the General was in no hurry and would stay awhile.

He replied that he was going to visit his old friend Ned Netherby and planned to stay the night at an inn about four miles on and then go to Netherby the following day.

"But you cannot do that," cried my mother. "You must stay here for the night. We wouldn't hear of your going to stay at an inn, would we Leigh?"

Leigh said that the General must stay and the latter needed little persuasion.

"Then that is settled," said my mother. "You will excuse me and I will see that they get your room ready. Carlotta, Damaris, come along and help."

We went out with her.

"I could see that the General wished to talk to your father," she said. "They will have memories to share. I know they served together at one time."

I went to my room and Damaris went to help my mother. I was mildly excited as I always was by visitors; and there was something about the General which made me feel that this was not an idle call. There was something purposeful about him. He was an attractive man. He must have been about six feet tall and a little older than Leigh, I imagine. He had a very military bearing and there was no doubt that he was a soldier. There was a scar on his right cheek to confirm this. It added to rather than detracted from his rugged good looks.

I had an idea that he might have come to persuade Leigh to come back to the army. A thought I was sure could not have occurred to my mother or her welcome would not have been so warm.

At dinner there was a great deal of talk about the old army days and Leigh quite clearly enjoyed these reminiscences.

The General talked about the King, whom he clearly did not like. "The Dutchman," he called him and used the term as one of contempt; and when he mentioned his name his colour deepened and the scar showed up whiter in contrast to the reddish tinge of his skin.

We left them talking together over their wine and my mother said to me: "He is a charming man but I hope he is not reminding Leigh too much of his life in the army. He talks about it as though it is some sort of paradise."

"My father would never want to leave you again, mother," said Damaris.

My mother smiled. Then she said: "I wonder why the General came?"

"It is because he was passing on his way to Netherby Hall," said Damaris. "He said so."

I smiled at my dear innocent sister. She believed everything everyone said.

The next day was Sunday and we were going to Eversleigh to dine, as we always did on Sundays. Although Leigh and my mother had bought the Dower House, they both regarded Eversleigh as their home. I had lived part of my life there and my mother all her life until recently. Damaris had been born there and it was only within the last year or so that Leigh had bought the Dower House. There was a walk of five minutes between the two houses and my grandparents became indignant if we did not call frequently. I loved Eversleigh, although perhaps Harriet's Eyot Abbass was more like home to me.

It was dinnertime and we were all at table in the great hall. My grandmother Arabella Eversleigh loved to have us all together. Damaris was a special favourite of hers, in a way that I could never be; but my grandfather Carleton had always had a special feeling for me. He was a most unconventional man, of fiery temper, arrogant and obstinate. I felt especially drawn towards him and I believe he did to me. I think he was rather amused by the fact that I was his daughter's bastard and there was a grudging admiration in him because my mother had defied conventions and produced me. I liked Grandfather Carleton. I fancied our characters were not dissimilar.

The house had been built in the days of Elizabeth in the E style with a wing on either side of the main great hall. I was attracted by that hall with its rough stone walls and I liked the armoury which adorned it. There was a military tradition in the Eversleigh family. Carleton had only briefly been a soldier; he had stayed home after the Civil War to hold the estates until the Restoration; the part he had played, I had always heard had demanded far more courage than a soldier needed and infinitely more skill; for he had posed as a Roundhead when his sympathies were Royalist in the extreme and so saved Eversleigh for posterity. I could well imagine his doing that. Every time he looked up at the vaulted ceiling with its broad oak beams, every time he glanced at the family tree which had been painted over the great fireplace, he must have reminded himself: If it had not been for my courage and resource during those Commonwealth years all this would have been lost.

Yes, the military history of the family was apparent everywhere. Leigh had been a soldier until recently; my grandmother Arabella's son by her first marriage was Edwin, the present Lord Eversleigh, and he was away from home now in the army. Jane—a rather colourless female—and their son, Carleton—called Carl to distinguish him from Carleton—lived at Eversleigh, which was indeed Edwin's, although my grandfather regarded it as his, which was not surprising since he managed the estate for years and had saved it for them in any case. There would not have been an Eversleigh Court but for him. My grandmother's father had been General Tolworthy who had distinguished himself in the Royalist cause. I remember that Beau had been in the army for a while. It was during the Monmouth Rebellion, he told me once and had seemed secretly amused by this. Even Carleton himself had been in the army then—on the side of Monmouth. Not that he had been a professional soldier. He had just been fighting for a special cause then.

So we were sure that our guest General Langdon would feel at home in such a household.

At the table on this day were my grandparents, Carleton and Arabella, Edwin's wife, Lady Eversleigh, and young Carl; Priscilla, Leigh, myself and Damaris. Also present were our neighbors of Grasslands Manor, Thomas Willerby and his son, Thomas Junior, who was about a year or two younger than I. Thomas Willerby was a widower whose wife had died recently. He was very sad about this, for it had been an exceptionally happy marriage. My mother felt the death of Christabel Willerby deeply, for Christabel had been a governess companion to her before her marriage and remained a good friend. There was another Willerby child at Grasslands—a baby girl. She was probably a year old and had been named Christabel after the mother, who had died bringing her into the world. My mother had made the tragedy hers, and the Willerbys were constant visitors at our house. She had insisted that Christabel come to our nursery for a while until arrangements could be made; and Sally Nullens, our old nurse, and Emily Philpots, who acted as governess to the children for years, were delighted with the arrangements. As for Thomas Willerby, he was so overcome with gratitude towards my mother that his eyes filled with tears almost every time he looked at her. He was a very sentimental man.

Both my grandparents welcomed General Langdon warmly and the conversation at the dinner table for the first fifteen minutes was all about the army.

Then Priscilla said rather pointedly, so I knew that she was giving voice to something which had been occupying her mind for some time: "It seems to me that Enderby Hall should not be left standing idle. It never did a house any good to remain empty."

"True," said Thomas, always ready to back her up. "They get damp. Houses need fires and people. They need living in."

"Such a lovely old house," said Jane Eversleigh. "Though I don't think I should like to live in it. I get the shivers every time I pass by."

"Only because you listen to gossip," said my grandfather. "If this talk of ghosts hadn't got around, no one would think of ghosts."

"Are you interested in ghosts, General Langdon?" I asked.

"I have never seen one," he said, "and I am inclined to need the evidence of my eyes."

"Oh, you have no faith," said Arabella.

"Seeing is believing," said the General. "How did the gossip start?"

"I think it began when one of the occupiers tried to

hang herself. She did not have a long enough rope and was badly injured. She died soon after."

"Poor woman, what made her do such a thing?"

"Her husband was involved in a plot."

"The Popish Plot," said Carl.

"No," I said, "that was my father. This was the Rye House Plot, wasn't it?"

"Yes," said Priscilla, rather uneasily I thought.

"They plotted against the King," said Carleton. "It was a foolish and criminal thing to do."

"I cannot understand why people have to do these things," said Priscilla.

"My dear lady," said the General, "if they feel something is wrong some men have the urge to put it right."

"And endanger lives," said Arabella fiercely.

"Oh, it is all past and done with," said Carleton. "But that is just how the house got its reputation."

"I should like to see a nice family settled in," said my mother. "It is pleasant to have good neighbors."

She was nervous and Leigh was watching her anxiously. I thought: They have talked about this together. I was sure then that my sister had reported finding me lying on the four-poster; she might even have mentioned that she thought I was talking to someone called Bow.

"It does happen to be my house," I said. I turned to the General. "It was left to me by my father's uncle. He was Robert Frinton."

The General said: "I knew the family. A great tragedy."

My mother was clenching her hands uneasily. She was very nervous today. It was the General who was making her so.

"There are a few months to go before you can claim possession," said my grandfather. "But I don't doubt that if a sale was arranged it would be approved."

"I am not sure that I want it sold."

"Perhaps you like ghosts, Mistress Carlotta," said the General.

"I should be interested to see one. Shouldn't you, General?"

"I think it would depend on the ghost," he replied.

25

Leigh said: "You *should* sell it, Carlotta. You'll never want to live there. But perhaps you could find a tenant and let it."

I was silent, very much aware of them all. They were tense. I wondered whether the General noticed. For some reason they wanted me to be prevented from going there, wandering through those empty rooms; Damaris must indeed have reported what she had seen and heard, and they would know I was still hoping to find Beau again.

"Think about it," said my grandfather.

"Do you know, I've been pondering in my mind whether or not I won't give up Grasslands," said Thomas Willerby.

"Give up Grasslands, Thomas!" cried my mother. "But *why?*"

"So many memories," he said, and there was silence at the table.

After a pause Thomas went on, "Yes, I've been thinking it might be easier to go back north. Try to build a new life. That was what I came here for and thanks to you all . . . and Christabel . . . I had a good one. Perhaps it would be best for me to move on now. . . ."

My mother looked sad, but I could see she was working out a future for him. Let him go and find a new wife . . . a new life and perhaps come back then.

"Oh, it's all in the future," said Thomas. "There's a lot to be thought about yet. But I do believe something should be done about Enderby."

To stop them talking of Enderby I said that I heard the Lady Elizabeth Villiers was to have the Irish estates of James the Second bestowed on her.

The General's face went deep red and he murmured, "Monstrous."

"Let the King please his mistress," said Carleton. "I'm surprised he has one. I wish him joy of the lady."

"It is a pity," said Arabella, "that things turned out as they have. Daughters against their father . . ."

"True, my lady," said the General. "I think Queen Mary must have been deeply troubled by her conscience. As indeed Anne will be if she takes the crown."

"Not a bit of it," cried Carleton. "England will not

tolerate a Papist King. They got rid of one Papist. James is where he belongs—in exile. That's where he'll stay till he dies. And if William should go . . . God forbid that he should, for he's been a good ruler of this country . . . then it will be Anne to follow him and she'll have the support of all those who wish this country well."

I could see that the General was striving hard to control himself. Leigh looked uncomfortable. He knew something of the General's thoughts in these matters and it was typical of my grandfather to state his views and not consider whether he was offending anyone.

"Usurpation of a throne," said the General in a quiet controlled voice, "often brings sorrow to those who take it."

"It was hardly that. James was useless. His daughter Mary was next and William was in the line of succession too. I was against him as soon as we heard of his Papist views and I would have put Monmouth on the throne rather than let that Papist rule over us. James was defeated and he's in exile. Let him stay there."

"You are vehement, sir," said the General.

"Are you not, sir?" said Carleton. "I tell you this. I feel strongly about these matters."

"That much is obvious," said the General.

Arabella changed the conversation tactfully and we talked of trivial matters such as whether we should have a bad winter, and even that recalled the time when the Thames was frozen and reminded poor Thomas of his meeting with Christabel.

I was rather glad when we went back to the Dower House. The General was silent and I fancied he had not greatly enjoyed his visit to my grandparents.

He and Leigh were alone together that evening and early the next morning the General took his leave of us and left.

My thoughts were occupied by Enderby. I wondered how I should feel if I could no longer go there. New people there would change the place. It would be a different house. Did I want to keep a monument to the lover who had deserted me? Would I be happier if I could no longer go to the house and brood?

It was strange but something had happened to me.

An anger had come to me; it soothed my misery a little because it hurt my pride. Could it really be true that he had deliberately gone away, that he had found a richer heiress? That was what they had said. He had borrowed money on the prospects of marriage with me; he was mercenary; he had gone in pursuit of richer game. Someone abroad... in Paris... in Venice perhaps. He had always talked a great deal about Venice. He had never pretended that he possessed the honour of a gentleman; he had constantly stressed the fact that he was no saint. "I have a lot of the devil in me, Carlotta," he had once said. And he made me search in his head to see if horns were sprouting there. "But then that's what you like," he said. "Because, let me tell you, Carlotta, there's a bit of the devil in you."

What a fool I was to dream that he would come back. It was more than a year now since he had gone. I pictured him living in some strange city—a castle on the Rhine, a palazzo in Italy, a château in France—with an heiress who was richer than I was. And he would laughingly talk about me, for Beau would talk about his mistresses. He jeered at that code of honour which gentlemen were supposed to respect.

I nursed my anger against him and found it was a kind of balm.

Yes, I thought, why should not Enderby be sold or let? What was the point of keeping a shrine to a false lover?

September had come. In a month's time I should reach my eighteenth birthday and that would be a very important occasion in my life, for on that day I should receive my inheritance. I would have come of age.

There must be a special celebration, Priscilla declared, and of course my grandparents insisted that it should be held at Eversleigh, which was so much more suitable than the Dower House.

Eversleigh was full of visitors and I knew that Leigh and Priscilla had invited some eligible young men in the hope that I should display some interest in them.

Harriet came with her husband, Gregory, and Benjie. I was happy to see them again. "We don't see enough
28

of each other," was Harriet's comment. She always amazed me. She was no longer young but she still retained that marvellous beauty. It was true that she took great pains to preserve it. Her hair was still dark ("my special concoction," she whispered to me, when I commented on it. "I will give you the recipe so that you will be prepared when you need it").

They were to stay for a week. "Why don't you come to Eyot more often?" asked Benjie.

I had nothing to answer to that. I couldn't tell Benjie that I was still hoping Beau would come back.

We rode a great deal together; I found I was enjoying those rides. I loved the cool damp September air; I began to notice the countryside as I never had before; I loved the tawny leaves of the beeches and the cones which were beginning to appear on the pines. Everywhere were the spiders' webs—a feature of autumn—and I thought they looked enchanting with the dewdrops sparkling on them. It had always been unlike me to notice nature. I began to feel as though I was awakening from a long nightmare.

Benjie was an exhilarating companion; he had always been ready to laugh, easy going, good natured, more like his father than his mother. Sir Gregory Stevens might not be the most exciting person I had ever met but he was certainly one of the kindest.

Benjie was twelve years or so older than I but that did not seem a great difference to me. I compared everything and everyone with Beau, who had been more than twenty years older. Oddly enough I felt as old as Benjie in experience of life. Beau had done that for me.

One day when we had been riding in the woods we came home past Enderby Hall.

"Dreary old place," said Benjie. "I remember once you followed your uncle Carl and me there."

"I remember well," I said. "You were horrible boys. You would have none of me. You told me to go away and not pester you."

"Put it down to our ignorant youth," said Benjie. "I promise I'll never say that to you again, Carlotta."

"I must have been an impossible child."

"No . . . just certain that Carlotta was the centre of the universe and all must bend the knee to her."

"Except Benjamin and Uncle Carl."

"Idiots we were."

"But it was all for the best. I followed you there, went to sleep in a cupboard and that was how we all got to know Robert Frinton, who turned out to be my father's uncle. . . ."

"Fell victim to your charms and left you his fortune. It's like a story in a ballad and just the kind of thing that would happen to you."

"I don't think there's much of the fairytale heroine about me, Benjie. Didn't you say yourself that I thought I was the centre of the universe. I imagine I haven't changed much and that means I am an extremely selfish creature."

"You're an adorable one, Carlotta."

He was looking at me with a certain intensity, and under Beau's tuition I had learned what that meant.

I said on impulse: "Let's go and look at the house."

"Isn't it locked up?"

"I have the key. I always carry it on my belt. Just in case I take the fancy to go in."

He looked at me oddly. He knew about Beau—the whole family did. But I did not think they knew he had stayed at Enderby.

We tethered our horses and walked towards the front porch. Being with Benjie was arousing certain emotions in me. I didn't understand myself. I had a sudden fancy to know what it would be like to make love with Benjie. Perhaps I was as Beau had suggested, the sort of woman to whom physical passion is a necessity. Beau had said he had never met such a ready virgin; meaning of course that I had not shrunk from him even in the first encounter. Like a flower opening to the sun, he had said. I remembered in the days before I had met Beau I liked to be with Benjie, and the knowledge that he felt something special for me had filled me with a gratified delight.

I opened the door. I had a feeling then that it might be possible to dispel the image of Beau for ever.

"It is an eerie place," said Benjie. "Don't you think so?"

"That's all in the mind," I retorted.

"Yes. I suppose you're right. It doesn't look eerie now with you standing there. Carlotta, you are beautiful. I only ever saw one other woman as beautiful as you and that was my mother. I was very proud of you when I believed you were my sister."

"Your pride did not extend to letting me accompany you on your jaunt to Enderby."

"I've told you you must put that down to boyish stupidity."

He was looking at me earnestly and I knew that in a moment he was going to kiss me. I started to cross the hall, looking up at the minstrels' gallery to remind me. The old ache was still there. There would never be anyone like Beau. I started to walk up the staircase, Benjie following close . . . past the haunted gallery. I was thinking, Why should I continue to brood on you, Beau. You went away and left me.

We looked into the rooms and we came to the one with the four-poster bed.

I stood looking at it and the bitterness and longing seemed strong as ever. Benjie was beside me. He said: "Carlotta, you're no longer a child. I've been wanting to speak to you for a long time, but you seemed so young. . . ."

That made me want to laugh. How much younger I was when I had frolicked on that bed with Beau! How . . . unadventurous! How different from Beau.

"Carlotta, I think they are expecting it."

"Expecting what?"

"Us to marry."

"Are you asking me?"

"I am. What do you say?"

I seemed to see Beau laughing at me. "It is what they expect. Your laggard lover has waited until you are of a ripe age. That makes us laugh, does it not, Carlotta? Bless you, my dear, you were ripe from the cradle. Such as you are. Marry your quiet Benjie. You will have a secure life, a safe one, and I promise you an incredibly dull one."

31

I knew I had not escaped from Beau. If I said yes now to Benjie I would feel no elation, no exhilarating anticipation such as I had felt when I entered this house to meet Beau.

"No," I said to Benjie. "No." And something made me add: "Not yet."

Benjie was all understanding. "I have hurried you," he said.

Hurried me! I thought. I have known your feelings for a long time. He had no notion of the sort of person I was. I imagined Beau in similar circumstances. If I had refused him he would have laughed at me. He would have forced me onto that bed.

Did I want that sort of lover?

Again I seemed to hear Beau's laughter. Yes, you do. You do.

He would think it a great joke that here in this very room where, as Beau would have said, we had sported so merrily, Benjie should ask me to marry him and when I said no imagine that he had hurried me, and suggested marriage when I in my innocence was not prepared for it.

No, I had not escaped from Beau.

We went out to our horses.

"Don't be disturbed, dearest Carlotta," said Benjie. "I am going to ask you later."

Harriet came to my room. She was sparkling with good health and I was sure that she was no less beautiful than she had been ten years before. She was plumper perhaps but not in an unsightly way; in fact the extra flesh did not detract from her beauty. She saw to it, she said, that it appeared in the right places.

I think she knew that Benjie had asked me to marry him. Some of the servants believed she had special powers and I was inclined to agree with them. Those incredibly beautiful violet eyes with the heavy black lashes were unusually discerning and there was little they missed.

"So, my little seductress," she said, "you have failed to make my Benjie a happy man. He asked you today, didn't he?"

I nodded.

"And you said no. My deduction is that you added the rider 'not yet,' for he is not so dejected as I would expect him to be if he had received a blank refusal."

"Harriet, you are right as usual."

I was laughing with her. She always lightened my spirits. I suppose I loved Harriet more than anyone except Beau. It was due to the fact that during the formative years of my childhood I believed her to be my mother. No, it was more than that. She was what I thought of as one of us—that meant that she was like Beau and myself.

We were the adventurers of this world, determined to have what we wanted and, if circumstances warranted it, were none too scrupulous as to how we got it.

It suddenly occurred to me that we had all been sent into the world with outstanding beauty. Beau and Harriet had that and it would have been false modesty on my part not to agree that I had it in some measure. By some strange quirk of nature I might have been Harriet's daughter. I was dark though not quite as dark as she was; I had blue eyes and they were deep blue rather than violet; but I did have similar black lashes and brows. There the resemblance ended, it was true. My oval face and high cheekbones, full lips and straight nose were pure Eversleigh. My nature resembled Harriet's and perhaps that, as much as our looks, made us seem alike.

However, we were in harmony and I could talk to Harriet more easily than to anyone else. My mother must have felt the same because it was to Harriet she had gone when she knew she was going to have me and was afraid to face her family.

"My poor Benjamin," she said. "He has long loved you. From the moment he learned that you were not his sister the idea began to form in his mind. He has lived for the day when he will take you to the altar. And I must say that I should very warmly welcome my new daughter."

"Dear Harriet, it is an alluring prospect to have you as my mother-in-law, but even so it is not a strong

33

enough reason for marriage."

"It would be good for you, Carlotta. Benjie will be good for you. He's like his father, and a woman could not have a better husband than my Gregory." She looked at me seriously: "You would have been very unhappy with Beaumont Granville," she added.

I turned away and she went on: "Yes, you would. Oh, I admit he is a fascinating creature. I can picture him now living in splendour, congratulating himself on his cleverness. He cannot return to England. His creditors would descend on him like vultures. I wonder where he is. I don't think it is Venice. I have written several times to a very dear friend of mine, the Contessa Carpori who owns the palazzo where you were born. She knew Beau. He was quite a well known figure in Venice. She says he is not there. If she hears of his turning up in any other Italian city she will let me know. Stop thinking of him. Get him out of your thoughts. It was fun while it lasted, was it not? Can you look on it as experience."

"It was such a wonderful experience, Harriet."

"Of course it would be. He would be a superb lover. But there are others in the world. It was your fortune he wanted, Carlotta."

"Then why did he not stay to take it?"

"It could only be because some more attractive proposition presented itself. That is the only thing I can think of. He owed money all round. He could not stay and face his creditors. It might be that your grandfather threatened him. Carleton Eversleigh has great influence at Court. He could ruin Beau if he set out to. But I don't think Beau is the type to give way lightly. You should face the facts, Carlotta, even when they're not very pleasant. The only solution seems that he scented a better proposition somewhere else and went off to pursue it."

"Harriet, it is nearly three years."

"And you have come of age. Forget him. Strike out anew. You have everything a girl could ask for. Beauty of the kind which will make you irresistible to almost any man; you have wealth; my dear child, what would

I have done for your fortune when I was your age!"

"You managed very well without it."

"I had to face years of struggle. I enjoyed it, yes. It's the adventure in my bones, but sometimes I had to do certain things which I had rather not. Carlotta, turn away from the past. Look ahead. The future's bright. Don't take Benjie if you don't want to. But I hope you will for many reasons...."

"The fortune being one."

"The fortune being one. But let me tell you that doesn't count with Benjie. He's a good boy, my Benjamin. He takes after his father, and believe me if it's a husband and not a demon lover you are looking for, you couldn't find a better man."

Harriet kissed me and showed me what she was going to wear to the banquet which was to celebrate my coming of age.

She had had an effect on me as she always did. Eversleigh Court was full and there were guests in the Dower House too. It was a solemn as well as a festive occasion. My coming of age. I had to listen to Sally Nullens telling me that I was the naughtiest of all her children and I had the best pair of lungs she had ever encountered which I used to get what I wanted. "There's some who would have given it to you," she commented. "But that was not my way. I could give a sharp smack where it hurt most and that's what you got from me and didn't bear a grudge for it—I will give you that." And there was Emily Philpots: "I'll say this for you, you might have got your pretty clothes in a mess but you did look lovely in them and it was a pleasure to sew for you. You haven't changed, Mistress Carlotta. I pity the man who gets you, yes I do." I might have said that as no man had ever tried to get Emily she might not be the best authority on the subject, but I loved them both in my way. They had been part of my childhood.

Damaris followed me around with a look of awe-struck wonder on her face. She was eleven now—rather gauche and too fat; her adoration irritated me. I was not very kind to Damaris, I'm afraid. She was always nursing sick animals and unhappy because some of them had died. She loved her horse and was quite an expert horsewoman. She was the pet of Sally Nullens and Emily Philpots. I gathered she had had the right sort of lungs and had rarely been beaten where it hurt most; and I was sure that she kept her clothes tidy and I felt a mean gratification that she hadn't looked as beautiful in them as I had in mine.

My mother, Leigh and even my grandparents were all hoping I would marry Benjie. It seemed they all knew that he wanted me to. There was a certain watchfulness about everyone. Almost as though they wanted to see me settled so that they could write "Finish" to the episode between Beau and me. I think they had the facile thought that once I was married it could be as though I had never known Beau.

I was desperately unsure, but I wanted to find out whether they were right and I suppose that was a step forward.

So I rode with Benjie; I danced with Benjie. I liked Benjie. I felt a mild excitement when he held my hand or touched my arm or now and then kissed me.

It was not that wild leaping of the senses I had felt with Beau but there was some response in me.

I imagined Beau laughing at me.

"You are a passionate young lady," he had said.

Was I? Was it just the need for physical satisfaction which Beau had led me to appreciate that I wanted now, or was it Benjie?

I was unsure. But I had made one decision. I was going to sell Enderby Hall. Perhaps that was symbolic, an acceptance of the fact that Beau would never come back now.

Mistress Elizabeth Pilkington had come to look at Enderby Hall. She had arrived the day before and was staying with friends a few miles from Eversleigh. She said she would ride over to look at the house if someone would meet her there.

Priscilla had thought Leigh should go but I had refused to allow that. They had to forget I was a child. I was a woman of means now and in any case Enderby Hall belonged to me. I wanted to show them my independence, so I would meet the lady and show her the house myself.

It was November and ten o'clock in the morning. I had suggested that time as it grew dark soon after four o'clock and if Mistress Pilkington came in the afternoon there would be little time for viewing. She agreed. She wanted to see the house in daylight of course.

I was conscious of a certain feeling of relief. I had at last come to the conclusion that once I no longer owned Enderby I should really be able to start afresh.

There was a chill in the air. I had never liked November. The winter lay before us and it seemed a long time to the spring. The trees had now lost most of their leaves and I fancied there was a melancholy note in the snatch of song I heard from a blackbird. He sounded as though he were trying to throw off his melancholy and couldn't succeed.

There was a little mist hanging about the trees. It glistened on the yews and there seemed more spiders' webs than ever. The end of the year was close; the end of a phase of my life perhaps.

She was waiting for me. I was rather surprised by her appearance. She was extremely elegant and had the most attractive reddish hair. Her riding habit was in the very latest fashion and most becoming. It was dark green in colour and she wore a hat with a little brown feather in it which matched that strikingly beautiful hair.

"Mistress Pilkington," I said. "I am afraid I have kept you waiting."

"Indeed not." She smiled, showing a beautiful set of teeth. "I arrived early. I was so eager to see the house."

"I hope you are going to like it. Shall we go inside?"

"Please."

I opened the door and we stepped into the hall. It looked different already. Much of the eeriness seemed to have disappeared. She looked up at the roof.

"It's impressive," she said. Then she turned and studied me carefully. "I know you are Mistress Carlotta Main. I did not expect I should have the pleasure of meeting *you*. I thought someone. . . ."

"Someone older," I finished for her. "No. This is my

37

house and I prefer to deal with business matters myself."

"Hurrah for you," she said. "I am like that too. The house was part of your inheritance."

"You seem to know a good deal about me."

"I move in London society. I remember the time when there was a great deal of talk about your betrothal to Beaumont Granville."

I flushed. I had not expected this.

She went on: "It was so very strange, was it not . . . his disappearance?"

She was looking at me intently and I was beginning to feel very uncomfortable indeed.

"There were all sorts of theories," she continued. "But he went, didn't he?"

"Yes," I said rather shortly. "He went. Those are the screens. Would you like to look at the kitchens or perhaps go upstairs first?"

She smiled at me as though to say, I understand, you do not want to talk of him.

"Upstairs please," she said.

I showed her the minstrels' gallery.

"Enchanting," she said.

We went through the rooms and she paused in the bedroom with the four-poster bed, that room with such poignant memories.

"What of the furnishings?" she asked.

"Those are for sale too if they are wanted. If not they can be disposed of elsewhere."

"I like them," she said. "I have a house in London which I do not think I would want to give up, so the furnishings would suit me well."

She went from room to room; then I took her behind the screens to the kitchens and then to the outhouses.

"Charming, charming," she said. "I cannot understand how you can bear to part with it."

"It has been uninhabited for a long time. There seems little reason why it should remain so any longer."

"No indeed. My son will be delighted with it, I am sure."

"Oh, you have a family then?"

"Just a son."

"Your husband . . . ?"

"I have no husband," she answered.

She smiled at me brightly. I was conscious that all the time she had been looking at the house she had been casting covert glances at me. It was almost as though I were at least of equal interest.

She must have sensed that I was aware of her scrutiny for she said: "Forgive me. I am afraid I embarrass you with my interest. You are a very beautiful young lady, if you will forgive my saying so. I am very susceptible to beauty."

I flushed a little. Not that I was averse to receiving compliments. I liked to feel I was attracting attention and I was quite accustomed to people taking a second glance. But there was something in her manner which disturbed me. I had a fleeting thought that she was not interested in the house but had some ulterior motive for coming here.

She herself was a very attractive woman and I thought it incumbent on me to return the compliment.

"You are very handsome yourself," I said.

She laughed, well pleased. "Past my prime, alas. There was a day . . ."

She struck a dramatic attitude almost as though she were performing for an audience. I said: "No, no, you are mistaken. That day is now."

She laughed and said: "I think we shall get along well together. It is good to get along well with one's neighbors. I know this is quite close to Eversleigh."

"It is very near. I live at the Dower House with my mother, but my grandparents are at the Court. There are three big houses fairly close together here. Eversleigh, Enderby and Grasslands Manor."

"That," she said, "sounds very cosy. Shall we look at the grounds?"

We went out into the misty air and together we walked through the gardens and the shrubberies.

"They are not as extensive as I thought they would be," she commented.

"Oh, they were bigger. But when my stepfather

bought the Manor he took over some of the land which had belonged to Enderby."

"Interesting. What did he buy? It would be interesting to see what I might have had."

"He had a wall built round it and it now joins our lands at the Dower House."

"Is that the wall?" she asked.

"Yes."

"He seemed determined to keep people out."

"The plan at one time was to use it for growing something. . . . He has not gone on with the idea yet."

"It looks rather wild in there."

"It's been neglected but it will be cleared up one day, I don't doubt."

"Well, I have to thank you, Mistress Main. I am enchanted with the house. I shall want to see it again."

"Certainly. I shall be delighted to show you."

"I was going to ask a favour. I am spending a week or so with my friends the Elsomers over at Crowhill. Do you know them?"

"Yes, we have met."

"Then you know you can trust me. Would you allow me to have the key of the house so that I might come over at my leisure in a day or so and look at it in detail?"

"But of course." I said readily. I could understand her wanting to see the place alone, and although it was furnished, it was only with the things which could not easily be removed. I had no fears of her taking anything. Although she engendered a certain uneasiness in me, I could not imagine her stealing.

Readily I gave her the key. I had another at home so that I could come back when I wished to.

We went out to our horses. She mounted with grace, bade me farewell and rode back to Crowhill.

I heard nothing for three days and one afternoon I was overcome by a longing to be in Enderby, for if I was going to sell it I should not have many more opportunities.

It was a misty afternoon; that morning it had been quite foggy and it seemed certain that the fog would
40

descend again as soon as it was dark. Now the mist hung in swirls; everything was damp, the bushes, the trees, my hair. Christmas will soon be here, I thought. We would go to Harriet's or she would come to us. I should be with Benjie again. He would certainly ask me once more to marry him. Perhaps I should say yes. Selling Enderby would be one small step away from the past and Beau; marrying Benjie would be a big one.

I was thinking of Mistress Pilkington and how interested she had been in everything—no less in me and my betrothal to Beau than in the house. She had sharp, lively eyes, tawny eyes I remembered, and they matched that magnificent red hair. She had a well-groomed look about her which suggested she was a woman who knew how to take care of her appearance and spared no pains in doing so. I was sure that she moved in Court circles, and there must have been a great deal of talk about Beau and me before he disappeared. I daresay there were cruel comments about my being an heiress. He had long ago attempted to abduct an heiress, Harriet told me when she was trying to soothe me, and had been prevented from marrying the girl by her father. "Poor Beau!" Harriet had said. "He was unlucky in his elopements." And then Beau's disappearance must have meant that he would be talked of even more.

So it was only natural that this elegant Mistress Pilkington would have heard of the matter and be interested when she came to see a house which belonged to the heiress in the case.

I opened the door and went into the house. I stood for a moment looking up at the gallery. It was so quiet. I found myself listening.

I should be rid of these fancies when Mistress Pilkington was installed here with her family. I expected I should be asked to call. It would all be so different then. That was what I wanted. I had done the right thing.

I walked up the staircase and turned into the minstrels' gallery. Something was different there. Oh yes, one of the stools had been moved forward and there was an impression on it as though someone had recently sat there.

Of course, Mistress Pilkington had been here.

Then I smelt the scent. It was unmistakable. It gave me a shock and set my heart hammering against my side.

It was that smell of musk. It brought back Beau so clearly. I could see his face, hear his voice. He had told me that he liked the scent because of its strength. He was interested in perfumes; he distilled them himself. Musk was the erotic perfume, he said. It was often added to others to give them a touch of the erotic. It was the aphrodisiac perfume. "Do you know, Carlotta, that it is absorbed by everything that comes near it. It stimulates desire. It is the love perfume."

That was how he talked, and the strong odour of the musk smell brought him back more clearly than anything could.

My mood changed at once. If I thought I had escaped from the spell he had laid on me I was mistaken. He was back as strong as ever.

For the first few seconds I was so overcome by my emotion that I did not ask myself why I should smell this in the minstrels' gallery. I just stood there with the longing to see him again so strongly with me that I could think of nothing else.

Then I thought to myself: But how did it come here? Someone has been here, someone so scented with musk that it remains after he or she has left.

Mistress Pilkington. Of course. But I had not noticed she was using musk when I had shown her round the house and I could not have failed to notice if she had. I recalled there was a delicate perfume clinging to her. It was of violets as far as I remembered.

She had the key. That was the answer. Why was I standing here in this dazed fashion? There was a perfectly logical explanation. Beau was not the only person who had used musk to scent his linen. There was quite a fashion among the fastidious gentlemen of the Court. It had come in with the Restoration. Beau said there were so many evil smells in London, and all over the country, for that matter, that a man must do something to prevent their assaulting his nostrils.

I must not be foolish and fanciful.

I would leave at once. There was no point in going through the house. I was too upset. No matter what explanation I could offer, the scent had conjured up too vivid a picture of him. I wanted to get away.

And then suddenly I saw it glinting on one of the floorboards. I stooped and picked it up. It was a button. A very unusual button, gold, and very delicately engraved.

I had seen that button before. It had been on a coat of claret-coloured velvet. I had admired the buttons very much. Beau had said: "I had them especially made for me by my goldsmith. Always remember, Carlotta, that it is the finishing touches to the garment which give it quality. Now these buttons make this coat unique."

And here . . . lying on the floor of the minstrels' gallery was one of those buttons.

Surely it could mean only one thing. Beau had been here.

"Beau," I whispered, half expecting him to materialize beside me.

There was nothing but the silence of the house. I turned the button over in my hand. It was real. This was no hallucination. It was as real as the scent which hung about the place—Beau's scent.

It is a sign, I thought. It is a portent because I am proposing to sell the house.

I sat down on one of the stools and leaned my head against the balustrade. The indentation on the chair, the scent . . . they could have meant anything. But the button, that was proof positive.

When had I last seen him wearing that coat? It was in London. Yes. He had not worn it here as far as I remembered. Yet here was this button. He could not have lost it while he was here. Surely it would have been found before if he had.

I was bewildered. I was overcome by my emotions and found it difficult to understand them. I did not know whether I was wild with joy or filled with misery. I was lost in limbo, black and uncertain. I called his name again. My voice echoed through the house. That was no good. What if that stupid little Damaris was hiding somewhere, spying on me? No, that was not fair. Damaris did not spy. But she did have a habit of turning up when she wasn't wanted.

Beau! What does this mean? Are you there? Are you hiding? Are you teasing me?

I went out of the gallery. I was going to look through the house. I went to our bedroom. I could smell the musk there.

It was awe inspiring, and the darkness would soon fall. The ghosts would come out—if ghosts there were.

"Oh, Beau, Beau," I whispered, "are you here somewhere? Give me a sign. Let me understand what this means."

I could feel the button growing hot in my hand. I half expected it to disappear but it was still there.

I went out of the house to my horse.

It was dark when I reached the Dower House. Priscilla was in the hall.

"Oh, there you are, Carlotta. I knew you were out. I was beginning to grow anxious."

I wanted to shout: Leave me alone. Do not watch me and worry about me. Instead I said coldly: "I can take care of myself."

I hesitated a moment and then went on: "I don't think I want to sell Enderby after all."

There was consternation at my decision. My grandfather said it was absurd that a chit of a girl should have a say in such matters. The house was neither use nor ornament and should be sold. My grandmother, I think, agreed with my grandfather; Leigh was tolerant and said it was my affair, and Priscilla, of course, started to worry about my strangeness in the matter. She knew it was something to do with Beau and she was upset because she had begun to think I was getting over that affair.

I sent a messenger to Mistress Pilkington at Crowhill to tell her that I had changed my mind. She sent back the key with a message that she was disappointed but understood how difficult I found it to part with such a house.

Christmas was coming and there was the usual bustle of preparation. Priscilla did all she could to arouse my interest; but I knew that I was difficult. My temper burst out at the least provocation, and Sally Nullens said I was like a bear with a sore head. Harriet sent a message to say that she, Gregory and Benjie would be joining us. We either spent Christmas at the Abbas or they came to Eversleigh. My grandmother insisted. She was very fond of Harriet; they after all had been friends almost all their lives and had met in France before the Restoration. My grandmother sometimes showed a certain asperity towards her, which seemed to amuse Harriet. Anyone who knew their history would understand it, because for a time Harriet had been Arabella's rival and Edwin Eversleigh had been the father of Harriet's son, Leigh, now Priscilla's husband. We were a complicated family. It had all happened long ago and in Harriet's eyes should be forgotten. But I could understand Arabella's resentment towards her. Then Priscilla had gone to Harriet when I was about to be born. I could imagine Arabella resented that too. However, Harriet stayed at Eversleigh, and there was a very firm bond between her and my grandmother just as there was between my mother and Harriet, and myself and Harriet for that matter. Harriet had played a major part in all our lives and she was like a member of the family. My grandfather was the only one who disliked her and he was a man who would not bother to hide his feelings, this was obvious. But there again I think he enjoyed his battles with her and I was sure she did. So it was always good when Harriet arrived.

It was the usual Christmas, getting in the yule log, decorating the great hall, giving the carol singers mulled wine out of the steaming punch bowl, feasting and dancing under the holly and mistletoe.

The Willerbys were there of course. Little Christabel was taken off to the nursery by Sally and she and Emily shook their heads and muttered about the less efficient methods employed at Grasslands compared with those at Eversleigh.

As we sat drowsily over the remains of the Christmas dinner, our goblets full of the malmsey and muscadel of which my grandfather was justly proud, Thomas Willerby again raised the question of his giving up Grasslands.

"I don't know," he said looking at my mother, "there is too much to remind us of Christabel."

"We should hate you to go," said Priscilla.

"And it would be so strange to have someone else at Grasslands," added my grandmother.

"We're such a happy community," put in Leigh. "It's really like one big family."

Thomas's expression grew very sentimental. I guessed he was about to say again that he owed his happiness to the Eversleighs.

Christabel had been my grandfather's illegitimate daughter. He was a wild man, my grandfather; it always delighted me, though, to see how devoted he was to my grandmother. Harriet once said: "He was a rake till he married Arabella. Then he reformed." I liked to think that that was how Beau would have been had we married.

"It is only the thought of leaving you all that has stopped my going before," went on Thomas. "When Christabel went I knew I could never forget while I was here. There's too much to remind me. My brother in York is urging me to go up there."

"Dear Thomas," said Priscilla. "You must go if it makes you happier."

"Try it for a while," suggested Harriet. "You can always come back." She changed the subject. She was a little impatient of this sentimental talk, I knew.

"Strange if there were two houses for sale," she said. "Ah, but Carlotta has changed her mind. She is not going to sell Enderby ... for a while. I wonder what our new neighbors would have been like."

"Carlotta was rather taken with her, were you not, Carlotta?" said my mother.

"She was very elegant. Not exactly beautiful but attractive with masses of red hair. I was very interested in Mistress Pilkington."

"Pilkington!" said Harriet. "Not Beth Pilkington!"

"She was Mistress Elizabeth Pilkington."

"I wonder, was she tall with rather strange-coloured
46

eyes—topaz colour she used to call them? In the theatre we said they were ginger like her hair. Good Heavens. Fancy that! If Priscilla would have allowed her to, Beth Pilkington would have bought Enderby. She was a considerable actress. I played with her during my season in London."

"I see it now," I said. "She was an actress. She said she had a son."

"I never saw him. I believe she had a rich protector. He would have to be rich to satisfy Beth's requirements."

My mother looked uneasy and said she thought it was going to be a hard winter. She disliked what she would think of as loose talk before Damaris and me. Leigh, who was always protective towards her, came in to help and talked about what he intended to do with some of the land he had acquired. My grandfather looked sardonic and I thought he was going to pursue the subject of Beth Pilkington, but Arabella gave him a look which surprisingly subdued him.

Then the talk turned to politics—beloved by my grandfather. He was fierce in his views—a firm Protestant and never afraid to state his feelings. These views of his had nearly cost him his life at the time of the Monmouth Rebellion, in which he had taken an active part and come before the notorious Judge Jeffreys. It was rarely mentioned in the household but I had heard of it. It upset everyone very much if that time was ever hinted at. However, he was safe enough now. Protestantism had been firmly established in England with the reign of William and Mary; although there was always a faint fear that James the Second might try to return, and I knew that a lot of people secretly drank to The King Across the Water, meaning James, who was sheltering in France as the guest of the French King.

Now there were whispers that King William was ailing. He and his wife, Mary, had had no children; and when Mary died, William had not married again. He was a good King though not a very likeable man, and when he died there was a possibility that James might attempt to come back.

I knew this was a source of anxiety to both my mother and grandmother. They had a woman's contempt for wars in which men liked to indulge generally to no purpose, as Harriet said.

Someone mentioned the death of the little Duke of Gloucester, the son of the Princess Anne, sister of the late Queen Mary and sister-in-law of the King. The little Duke had lived only eleven years.

"Poor woman," said Arabella. "What she has gone through! Seventeen children and not one of them to live. I hear she is heartbroken. All her hopes were centred on that child."

"It's a matter of concern to the country also," said my grandfather. "If William is not to last long, the only alternative is Anne, and if she does not produce a child what then?"

"There'll be many eyes turned towards the throne during the next year or so, I'll swear," said Leigh.

"You mean from across the water," added Thomas Willerby.

"Aye, I do," agreed Leigh.

"Anne has many years left to her. She is thirty-five or thereabouts, I believe," said Priscilla.

"And," said my grandfather, "she has shown she cannot bear healthy children."

"Poor little Duke," said my mother. "I saw him when we were in London once exercising his Dutch Guards in the park. He was a real little soldier."

"A sad creature," said Harriet. "His head was too big for his body. It was clear for a long time that he couldn't last long."

"Eleven years old and to die! The King was fond of him, I think."

"William has never had much affection to spare for anyone," said Leigh.

"No," agreed my grandfather, "but a King's duty is not to spare affection but to rule his country and that is something William has done with commendable skill."

"But what now, Carleton?" asked Thomas Willerby. "What now?"

"After William...Anne," said my grandfather.

"Nothing for it. We can hope that she produces another son . . . this time, a healthy one."

"If not," said Benjie, "there may be trouble."

"Oh enough of all this talk of strife," cried Harriet. "Wars never brought any good to anyone. Is this Christmas talk? Let us have a little more of the season of peace and goodwill and less of what will happen if. . . . If is a word I never did greatly like."

"Talking of wars," said my grandfather with a malicious glance at Harriet. "There is going to be trouble over Spain. What do you think"—he glanced towards Leigh and Benjie—"of the grandson of the French King taking the crown of Spain?"

"Dangerous," said Leigh.

"Not good," agreed Benjie.

"Now what has Spain to do with us?" said my grandmother.

"We can't have France in command of half of Europe," cried my grandfather. "Surely you see that."

"No, I don't," said Arabella. "I do believe you like trouble."

"When it's there, we're not so stupid as to turn our faces from it."

Harriet waved her hands to the gallery and the minstrels started to play.

My grandfather looked at her steadily. "Have you ever heard of an Emperor who took his fiddle and played while Rome was burning?"

"I've heard of him," said Harriet, "and I have always thought he must have been devoted to the fiddle."

"You don't believe me, do you?" said my grandfather. "Let me tell you this, that in the life of our country things happen which at the time seem of small importance to those who are too blind to see their real significance, or who are so bemused by their desire for peace that they look the other way. And what affects our country affects us. A little boy has died. Prince William, Duke of Gloucester. That little boy would have been King in due course. Now he's dead. You may think it is unimportant. Wait and see."

"Carleton, they should have called you Jeremiah," said Harriet mockingly.

"You get too excited about things which may never happen," put in my grandmother. "Who is going to lead the dance?"

My grandfather rose and took her by the hand. I was not the least bit interested in this talk of conflict about the throne. I didn't see how it could affect me.

How wrong I was, I was soon to discover.

It was the following day. We were all seated at table again when we had a visitor.

Ned Netherby had ridden over from Netherby Hall and he was clearly distraught.

He came into the hall where we were gathered.

"You're just in time for dinner," my mother began.

Then we were all staring at him, for he had obviously ridden over in great haste.

"Have you heard?" he began. "No . . . evidently not. . . ."

"What's wrong, Ned?" said my grandfather.

"It's General Langdon."

"That man," said my grandfather. "He's a Papist, I truly believe."

"He obviously is. They've caught him. He's a prisoner in the Tower."

"What?" cried my grandfather.

"He was betrayed. He tried to drag me in," said Ned. "Thank God he didn't."

My mother had turned pale. She was avoiding looking at Leigh. I could sense the terrible fear which had come to her.

No, I thought, not Leigh. He won't get caught in any plots.

"That's why he was here . . . a little while ago," went on Ned Netherby. "He was trying to recruit . . . an army, I suppose. He's been discovered, caught. It'll be his head, you'll see."

"What was his plan, do you think?" said Carl.

"To bring James back and set him up on the throne, obviously."

"The rogue!" cried my grandfather.

"Well, it's come to nothing," said Ned. "Thank God I kept out of it."

"I should hope you would, Ned," said my grandfa-

50

ther. "Papists in England! No. We've had enough of their like."

"I thought I'd come . . ." Ned was looking at Leigh.

"Thanks," said Leigh. "I am not involved either. It was good of you, Ned."

"Thank God for that. I knew he had been here. Do you think we shall be suspected?"

My mother put her hand to her heart, and Leigh immediately laid a hand on her shoulder.

"Of course not," he said. "Everyone knows our leanings. We're staunchly behind William and we shall be with Anne."

"*And* after her the Hanoverians if she has no issue!" roared my grandfather.

"The same with us," said Ned. "But I thought I'd let you know."

"So he is in the Tower. It's where he belongs. My grandfather beat his fist on the table, a habit of his when he wished to show authority or vehemence. "What do you think he was going to do, eh, Ned?"

"He hinted when he came here," said Leigh. "He's sounding people out to find out how many would rally to James's banner if he came back. I don't think he found many. We've all had enough of war. As for civil war, there's not a man in the country who wants that. James will be wise to stay where he is."

"Well then," said Harriet, "the plot is over. I wonder what will happen to our General?"

"It'll be his head," growled my grandfather. "We cannot afford to have his like prowling around. It's a sorry state of affairs when generals in the King's army are ready to play the traitor."

"The trouble is," said Harriet, "he would think it was you who were playing traitor to James, who was after all the King."

My grandfather ignored her and my mother said, "Ned, do sit down and join us."

She was very grateful to him but I knew she was going to be uneasy for some time to come. Ever since my grandfather had been taken during the Monmouth Rebellion she was terrified of our men becoming involved in some intrigue.

She was at her most fierce when she spoke of their folly in this respect.

That evening had lost its festive air. I was melancholy thinking of the gallant General in a comfortless cell in the Tower of London and contemplating how easily ill fortune could come along.

We heard more of the affair as the days passed. It was not being generally regarded with any great surprise. There had been so many who wanted James back and the Jacobite Movement was known to flourish throughout England. The only different was that this might be considered to be of more importance than most of the plots because it was being organized by one of the generals of William's army.

However, no one we knew was implicated. We heard that the General had not yet been tried but soon would be, and as the days passed I, at least, forgot about it.

I had other matters with which to occupy myself, for during those Christmas holidays Benjie again asked me to marry him.

I still declined to give him a definite answer but he was a great deal in my mind.

He said: "You don't still think of Beaumont Granville, do you?"

I hesitated.

"Oh, but he's gone, Carlotta. He'll never come back now. If he had intended to he would have done so long ago."

"I think I must be the faithful kind, Benjie."

"My dearest Carlotta, do you know what Harriet said to me the other day? She said: 'Carlotta cherishes a dream. It's about a man who never existed.'"

"Beau existed, Benjie."

"Not as you see him. What Harriet means is you built up a picture about him and it was a false one."

"I knew him very well. He never pretended to me that he was other than he was."

"He's gone, Carlotta. He could be dead."

"Sometimes," I said, "I think he must be. Oh, Benjie, if only I could find out the truth and if he is dead how he died . . . I think I could begin to start again."

"I'm going to find out," said Benjie. "He's abroad

52

somewhere, and Harriet said that he would be in some fashionable city. He would never bury himself in the country. I'm going to marry you, Carlotta. Remember that."

"You're good to me, Benjie," I said. "Go on loving me . . . please."

Perhaps that was an admission. Perhaps I knew that I would one day marry Benjie.

At the end of January Harriet, Gregory and Benjie went back to Eyot Abbass. Harriet had now firmly decided that the sooner I married Benjie the better. She asked me to go and stay with them soon.

"When the spring comes," she said, "I shall expect you."

It was May when I set out to visit Harriet.

My mother was in a happy state of mind. It was clear now that there would be no reverberations about General Langdon and I was sure she believed that when I returned I would announce my betrothal to Benjie. It was what she wanted. It would bind us all more closely together.

Leigh was always busy about his land. He was cultivating more and more. They were all very pleased that there had actually been a new Act of Settlement which declared that Princess Anne was next in the line of succession to William, and that if she died without heirs the throne should go to the descendants of Sophia of Hanover, providing they were Protestants.

Leigh said: "It's sensible. It shows clearly that we'll never have James back. And it means that England will never consider any but a Protestant King."

I felt impatient with all this talk about religion. "What difference does it make?" I cried. "Who cares whether we have a Protestant or Catholic King?"

"It makes a difference when men start quarrelling about it and insist that others think as they do," explained Leigh.

"Which is just what they are doing with this Act of Settlement," I pointed out.

I didn't really care. I just wanted to be argumentative. Perhaps I did feel a little resentment at the treatment of the Catholics, as my father had died because he was one and dear old Robert Frinton, who had left me his fortune, had been a staunch adherent of the Catholic Church. And now General Langdon was going to come to a tragic end. I knew these men courted danger—all of them—but I was impatient with their intolerance towards each other.

However, the fact that the King was obviously ailing, although there was an attempt to prevent this becoming public knowledge, did not matter as much because there was the Princess Anne to step onto the throne if he should die; and although she was without heirs, she was only in her thirties and there was always the Electress Sophia with her brood in the background.

So I prepared to leave for Eyot Abbass.

Damaris was sent by my mother to help me sort out my clothes. My mother was always trying to bring us together and created a fantasy in her mind that we were devoted to each other. That Damaris had a blind adoration of me I knew. She loved to brush my hair for me. She liked to put my clothes away; and when I was dressed ready for dinner when we had guests or was going riding, she would stand before me, that little round rosebud mouth of hers quite eloquent in her admiration.

"You are the most beautiful girl in the world," she once said to me.

"How do you know?" I asked. "I suppose you're a connoisseur of the beauties of all countries, are you?"

"Well," she replied, "you must be."

"Why, because I'm your sister and you think everything connected with our family is better than everything else?"

"No," she answered. "Because you are so beautiful nobody could be more so."

I should have been pleased by this simple adoration but it irritated me. She was all that I was not. Born in wedlock of a happy marriage. A good child, truly enjoying going with my mother to visit the poor and taking baskets of food to them. She really cared when somebody's roof leaked and she would even beard our grandfather in his private chamber and beg him to do

54

something about it, although he terrified her. She was not the sort of child he was interested in and characteristically he made no effort to pretend he was. He did everything he could to intensify her fear of him. Grandmother Arabella scolded him for it and was particularly sweet to Damaris because of it. My grandfather preferred a rebel like me. He had not really wanted to stop my marriage to Beau, although he had ridden out after us when we eloped. He thought it would be good for me to learn my own lessons. There was a great deal of him in me and he knew it, and as he thought what he was was the right thing to be, he had an affection for me which he never would have for Damaris.

She folded my gowns, stroking them as she did so.

"I love this blue one, Carlotta," she said. "It's the colour of peacocks' feathers. The colour of your eyes."

"Indeed it is not," I said. "My eyes are several shades lighter."

"But they look this colour when you wear this gown."

"Damaris, how old are you?"

"Nearly twelve," she said.

"Then it is time you started thinking about what brings out the blue in your own eyes."

"But mine are not blue," she said. "They're no colour at all. They're like water. Sometimes they look grey, sometimes green, and only a little blue if I wear something of a very deep blue. And I haven't those lovely black lashes; mine are light brown and they don't show very much."

"Damaris, I can see what you look like very well and I don't want a detailed description. What shoes have you packed?"

She started to enumerate them, smiling in her usual good-tempered way. It was impossible to ruffle Damaris.

Twelve years old, I mused. I was just past twelve when I first met Beau. I was very different from Damaris. Aware even then of those glances that came my way. Damaris never saw anything but sick animals and tenants who were in need of repairs to their dwellings. She would make a very good wife for someone as stolid and virtuous as herself.

"Oh, get along, Damaris," I said. "I can do this better myself."

Crestfallen, she went. I was unkind to her. I should have tried to deserve a little of that admiration which she gave me so unstintingly. Poor pudgy little Damaris, I thought. She would always be the one to serve others and forget herself. She would live pleasantly . . . for others and never really have a life of her own.

If I wasn't so impatient with her I could find time to be sorry for her.

I was to leave the next day; and there was quite a ceremonial supper at Eversleigh, for my grandmother always insisted on our going over on occasions like this.

My uncle Carl, my mother's brother, was home on leave. He had followed the family tradition and gone into the army. He was very like his father and Carleton was rather proud of him.

My grandmother gave me lots of messages for Harriet and had prepared some herbs and lotions which she thought might interest her. They would go with my baggage on one of the pack horses. It was a three-day journey taken in easy stages, and they were discussing the route by which I should go. As I had done it many times before this seemed unnecessary.

I protested that they were making it seem like the feast of the Passover.

Grandfather laughed and said: "Oh, our lady Carlotta is a seasoned traveller."

"Enough of one to feel that all this discussion is unwarranted," I said.

"I heard that the Black Boar is a most reliable inn," put in Arabella.

"I can verify that," said Carl. "I spent a night there on the way here."

"Then you must go to the Black Boar," said my mother.

"I wonder why they call it the Black Boar," asked Damaris.

"They keep one there to set on the travellers they don't like," said my grandfather.

Damaris looked alarmed and my mother said: "Your grandfather is teasing, Damaris."

Then the political talk started and once that had begun my grandfather would not let it stop. My grandmother suggested that we leave the men to fight their imaginary battles while we gave ourselves to more serious matters.

So the females sat in the cosy winter parlour and talked about my journey and what I must take, and that I must not allow Harriet to keep me too long. I was delighted when we left for the Dower House.

The next morning I was up at dawn. My mother and Damaris were in the stables and my mother assured herself that everything I should need was on the two packhorses. Three grooms were accompanying me and one of them was to look after the packhorses. My mother wore her anxious look.

"I shall expect a messenger to be sent back to me as soon as you arrive."

I promised this should be done.

Then I kissed her and Damaris and set out, riding behind two of the grooms while one rode behind me; and the packhorses came a little way behind him. It was the usual procedure for the roads, for although they had improved in late years, they could still be unsafe.

I had had instructions, which I had agreed to obey, that I would not travel after dark.

I was on my way to Harriet.

An Encounter at the Black Boar

It was a beautiful morning and I felt my spirits rise as
we rode along the familiar lanes all gay and full of
flowers—meadsweet, stitchwort and ground ivy. I could
smell the sweet hawthorn as we passed fields in which
the buttercups and daisies abounded, and in the orchards the apple and cherry trees were a riot of rose
and white.

The fresh morning air, the beauty of the countryside,
could not fail to have their effect on me. I felt more
carefree than I had since I lost Beau and it seemed as
though nature was telling me that I must not go on
brooding forever. One season was past but another was
beginning. Beau had gone and I must face that.

And yet what of the button I had found in Enderby?
What of the scent of musk that had hung in the air?
I had gone there again and there was no longer perfume
in the air. There was nothing. I could have believed I
had imagined it all but for the button. He must have
left it there before he went away. It could have remained in a corner, and perhaps when Mistress Pilkington went through the house she disturbed it. Yes,
a possibility, but what of that scent?

You could have imagined it, I told myself.

Perhaps I wanted to think that on this May morning.
I began to think of riding in the woods near Eyot Abbass with Benjie and rowing over to the Eyot with him.
We could picnic there and stroll among the ruins. I was
conceived there. My mother had told me that much.

And when she and my father, Jocelyn, had returned to the mainland he had been captured and taken off to his execution. Yes, it was not to be wondered at that I had a special feeling for the Eyot.

We rode for a long time along the coast road and made good progress the first day. The weather was ideal and we put up at dusk at the Dolphin Inn, where I had stayed on other occasions and was known to the host. He was delighted to see me and my party and served us some very good pike. There were quarters for us all at the inn, and following a good night's rest we left early in the morning after a hearty breakfast of ale and cold bacon with freshly baked bread to which we did justice.

The morning began well. The sun was warm and the roads fairly good, and just before midday we stopped at the Rose and Crown and there partook of pigeon pies with the inn's special brew of cider, which was a little more potent than we realized. I had very little of it but the groom in charge of the saddlebags was less abstemious and by the time we were ready to go he had fallen into a deep sleep.

I roused him but I could see that he would be little use on the road until he had a rest.

I said to Jem, the chief of the groom guards: "We can either wait or leave him."

"If we wait, mistress," answered Jem, "we'll not reach the Black Boar by dusk."

"We could stop somewhere else, perhaps."

"I know of no place, mistress, and your mother was insistent that we stay at the Black Boar."

I shrugged my shoulders impatiently. "We will find somewhere else. It only means that we shall be a little late arriving at Eyot Abbass."

"I know of no inn other than that of the Black Boar in the district; and we have to be careful. There are all sorts of wicked people on the roads. My lady impressed on me that we were to keep to the main roads and to stay only at inns which we knew could be trusted."

"There is so much fuss," I said.

"Mistress, I am to guard you and I dare not disobey my orders."

"Well, I'm giving orders now," I said. "We have to decide whether to leave that oaf to sleep off his drunkenness and go on without him or wait."

"To go on without him means there are only two of us to look after you."

"Oh, come, I am not a helpless invalid. I can give a good account of myself if necessary. Give him an hour and if he is not fully awake by then we'll leave him here. He can follow us with the saddle horses and at least we will get to the Black Boar tonight."

This was what we did. The grooms were very uneasy. I laughed at Jem. "You are looking over your shoulder all the time, Jem," I cried. "Just because Old Tom gets tipsy on cider we are in no greater danger. I'll swear he would be little good to us if we were attacked and we shall get away more easily without the packhorses. Moreover we have less to be robbed of."

"There's bad omens, mistress," said Jem shaking his head, "and I never like it when things start to go awry."

"He'll get a good scolding when arrives at the Abbass, I promise you."

"Oh, mistress, he weren't to know how strong the cider were."

"We knew by the first mouthful," I protested.

In fact we were able to get along more quickly without Tom and the saddle horses, even so twilight was fading when we reached the Black Boar.

As we rode into the courtyard I was astonished by the activity there. Grooms were running about attending to the horses and there was a general air of bustle, which was unusual.

Jem helped me dismount and I went into the inn. The host came out to meet me rubbing his hands together with an air of consternation.

"My lady," he said, "Oh, my lady, we are in such a turmoil. We are full to overflowing."

I was dismayed.

"You cannot mean that you have no room for us?" I cried in dismay.

"I fear so, my lady. I have let the whole of the floor to a party. They are most important gentlemen and one of them is sick."

60

I felt a twinge of apprehension. I remembered Jem's saying that if one thing went wrong, it started a chain of events. If it had not been for that stupid groom drinking too much cider we should have arrived two hours earlier and have had our rooms before the important gentleman came. Always before there had been room at the Black Boar. It was not as though it was one of those inns on the main road to a big city. It was quite off the beaten track, and never before when travelling back and forth between Eyot Abbass and Eversleigh had I encountered such a situation.

"What can we do?" I cried in distress. "It will be quite dark soon."

"There's only the Queen's Head as I can think of and that's ten miles on."

"Ten miles. We couldn't do it. The horses are tired. There are only three of us—the grooms and myself. I have left one behind at the Rose and Crown to sleep off a surfeit of cider. It is because of him that we have arrived so late."

The innkeeper's face lightened a little. "Well," he said, "I do wonder ..."

"Yes." I said. "Yes. You wonder what?"

"There is a little room—well, 'tis scarce worthy of the name. A big cupboard more like. But there is a pallet in it and a table and chair ... no more, mind. 'Tis on the same floor as the gentlemen have took. I said naught about it. One of our maids sleeps there sometimes."

"I'll take it," I said. "After all, we shall be off early tomorrow morning. What about my grooms?"

"Well, I be thinking of them too. There's a farmhouse a mile along the road. Reckon they could sleep in the loft over the stable if they was prepared to pay for it."

"I will pay," I said. "Now show me this ... cupboard."

"'Tisn't what I like to offer you, my lady. ..."

"It will suffice, I'm sure," I said. "It will teach me to be early in future."

He was immensely relieved and I followed him up the stairs.

We were on a landing which I remembered from the

past. The first door was that of my cupboard. There were four other doors on the landing.

The innkeeper opened the door. I was dismayed, I had to admit. It was indeed little more than a cupboard. The pallet occupied one side of it and a stool and a small table were all else that it contained. There was a small window in it which would make it just tolerable.

The innkeeper was looking at me dubiously. I said: "It will have to do." Then I turned to him. "There are four good rooms on this floor," I went on, "and only six in the party, you say. Perhaps they would agree to share more evenly, so that I could have one of the rooms."

The innkeeper shook his head. "They were most certain what they wanted. It was all that floor. They paid me well for them . . . right on the nail. They said the whole floor. They had this sick gentleman. They said they didn't want him disturbed. Best say nothing, my lady. They said the whole floor. They was most insistent on that. I hadn't thought of this little place, see."

"Well, I'm grateful to get it. I'll see my grooms and send them off to the farmhouse. Then will you send me some hot water so that I can wash the grime of the road from my hands and face."

"I will have it sent, my lady."

I followed him down, saw the men and told them that they were to ride to the farmhouse. I would be up soon after dawn and pick them up as it was on our way.

Then I went back to my room and had not been there a few minutes when a maid arrived with some hot water for me. She set the bowl on the table and I felt a little better when I had washed and taken off my hat and shaken out my hair.

I would have something to eat in the dining room. The innkeeper had said there was sucking pig and I knew that it was a specialty of the inn and few people served it in a more tasty fashion than the innkeeper's wife.

It had been a bad moment when I thought I was not going to find shelter for the night, but I had my little cupboard and it was only for a few hours. I should not undress. There was no room. Besides, anything I should need would be in the saddlebags.

A plague on the drunken groom. He would be roundly scolded by Harriet and Gregory when I arrived. It was a good thing we were not going back to Eversleigh. Priscilla would have been reduced to great anxiety—as for my grandfather, he would be capable of dismissing the groom on the spot.

Well, here I was and tomorrow I should have forgotten the incident.

I opened my door and stepped onto the landing. As I did so a man opened one of the other doors and came out. He stared at me in amazement. I felt a sudden tremor of excitement which I could only suppose was because he reminded me of Beau. Not that he looked the least bit like him. It was just his height and the fact that he was dressed with that fashionable discreet elegance which few men of my acquaintance possessed. His coat was square cut and as it was unbuttoned his embroidered waistcoat was just visible beneath it. His long shapely legs were encased in blue stockings with silver clocks and there were silver buckles on the garters just below the knee. The lower part of his coat was stiffened with wire, I imagined, and beneath it I caught a glimpse of a sword. He wore square-toed shoes with rather high blue heels and the silver buckles on his shoes matched those on his garters. His peruke was long and formally curled and on it he wore a three-cornered hat trimmed with silver galloon. It seemed strange to notice what a complete stranger was wearing. Afterwards I said it was because he had clearly taken such pains with his appearance that it seemed impolite not to notice it. There was a faint perfume emanating from him and that perhaps more than anything reminded me of Beau. He was a dandy—like Beau—and they were habitually users of scent. Beau once said that there were so many evil smells about that they must protect themselves. This man looked like someone one would meet at Court rather than in a country hostelry.

I did not have long to take in all this for he was clearly astonished to see me. I was about to shut the door of my cupboard room when he burst out: "Who are you and what are you doing up here?"

I raised my eyebrows to express my surprise.

He went on impatiently, "What are you *doing* on this landing? I have paid for the use of it, and have particularly asked that there should be no intruders."

"*I*," I replied haughtily, "have paid for this room . . . such as it is, and let me tell you, sir, I deeply resent your manner."

He said: "*You* . . . have paid for a room here!"

"If you can call it a room," I said. "I have taken space for the night, understanding that you and your party have taken the rest of the rooms."

"How long have you been here?"

"I fail to see that is any concern of yours."

He walked past me and went downstairs. I heard him calling for the innkeeper.

I stood where I was, listening.

"You rogue. What do you mean by this? Did I or did I not pay you for the use of your rooms this night and was it not on the understanding that I and my party were not to be disturbed?"

"My lord . . . my lord . . . the lady has only this small room. It could be of no use to you. That was why I did not mention it. The lady comes frequently. I could not turn her away, my lord."

"Did I not tell you that I have a very sick man up there?"

"My lord . . . the lady understands. She will be very quiet."

"I have expressly commanded . . ."

I went downstairs and swept past them, for they were standing at the foot of the stairs.

I said: "Your sick friend will be more disturbed by all the noise that you are making than he possibly can by my presence on that floor."

Then I went into the dining room.

I was aware of him looking after me. He turned and went back upstairs.

The innkeeper's wife was in the dining room. She was clearly disturbed by all the fuss that was going on and tried to pretend that she was not.

The sucking pig would be served at once, she told me, and I said I was ready for it. She brought it herself. It was succulent and appetising and there was cold venison pie with a mulled wine to wash it down with. This was followed by apples and pears and biscuits flavoured with tansy and some herbs which I could not recognise.

It was when I was eating the biscuits that the man entered the dining room.

He came to my table and said: "I wish to apologise for my behaviour."

I inclined my head to imply that an apology was needed.

"I was so anxious about my friend."

"I gathered that," I answered.

"He is a very sick man and is so easily disturbed."

"I promise I shall not disturb him."

I had an opportunity now to look at his face. It was an interesting one. He was deeply bronzed, and his peruke was dark but I imagined beneath it his hair would be fair; his eyes were light brown, almost golden, and he had strongly marked dark brows. It was a strong face—a deep cleft in the chin and full lips—sensuous lips, I decided, which could be cruel; there was a merriment in his eyes which contrasted with the mouth. His was a disturbing personality; or perhaps, as Beau had hinted, I enjoyed the company of the opposite sex in what he had called a normal, healthy way.

I wished I could stop remembering what Beau had said and comparing everyone with him. My interest in this man was because there was something about him which reminded me of Beau.

"May I sit down?" he said.

"This is the general dining room, I believe. And I am about to go."

"You understand my discomfiture when I discovered that others were close by my sick friend."

"Others? You mean when you discovered I was."

He leaned his elbows on the table and studied me intently. I saw the admiration in his eyes and I had to admit that I was gratified.

"You are a very beautiful young lady," he said. "I am surprised that you are allowed to travel alone."

"This is hardly to the point," I said coldly, then feeling it might be unwise to let him think I was alone added: "I am not travelling alone. I have grooms with me. They, alas, have had to find accommodation elsewhere. I make this journey frequently, but this is the first time something unfortunate like this has happened."

"Please do not think of it as unfortunate. I was angry, I admit. Now I rejoice that I have been given this opportunity to make your acquaintance. May I know your name?"

I hesitated. I could understand his annoyance and he was clearly a quick-tempered man. He was doing his best to apologise now and I did not want to appear ungracious.

"It is Carlotta Main. What is yours?"

I saw that he was surprised. He repeated: "Carlotta Main. You belong to the Eversleigh family."

"You know my family?"

"I know of them. Lord Eversleigh is your..."

"He is my grandmother's son by her first marriage."

"I see. And Leigh."

"He is my stepfather. We are a rather complicated family."

"And a military one. I believe the great General Tolworthy was a connection."

"That's so. It seems that I am no stranger to you. I wonder if I have heard of your family. What is your name?"

"It is...John Field."

"No. I have never heard of any Fields."

"Unexplored pastures," he said with a hint of humour. "I wish we had met in happier circumstances."

"And I wish that you get your friend safely to London."

"Thank you. He needs skilled attention quickly. It is a great anxiety....

I realized that he was apologising again and I stood up. I felt I should retire. There was something too bold and disturbing in his looks. He studied me too intently, and having had some experience of such matters I was well aware that he was assessing me and for what purpose. He was too like Beau for my comfort, and Beau had taught me so much about the ways of men.

The more I was close to this one, the more uneasy I became.

He stood up with me. He bowed and I went out of the dining room. I took a candle from the table in the hall and started up.

I met the innkeeper's wife on the stairs with the serving maid. They were carrying food up the landing. It was evidently being served in one of those four rooms. So this John Field had come into the dining room just to apologise to me.

I went into my room and was relieved to see that there was a key. I turned it in the lock and felt safe.

It was stiflingly hot in the little cupboard so I went to the window and found to my delight that I could open it, and when a little air came in the atmosphere was more bearable.

I sat down on my stool. It must be nearly ten o'clock. We should leave early in the morning. There was not a great deal of time to be spent here, and how glad I should be when the dawn came.

Then suddenly a gust from the open window doused my candle. I sighed but did not attempt for a while to relight it. There was a half-moon and it was a clear night, so as my eyes grew accustomed to the gloom I could see well enough.

It was then that I became aware of the crack of light in the wall. Perplexed, I stared at it; then I got up to examine it.

Good heavens, I thought. There must have been a door there at one time. It has been boarded up.

Yes, that was it. Boarded up and not too expertly done. This cupboard room of mine must at one time have led from the room next to it—perhaps it was a kind of dressing room—and there had obviously been a small communicating door between the two rooms. Someone must have decided to shut it off completely to make a maid's room of it.

There was this slight crack at the side which would

67

hardly have been visible if I had not been in the dark and there was light in the room behind the partition. And as I was examining it, I heard the mumble of voices. At first I thought they came from the corridor. Then I realized that they were coming through the crack in the wall.

John Field and his friends were in urgent discussion. I shrugged my shoulders. I imagined them sitting down to the sucking pig, which had been brought up by the innkeeper's wife and her serving woman.

Then suddenly I heard my name and I was alert. I put my ear to the crack.

I recognised the voice of John Field. "Carlotta Main ... the heiress ... one of the Eversleighs ... That she should be here this night."

A mumble of voices.

"I could murder that innkeeper. I said clearly that we were not to be disturbed...."

"It's only a girl...."

"Yes ... but one of the Eversleigh family...."

"You spoke to her?"

"A real beauty." I heard him chuckle. "A young lady with a high opinion of herself."

"You were clearly taken with her. Trust you, Hessenfield."

Hessenfield, I thought. He had said he was John Field. So he had given me a false name. This was no ordinary mission of taking a sick man to a doctor. And why should it need six men to do this? Unless of course they were servants; but from that scrap of conversation I had heard it did not seem that this was the case.

Then I heard him again: "A fiery creature, I imagine. A real beauty."

"This is not the time for dalliance of that nature."

"You've no need to remind me. We'll have no trouble with the haughty young lady. She'll be off at dawn. I gathered that from her."

"Do you think it was wise ... ?"

"Wise? What do you mean ... ?"

"Making yourself known ... going to speak to her ..."

"Oh, an apology was needed, you know."

"Trust you to play the gallant. What if she recognised you?"

"How could she? We've never met." .

"Well, gave an account of you..."

"The occasion won't arise. We'll be out and away within the next few days.... Stop fidgeting, Durrell. And now ... let's go and eat."

I heard the shutting of the door and there was silence. They would be partaking of the sucking pig in the next room.

I lighted my candle and went back to my stool.

There was something very mysterious going on and in a way I was caught up in it. It was disconcerting to know how much my presence disturbed them. What had he meant when he said I might recognise the man who called himself John Field? And his real name was Hessenfield. Why should he have given a false name? Because if he were found out in whatever he was doing, he did not want it to be known.

There was a long night to be lived through and I did not expect to get much sleep.

I took off my jacket. I did not intend to undress completely. I had no nightclothes in any case. They were in the saddlebags.

I lay down on the pallet, blew out my candle and found myself watching the crack in the wall.

It must have been past midnight when I saw a flicker of light. I went to the wall and put my ear to the crack. There was no conversation. Evidently someone was in the room alone. In due course the light went out.

I dozed fitfully through the night and as soon as the first streaks of light were in the sky I was preparing to leave. I had settled my account with the innkeeper the previous night and told him that I might be leaving before the household was astir. He had left me some ale and cold bacon with bread on the table and there was a can of water and small ewer. I used these as silently as I could and ate my breakfast.

While I was doing this I heard signs of activity on the landing and guessed that my neighbours were astir also.

I looked out of my window and saw one of them going to the stables.

Then I heard the creaking of stairs.

I was ready. I opened my door and looked out. It was silent. Then I heard the sound of heavy breathing and a gasp as though someone were in pain.

I went along the landing. A door was half open. Then I heard the gasp again.

I pushed open the door and looked in. "Can I help?" I said.

I have often thought afterwards how one moment in time can affect our whole lives and wondered how different everything might have been if I had remained in my room until the party who had shown such a desire for secrecy had gone.

But my curiosity got the better of me and I took a fatal step when I pushed open that door and looked in.

A man was lying in the bed. There was blood on his clothes and his face was the colour of whey. His eyes were wide and glassy and he looked very different from when I had last seen him.

But I recognised him at once. I ran to the bed.

"General Langdon," I said. "What are you doing here?"

And as I spoke I was aware that someone had come into the room. It was not the man who called himself John Field but one of the others.

He was looking at me with horror. He drew his sword and I thought for a moment that he was going to run it through me.

Then John Field was there.

"Hold!" he cried. "What are you doing, you fool?"

He had knocked the sword out of the other's hand. I heard it clang to the floor and I stared at it in horror.

"She . . . knows him," said the man. "By God, she's got to die."

"Not so fast," said John Field Hessenfield, and it was clear to me that he was the leader. "Kill her . . . here! You must be mad. What would happen then? They would be after us and we should never get across."

"We've got to finish her," said the man who would

have killed me. "Don't you understand? She knows ...she knows who he is."

It is a strange feeling to look death in the face but that was what I was doing now. I was bewildered and I could only think that I might so easily now be lying on the floor of this room with a sword through my heart.

"We'd better get out of here quickly," said the man Hessenfield. "Not a moment to lose."

He took a step towards me and gripped my arm so firmly that I winced.

"She'll have to come with us," he said.

The man who would have killed me relaxed a little. He nodded.

"We can't get rid of her here, you fool," said Hessenfield.

"Come on." Others had come into the room.

"What's this?" said one.

"Our floor neighbour," said Hessenfield. "Come on. Get the General out. Carry him carefully. And be quiet, for God's sake be quiet."

He pulled me to one side and two of the men came forward. Carefully they lifted the General. He groaned. I watched wide eyed and silent while they carried him from the room.

Hessenfield was still holding my arm.

"Come on," he said.

I was forced along the landing. At the door of my room we paused and he flung open the door. "Nothing must be left behind," he said.

"There is nothing. What are you doing?"

"Silence," he hissed. "Do what I say or that will be the end of you."

The clear morning air filled my lungs and I began to think clearly. What was General Langdon doing with these men? The last I had heard of him he had been a prisoner in the Tower.

There was no time to think. I was being hustled to the stables.

One of the men mounted a horse and the General was put on with him.

I was set on a big black horse and Hessenfield bounded up beside me.

"Don't leave her horse behind," he said. "We'll have to bring it with us. Ready."

Then we were riding through the dawn.

I shall never forget that ride. I tried to talk but he would not answer. They let my horse go free when we had gone some five miles. He was an encumbrance. Then we went on.

It was no use trying to protest. I was held fast against my captor. I knew that I was in imminent danger; that the reason this man had been so angry to find me on that floor was because he had something of great importance to hide. I knew what it was now. It was the presence of General Langdon.

My thoughts started to form into some sort of order.

General Langdon had come to Eversleigh, trying to recruit men to the Jacobite cause. He wanted to raise them against the present King and bring James back to the throne. Then he had been discovered and sent to the Tower. Now here he was—obviously very ill, but free.

It must have been about midday when we came to a wood. We rode into this and pulled up for a while. They evidently knew where we were and had been making for this spot. There was a stream where the tired horses were able to drink. The General was laid on a blanket and one of the men brought out some bread and bacon with a flask of ale.

"So far so good," said Hessenfield.

He looked at me sardonically, I thought.

"I am sorry we have to inconvenience you like this, Mistress Main. But you do realise, do you not, that you have inconvenienced *us* far more."

"What is all this about?" I demanded, trying to hide my fear with a show of bravado.

"Dear lady, it is not for you to ask the questions. From you—if you value your life—we expect blind obedience."

"Don't dally with the wench," said the man who had been ready to kill me. "This would be a good spot to be rid of her."

"Do not be so impatient, my dear fellow. We have one purpose ahead of us. All that matters is that we fulfil it."

"She's a danger."

"A small danger which we do not want to turn into a big one."

"I see that you have other plans for her. We expect that of you, Hessenfield."

Hessenfield suddenly struck out and the man was lying on the grass.

"Just a little reminder, Jack," he said, "that I give the orders. Never fear, I shall see that we are not betrayed. The lady shall be dealt with...but when dealing with her can bring no trouble to us." He turned to me. "You must be tired. We have ridden far. Sit down...here."

I moved away and he caught my arm.

"I said, sit here," he told me, raising his eyebrows. His eyes were twinkling but his mouth was cruel. I was aware of the sword he wore at his waist. I shrugged my shoulders and sat down.

He sat beside me. "I am glad you are sensible," he said. "Good sense is a great ally. And you need all the allies you can muster, Mistress Main. You are in a somewhat dangerous position. You understand?"

"What are you doing with General Langdon?"

"Saving his life. Is that not a commendable thing to do?"

"But he...he is the King's prisoner."

"He was," said Hessenfield.

"You mean...?"

"I told you, Mistress Main, that it is not for you to ask the questions. Do as I tell you and who knows, you might save your skin."

I was silent. He stood up and moved off. Then he came back with some bread and bacon for me. I turned my head away.

"Take it!" he thundered.

So I took it.

"And eat it," he said.

"I do not wish to eat it."

"But you will eat it all the same."

73

He stood there, legs astride, looking down at me. I ate a little of the bread and bacon. Then he came back with a flask of ale. He threw himself down beside me and offered me the flask. I drank a little. He smiled and put it to his lips. "We shall share the flask," he said. "One might say it is a loving cup."

Then I was conscious of a tingling fear because there was that in his eyes which I understood. I thought of what one of the others had said: "You have other plans for her. We expect that of you, Hessenfield."

I saw that I was completely at his mercy. The others would have killed me and thrown my body in a stream or buried it under the trees and nobody would ever know what had become of me. I would disappear ... as Beau had disappeared.

He stretched out beside me eating bread and bacon and drinking from his flask.

He said: "You are a bold young lady, I know. Don't think I don't see those flashing eyes. You must realise that you are in acute danger. Your hope is in me. You know that. You have stumbled on something which is a matter of life and death ... your death as well as others. You were too curious, mistress. Why did you not go on when there was no room at the inn? Why did you walk into that room when you had no business to?" He leaned towards me. "But, do you know," he went on quietly, "I am glad you did."

I did not answer.

I wondered what would happen to me next. I knew he desired me. I knew that he was a man who would have mistresses throughout the country. He was so like Beau in many ways. He did not want to kill me as the others did, at least not until after he had been my lover.

Death was very close but, strangely enough, I felt more alive than I had since Beau had died.

We were in the wood for two hours before we set out again. I was very conscious of his proximity and he was aware of this. I could see by the expression in his eyes that this amused him; but I warned myself against him. He was as ruthless as the rest of them.

They seemed to be making for some special place

and I very soon realised that we were heading south. I was all right for now and then I fancied I caught the tang of the sea. We kept away from main roads and at length we came to a house in a very isolated part of the country. It overlooked the sea but there appeared to be no other dwelling for miles around.

We rode into the courtyard and dismounted. As we had ridden along I had been trying to think of ways of escaping from them. That was not going to be very easy, I could see; but the thought exhilarated me. I imagined their rage and fear when they discovered I had gone, and that gave me a certain pleasure.

One thing I had gathered was that General Langdon was no unwilling prisoner; and I came to the conclusion that they had rescued him from the Tower. Surely quite an undertaking, but I already knew that if Hessenfield made up his mind to do something he almost certainly would.

Could it really be that these men were members of that often spoken of Jacobite community who were determined to put James on the throne? That General Langdon was one of them I already knew. I could see what a dangerous intrigue I had fallen into without caring one way or the other for their aims.

I was hustled into the hall. There was an air of absolute quiet about the place.

Hessenfield said: "Better search thoroughly. Every room, every possible spot."

I looked about the hall.

"Pleasant place," said Hessenfield conversationally. "We're lucky to have it."

"How did you know it would be empty?"

He held up a finger almost playfully. "Really, my dear, must I tell you again not to ask questions?"

I turned away impatiently and I saw the excitement leap up in his eyes and it sent a shiver of apprehension through me which I could not honestly say did not hold a slight touch of pleasure.

One of the men, who was called Geoffrey, returned to the hall.

"All in order," he said.

"Good. Now for a council of war. First get the invalid to a bed."

I said: "His leg is bleeding badly. It needs attention." They were all looking at me.

"She's right," said Hessenfield. "One of you had better see about that doctor. You know where to go."

Durrell said: "I'll go."

"At once."

"The bleeding should be stopped at once," I said.

"Help him up and we'll look at his leg again," said Hessenfield. He was gripping my arm and two of them carried the General up the stairs. Hessenfield and I followed.

The house was in good order. I could not understand why it should be deserted. There was a wide staircase leading to a landing, and the General was taken into a bedroom and laid on a four-poster bed.

His hose were removed and his breeches cut away. There was an ugly wound on his thigh. I said it should be bathed and bandaged. That might stop the flow of blood.

"Get water for her," said Hessenfield.

"I want bandages too," I said.

It seemed that there were no bandages, but one of them found a man's shirt in a cupboard and we tore it up. It served well enough.

"How did this happen?" I said.

And Hessenfield gripped my shoulder and laughed at me, reminding me that I was at it again. Questions were forbidden—at least coming from me.

"You understand we have to stop the flow of blood," I said. "If we don't he'll die. I think I know how to do it."

I was remembering an occasion when Damaris had cut her arm badly and Leigh had stopped the bleeding. I had watched him fascinated and now it came back to me.

"I need a strong stick," I said.

There was silence and then Hessenfield said: "Find something for her." They found a back scratcher on the dressing table; it was long and thin, yet strong, made of ebony and had carved claws at the end.

I found the throbbing point and put a pad of cloth over it; then I tied a strip of bandage over it leaving a half-knot in which I placed the back scratcher before tying it firmly. Then I carefully turned the wood, tightened the bandage as I had seen Leigh do. It was not long before the profuse bleeding had stopped.

I sat by the bed and anxiously watched the General. The men were looking at the wounded man. I could see that he was badly injured and wondered how he had affected his escape from the Tower.

It seemed a long time before the doctor came. He was obviously nervous and I guessed that he was a Jacobite and would not have been brought to the house otherwise.

I explained to him what I had done. He said: "Good. Good," and I felt an immense lifting of my spirits.

"He has lost a lot of blood," he said. "A little more could have been fatal. This action may well have saved his life."

I was overwhelmed with joy. Hessenfield was looking at me with a sort of proprietary pride which amused me and I must say gave me a certain exhilaration.

I was walked out of the room by the man called Durrell and put in the next one. He stood guarding me. I knew that he would have despatched me on the spot if he had had his way.

He was not young; he must have been about fifty. There was fanaticism in his face; I guessed he was a man who would take up a cause and give everything to it. He was different from Hessenfield, to whom I was sure life was intended to be enjoyed however serious the undertaking. Hessenfield must be at least twenty years younger than this man. I guessed him to be about thirty, though, like Beau, he appeared to be younger. I wished I could stop comparing him with Beau.

I heard the doctor leave. Hessenfield came into the room. He was smiling. "He'll be all right," he said. "He couldn't have afforded to lose much more blood. You see, Durrell, our lady is proving a useful member of the party. Perhaps she will prove to be more useful. Who knows? There is usually some good to be found in feminine society."

Durrell went close to him and whispered: "Do you realise someone has to guard her all the time?"

"I shall make that my special pleasure."

"All the time . . . have you thought what that means?"

"All the time will be only a day or so."

"It might be a week."

"No! Three days at most."

"Weather permitting," said Durrell.

I guessed then that they were here to wait for a ship to take them to France.

I was beginning to piece the story together.

The two men went out and one of the younger ones, named James, was sent to guard me. James was very young, about eighteen, I supposed, an earnest boy who I was sure was longing to die for his cause.

I was getting to know them all. Hessenfield, Durrell, James, Shaw and Carstairs. James was the son of Carstairs. They were of the nobility, I believed, and at one time had been at court. Hessenfield was clearly the leader—which was fortunate for me, for there was no doubt that had it been left to Durrell I should have been dead by now. Durrell believed that I was an encumbrance and I could quite see his point. At least I had been useful in attending to the General, and the General's life was of the utmost importance to them otherwise why should they all have risked their own to save it?

It was like living in a dream. In fact, I kept thinking that I was going to wake up and find it really was one. It was so fantastic to find myself in a mysterious house which looked as though it had been inhabited a few minutes before we arrived and then was miraculously empty. In the kitchens, I was to discover, were hams and joints of beef and mutton. There were pies in the larder—ample food to feed a party of men for at least a week. It was clear that we had been expected. And here was I in the heart of this fantastic adventure with a sword of Damocles hanging over my head, for I was here on sufferance. One false step and that would be the end of me. I was being allowed to live because of some purpose the man called Hessenfield had in store

78

for me. I had stumbled on a dangerous plot and become part of it.

I did not need an explanation of what was happening. It was obvious. They were Jacobites; General Langdon had tried to raise an army to fight for James; he had been discovered, imprisoned and would have been condemned to death. Then a band of bold conspirators, headed by Hessenfield, had rescued him from the Tower and they were trying to get him out of the country. That was why they were in this house waiting for the ship which would take them across to France where they would join King James at St. Germain-en-Laye.

For me to have discovered so much without being told explained how very vulnerable they all were. If I escaped and gave the alarm before they were able to get out of the country it would be the hangman's noose or the executioner's block for the lot of them.

So it was not surprising that it should be deemed wise to despatch me on the spot, bury my body somewhere and let my disappearance remain the mystery which Beau's death was. That set me wondering if something like this had happened to Beau.

Darkness fell.

We went down to eat in the great kitchen. The doors were bolted and barred and no one could have got in easily.

I sat at the table with them and there was little conversation. I made that impossible. Durrell was afraid to say too much in front of me. My impression grew that he would kill me if he had a chance.

They ate heartily, which was more than I did. They drank openly to the true King. No secret drinking to the King Across the Water here.

Hessenfield said: "We shall retire early. It may be that our deliverers will be here by morning."

"I pray God we will be gone by this time tomorrow," said Durrell.

"Aye, I hope He will hear your prayers," said Hessenfield.

Durrell was looking at me.

79

"You may leave her to me," said Hessenfield; and I saw the rather sour smile on Durrell's lips.

Hessenfield had me by the arm.

I said: "I will stay here. I will give you my word..."

"That you will not try to get away?" said Hessenfield. "I'd feel safer with you in my care."

Again that smirk.

He nodded to everyone, and still holding my arm he took me from the room.

We went to that one which he had chosen for himself. It was a very fine bedchamber with a four-poster bed draped with green velvet curtains.

He locked the door and turned to face me.

"Here we are at last," he said. "I am sorry, Mistress Main, that you must remain our prisoner but we must make the best of it, do you agree?"

"It is always wise to make the best of everything," I muttered.

"And you are wise. I see that... almost always wise. But perhaps not so wise as usual when you pried into matters which did not concern you this morning."

"I did not intend to pry. Let me tell you that I am not interested in your plots and counterplots."

"Well, interested or not, you have become part of this one."

He removed his coat and started to unbutton his waistcoat.

"I think," he said, "you will find this bed more comfortable than the one you had last night. A wretched affair, was it not? I was so sorry that you were forced to use that. I'll warrant you slept little."

I went to him and laid a hand on his arm. "Let me go," I said. "What do you think will happen? Do you think my family will stand aside and allow me to be kidnapped in this way?"

"My dear Carlotta. May I call you that? Mistress Main does not suit you in the least. Carlotta, my dear. They are not going to find you. You left the inn with your horse early in the morning as was arranged; you went to join your grooms a mile up the road. It was early morning. There was no one about. Lying in wait for you was some footpad. He stole your possessions.

Being you, you put up a fight, in which you were killed. He buried your body in a wood or threw it in a stream or something such. A far more plausible explanation than that you fell in with a band of desperate men, one of whom is so gallant that he is going to let you live awhile . . . if you deserve to."

"It pleases you to joke about this matter."

"It pleases me because I am so happy to be here with you."

He took hold of me then and held me powerless in his arms.

"Presumably," I said, "you are displaying your superior strength."

"Rather unnecessary, is it not? One should never stress the obvious. I find you most desirable."

"I am sorry I cannot return the compliment."

"You will change your mind."

"So you saved my life . . . for this."

"A worthy cause," he said.

"You are . . . wicked."

"I know. But you are not so very virtuous yourself, are you, Carlotta?"

"I don't think you know anything about me."

"You'd be surprised how much I do know."

"You know my family. That should be enough to tell you they will not stand aside and allow me to be treated like this."

"I could take you very easily, you know . . . now . . . this moment. You are looking round for means of escape. You could scream. Who would care? In fact that might bring Durrell with his sword. You are trapped, sweet Carlotta. At the mercy of your ravisher. There is nothing to be done in such circumstances but to submit. It saves a great deal of trouble."

I wrenched myself away from him and ran to the door. I pummelled on it with my fists.

"Now that," he said, "is an action scarcely worthy of you. Who in this house is coming to your rescue? Save your energies for more worthy purposes."

He had taken me by the shoulders and led me back into the room.

"You are irresistible and we shall be lovers this

81

night," he said. "It is what I wanted from the moment I saw you. You are such an attractive creature, Carlotta. You invite. You promise. You are meant for love...our sort of love."

"Love," I cried. "I should think that is a subject you know nothing about. You mean lust, do you not? I am at your mercy. You are intent on rape—a very gentlemanly activity, I believe, and I have no doubt you are well versed in it. It is easy, is it not, to seek out helpless women who are unable to fight against you. Oh, very gallant. I despise you...Field...Hessenfield, whatever your name is. You haven't even the courage to own up to that and have to masquerade under a false name. Let me tell you this, if ever I get out of this place I shall not forget you."

"I hope not," he said. "I intend to make you remember me for the rest of your life."

"With a shudder...with loathing....Yes, you are probably right. That is how I shall remember you."

"No," he said, "perhaps otherwise."

His arm was about my shoulder and there was a curious gentleness in his touch. He forced me onto the stool and knelt at my feet and taking my hands in his smiled up at me. His eyes were shining. I noticed that they were golden coloured. Again he reminded me of Beau. He had looked like that before we made love.

He kissed my hands just as Beau used to and he said: "Carlotta, you have been very unhappy. I am going to change that."

I tried to snatch my hands away. "You know nothing about me," I cried.

"I know a great deal," he answered. "I knew Beaumont Granville...well."

I closed my eyes. There was something unreal about this scene. If he had taken me by force, roughly, crudely, it would have seemed the natural outcome and in any case I had been expecting it. But this talk about Beau was unnerving.

"He was a friend of my father," he said. "He often came to our house. He took a fancy to me. He used to talk a great deal to me."

"Did he talk of me?"

82

"He talked of all his women."

"All his women!"

"They were legion. There had been women in his life since he was fourteen. He was very frank with me. He said he would undertake my education. What aspect of that education I don't need to explain."

"I don't want to hear any more."

"My dear, it is for me to say what shall and shall not be. I know you still think of him, don't you? How long is it since he disappeared? Three years. Four years. What happened to him do you think?"

"Perhaps he was killed as you intend to kill me."

He was thoughtful. "He had many enemies. A man like Beaumont Granville would. It is generally thought that he went abroad... in search of higher game. It was not unusual for him to disappear for periods at a time. Usually creditors or having involved himself in some affair that was giving him trouble was the cause."

"Why are you telling me all this?"

"Because you must get him out of your mind. You have set up a great memorial to him. He is not worth it, Carlotta."

"Another quality I have discovered in you. Such loyalty to your friends."

"Yes, he was a friend in a way but you mean more to me."

I laughed. "This time yesterday I saw you for the first time. I wish to God I never had."

"I do not think that is exactly true." He laid a hand on my wrist. "I can feel your heart beating fast, Carlotta. Oh, it is going to be wonderful between us. I know it. But I want you to stop comparing me with Beaumont Granville."

"I did nothing of the sort...."

"You should keep to the truth, Carlotta. The truth is so much more interesting than lies."

"Oh, let me out of here. I promise I will not say a word of what I have seen. Give me a horse. Let me go. I will find my way to Eyot Abbass. I will say I lost my way. I will make up some plausible tale. I promise you,

83

you and your band shall not be the worse for anything I shall say."

"Too late," he said. "You are here, Carlotta, in the trap. A most delightful trap, I promise you."

"With death at the end ... ?" I asked.

"It will depend on you. You will entertain me and each night I shall look forward to more shared joys. Have you heard of Scheherazade? She told stories and for her skill was allowed to live through another day. You are a Scheherazade of sorts, Carlotta, and I am your sultan."

I put my hands over my face. I did not want him to see my expression. His talk of Beau had brought back so many memories of the room in Enderby Hall. This room was not unlike it. He reminded me more and more of Beau. I was afraid of myself. I felt that if this man touched me I should not be able to fight off the fantasy. I should let myself slip into the dream.

"Stop regretting Beaumont Granville," he was saying. "You would have been wretched with him. Your people were right to try to stop the marriage. Beaumont could never be faithful to one woman for more than a week. He was completely cynical about them. He talked of them to me ... to others too, I don't doubt. He talked of you, Carlotta."

I repeated blankly: "He talked of me!"

"He was going to marry you because of your fortune. Solely because of your fortune, Carlotta. He wasn't in the least reluctant, though. A nice fortune and a loving little wife. He told me how it was with you. He described those times you spent together in Enderby Hall, wasn't it? He talked about women like that. He used to talk about Naturals. They were born for it, he said. Lovely passionate creatures. They are as eager as you are. Carlotta, he said, is like that. He was glad, he said. One grew tired of the shrinking kind who had no heart in the romp."

"Be silent," I cried. "How can you? I hate you. I hate you. If I could I would ..."

"I know. If you had a sword here you'd run it through me as Durrell would have run it through you this morning. You owe me your life, Carlotta."

84

I could not explain my feelings. There was shame there, shame for what Beau had said of me. I never wanted to see that room at Enderby again. My mother had done everything she could to stop me and she had been right. I could not bear to think of him—discussing me and my emotions and my reactions to this . . . disciple of his.

His fingers were on my coat. "Come, dear Carlotta," he said. "Forget him. He is past. Perhaps he lies mouldering in some grave. Perhaps he is at this moment lying with someone who can give him more than you could. Forget him. I know you and love you already. You are no stranger to me, Carlotta."

He had taken off my coat. He was undressing me with unexpectedly tender hands.

I wrenched myself free suddenly. I looked about the room. He took my face in his hands and said: "Caught. Trapped, like a little bird in a net. Sweet Carlotta, life is fleeting. Who knows, perhaps this very night men will come to this place and take me. Perhaps in a week, a month, my head and shoulders will have parted. Life is short. It has always been my motto. Enjoy it while we can. That should be yours, too. Who shall say what tomorrow shall bring to either of us? But there is to-night."

Then he picked me up and carried me to the bed.

He laid me there and I closed my eyes.

Resistance was useless. I was completely in his power. I knew the sort of man he was. Beau's sort. He was moving about the room. Then he blew out the candle and was beside me.

I wanted to cry out in protest. But cries, as he had pointed out, were useless. I was in his power.

I heard him laugh in the darkness. I think he knew me better than I knew myself.

It is difficult to understand myself. I suppose I should have felt degraded and humiliated; and in a way I did, and yet. . . . It is hard to explain except to say that I am a woman who was meant to experience physical passion and I was beginning to understand that it was not so much Beau himself that I had missed as the opportunity to match my physical needs with one with whom I was in complete bodily harmony. This was how it was with Hessenfield. We were as one flesh; I forgot the reason for my being where I was and although I brought out all my pride—and that was considerable in ordinary circumstances—I could not hide the fact that I found pleasure in this encounter.

Hessenfield knew it; he exulted in it, and he was by no means a rough or uncouth lover as might have been expected in the circumstances. He behaved as though his great desire was to please me and he made no secret of his delight in me.

He told me that I was wonderful; that he had never enjoyed such an experience as much as he had with me.

In the darkness he whispered to me: "I could so easily fall in love with you."

I did not jeer at him; I remained silent. I was overcome by a mixture of shame and ecstasy.

We were as suited as lovers as Beau and I had been. There was an overpowering sensuality in us both which gave us a rare appreciation of the sensations we could evoke in each other. Whatever happened to me, I could not wholeheartedly regret this adventure.

He knew it even as I did. He certainly behaved like a lover after that first onslaught. It was as though he was telling me that he was sorry it had happened in this way.

When the first streaks of light were in the sky he was at the window. He was looking for the ship.

"There is nothing there," he said; and there was almost a relief in his voice.

Another day passed. A long day it seemed. They were all watching for the arrival of the ship. I dressed the General's wound. I seemed to be more adept at nursing than any of the others and they let me do it. They seemed glad that I could.

The General was not quite sure where he was, so he did not question my presence. I was glad of that. Later I went down to the kitchen and prepared the food for them. It was only a matter of setting it out on the table for whoever this house belonged to had left it well stocked with food.

I was embarrassed to meet Hessenfield's gaze during that morning. He was so knowledgeable; he would know exactly how I was feeling, and I could scarcely pretend to be as outraged as I should be. He had been fully aware of the passion in me which had matched his own. He was too experienced not to understand my nature. At one time he came up behind me, caught me and held me against him; I felt his lips on my ear. He was behaving as a true lover might. It was disconcerting.

I felt ashamed to face the others, for they all knew what had happened. Hessenfield undoubtedly had a reputation for his amorous adventures. Beau's pupil, I thought.

He had taught me something. It was that it was not so much Beau whom I wanted but a man who could satisfy me in the way Beau had.

The night came and we were alone again. As he held me tightly against him he said: "I am glad the ship did not come today."

"You are a fool," I said. "Every day your danger grows."

"It's worth it," he answered, "for a night with you."

We lay together in the big four-poster bed just as I had lain in that other with Beau.

He said: "I believe you love me a little."

I did not answer and he went on: "At least you do not hate me. Oh, Carlotta, who would have thought this would have turned out so. Since I saw you in the inn I wanted this. I wouldn't have anything changed. . . ."

Then he kissed me and I tried to ward off the desire which he knew so well how to kindle.

"You should never pretend, sweetheart," he said. "There is nothing wrong in being a vibrant woman. Oh, God, how I wish that things were not as they are. I like to think that these traitors had not arisen, that you and I had met perhaps at some court function. And I saw you and loved you and asked for your hand in honourable marriage. Think of that, Carlotta."

"I should have to agree, you know," I reminded him.

"You would. There would have been no objection from your family, I promise you, and if there had been from you I should have brought you to some place like this and proved to you how necessary I was in your life. You would have accepted me then, Carlotta, would you not?"

"I suppose if you had seduced me I should have to," I retorted.

"Sweet Carlotta. I shall pray that the ship does not come tomorrow."

I said nothing. I was afraid to betray my feelings with words as I had in other ways.

In a strange way I was in love with him. It must be remembered that we were all in a highly emotional state. Death hovered over all of us. It seemed unlikely that they would allow me to live. I knew too much. Durrell was right. Although they guarded me night and day it would not have been impossible for me to escape their vigilance and then, considering what I knew, I could be a terrible danger to them.

I thought of it. While Hessenfield lay sleeping beside me I could have risen, found the key to the door, unlocked it, got out of the house, taken one of the horses from the stable and been away. Hessenfield was taking a great risk in letting me live. And they no less than I were close to death, and that knowledge must have its effect. I was conscious of a great desire to go on living—a lust for life which I had not noticed before. In the last day or so I had moved away from the past. I had changed. I was not exactly happier than I had been, but I can only say that I was more alive.

I lived from hour to hour. I did not want to look ahead to the time when I should gaze out and see the ship there. God knew what would happen to me then. Hessenfield would say good-bye to me. Would he do it with a sword? No, I could not believe he would harm me. Yet he would have imposed himself upon me however reluctant I had felt. He would have raped me and exulted in it.

And yet there had sprung up these strange emotions between us. Our natures went out to meet each other;

in a way we belonged together. He was a man of power. Perhaps that was what I looked for in men. He was a natural buccaneer, an adventurer, a leader of men. He had grace, elegance and an air of gallantry; he was a man of the world; he combined fastidiousness with a kind of primitive strength. He was virile yet he was tender; he had the ability to make me feel that I was more important to him than anyone had ever been before and I thrilled to that, although I could not entirely believe it. Beau had that, I reminded myself. And to him I had just been a fortune—and the means of providing amusement for an hour or so.

There was no doubt that my emotions were in turmoil; my senses were heightened. I was living again—and more than anything I wanted to go on living.

It was the third day. They were beginning to get restive.

"What has delayed them?" I heard Durrell say. "It can't be the weather. God help us, at any moment a storm could arise ... gales ... anything. That would be understandable ... but it's calm enough out there."

The weather had turned warm and the sun beat through the windows. I looked longingly out at the green lawns and the shrubbery.

The house was built in a small valley and it was only from the second and third storeys that the sea was visible.

Hessenfield, seeing me gaze out with longing, came to stand beside me. He laid a hand on my shoulder and I felt the tremor run through me.

He said: "It looks inviting out there."

"We have been cooped up so long," I replied.

"Come," he said. "We'll take a walk."

I was delighted, and I couldn't help showing my pleasure.

"I don't think you'll try to run away," he said. "In any case you wouldn't have much chance, would you?"

I did not answer.

"Come," he said. He unlocked the door and we went out. I stood for a moment breathing in the fresh air. It was exhilarating.

"A pleasant spot," said Hessenfield. He gripped my arm. "Ah, it is good to be out of doors again."

We walked in silence up the slight incline and now we were facing the sea. It was calm as a lake and of a beautiful mother-of-pearl translucency.

"Sometimes I think our ship will never come," he mused. "Or come too late for us."

"What shall you do if it does not come?"

"If it does not come our chances are slight. With every day that passes the danger becomes more acute." He turned to me suddenly and looked intently at me. "And each morning I have said, 'Not today. Give me another night with my love.'"

"You do not deceive me. You are as eager as the others for the ship to come."

He shook his head, and we were silent for a while.

We had come out to the path which was close to the cliff edge. There was a narrow gully leading down to the beach.

I said: "I should like to go close to the sea . . . to touch it."

"Why not?" he said. "Come on." He took my hand and we ran down the slight slope. I crouched by the water and let my hand trail in it.

"So peaceful here . . . so quiet," he said. "I wish . . . Ah, since I met you, Carlotta, I have done little but wish things were otherwise. Do you believe me?"

I said: "We often feel something at a certain time and think it is all-important. Then life changes and we see that which was so important to us was of small significance."

"And you think this . . . our encounter . . . is of small significance?"

"If you kill me it will be of small significance to me, for I shall be dead."

He turned away from the sea, and, holding my arm firmly, as though I had reminded him of the need to guard me, we walked up the incline to the path.

As we reached the top I heard him catch his breath. I glanced along the path and saw why. Four horsemen were riding towards us.

Hessenfield's grip tightened on my arm. We were

too late to turn back or to hide ourselves. They would have seen us as soon as we saw them.

Now, I thought. It is my chance. This is what they feared. Oh, Hessenfield, I thought, you have made a grave mistake. You should never have left the house with me.

The tables were turned. His life was in my hands now.

Triumphantly I saw that the men were soldiers of the King's army and it could well be that they were on the trail of the conspirators who had rescued General Langdon from the Tower.

Hessenfield pressed himself against me. It was as though he was reminding me of everything we had been to each other. He said nothing. This was no time for words.

All I had to say was: "They are holding me prisoner because I know what they have done." And I would be free.

The men were now within calling distance.

"Good day to you," they shouted.

"Good day," called Hessenfield. I said "Good day" too.

The horsemen drew up and looked at us keenly. They saw an elegant country gentleman and his woman in a well-cut riding suit.

"You live hereabouts?" asked the horseman.

Hessenfield waved his hand in the direction of the house.

"Then you know the district?"

"You could say so," said Hessenfield. I was amazed by the calmness of his voice.

"Have you seen any strangers pass this way?" asked the horseman.

"Strangers? I have noticed nothing."

"And you my lady?"

It seemed a long silence. I heard the shriek of a gull—mocking in a melancholy way. Revenge. Your chance. They will lose their heads, every one of them.

I heard myself say: "I have seen no strangers."

"I'm afraid neither I nor my wife can help," said Hessenfield and there was a lighthearted joy in his voice which I thought must be apparent to them. "Is it anyone in particular you are looking for?"

"No matter," said the horseman. "But perhaps you can tell us how far it is to Lewes."

"Five or six miles along the road," said Hessenfield.

They doffed their hats and bowed. We stood for a moment looking after them. Then he turned to me. He said nothing. He just took me in his arms and held me tightly.

I had shown him my true feelings for him. It was like ridding myself of a burden.

There was no longer any need to pretend.

That night it was different.

We were lovers now in truth.

"Do you realise, foolish one, that you have declared yourself for us?"

"I care nothing for your plots."

"That makes it all the more important. Oh, Carlotta, I love you. I would have loved you if you had betrayed us. But I don't think I was ever so happy in my life as I was that moment when you stood there and declared yourself for us."

"For you," I said.

"Dearest Carlotta," he said. "My love. A week ago I did not know you, now you are here and you have changed my life."

"You will forget me," I said.

"As you will forget me?"

"I don't forget easily."

Then he kissed me and we made love with an intensity as though we had some premonition that this would be our last night together.

We found sleep impossible.

We lay awake talking. There was no barrier between us now. I had held his fate in my hands and had shown clearly that I would save him at risk to myself. Nothing could have been more explicit.

He told me of the necessity of taking the General to France.

"We are determined," he said, "to rid the country of the imposters. The throne belongs to James Stuart and

92

his son after him. William has no right to it. Anne is not the true heir while James lives and has a son to follow him."

"Why should such matters be of great importance to us? William is a good king, most people agree. Why should we risk our lives just so that one person shall wear the crown instead of another?"

He laughed at me. "Women's reasoning," he murmured.

"And none the worse for that. In truth, reasonable reasoning."

He ruffled my hair and kissed me.

Then he told me of the disappointment over the plot that failed and the consternation in St. Germain-en-Laye when it was discovered that General Langdon was in the Tower. "We planned carefully. It was the usual escape. Wine smuggled in ... drunken guards, stolen keys. Unfortunately at the last lap it was necessary for the General to jump to freedom. The rope he used was not long enough. He crashed to the ground. Hence his injuries. We got him away by boat to a spot on the river where horses were waiting. That was how we got to the Black Boar."

"And if you were caught ..."

"Our heads would be the price we should pay."

I touched his head—his thick light brown hair with the tawny lights in it, which was so much more becoming, I thought, than the fashionable peruke.

"Yes," he said, "and you have saved it this day, my love. Although we should have put up a good fight if you had betrayed us. Oh, I was so proud of you, so happy for myself when you stood there and told them you had seen no strangers pass by. You hesitated, though. Just a split second. You knew you could save yourself. Yes, you could ... but at my expense ... perhaps the cost of my life. And then you knew what you wanted to do. Never, never shall I forget."

He told me of the Court at St. Germain-en-Laye where the sad old King lived out his days, an exile in a strange land, deserted by his people, betrayed by the daughters he had loved so well, living on the bounty of the King of France when he should be in his own Palace of Westminster.

"But he will come back," said Hessenfield vehemently. "There are many in the country who want him and hate the usurpers. You see what support we have. This house was put at our disposal. The people who own it are good Jacobites. They moved out with all their servants and left it in readiness for us. The owner will return in a few days to see if we are gone. If we have he and his family will return. The doctor who came to see the General is another of us. You see we are scattered throughout the country and only awaiting the call...."

"They are foolish," I said. "No good can come of civil war. That was proved years ago."

"We are fighting for the true King, the King Across the Water, and we shall not cease until he is back where he belongs."

"And if the ship comes you will go back?"

"When the ship comes, Carlotta, I shall go."

I sighed and we lay in silence for a while.

As soon as it was light he went to the window. I heard him gasp and I leapt out of bed to stand beside him.

There was the ship.

He gripped my hand. "At last...it has come," he said. Then he turned to me. "Get dressed. Lose no time."

I did so and when I was ready so was he.

"Come," he said, "quickly."

I followed him to the stables where he selected a mount for me.

I said: "You are sending me away?"

"Before the others know the ship is here."

"Durrell would kill me," I said.

"He thinks it the only way. You must get away from here as soon as possible. You are some twenty miles from Eyot Abbass. You can do it today. Ride on to Lewes and there ask instructions. You will say you have lost your party."

"And you will go to France?"

He put his arms about me and held me fast.

"I had thought to take you with me. But I dare not. It is too dangerous. You must go back to your home."

"So it is good-bye."

"I shall come back," he said.

I shook my head and turned away.

"Come," he said. "There is no time to lose. I want you away from here before Durrell wakes. The first thing he would want to do is kill you."

"You would not let him. You would save me as you did before."

"There might come that unguarded moment. Who knows? I cannot risk it. But I tell you this, Carlotta, I shall come back."

He led my horse out of the stables. Anxiously he looked back at the house.

He patted the horse's flanks. Then he took my hand and kissed it and then laid it against his cheek for a few seconds holding it there.

"Farewell, my sweet Carlotta," he said.

Then I rode on.

I did not see where I was going. I could only see his face. After a while I looked back and he had gone.

I came to a small hill and I rode up this and as there was a clump of trees there, I dismounted, tethered my horse to a tree stump and looked back.

I could still see the ship.

And as I stood there I saw a boat lowered from the side of the ship and rowed ashore. Then I saw them lifting the General into the boat.

I watched and I waited there until the boat had reached the ship and they were all on board.

Then I untethered my horse and rode on to Lewes.

The episode was over.

A Child Is Born

It was dark when I arrived at Eyot Abbass. I had received instructions in Lewes and at length I had come to a road which was familiar to me.

I rode into the courtyard and one of Harriet's grooms who was there gave a great shout when he saw me.

I called out: "Yes, I'm here. At last I have arrived."

He rushed to help me dismount. "I must go and tell the mistress. They've been that worried."

"Yes," I said. "I'll come with you."

We ran into the house. I was shouting: "Harriet. Gregory. Benjie. I'm here."

Harriet was the first to appear. She stared at me for a few moments and then she ran to me and caught me in her arms. "Oh, Carlotta," she cried. "Wherever have you been? We've been worried to death. Gregory. Benjie. She's here. Carlotta's here."

Benjie came running into the hall. He swept me up into his arms. There was no mistaking his joy.

Then there was Gregory—dear quiet Gregory, who might be less effusive but who was as delighted to see me as the rest.

"You've come alone. . . ."

"Harriet, I've had such an adventure. . . ."

"But you're worn out. You need something to eat and your clothes . . ." That was Harriet.

"The grooms came here without you. They said you must have been attacked on the way from the inn to the farm where they were staying."

"I'll tell you all about it. I hardly know where to begin."

"I do," said Harriet, "with food and a wash and change. Your saddlebags arrived. I can tell you we've been frantic. Now you men, leave Carlotta to me, and, Gregory, go and tell them to speed up supper, but first some chicken broth for Carlotta and it is to be brought to her room."

Harriet took me up to the room I always occupied at Eyot Abbass. She brought out a gown from my baggage and almost immediately the chicken broth arrived. I took it greedily and then I washed in the hot water which was brought to me and changed into my gown.

Harriet came back to see how I was getting on.

"You've had an adventure," she said. "A pleasant one."

"I narrowly escaped being murdered."

"You look elated. We're longing to hear. I won't question you now, my dear. You can tell us all over supper."

So I told—at least what I wanted them to know. I had decided on my way here that there must be some truth in my story. I would soon be caught out if I made up something entirely different, which at first I had felt inclined to do because I did not want to put Hessenfield in danger. But he was safe now. I had watched him board the ship. He would probably be in France at this moment.

So I told them of our late arrival at the Black Boar and how all the rooms were taken by a party of six men and how all I could get was the small room on the same floor, which had not pleased them.

I went on to tell them how I had discovered that they had with them a sick man whom I recognised as General Langdon.

"Why, he has escaped from the Tower!" cried Benjie.

"Exactly," I said. "They had rescued him. They were going to kill me because I knew who the General was, but one of them wouldn't allow it."

I wondered if a soft note had crept into my voice. I thought it might be so because Harriet looked especially alert.

97

"They took me with them to a house on the coast. A ship came and they went away in it."

"And they released you then?" said Gregory.

"I suppose they thought they were safe, the vile wretches," added Benjie.

"They believed in a cause," I pointed out. "They really believe it is right to restore James to the throne."

"Have they made a Jacobite of you?" said Harriet.

"Of course not. I'm not interested in their stupid causes."

"What a terrible ordeal," went on Harriet. "We've been frantic."

"My mother?" I began.

"I didn't tell her. I thought I'd wait awhile. I had a notion you were safe, and you know what she is. She would imagine the worst. But it couldn't have been much worse. You...in the hands of those desperate men."

"I don't think Hessenfield would have let them kill me. Right from the first he saved me before..."

I was tired. I wasn't thinking what I was saying and Harriet could always see farther than most people where human emotions were concerned.

"Hessenfield!" cried Gregory.

"Hessenfield," repeated Benjie.

"Great heavens!" cried Harriet. "Lord Hessenfield, of course. We have met him in the old days. He was a close friend of James's. Of course, he's a leading Jacobite. All the Fields were hand in glove with James."

"Fields!" I said blankly.

"The family name, dear. John—he's the eldest of them. I remember his father before he died. My dear Carlotta, so it was Hessenfield who got General Langdon out of the Tower. Quite a feat. Typical of Hessenfield."

John Field, I thought. He told me he was John Field. He had not lied about his name.

They were plying me with questions. I told them how I had ridden out with them and how we had stayed at a house on the coast in which we had lived for three days.

"My dear Carlotta," said Harriet, "some of us have strange adventures. They somehow attract them. You certainly attracted one this time. Now what you want more than anything is rest, and I am going to insist that you go to bed at once. You can tell us more tomorrow. What you need is a good sleep, and I'm going to bring you some of my black currant posset. So off you go. Say good night to them and I'll be up with the posset shortly."

I knew Harriet. She wanted to talk and she wanted to do so more freely than she could before her son and husband.

She came to my room with the posset. By that time I was in bed. She was right, I was exhausted, and yet at the same time I knew I should not find sleep easily.

I kept thinking: This time last night I was with him. And I could not get out of my mind the memory of his face when he had kissed me good-bye.

Harriet handed me the posset and seated herself by my bed.

"Something else happened," she said.

I raised my eyebrows to express innocence of her meaning.

"Hessenfield?" she said. "I remember him well. A fine gentleman." She smiled. "And he saved your life. And you were with them for three days."

I was silent.

"Do you want to tell me, Carlotta?" she asked.

"Harriet, I don't feel I can talk about it . . . yet . . . even to you."

She said: "I think I understand. You will tell me in time. My dear child, how glad I am to have you back. I have been terrified. . . . There are so many things that can happen to women in this world. But somehow I knew that you would know how to take care of yourself. You're a natural survivor, Carlotta. I know them when I see them. I'm one myself."

She bent over and kissed me and took the posset from my hand.

I believed she knew that Hessenfield and I had been lovers.

I could not have come to a better place in which to try to regain my composure. Gregory and Benjie were such dear, uncomplicated people. They accepted my story; they could only be thankful that I had come out of it alive. All they thought I needed was rest and feeding up a bit to make up for the discomforts I had endured.

It was different with Harriet. She knew something had happened, and being Harriet she guessed what. She understood, perhaps, and she had made in the past the acquaintance of Hessenfield. She knew how it would be with two people such as we were shut up for three days, with death hanging over us and me in their power.

But Harriet's chief charm was that she never probed. I was aware—and my mother had discovered this too—that in any difficulty Harriet would bring out all her resources—and they were formidable—to one's aid. But she behaved as though whatever had happened, however tremendous it might seem to other people, was in her eyes merely another piece of life. Never to be judged or condemned by others who could never see it in all its complexities. If it was good, enjoy it; if not, find a way to extricate oneself. Harriet was by no means what would be called a good woman, but she was a comforting one. She was engrossed in her own life, determined to get the best of it—and none could deny she had. She was by no means scrupulous; she was fond of the good things of life and would go to great lengths to get them. I suppose one of the comforting things about her was that one knew whatever one had done she had probably done also; she would understand the motive, and even if she didn't she would never get lost in the devious paths of right or wrong.

I knew she would understand without question that what had happened between myself and Hessenfield was natural. In time I would talk to her as I never could have talked to my mother. One might say your mother gave birth to you—a bastard, born out of wedlock. Oh, yes, that was true but all that happened was that she had on one occasion forestalled her marriage vows, which had never been uttered because of the executioner's axe. My mother was at heart an unadventurous woman with a deep respect for conventions. I was not and never would be. Nor was Harriet.

For the first few days I absorbed the peace of Eyot Abbass, that lovely old house which Gregory had inherited when he came into the title on the death of his elder brother. I had always loved it. In a way it was more my home than Eversleigh, for in the early years I had believed Harriet and Gregory to be my parents. I knew every nook and cranny of the house. I loved the hilly country round about. It was so flat at Eversleigh. In the country lanes I had ridden my first pony, in the paddock I had ridden round and round on a leading rein with Gregory or Benjie or one of the grooms in charge of me. It was home to me. It was about a mile from the sea, but as the house was built in a slight hollow—as a good protection against the southerly winds—the Eyot could only be seen from the topmost windows. A lovely old house built as most houses were in the Elizabethan style—hall in the centre with the west and east wings on either side. A house of towers and turrets and red Tudor bricks and a beautiful garden which was rather wild because Harriet liked it that way and Harriet's will was law in that house.

From my window at the top of the house I often looked at the Eyot, about a mile out to sea. There had been a monastery on it before the dissolution and it had always been a specially exciting place to me.

I had loved to play hide-and-seek there in the summer days when we rowed over with picnics. When I learned the truth about myself I believed the Eyot was a special place to me because I had been conceived there. Very few people can be absolutely certain of where their conception actually occurred. I could, for the only time my mother and father had been lovers was on the Eyot. Poor star-crossed lovers. Then suddenly I thought it is like a pattern...in a way. She lost her lover because of some silly plot in which he was involved. And I...

I was not sure that I thought of Hessenfield as a lover. Our encounter was very different from that of my parents. They had met; she had tried to save him; they had loved romantically and the result was myself.

101

I am sure that what had passed between them had been very different from my adventure.

I had to forget him now as I had to forget Beau. Was I destined to love so tragically?

I had been a week at the Abbass when I talked to Harriet. I had not meant to. She was sitting on a wooden seat in the garden. I saw her from the house and I felt the impulse to go down and join her.

She merely smiled when I sat down beside her.

"You are feeling better now," she said, stating a fact. "And yet you are still not here half the time."

I raised my eyebrows questioningly and she went on: "Still in that mystery house by the sea."

She asked no questions. She sat there waiting and I knew that the time had come to tell her. I could hold it in no longer.

"Yes," I said. "Still thinking of it."

"It is bound to have its effect on you."

"Harriet," I said. "You know how it was between Hessenfield and me."

"I guessed," she said. "Knowing him...knowing you. Did he force you?"

I hesitated. "Well, in a way..."

She nodded. She understood perfectly. "Hessenfield is a born charmer," she said. "He's another such as Beaumont Granville. Not such a villain, I hope. But there is a similarity."

"You think Beau was a villain but you didn't try to stop my marrying him as the others did."

"I thought it was something you had to learn yourself. You've been brooding a lot about him. And now we have Hessenfield. But he's gone now. It was inevitable that he would. He's lucky. He did what he came to do and got away with it and his life; and I gather from you that some of his time here was spent very pleasantly."

"Harriet, you are not shocked?"

"My dear child, should I be shocked...by life?"

"You have had a lot of lovers, Harriet."

She did not answer. Her eyes had become vague as though she were looking a long way back, seeing a procession of them, men she had loved, and some of
102

whom she had forgotten now. The words came falling out then and I could not stop them. I explained to her how he had saved my life when the man Durrell would have killed me; how he had made it plain what he would expect of me and how when it happened I had wanted it to.

"There. Can you understand that?"

"Indeed I can. I have seen him. It must have been as great an experience for you as it was with Beau."

"Beau and I were lovers too, Harriet."

"Of course you were. Beaumont Granville wouldn't have played it otherwise. My dear child, you will have lovers. You are not like those good women, your grandmother and your mother. You can reach heights of passion which they wouldn't dream of. It is nothing to be ashamed of. You are more sensitively moulded. That's all. Do you know, you are very like me. I think when I decided to play the role of mother, fate was amused and made you my child. You even look a little like me. Do you mind?"

"Harriet, there is no one I would rather look and be like."

"Said with more affection than wisdom, but bless you for it. Now there is something that has occurred to me. You spent three nights with Hessenfield. What if there should be consequences? Have you thought of that?"

"Yes, I have. When I look out of my window at the Eyot and remember how I was conceived there, I think to myself, what if I should have Hessenfield's child?"

"Well, what conclusion did you come to, suppose that passionate relationship should bear fruit?"

"I am a little frightened at the thought and yet at the same time . . ."

"I know . . . elated."

"It would be wonderful in a way to have a child to remember him by."

"Children of such affairs make a good deal of pother when they make their entry into the world. You yourself made a most spectacular entry."

"Only because you were stage managing it." I began to laugh faintly hysterically, I must admit, for now that

103

I had brought that possibility which had haunted my thoughts into the daylight I was indeed disturbed.

Harriet patted my hand suddenly. "If it should be so we shall have to consider what is to be done. Of course, it may not be so. It happened to your mother somewhat similarly. Life does not usually work out to such neat patterns. But let us be prepared, eh?"

"Oh, Harriet," I said, "it is good to be with you. I suppose my mother must have felt like this all those years ago."

She was silent with that glazed look in her eyes, again remembering the past. She must, I calculated, be quite sixty years old, but she had retained a certain youthfulness by her nature as well as artificial aids and in that moment she looked like a young girl.

Yet it was like repeating a pattern, for I did discover that there was to be a child.

I did not now know quite how I felt. I was dismayed, it was true, and yet I was conscious of an overwhelming excitement. I realized how dull life had been after Beau's disappearance until my capture by the Jacobites. Then I felt that I had started to live again, and I wanted to live desperately; it was necessary to me even if it meant that I might have to endure dangers.

I wasted no time in telling Harriet. She was excited. I understood her perfectly. She liked things to happen even if they were going to present difficulties, and the more insurmountable those difficulties seemed the more excited she became.

It was the greatest comfort to be with her. She discussed my condition with verve. "It is different from your mother's case. She was a young and innocent girl. To produce an illegitimate child seemed to her unthinkable. Yet there you were, my dear Carlotta, waiting to be born. We had to practice a good deal of subterfuge."

"I know. Venice. That magnificent palazzo and then the pretence that I was your child."

"It would have made a good play. But here we have a different situation. You were forced into this by that adventurer. To what children owe their lives! You
104

might say that the one you have conceived owes his or her existence to a goblet of potent cider.... But what are we going to do, Carlotta? You are a rich woman. You could defy them all if you wished. You could say: I am having this child and if you are going to criticise me for it, I shall snap my fingers at you. On the other hand, it is good for a child to have a father. Two parents are better than one, and it is not easy to flout society. I would like a father for the baby."

"Its father will never know of its existence."

"How can you be sure of that? But we waste time. Not that there is any *immediate* hurry, but it is well to plan ahead."

I started to think of my mother and my grandmother. There would be consternation in the family. My grandfather would want to kill Hessenfield, and as he was a Jacobite into the bargain—my grandfather being a stern Protestant—I had no doubt of the rage he would feel. Then there was Leigh. Although he appeared to be mild enough, he had a fierce temper. I had heard how he had once attacked Beau when he had been, as Leigh called it, too friendly with my mother. I had seen the scars on Beau's body inflicted by Leigh. And all for a mad escapade, Beau had told me that Leigh had come to his apartment and caught him unawares, and had inflicted those wounds on him.

So I could imagine my mother's distress and the effect this matter would have on Leigh, and I should have to tell them of course that I had been caught up in the plot to rescue General Langdon, and they would insist that I had been raped and that the child was the result of that.

Oh, yes, I could well imagine an outraged party from Eversleigh even attempting to go to St. Germain-en-Laye to wreak vengeance.

I mentioned this to Harriet and she agreed.

"There is one other possibility which has occurred to me. I wonder if it has to you."

"What?" I asked.

"Benjie," she said.

I looked at her in amazement.

"Marry Benjie," she said. "He would be a very nice father for the child."

"Your son!"

"Well, there's no doubt he's that. No doubt that he's Gregory's either, though I had to pretend he was Toby Eversleigh's for a long time. These contretemps occur and it is better to tackle them in the way which will bring less trouble to everyone. Listen. If you marry Benjie you can have a child—a little prematurely perhaps, but that is soon forgotten. You will have a husband, the child will have a father, and they are useful assets on most occasions."

"Are you suggesting that I should deceive Benjie just to . . . to acquire these useful assets?"

"Not necessarily deceive him. Tell him the story of your capture, how your life was in danger and to preserve it you had to submit. That's true, it is not?"

"It's not the whole truth, Harriet. We . . ."

"I know what happened. You tasted excitement with Beau; you missed it and thought it was your love for him you missed. It was more than that, though, and then the dashing Hessenfield arrived and threw a little light on the subject. You're not like your true mother, dear child, you take after me. It was a great adventure, was it not? While it lasted you were deeply involved in it. But there are other men in the world like Beaumont Granville and John Hessenfield. Benjie is not one of them. But that is all to the good. He's the best kind to marry. He loves you truly. And there is a great deal to be said for true love. Look how I have settled down to happiness with his father."

"You want my fortune for Benjie, don't you, Harriet?"

"Of course. I'm not going to deny that it adds to your many attractions."

"That was what Beau said. But I couldn't marry Benjie without telling him."

"I was not suggesting that you should. Benjie will love you none the less because he is going to play the saviour. That will suit him well. He'll want to protect you. Yes, Benjie is the best answer."

I shook my head.

"One can't use people like that, Harriet. It's not the way to live."

"You still have some growing up to do," she said.

Harriet was noted for taking matters into her own hands. She had with my mother; and she had always managed her own affairs with skill.

She spoke to Benjie without telling me, and his reaction was to seek me out at once.

He was tender; he was protective, all that she had known he would be.

"My dear little Carlotta," he said. I noticed that I had become little, although I was a tall girl, as tall as he was. "Harriet has told me."

"What has she told you?" I asked.

"There is no need to talk of it. It makes me furious. I wish he were here. I would kill him. . . . But there is something I can do and I'm going to do it."

I turned away from him but he caught my arm and said: "We're going to be married. We're going to be married from here, soon. Harriet and Gregory will arrange it. You know they always wanted it. You've been their special darling all your life. Mine too, Carlotta."

I said: "Listen . . . you don't know what you're doing."

He laughed. "Dearest Carlotta, it was no fault of yours. That black villain took advantage . . ."

"It was not quite like that, Benjie."

He wouldn't listen to me. He knew how it was. Harriet had told him, and, like his father, he had been listening to what Harriet had told him for a very long time.

I was shocked, he insisted. Who wouldn't be? I had had a terrible experience. It was all so easy to understand and because of it I was going to have a child. That child would be his child. No one should know he was not the father. He was going to take care of me.

He had his arms about me and I had always been comforted by Benjie. When I started to grow up I was aware of the immense power I could wield over him and I shall never forget his joy when he discovered that I was not his sister. I knew he had planned to marry me from that moment.

107

It was a way out. I imagined what it would be like at Eversleigh if I had a child without a father. However independent one felt, however ready to fly in the face of convention, when it came to doing it there were complications which made it unpleasant. There would be disadvantages for the child also.

I could of course take the path which had been taken in so many cases. Go away secretly and have the baby, get someone to take it. Oh, no, I did not want that.

The alternative was to marry Benjie. Our marriage would surprise no one. For some time our families had been hoping for it.

I was not deceiving Benjie. If he liked to put his own construction on what had happened—and I could see that nothing I could say would make him do otherwise—then I must be thankful that I was provided with such an easy solution to my dilemma.

Harriet threw all her energies into making the arrangements. My mother was going to be put out because I had married from Eyot Abbass instead of from my own home in the conventional manner. But as soon as she knew that I was pregnant she would understand. She would believe that Benjie and I had forestalled our marriage vows and that the need for the wedding was urgent.

I could imagine my grandfather's sly smiles and my grandmother's telling my mother that she wouldn't be surprised if Harriet had arranged the whole thing.

We were married in the nearby church. It was a simple ceremony and it took place exactly six weeks after my meeting with Hessenfield.

I vowed to myself that I would be a good wife to Benjie, and I did make him very happy.

Harriet was delighted, and commented that nothing could have pleased her so much and that all was well that ended well. It did occur to me that this was not the end, but I said nothing. I could only feel at that time an overwhelming gratitude to them all—my husband, Harriet and dear Gregory. Eyot Abbass would now be my home.

My mother arrived the day after the wedding, for Harriet had sent a letter to her telling her of the proposed marriage.

She was indignant. She believed that I had come over with the idea of marrying Benjie and that it was some plot concocted by Harriet to arrange the marriage for me.

She suspected that Harriet, having played such a major part at the time of my birth, wanted to control my life and play the part of my true mother. To console her I told her at once that the reason for the hasty marriage was my pregnancy.

She was shocked and then confused because we all knew that I was her love child. There was nothing she could say then but wish me happiness.

"Benjie is a good man," she said. "You must make sure you make him a good wife."

"I shall do my best," I promised her.

I could see that she was working it out according to the rules. When the child was born they would say it arrived prematurely. No one would believe it, but they would all pretend to.

I wanted to laugh at such conventions; but when I considered how ready I had been to fall in with them, I could hardly do that.

Shortly after my marriage Benjie and I went back to Eversleigh. Harriet came with me, so did Gregory. It was to be some sort of celebration.

"The bride is supposed to be married from her home," said Harriet. "You know how your mother likes to do things according to the book . . . except of course on very special occasions."

My mother had her way and there was a feast and people were invited.

My sister, Damaris, thought it was all so wonderful.

"Exciting things always happen to you," she said.

I looked at her with a kind of affectionate scorn. Dear little Damaris, the good girl. Men like Beau and Hessenfield were not for her. She would marry some young man her parents would find for her and she would be perfectly content because it was what they wanted.

The visit went well and predictably and I was rather glad when we were on our way back.

When it was suggested by Harriet that we stay at the Black Boar, Benjie protested.

"It would be unpleasant memories for Carlotta," he said.

"In my opinion," said Harriet, "it would be a good idea to lay the ghost."

When she said that, I had a great desire to see it again, wanted to find out what my real feelings were. I loved Benjie. He was delighted to find me a passionate wife. I think he had thought that after my adventures I might have felt some reluctance. I surprised him. I was fond of Benjie; it could never be Beau or Hessenfield of course—he lacked entirely that buccaneering spirit—but he was virile and adoring and he offered me the balm I needed at this time. I promised myself that I was going to be happy. Hessenfield had laid the ghost of Beau and Benjie would lay that of Hessenfield.

When I said I would like to go to the Black Boar that settled it and we went.

It was strange arriving there and being greeted by the innkeeper and his wife.

The innkeeper was full of apologies to Harriet and explained to her what she knew already, that he had been so upset to have let his floor to the party of noble gentlemen. I assured him that I quite understood and reminded him that he had most kindly, to their dismay, put me into the cupboard room.

"I am overcome with shame to have offered you such a place," he said.

"You did everything you could."

We had the floor to ourselves. Benjie and I in the room where the General had lain. It was a strange night. I dreamed of Hessenfield, and even when I was awake I kept fancying that it was he who lay beside me, not Benjie.

The next morning before we left, Harriet and I found ourselves alone together.

"Well?" she said. "What do you think now?"

I was silent and she went on: "That place they took you to must be near here."

"It was not very far, I suppose."

"Do you know where?"

"Yes. I discovered when I found my way back to you. It is five miles from Lewes." I remembered so clearly then how we had stood there while the horseman looked at us searchingly. I could smell the tang of the sea. I could remember how time seemed to stand still and how Hessenfield had waited on my words. And when I had declared myself for him and the horseman had ridden on, how he had turned to me and held me against him. I had rarely been as happy in my life as I was in that moment.

"I could find it."

"I'd like to see it," said Harriet.

"We could hardly go there."

"I have a plan. Leave it to me."

The men joined us for breakfast in the inn parlour, and as we were partaking of hot bread and bacon, Harriet said: "I have a friend who lives nearby. I should so like to see her."

"Could you not do so?" asked Gregory, always ready to indulge her.

"It seems odd to call after so many years without warning her. I could find her place. I visited it long ago, I remember, when she married. But I should like to look her up . . . and surprise her."

Gregory said: "Let us look in then. It is far out of our way?"

Harriet said it would be a good idea. Then it occurred to her that perhaps it would not be fair for us all to descend upon her. Why should she and I not go alone? We could take one of the grooms with us if they were going to protest, and she knew they would.

"Let us spend another night at the Black Boar. And Carlotta and I can go and do our little visiting. You have always said, Gregory, that you like this country-side. Now is the chance for you to explore it."

Harriet had a gift for making people believe that what she suggested for them was exactly what they wanted for themselves, and the outcome was that later that morning she and I, with a groom in attendance, were riding out along that road which I had been taken on that memorable night.

The smell of the sea was strong that morning. There

was a faint breeze which ruffled the waves and set a frothy frill on them where they rose and fell on the sand.

I saw the roof of the house and I was overcome for a moment by the power of my emotions.

"Perhaps there's no one there," I said.

"Let's go and see."

We rode down the slight incline to the house.

There was a woman in the garden.

"Good day to you," she said. She had a basket full of roses. She looked so much at home, and when I thought of arriving at that mysteriously empty house which at the same time showed obvious signs of recent habitation, I marvelled.

She obviously thought we had lost our way and were asking for instructions.

"We have come from the Black Boar," said Harriet.

She smiled. "And you are not sure of the road. Where do you want to go?"

I said: "Could I have a word with you?" She changed colour slightly. "You must come in," she said.

We tethered our horses by the mounting block and followed her into the hall which I remembered so well.

"I will send for refreshment," she said. "I am sure you would like to rest awhile before you continue your journey." A servant appeared from behind the screens and she said, "Bring wine and cakes, Emily. To the winter parlour."

And so within ten minutes, during which we had made conversation mainly about the weather and the state of the roads, wine was brought with wine cakes. Then the door was firmly shut and she was looking at us expectantly.

"You have brought a message for me?" she said.

Harriet was looking at me and I said: "No, there is no message. I was wondering if you could give me some information. I am a friend of Lord Hessenfield."

She looked alarmed. "All is not well?" she asked.

"I believe nothing to have gone wrong," I said.

"What we want to know"—Harriet could not stop coming forward, for what she hated was to play what

112

she called a standby role—"is, did he reach his destination safely?"

"You mean . . . when he left here?"

"Yes," I said. "That is what we mean."

"But that is weeks ago. They had a rough crossing but made it in safety."

"And they are now with the King?"

She nodded. "You must tell me who you are," she said.

"Friends of Lord Hessenfield," said Harriet firmly, and I could see that we had been accepted as workers in the Jacobite cause.

"I was with them when they brought the General here," I said. "What we should have done without your house I cannot think."

"It was a small thing to do," she said. "We ran no risks. We just went away with the servants for a week. That was all."

"It was our salvation," I said. "But we must not stay. I just wanted to meet you."

She filled up the wine and we drank to the King, which meant James the Second, not William the Third. Then we told her we were going back to the Black Boar.

She walked with us to our horses, and as we rode away Harriet said: "Well done, my little Jacobite. I am sure the good lady thinks there is some significance in our visit. As good Jacobites we should have known that Hessenfield is safe at St. Germain-en-Laye. The lady was a little puzzled, methinks."

"You certainly think up the wildest things to do. You're a lady of intrigue."

"Well, what was that? Just a little exercise in deception of the mildest kind. I wonder how many Jacobites there are in this country, all waiting for the moment, eh? At least we know Hessenfield and his merry men made it safely. They are now at St. Germain planning fresh moves, I'll warrant."

I felt a great relief because he was safe.

Preparing for the birth of a baby was a new and enthralling experience.

As the weeks passed into months I became more and

more absorbed by it, and when I was aware of the life within me I thought of little else but the time when my child should be born.

In September, four months after my child's conception, news was brought to us that King James had died at St. Germain-en-Laye. There was a good deal of talk then and I remember Gregory's saying that this would not be an end of the Jacobite movement. James had a son who would be considered the rightful heir.

"Poor James," said Harriet, "what a sad life he had! His own daughters to turn against him. They say he felt it deeply."

"He did not want to return to England and to his throne," said Benjie. "To become a Jesuit as he did meant that he had finished with the world."

I wondered what effect his death would have on Hessenfield, and I guessed that his efforts would not cease. He had a new pretender to replace the old one, and I wondered then if he would ever come to England and what his feelings would be if he knew I had borne him a child.

James was buried with honours and his body placed in the monasteries of the Benedictines in Paris and his heart sent to the nunnery at Chaillot. Most significant of all Louis the Fourteenth, the French King, had caused the young Prince to be declared King of England, Scotland and Ireland as James the Third.

There was much talk about this and as there were rumours that the health of our King William was not very good a certain speculation was growing up everywhere. Even the servants talked of it and, I believed, took sides.

To show his disapproval William recalled his ambassador from the French Court and ordered the French ambassador to return to France.

The next we heard was that England had entered into an alliance against France. This was called the Grand Alliance; it looked as though war might be imminent. This was not concerned with bringing back James but the Spanish Succession and the threat of war was disturbing, but through it all I remained wrapped up in the thoughts of my child.

At Christmas my mother and Leigh came to Eyot Abbass with Damaris.

My mother was very eager to hear how I was and she had brought garments and advice about the baby. She was determined, she said, to stay until my child was born and nothing was going to shift her. She said this almost defiantly, thinking of Harriet, I was sure, which was absurd really for Harriet had no desire to usurp her position as a mother. My mother would never understand Harriet. This ridiculous rivalry had only grown through me, I believed. Before my birth she must have felt much the same towards her as I did since she had gone to her for advice.

We had the usual Christmas festivities. I was getting large at that time, having only two months to go.

And on a bleak February day my child was born.

It was a strong healthy girl.

As I held my child in my arms I marvelled that out of that encounter, which had been so closely concerned with death, life should have come. A new life.

"What shall you call her?" asked my mother gloating over the child.

"I have decided to call her Clarissa," I said.

DAMARIS

The Cellar of Good Mrs. Brown

I suppose all my life I have been overshadowed by Carlotta. She is seven years older than I, which gives her a certain advantage, but age has nothing to do with it. Carlotta is herself, and as such the most fascinating person I have ever met.

People turn to look at her when she comes into a room. It is as though the desire to do so is irresistible. Nobody could understand it better than I because I feel this deeply and always have. She is of course startlingly beautiful with that dark curling hair and those deep blue eyes; if one is the sister of such a creature one is immediately dubbed plain merely by comparison. I don't doubt that if I had not had Carlotta for a sister I should have passed as quite a pleasant-looking, ordinary sort of girl; but there was Carlotta, and I became accustomed to hearing people refer to "the beauty." I quickly accepted this and I didn't mind nearly as much as my mother thought I might. I was one of Carlotta's worshippers too. I loved to watch those deep-set eyes half closed so that the incredibly long dark lashes spread fanlike on her palish skin; then her eyes would open and if she were angry flash with blue fire. Her skin was pale but with a certain glow. It reminded me of flower petals. It was the same colour and texture. I was pink and white with straight brown hair which did not curl very easily and never stayed where I wanted it to. My eyes seemed to have no definite colour; I used to say they were water colour. "They are like you," Carlotta once said. "They have no colour of their own. They take colour from whatever is close. You're like that, Damaris. The good girl. 'Yes, Yes, Yes,' you say to everything. You never have an opinion that is not given to you by someone else." Carlotta could be cruel sometimes, particularly when someone or something had annoyed her. She liked to take her revenge on whoever was near—and that was often myself. "You're such a *good* girl," was her constant complaint, and she made it sound as if goodness was a despicable thing to be.

My mother was always trying to let me know that she loved me as much as she loved Carlotta. I was not sure about that, but I did know that I did not cause her the anxiety that Carlotta did.

I overheard my grandmother once say to my mother, "You'll have no trouble with Damaris, at any rate."

I knew they were comparing me with Carlotta.

Carlotta was constantly involved in some controversy. Exciting things happened about her and she was generally the centre of them all.

Not only was she beautiful but she was rich. She had charmed Robert Frinton, who had lived at Enderby Hall, and so completely had she done this that he left her his fortune. Then there was all the fuss about her elopement with someone called Beaumont Granville. I never saw him but there was a great deal of talk about him and his name was on everybody's lips—even the servants'.

That was over a long time ago and now she was married to Benjamin Stevens—dear Benjie, whom we all loved so much, and my mother was particularly pleased as there was a little baby.

We had spent Christmas at Eyot Abbass and everything had circled round Carlotta then.

My mother insisted on staying until the baby—a little girl called Clarissa—was born and my father and I had come home.

"Now she has a baby," my mother said, "Carlotta will settle down."

120

"Settle down!" cried my grandfather with a chuckle. "That girl will never settle down. Mark my words, she'll always be the centre of some storm."

My grandfather had a specially warm spot for Carlotta. He never seemed to notice me. My mother said that he had not been like that with her. It made his affection for Carlotta even more remarkable.

My mother was coming home shortly. There was no longer any reason why she should stay away. She had seen her granddaughter safely into the world, and Eyot Abbass was Carlotta's home now that she had married Benjie. She had more or less returned to the scene of her childhood, for her early years, when everyone thought she was Harriet's daughter, had been spent at Eyot Abbass.

Yesterday one of the Stevens's grooms had ridden over with letters. My mother would be setting out at the end of the week. The journey was not long. It usually meant two nights at an inn, and that was taking it slowly. The grooms managed it in two days and they were always trying to do it in record time.

It was a sparkling morning. March had just come in like a lion, as the saying goes, and we were hoping it would prove the old saying true by going out like a lamb. There was a feeling of spring in the air. The long winter was over; the nights were getting shorter, and although there was not much warmth in the sun yet, it gave a promising radiance to the fields and hedgerows. I loved to ride out into the country; I loved to watch for the changing of the land. I had a great fondness for the animals too. Apart from my dogs and horses I loved the birds and all wild things. They came to me first and always seemed to understand that I would not dream of hurting them and above all wanted to help. I knew how to speak to them, how to soothe them. My father said it was a natural gift. I had tended rabbits and sparrows and once there was a redshank which I found on the marshes. He had a broken leg and I had set it for him. It was amazing how it healed.

I loved the country life; I knew that the time would come when I would go to London with my family and there would be balls and such things for me, the object being to find me a husband. I dreaded that; but there was one consolation, neither of my parents would force me into marriage if I didn't want it; and their great desire was to see me happy.

In any case I was only thirteen and that was in the future. I remembered that Carlotta had not been much more when she had fallen in love with Beaumont Granville. But Carlotta was Carlotta.

"She was born with all the wiles some women take a lifetime to learn," said my grandfather. "And then only get half of them."

He spoke with approval. I quickly realised that I had been born with none of those wiles.

On this particular March morning I did not care. I saw that the rooks were busy making their nests and I saw some meadow-pipits, which we sometimes called tit-larks. They were a little like larks and could be mistaken for them by some who had not studied them as I had. I loved to see them on the ground, where they ran instead of hopped. I heard the cry of a redshank— a sort of whimper. I would not go near her because the nest would not be far off and it would throw her into panic if anyone approached her young.

I came past Enderby Hall. No one lived there, which was rather absurd, said my father. A big house like that, furnished, standing vacant just because Carlotta had some caprice to keep it so. The house had been left to her by Robert Frinton with the rest of his fortune, and at one time she had thought to sell it and suddenly and capriciously, said my father, had changed her mind.

I didn't like Enderby very much. When we were young Carlotta had tried to frighten me there. She told me how when she was very small she had wandered in there and been lost. They had all been in a panic and finally she was discovered in a cupboard fast asleep. Robert Frinton had been so taken with her that he had called it Carlotta's cupboard.

She enticed me into it and tried to lock me in but I had known what she might have in mind too and for once in my life had been too quick for her. "Silly!" she had said afterwards. "I wouldn't have kept you there.

I just wanted you to learn what it feels like to be shut up alone in a haunted house." She had looked at me with that trace of malice she often showed. "Some people's hair turns white overnight," she said. "Some just die of fright. I wonder what you would look like with white hair? It might be better than no real colour at all."

Yes, there had been times when Carlotta had been merciless. But I had never faltered in my admiration and I always sought her attention and was gratified to receive it even when it could result in ghoulish experiments such as she had planned for me in the cupboard in Enderby Hall.

I rode past, skirting the land which my father had bought and which had once belonged to Enderby. There was a wall about it now.

I came past Grasslands Manor, the home of the Willerbys, and young Thomas Willerby saw me and called to me.

I would have to go in. They expected it; and old Thomas loved to have callers. He was particularly fond of everyone from our family.

I took my horse to the stables and Thomas and I went into the house together.

Old Thomas was delighted to see me. I told him the news while he sent for wine and cakes, which I should have to take because he would be hurt if I didn't. He loved to show his hospitality.

I told him my mother was returning home and he said how glad we must be and how happy to have an addition to the family.

I admitted I was longing for my mother's return. She would have all the news of the baby and Carlotta to tell us.

He said: "I have some news too. I have bought a place near York."

"Oh," I said, "You really will be going then."

"As you know, my dear, I have been shilly-shallying for a long time, but now I really have made up my mind."

"And what of Grasslands?"

"I shall sell it."

I was thinking it strange how there seemed no lasting luck in either Grasslands Manor or Enderby Hall. I wondered if there was such a thing as ill fortune, for these houses seemed to have incurred the wrath of fate. Even the Willerbys had not escaped, though at one time they had been very happy. Then Thomas's wife had died giving birth to young Christabel. It was all very sad.

"Yes," he said. "It may be that your parents will give me a hand with the selling. I don't want to wait here...now I have the new house."

"We shall all be delighted to show people round it. Have you spoken to my father yet?"

"No, I was waiting until your mother came back. Now she is coming. That is good news. Less happy news at Court."

"Is that so?"

"Yes, the King has broken his collarbone."

"That is not very serious, is it?"

"I heard he has been ill for some time," said young Thomas. "He was riding from Kensington to Hampton Court when he was thrown from his horse. The horse caught his foot in a molehill, they say. It didn't seem much at the time."

His father put in: "I hear the Jacobites are drinking to the Little Gentleman in Black Velvet, meaning the mole who in making his hill has done the country a service."

"It seems a pity that they must be so pleased about an accident. What of the horse? Was it badly hurt?"

"Now that I didn't hear. I suppose they thought it wasn't important."

While we were drinking the wine another visitor arrived. It was my uncle Carl from Eversleigh. He was in the army and home on leave.

"Oh, hello, Dammee," he said. He was very jovial, Uncle Carl, and thought it amusing to make a joke of my name, which he knew irritated my mother. "There's news. The King is dead."

"I thought it was just his collarbone," said Tom Willerby.

"He had several fits apparently, and he has been

trying to keep his weakness a secret from the people for some time. He died at eight o'clock this morning."

"There will be excitement across the water," said Thomas Willerby.

"Among the Jacobites, yes. They haven't a chance. Anne was proclaimed Queen this very day. Let's drink to the new reign, eh?"

So our glasses were filled and we drank to our new sovereign: Queen Anne.

The Eversleighs had always had close connections with the court. My grandfather Carleton Eversleigh had been a great friend of Charles the Second. After he had been involved in the Monmouth Rebellion he had fallen out of favor with James, of course, and although William and Mary had received him, he had never been on the same terms with them as he had with Charles. However, that we should go to London for the coronation was taken for granted and we made ready.

It was now April. Carlotta's baby was two months old and she was not going to London this time. Harriet was not either. It must have been one of the first times she had missed a royal function, but I suppose even she was beginning to feel her age. She was several years older than my grandmother.

Nevertheless it was quite a big party that set out from Eversleigh. My grandparents, my parents, Uncle Carl and myself.

"Dammee," said Uncle Carl, "it'll be good for you to see a bit of life."

"She is young yet, Carl," said my mother, "and her name is Damaris."

"Very well, sister," retorted Uncle Carl. "She is as yet a babe in arms and I'll remember not to call little Dammee Dammee."

My mother clicked her tongue impatiently but she was not annoyed. There was something very lovable about Uncle Carl. He was several years younger than she was and sometimes she talked about the old days and then she told me how their father had doted on Carl while he hardly seemed aware of her.

"There came a time when things changed," she said

125

once, and there was a note in her voice which made me want her to tell me more; but when I asked she shut her lips tightly together and wouldn't say a word more on the subject. Secrets, I thought. Family secrets. I should probably know them one day.

Well now we were going to London and there was all the fun of setting out. If Edwin had been home, as a peer of the realm, he would have played a big part in the ceremony. My grandmother regretted that he was away on foreign service. However, we were determined to make a jolly time of it.

"If you can't rejoice at coronations, when can you?" said my grandfather. "You have a new monarch and you can with a good conscience delude yourself into thinking all will live happily ever after. So let us all enjoy our coronation."

We were in high spirits as we set out. The family and six servants. We had three saddle horses, for we should need special clothes if we were to go to Court.

I was watching out for birds. I knew where to look for them—willow warbler in the open country, tree pipit always where there were trees and turtle doves in the woods. I loved to hear their joyous singing at this time of the year. They were so happy because the winter was over.

I told my mother that it made *me* feel happy just to hear them.

She gave me her warm approving smile. Later I heard her say softly to my grandmother, "Damaris will never give me one moment's cause for anxiety, I am sure."

And my grandmother replied: "Not of her own free will, Priscilla, but sometimes disaster strikes from unexpected quarters."

"You are in a strange mood today, mother."

"Yes," said my grandmother, "I think it's because we're all riding to London. It makes me think of the time when Carlotta eloped."

"Oh, how thankful I am that is all over."

"Yes, she is safe with Benjie."

"And now this child. A baby will sober even Carlotta."

126

They lapsed into a comfortable silence and in due course the grey walls of the Tower of London came into sight. We were almost at the end of our journey.

It was always exciting to arrive in London. The streets were teeming with life; there was noise and bustle everywhere; I had never seen so many people as I saw in London—all sorts of people, all different, all, I imagined, leading the sort of lives we of the country could only guess at. There were gentlemen in exaggeratedly elegant garments flashing with what could have been real jewels but might well have been imitation; ladies patched and powdered; vendors of all kinds of objects and apprentices standing at the doors of the shops calling out to passersby to buy their wares. There was the excitement of the river, which was always crowded with craft of all kinds. I could never tire of watching the watermen shouting for customers with the cry of "Next oars" and piloting their passengers from bank to bank and taking them for pleasure trips past the splendours of Westminster to beyond the Tower. I liked the songs they sang; and when they were not singing they were shouting abuse at each other. My mother had never wanted me to use the river. I had heard her say that people forgot their manners and breeding when they stepped into a boat, and even members of the nobility assumed a coarseness which would not have been acceptable to polite company ashore.

Although Carlotta would have called me rather slightingly a country girl, I could not help but be fascinated by the London scene. There was so much to see which we never saw in the country. The coaches which rattled through the streets containing imperious ladies and gentlemen so sumptuously attired fascinated me as did the street shows. One could see Punch and Judy in a booth at Charing Cross; and along Cheapside there were knife swallowers and conjurors and their tricks for the delight of passersby. There were giants and dwarfs performing all sorts of wonders; and the ballad sellers would sing their wares in raucous voices while some pie man would shout to you to come and test his mutton.

The greatest attraction was a hanging at Tyburn,

but that was something I had no wish to see—nor should I have been allowed to if I had wanted to. Carlotta had seen a hanging once and she had described it to me—not that she had enjoyed it, I believed, but she could become exasperated with me at times and liked to shock me.

Her lover had taken her to see it because, he had said, she must learn what the world was about. She said it was terrible to see the men to be hanged arriving in a cart, and although she had pretended to look she had her eyes shut. She said there were men and women selling gingerbread, pies, fairings and the dying speeches and confessions of others who had recently met their death in this way.

I had said: "Don't tell me. I don't want to hear."

But she had gone on telling me and, I believed, making it even more gruesome than it actually was.

On other visits to London I had walked with my parents in the Mall, which was delightful, and this fashionable thoroughfare was very much used by members of the respectable nobility. There one paraded and bowed to one's friends and acquaintances and sometimes stopped and talked and and made arrangements to meet at some place. I loved the Mall. My grandfather told me how he had played Pell Mell there several times with King Charles. Nowadays there were flower girls there with their blooms, girls with baskets of oranges, which they proferred to passersby; and one could come face to face with a milkmaid driving her cow and stopping now and then to take milk from the cow so that buyers could be sure of its freshness. Strolling by watching the people was a great excitement to me. I had always enjoyed it.

"You should see it at night," Carlotta had said to me; and she had described the gallants who went out prowling through the crowds searching for young girls who took their fancy. At night one could see the ladies patched and beribboned and sometimes masked. That was the time to stroll down Pall Mall. "Poor little Damaris! They'll never allow you to do that." And when I had said they wouldn't allow her either she had just laughed at me.

I could never stop thinking of Carlotta for long and here in this city of adventure she seemed closer than ever.

We were all installed in the Eversleigh town house which was not far from St. James's Palace, and my mother said I should have a good night's rest for we would be out early the next day to see the beginnings of the coronation ceremonies.

I woke early the next morning, excited to find myself in a strange bed. I went to my window and looked down on the street where people were already gathering. They would come in today from the surrounding country. It was the twenty-third of April, St. George's Day. The people were very excited. I wondered how the Queen felt. What would one's reaction be if one were taking a crown which did not by right belong to one. Of course the English would never have a Catholic on the throne. I had heard my grandfather expound at length on that subject. And King James could have retained his crown if he had given up his faith. He refused and lost it, and then we had had Protestant William and Mary, now both dead, and Mary's sister Anne was our Queen.

The Jacobites would be angry but the mood of the people seemed to indicate that they wanted Anne. Or perhaps they just wanted a coronation.

At eleven o'clock we rode into the streets and saw the Queen on her way from St. James's Palace to Westminster Hall. She was carried in a sedan chair because she was so troubled with dropsy and swollen feet that she could not walk. She was about thirty-seven years of age, which seemed young to be afflicted with such an infirmity, but she had given birth to so many children and not one of them had survived—the young Duke of Gloucester, on whom all her hopes were set, having died recently—that this had had its effect on her.

Prince George of Denmark, her husband, who was as devoted to her as she was to him, walked before her and he was preceded by the Archbishop of Canterbury.

It was a glittering sight with garter-king-at-arms

129

and the lord mayor and black rod with the high steward of England all in attendance.

The Queen looked calm and surprisingly beautiful in spite of the fact that she was very fat, a condition induced by a lack of exercise and a love of food; on her head was a circle of gold set with diamonds and its simple elegance became her.

We had places in the Abbey and we followed the procession treading our way through the sweet herbs which had been sprinkled on the ground and taking the places allotted to us.

It was an uneasy moment when Thomas Tennison, the Archbishop of Canterbury, presented the Queen to the assembly and asked the question: "Sirs, I here present unto you Queen Anne, undoubted Queen of this realm. Whereas all you that are come this day to do your homages and service, are you willing to do the same?"

It seemed to me that the pause following those words went on for a long time, but that was merely my imagination because I had heard so much talk about the Jacobites.

Then the shout was deafening: "God save Queen Anne."

The Archbishop had to repeat the question three times after that—for he had to face the east, west, north and south each time he said it.

It was a thrilling moment when the choir began to sing the anthem. "The Queen shall rejoice in Thy strength, O Lord. Exceeding glad shall she be in Thy salvation. Thou shalt present her with the blessings of goodness and shalt set a crown of pure gold on her head."

When I heard all those voices singing in unison I felt sure that Anne really was the chosen sovereign and the King Across the Water presented no threat to the peace of the land.

It was sad, though, to see the Queen having to be helped to the altar; but when she made the declaration her voice was loud and clear.

"Will you to the utmost of your power maintain the

laws of God, the true profession of the gospel, and the protestant reformed religion established by law . . . ?"

"I promise to do this," declared Anne firmly.

This was what the people wanted. After all, it was because her father had not been an upholder of the Protestant faith that he had lost his throne.

After that there was the ceremony of the anointing, which was carried out in accordance with the ancient customs. Anne must stand while she was girt with the sword of St. Edward and then she must walk to the altar to offer it there. The spurs were presented to her and she placed them beside the sword on the altar and then she was invested with the ring and the staff.

The ring, my father had told me, was called the wedding ring of England and was engraved with the Cross of St. George. When it was placed on the finger it symbolized that the sovereign was pledged to honour his or her country and offer all the service and devotion of which that sovereign was capable. It is like a marriage, added my father.

I was deeply moved by the ceremony, as one must be, and when the Queen was seated on her chair and the Dean of Westminster brought the crown for the Archbishop of Canterbury to place on her head I joined with fervour in the loyal shout of "God save the Queen." It was wonderfully inspiring to hear the guns booming out from the turrets of the Abbey and being answered by those of the Tower of London.

I watched the peers led by the Queen's Consort, the Prince of Denmark, pay their homage to the new Queen by kneeling before her and then kissing her cheek.

We had places at the coronation banquet. My parents had been wondering whether the Queen would attend, for her disability must have made her quite exhausted, but my grandfather immediately replied that she must be there, tired or not. Otherwise those sly Jacobites would be saying she dared not face the traditional challenge of the champion Dymoke.

I enjoyed every moment. I was delighted to be able to gaze on the Queen. I thought she looked very regal and hid her tiredness very well. I liked her husband, who seemed mild and kind and was clearly anxious on her account.

It was after eight before the banquet was over and as the ceremonies had been going on for most of the day, the Queen was clearly relieved to leave for the palace of St. James's. The crowds cheered wildly as she passed along in her sedan chair.

The banquet in Westminster Hall might be over but the people were going on carousing throughout the night.

My grandfather said we should get home before the streets became too rowdy, as they would later. "If you want to," he said, "you can watch from the windows."

This we did.

It was afternoon of the following day. My mother, my grandmother and I had shopped in the morning in the Piazza at Covent Garden, which was crowded with revellers still celebrating the coronation. My mother had admired some violets, one of her favorite flowers, and had meant to buy some, but we turned away, our interest caught by something else, and forgot about them.

As we sat there a young woman went by. She was young and very flamboyantly dressed; but something about her reminded me of Carlotta. It was only a fleeting resemblance of course. She was not to be compared with Carlotta. At that moment a young man walked past and stopped. I realised that he had been following her, that she was aware of it and was now waiting for him to make some proposition.

Of course I knew this sort of behavior was commonplace and that women came out, usually at dusk and at night, with the very object of finding companions, but I had never before seen it so blatantly undertaken.

The two went off together.

The incident had had an effect on me. Chiefly I think because the woman bore a slight resemblance to Carlotta and had brought memories of her. I thought, if she were with us she would not be sitting here looking out. What had she said to me once: "Damaris, you're a looker-on. Things won't happen to you. You'll just watch them happen to other people. Do you know why?

It's because you're afraid. You always want to be safe, that's why you're so dull."

Cruel Carlotta. She so often hurt me. Sometimes I wondered why she meant so much to me.

Then the thought occurred to me that it would be a lovely surprise for my mother to have her violets. Why should I not go out into the streets and buy them for her? I shouldn't have to go back to the Piazza. There were many flower sellers in the streets—even more than there usually were because of the coronation, for they were taking advantage of the crowds to do more business.

I was not supposed to go out on my own. I seemed to hear Carlotta laughing at me. "It was only to the end of the street."

I should be scolded, but my mother would be pleased that I had remembered.

I was sure that if I had not seen the woman and been reminded of Carlotta I should never have been so bold. I put on my velvet cloak, slipped my purse into the pocket of my gown and went out.

I reached the end of the street without seeing a flower seller, and as I turned the corner I was caught up in a howling mob. People were circulating about a man in a tall black hat and shouting abuse at him.

Someone pressed against me. I was wary and kept my hand on my purse.

A woman was standing near me. I said, "What is it? What has he done?"

"Selling quack pills," she said. "Told us they'd make you young again, bring the colour back to your hair and cure all ailments, make you twenty again. He's a quack."

I stammered: "What will they do with him?"

"Duck him in the river, most like."

I shuddered. I was made uneasy by the looks of the mob, for I suddenly realised that I myself was attracting some strange looks.

It had been rather foolish to come out alone. I must get away from the crowd, find my violets quickly and go home.

I tried to fight my way out. It wasn't easy.

"Here, who you pushing of?" demanded a woman with greasy hair falling about her face.

I stammered: "I wasn't pushing. I . . . I was just looking."

"Just looking, is it, eh? The lady's only looking at us common folk."

I tried to move away unobtrusively, but she was not going to let me. She started to shout abuse at me.

I didn't know which way to turn. Then suddenly a woman was standing beside me. She was poorly dressed but clean. She caught my arm and said: "Now let this lady alone, will you? She's not sport for the likes of you."

The other woman seemed so surprised at the interruption that she stared open-mouthed at the other, who took the opportunity to take my arm and draw me away. We were soon lost in the crowd.

I was grateful to her. I had simply not known what to do and how to escape from that woman who had seemed so determined to make trouble.

The crowd had thinned a little. I was not sure which end of the street I was at. I thought I would abandon the idea of getting the violets and go home as quickly as possible. I could see my mother had been right when she had not wanted me to go out alone.

The woman was smiling at me.

"You shouldn't be out alone on the streets, dear," she said. "Why, that's a beautiful velvet cloak you're wearing. Gives people ideas, see, dearie. Now let's get you back home fast as we can. What made you come out alone? Who are you with?"

I told her I had come up from the country with my family for the coronation and I had slipped out to buy some violets for my mother.

"Vi'lets," she cried. "Vi'lets. Now I know the woman what sells the best vi'lets in London and not a stone's throw from this here spot where we standing. If you want vi'lets you leave it to Good Mrs. Brown. You was lucky you was, dearie, to come across me. I know that one who was after you. She'd have had your purse in no time if I hadn't come along."

"She was a terrible woman. I had done nothing to her."

"Course you hadn't. Now have you still got your purse?"

"Yes," I told her. I had made sure to keep my hand on it after all the stories I had heard of the agility of the London thieves.

"Well, that's a blessing. We'll get them vi'lets and then, ducky, I think we should get you back home ... before you're missed, eh?"

"Oh, thank you. It is so kind of you."

"Well, I likes to do a bit of good where I can. That's why they call me Good Mrs. Brown. It don't cost nothing, does it, and it helps the world go round."

"Thank you. Do you know Eversleigh House?"

"Why, bless you, dearie, a' course I do. There ain't no place in these 'ere parts that Good Mrs. Brown don't know about. Don't you be afraid. I'll whisk you back to Eversleigh House afore you can say Queen Anne—that I will—and with the best vi'lets you can find in London."

"I shall be so grateful. They wouldn't want me to be out, you see."

"Oh, I do see, and right they are. When you think of what I just rescued you from. These thieves and vagabonds is all over this 'ere wicked city, dearie, and they've just got their blinkers trained on innocents like you."

"I should have listened to my mother."

"That's what the girls all say when they gets into a bit of trouble, now don't they? It never done no harm to listen to mother."

While she had been talking we had moved away from the crowd. I had no idea where we were and I saw no sign of flower sellers. The street was narrow, the houses looked gaunt and dilapidated as we turned up an alley.

I said uneasily: "We seem to be coming a long way."

"Nearly there dear. You trust Good Mrs. Brown."

We had turned into an alley. Some children were squatting on the cobbles; from a window a woman looked out and called: "Nice work, Mrs. Brown."

135

"May God bless you, dear," replied Mrs. Brown. "This way, ducky."

She had pushed me through a door. It slammed shut behind us. I cried out: "What does this mean?"

"Trust Good Mrs. Brown," she said.

She had taken my arm in a firm grip and dragged me down a flight of stairs. I was in a room like a cellar. There were three girls there—one about my age, two older. One had a brown wool coat about her shoulders and was parading up and down before the other two. They were all laughing but they stopped and stared when we entered.

It was now brought home to me that the fears which had started to come to me when we first turned into the labyrinth of back streets were fully justified. I was in a more unhappy position now than I had been when accosted by the woman in the crowd.

"Now don't be frightened, dearie," said Mrs. Brown. "No harm will come to you if you're good. It's not my way to harm people." She turned to the others. "Look at her. Ain't she a little beauty. Come out to buy vi'lets for her mamma. Feel the cloth of this cape. Best velvet. That'll fetch a pretty penny. And she kept her hand on her purse too, which was nice of her. She came near to losing it in the crowd."

I said: "What does this mean? Why have you brought me here?"

"There," said Mrs. Brown, "Don't she talk pretty. You two girls want to listen and learn how to do it. I reckon it would be a help to you in your work."

She laughed. It was amazing how quickly Good Mrs. Brown had become Evil Mrs. Brown.

"What do you want of me? Take my purse and let me go."

"First of all," said Mrs. Brown. "We want that nice cloak. Off with it."

I did not move. I stood there clutching it to me.

"Now, now," said Mrs. Brown. "We don't want any trouble. Trouble's something I never could abide." She took my hands in a firm grip and wrenched them from my cloak. In a few seconds it was off my shoulders.

136

One of the girls grabbed it and wrapped it round herself.

"Now then, now then," said Mrs. Brown. "Don't you dirty it, now. You know how particular Davey is. He wants it just as it comes off the lady."

"I see you brought me here to steal my cloak. Well, you have it. Now let me go."

Mrs. Brown turned to the girls and they all laughed. "She's pretty, though, ain't she?" said Mrs. Brown. "Such a trusting little piece. She took quite a fancy to Good Mrs. Brown, I can tell you. Was ready to follow her wherever she led."

I turned towards the door. Mrs. Brown's hand was on my arm.

"That's not all, ducky."

"No," I cried. "You want my purse as well."

"You did keep it nice and safe for us. It would be a pity not to have it after that, wouldn't it?"

They kept laughing in a shrill way which frightened me.

I took out my purse and threw it on the floor.

"Good. You see she's not one for trouble either."

"Well, you have my cloak and my purse. Now let me go."

Mrs. Brown was feeling the stuff of my gown.

"The very best cloth," she said, "only worn by the gentry. Come on, dearie. Off with it."

"I cannot take off my dress."

"Her servants has always done it for her," mocked one of the girls.

"We'll be her servants today," said Mrs. Brown. "I always believe in treating my friends in the way they're used to."

It was becoming more and more of a nightmare. They were pulling my dress over my shoulders.

"What shall I do?" I cried. "You are taking all my clothes. I shall be . . . naked."

"See, a nice modest little girl. Now listen, dearie, we wouldn't let you go out into the street starkers, would we, girls? Now that would cause a bit of a barney, wouldn't it?"

They all laughed hideously.

I felt numb with terror. How I longed to call back time. How I wished I was sitting at my window and that I had had the good sense to do what I had been told was the wise thing to do—never go out alone.

I was sure this was some sort of nightmare. It couldn't be true. Things like this did not happen.

They had stripped me down to my shift. How I hated their dirty fingers feeling the cloth of my clothes, gloating, as they took them from me, over the price they would fetch.

I stood there shivering with the awful realisation that if I wanted to escape I could not run out into the street with no clothes on.

Nevertheless I felt I could not endure to stay any longer in this terrible room with the piles of clothes lying on the floor. I saw that it was the profession of women like Mrs. Brown to lure unsuspecting people— children, it seemed mostly—into her den and there to rob them of their clothes.

"Well, dearie," said Mrs. Brown, "you was a nice little pick up. But listen here. I don't want no trouble. You understand. Trouble and Mrs. Brown is two that don't go together."

"You're a thief," I said. "You will get caught one day and you'll go to Tyburn for what you do."

"Not such a babe as we thought, eh?" She winked at the girls, who chortled with amusement.

"We're careful. We're good. Least I am. I wan't called Good Mrs. Brown for nothing. Give me that cloak, ducks," she said to one of the girls. The girl handed her a cloak which was rugged and torn.

"There, wrap that round yourself," she said.

I looked at it distastefully.

"Oh, it's not what you're used to, dearie. I know that. But it's better than going naked. It's more decent, see."

I wrapped the cloak round me and for a moment my disgust was greater than my terror.

"Now listen, dearie. We're going out of here. I'll take you back on your road, see. I don't want no trouble. I don't want nothing traced to me. Good Mrs. Brown keeps out of trouble. All she wants is the nice clothes rich little ladies and gentlemen wear. It don't mean much to them because they have others. But it means the difference between eating and starvation to Good Mrs. Brown. So I shall take you out with me. And if you was to shout I'd got your clothes nobody here would listen to you. Then I'll leave you to find your home on your own. Yes, when it's safe I'll leave you. Understand?"

I nodded. My one desire was to get out of this place with as little trouble as possible.

She gripped my arm. We went up the stairs. The relief to feel the fresh air again was great.

All the time she was taking me through the narrow streets she was talking to me. No one took any notice of us. She had had my shoes too, so I was barefooted and I could not walk easily on the cobbles.

She laughed at me because I stumbled.

"They are such pretty shoes," she murmured. Then she went on: "Listen to me, ducky. You've had a lucky escape. You lost your clothes. You could have lost more than that, dearie. Mrs. Brown has taught you a lesson. What a day for a rich little girl to go wandering out in her velvets and silks! Today, dearie, there's more rogues and vagabonds in this 'ere city than at any time . . . and there are enough of us, Gawd knows, without this new lot. They comes in from all over the place, coronation days, royal weddings, you know . . . such like. They're the times to make a picking. Well, you've been plucked, little pigeon, and thank your stars it was by Good Mrs. Brown. Now I don't want no trouble. You haven't been hurt, have you. I've even given you this 'ere cloak to cover yourself. They'll ask questions. You'll tell them it was Good Mrs. Brown . . . but you won't know where I took you, will you? So you won't be able to tell on me. You'll get over this. My what a scolding you'll get. Silly little pigeon. But they'll be that glad to get you back; I reckon you'll be petted more than ever. Thank Good Mrs. Brown. And you won't want to bring trouble on her, will you? Remember the good she's done you. Why, you might have been picked up by one of them old bawds and been sold to some loving old gentleman by now. See. You'll be prepared

139

next time. But I reckon there won't be a next time. You've learned a lesson from Good Mrs. Brown."

We had come out of the labyrinth of streets.

"There now," she said. "You want to get home fast. Just round the corner is the street where they was getting ready to duck the old quack. You know where you are from there. Get home . . . quick."

She gave me a little push. I looked round and she disappeared. My relief was intense. I started to run.

Yes, she was right. There was the street where it had all begun. If I turned the corner and went straight on I would come to Eversleigh House.

I turned that corner and ran full tilt into a woman who was walking along with a young man beside her.

She gave a little shriek of disgust and I think she put out a hand to ward me off. I fell sprawling to the ground.

"Gad," said the young man. "She's wearing nothing beneath the cloak."

"She was after my purse," said the woman.

"I was not," I cried. "I have just been robbed of my clothes."

They were startled by my voice, and having just come from Mrs. Brown's terrible room I understood why. It did not match my appearance.

The young man helped me to my feet. We must have looked odd together, for his appearance could only be described as exquisite. I could smell the faint perfume with which his clothes were scented.

The lady was beautifully dressed too and also perfumed. We must have made a strange contrast.

"What happened to you?" said the lady.

"I came out to buy some violets for my mother," I said quickly. "A woman started to shout at me in the crowd and then another woman came along. She said she would take me to buy the violets and she took me to a horrible room and made me take off all my clothes."

"There's quite a trade in it," said the young man. "It is usually young children who are the victims. Are you hurt?"

"No, thank you. I want to get home quickly."

"Where is your home?"

"It's Eversleigh House."

"Eversleigh House! So you are one of the Eversleighs," said the woman.

"Let us get her home quickly," said the young man. "They'll be anxious, I daresay."

They walked along beside me. I wondered what passersby thought to see this elegant pair in the company of such a ragged barefooted urchin. No one took very much notice. So many strange sights were seen in London that the people accepted them as commonplace.

I could have wept with relief when we arrived at the house. Job, one of our servants cried: "She's here. Mistress Damaris is here." I knew by his words that I had already been missed.

My mother came running into the hall. She saw me standing there in the horrible cloak, stared disbelievingly for a few seconds then, realising it was indeed her daughter, swept me into her arms.

"My darling child," she said, "whatever has happened? We have been frantic."

I could only cling to her speechless, I was so happy to be with her.

The lady spoke. "It's a trick they practice often," she said. "She was robbed of her clothes."

"Robbed of her clothes . . . !" my mother repeated.

Then she looked at the two who had brought me home. I saw her glance at the young man and as she did so a strange look came into her face. It was a mingling of all sorts of things, amazement, disbelief, a certain fear and a sort of horror.

The lady was saying: "We found her running away. . . . She ran into us, and then, when we heard who she was, we thought we would make sure she got home safely."

My mother stammered: "Thank you." Then she turned to me and hugged me against her and we just clung together.

My father appeared.

"She's here. She's home," he cried. "Thank God. Why . . . for God's sake."

My mother said nothing and it was the strangers who explained.

141

"It was good of you," said my father. "Come, dearest, let the child get rid of that awful garment. She had better have a bath quickly." I ran to him and he held me tightly. I had never loved them so much as I did at that moment.

My mother was terribly shaken. She seemed to be in a kind of daze and it was my father who took charge.

"You must have some refreshment," he said to the woman and the young man.

"It is not necessary," said the woman. "You will all be feeling very upset."

"Oh, come," said my father, "you must stay awhile. We want to tell you how grateful we are."

"The streets of London were never safe but they are becoming worse than ever," said the young man.

"Priscilla," said my father, "take Damaris up and look after her. I'll see to our guests."

I went upstairs with my mother. The cloak was taken away and given to one of the servants to burn. I washed all over in warm water and dressed myself while I told my mother exactly what had happened.

"Oh, darling," she said, "you shouldn't have gone out on your own."

"I know, but I only meant to go to the top of the street and buy you violets."

"When I think of what could have happened. That wicked woman . . ."

"She wasn't so very wicked, mother. She called herself Good Mrs. Brown. She didn't hurt me. She only wanted my clothes and my money."

"It is monstrous," said my mother.

"But she was poor and it was her way of getting something to eat, she said."

"My dear, you are such a child. Perhaps you should rest now."

"I don't want to rest, mother, and I think I should go down and thank the people who brought me home."

My mother stiffened in a strange way.

"Who are these people?" she asked.

"I don't know. I was running along and fell into them. I went sprawling on the ground and they picked me up. They knew this was Eversleigh House, and

142

when I told them it was my home they insisted on bringing me."

"Very well," she said, "let's go down."

My father was in the drawing room with them and they were drinking wine. They were still talking about the rogues who invaded London at a time like this. My grandfather and grandmother had joined them. They had not been aware that I had disappeared and had listened with horror to what had befallen me.

My grandmother rose up when I entered and embraced me with fervour, but the way my grandfather looked at me implied that he had never had much respect for my intelligence and had even less now.

My father said: "This is the strangest coincidence. This lady is Mistress Elizabeth Pilkington, who once thought of taking Enderby Hall."

"Yes, and I was very disappointed when I heard that it was no longer for sale."

"A caprice of my granddaughter's," said my grandfather with a curl of his lips. "The house belongs to her. It's a mistake to give women power over property. I've always said it."

"You have always nourished a feud against the opposite sex," said my grandmother.

"It didn't prevent my snaring you into matrimony," he countered.

"I married you to show you how you underestimated us," she countered.

"Alas," he retorted, "my opinions do not seem to have changed after . . . how many years is it?"

They were always like that together; it was a constant sparring match and yet their devotion to each other kept showing itself; and they were as happily married as were my parents. They merely had a different way of showing it.

"Speaking of houses," said my grandmother, "although Enderby Hall still stands empty, there is another in the district. Neighbours of ours—of whom we were very fond—are going away."

"Yes," said my grandfather, "there is Grasslands Manor."

"Are you still looking for a place in the country?" asked my mother.

"My mother is very interested in that part of the country," said Matthew Pilkington.

A faint colour had appeared in Elizabeth Pilkington's cheeks. She said, "Yes, I might like to take a look at this Grasslands Manor."

"Any time which is convenient to you we shall be pleased to see you at Eversleigh," my grandmother told her.

"It is so bracing there, I believe," said Matthew.

"If you mean the east wind favours us with its presence very frequently, yes," said my grandfather.

"An interesting spot, though," said Elizabeth.

"Roman country, I believe," added Matthew.

"Yes, there are some fine specimens of Roman remains," put in my grandfather. "Well, we're not far from Dover and there is the old Pharos there...the oldest in England."

"You must go and look at this Grasslands Manor," said Matthew Pilkington.

"Oh, I will," replied his mother.

They took their leave soon after that. They had a house in London close by, they said, and hoped we should meet again before we left for the country.

"Unfortunately we shall be returning the day after tomorrow," said my mother.

I looked at her sharply because we had made no arrangements so far.

My grandmother was about to speak but my grandfather threw a warning look in her direction. I felt there was something going on which was a secret to me.

"Well, I shall be down to look at this Grasslands place, I daresay," said Elizabeth Pilkington.

When they had left I was plied with questions. What had possessed me to go out on my own? I had been warned often. I must never do it again.

"Don't worry," I assured them. "I won't."

"To think how easily it could happen," cried my mother. "And what *might* have happened. As it is there's that beautiful new cloak and dress...."

144

"Oh, I am so sorry. I have been so foolish . . . ."

My mother put her arm about me. "My dear child," she said, "if it has taught you a lesson it was worth it. Thank God you came safely back."

"It was good of the Pilkingtons to bring her back," said my grandmother.

"I rushed into them. I was almost home then," I said.

"But they really were concerned," went on my grandmother. "Wouldn't it be strange if they took Grasslands?"

"There's something about them I don't like," said my mother, and there was a strange expression on her face as though she had drawn a veil over her features to hide what she really felt.

"They seemed pleasant enough," said my grandmother.

"And to have the means to buy the place," added my grandfather.

"Carlotta showed her over Enderby Hall," said my mother. "And then she decided not to let. She must have taken a dislike to her."

"Oh, it was just one of Carlotta's whims," said my grandmother. "That couldn't have had anything to do with Elizabeth Pilkington. She just did not want to sell the house."

"It will be strange if you have found a buyer for Grasslands, Damaris."

I thought it would be strange too. I rather hoped I had. I thought it would be rather pleasant to have the Pilkingtons as neighbours.

The next day Matthew Pilkington called.

I was in the hall when he arrived so I was the first to greet him. He was carrying a big bunch of violets.

He smiled at me. He was very handsome—in fact I think the most handsome man I had ever seen. Perhaps his clothes helped. He was wearing a mulberry-coloured velvet jacket and a very fine waistcoat. From the pockets low down in his coat a frilly white kerchief showed. His stick hung on a ribbon from his wrist. He wore high-heeled shoes which made him look very tall—he must be of a considerable height without them;

and the tongue of his shoe stuck up well above the instep, which, I had learned since coming to London, was the very height of fashion. In one hand he held his hat, which was of a deep shade of blue, almost violet. In fact his clothes toned beautifully with the flowers, so that I could almost have believed he had chosen them for that purpose. But of course that could not be so, violets having a special significance.

I felt myself flushing with pleasure.

He bowed low, took my hand and kissed it.

"I see you have recovered from your adventure. I came to enquire and I have brought these for your mother so that she shall not be without what you braved so much to get for her."

"Oh, but that is so good of you, " I said. I took the flowers and held them to my nose, inhaling the fragrance.

"From the best flower seller in London," he said. "I got them in the Covent Garden Piazza this morning."

"She will be so pleased. You must come in." I took him into the little winter parlour which led from the hall.

"Please sit down," I said.

He put his hat on the table in the hall and followed me.

"So," he said, "you are returning to the country tomorrow. I am sorry about that. My mother would so liked to have entertained you. She is anxious to hear more of this house which is for sale."

"It's a very pleasant house," I said.

"I wonder why the owners left it."

"The wife died having a baby and her husband can't forget. He came from the north originally and has gone back there. They were very great friends of ours and we have offered to show people the house if they are thinking of buying it. My grandmother has the keys at Eversleigh House."

"And what about this other house?"

"Enderby. Well, that is a fine house too, but it has the reputation of being haunted."

"My mother was most impressed by it."

"Yes, but Carlotta, my sister, who owns it, decided

146

not to sell. It was left to her, you see, by the previous owner, who was a relative."

"I see, and Enderby remains empty."

"It is extraordinary. Carlotta's whim, my grandfather calls it."

"Where is your sister?"

"She is married now and lives in Sussex. She has the dearest little baby. Tell me, do you live in London?"

"Well, I have a place in the country—in Dorset—a small estate to look after. I am there sometimes and sometimes with my mother in London. Of course now that there is war I may join the army."

I frowned. My mother hated wars so fiercely that she had imbued me with the same feeling.

"It seems ridiculous that we should concern ourselves with the problems of other countries," I said. "Why should what happens in Europe matter to us?"

I was really repeating what I had heard my mother say.

He said: "It is not quite as simple as that. Louis the Fourteenth, the French King, made an agreement with our late King and he has broken that agreement. His grandson Philip of Anjou has been made King of Spain. You see France will be dominating Europe. He has already put garrisons into the towns of the Spanish Netherlands. Worst of all he has acknowledged the son of James the Second as James the Third of England. War has been declared and we have strong allies in Holland and the Austrian Empire. It is necessary to go to war, you see."

"So you may become a soldier. My father was a soldier once. He gave it up. My mother was so much against it. He bought the Dower House at Eversleigh and farms the land there and looks after his tenants; he works with my grandfather, who is getting old now. You met him yesterday. My uncle Carl is in the army and so is my uncle Edwin. He is the present Lord Eversleigh. He lives at Eversleigh when he is home."

"I know yours is a family with a strong military tradition."

147

We were deep in conversation when my mother entered the room. She drew back in astonishment.

"Oh, mother," I cried, "we have a visitor. And he has brought some violets for you."

"That is kind," she said. "Thank you." She took them and buried her face in them.

"My mother asked me to try to persuade you to stay a few more days so that we could entertain you here in London," said Matthew Pilkington.

"That," said my mother, "is extremely kind but we have made our arrangements."

She sent for the customary wine and he stayed for an hour. I felt he was reluctant to go but I sensed that my mother was not eager for him to stay. I hoped he did not realise this and that I did only because I knew her so well.

When he left he said: "I believe we shall meet again soon."

"I hope so," I said warmly.

Later that day my mother told my grandparents that Matthew had called.

"A suitor for Damaris already," said my grandmother.

"Nonsense," retorted my mother, "she is far too young. In any case he brought the violets for me."

"An excuse of course," said my grandmother.

I suppose hearing Matthew referred to as my suitor set me thinking. He had seemed to like me. Then I realised that this was one of the rare occasions when Carlotta had not been present to demand attention.

Still, I rather liked the idea of having Matthew for a suitor.

We left London the next day. As we rode out of the town, passing through Temple Bar into Cheapside, where the stall holders and their customers made passage difficult, to Bucklersbury, where the tantalising smells which came from the apothecaries and grocers shops filled the air, and as I saw the grey walls of the Tower of London rising above the river I thought of what could have happened to me when I ventured into these fascinating but terrifying streets and how fortunate I had been to encounter no worse than Good Mrs. Brown.

Indeed I was beginning to bestow on her that benevolence she had been so eager to claim. Moreover, I remembered that she had brought the Pilkingtons into my life; and since Matthew had called with the violets I had been thinking about him a good deal.

My mother had been inclined to laugh at what she called his dandified appearance. My grandfather said it was the fashion and most young men looked like that nowadays. He thought fashions were less exaggerated than in his young days. "We were beribboned. Yes, that's it! Ribbons in every conceivable place."

My grandmother was rather pleased that Matthew had called again. She was sure he had come to see me. She had always felt that Carlotta overshadowed me and I knew that now she believed I should come into my own.

When I came to think of it I was rather pleased that Carlotta was not here. Then I fell to wondering whether I should ever see Matthew again.

So we left London and came into the country.

We stayed one night in an inn near Seven Oaks and the next day were home.

When I had assured myself that my dogs and my horse had been well cared for I was prepared to settle down to the daily routine, but somehow nothing could be quite the same again. We had a new sovereign; and I had had that adventure which was going to haunt me for quite a while. It did. I had a few nightmares dreaming I was in that horrible room with the three young girls and they were creeping up to me led by Good Mrs. Brown. I would awake calling out and clutching the bedclothes frantically to me. Once my mother heard me. She sat by the bed.

"How I wish we had never gone up to London," she said.

But after a while I ceased to dream, and then there was the excitement of Elizabeth Pilkington's coming to Grasslands Manor.

As soon as she saw it she declared that she liked it;

and this time the sale went through. By the end of the summer she was installed in the Manor.

Matthew by that time was serving with the army, and I did not see him, but I became friendly with her and we visited each other frequently.

I helped her move in and buy some of the furniture for the house, for she was still keeping her London residence.

"I am so used to town life," she told me, "that I can't abandon it altogether."

She was amusing and lively and talked a great deal about the theatre and the parts she had played. She reminded me of Harriet and indeed they had known each other at one time when they had played together in William Wycherley's *The Country Wife*. My grandfather liked her and she was often invited to Eversleigh. My mother became friendly with her too. Her dislike seemed to be for Matthew and now that he was in the army she seemed to have forgotten about him.

That Christmas we went to Eyot Abbass. Little Clarissa was quite a person now. She was ten months old and beginning to take an interest in everything. She was fair haired and blue eyed and I loved her dearly.

My mother said: "Damaris will make a good mother." And I thought more than anything I should like to have a baby of my own.

Carlotta was as beautiful as ever. Benjie adored her and was so delighted to be her husband. It was not so easy to know how Carlotta felt. She had always been unpredictable. There was a vague restlessness in her which I could not understand. She was the most beautiful girl in any gathering; she had a husband who clearly wanted to grant her every wish; she had a dear little baby, a gracious home; Harriet and Gregory were very fond of her and she had all her life been like a daughter to them. What did Carlotta want to make her happy?

I couldn't resist asking her once. It was four days after Christmas and I went out walking with Gregory's retriever when I came upon her sitting in the shelter of a cliff looking out to the Eyot.

I sat down beside her. "You are lucky, Carlotta," I said. "You just have everything . . . ."

She turned to look at me in amazement. "What has come over our little Damaris?" she asked. "She used to be such a contented little piece. Happy in her lot, ministering to the sick—animals mostly but not above taking a basket of goodies to the ailing of the district—goodness and contentment shining from her little face."

"You always made fun of me, Carlotta."

"Perhaps it was because I could never be like you."

"You . . . like me! You'd never want to."

"No," she said. "You're right there. What an adventure you had in the wicked city. Robbed of your clothes and sent out naked. My poor Damaris!"

"Yes, it was terrifying. But I ran into the Pilkingtons and because of that Elizabeth Pilkington is at Grasslands. Carlotta, isn't it strange how one thing that happens leads to something else which wouldn't have happened otherwise?"

She nodded and was serious. I could see her thinking of that.

"You see, if I hadn't gone out to buy violets . . ."

"I get the point," she said. "No need to elaborate."

"Well, it just struck me."

"You like this woman, don't you? I did when I showed her Enderby."

"Why did you decide so suddenly not to sell?" I asked.

"Oh, I had my reasons. She has a son, has she?"

"Yes . . . Matthew."

"You like him, don't you?"

"How . . . did you know?"

She laughed at me and gave me a friendly push. "That was the trouble, Damaris. I always know what you're going to do. You're predictable. It makes you . . ."

"I know," I said. "Dull."

"Well, it is nice to meet a little mystery now and then. So Matthew was very gallant, wasn't he?"

"He brought violets for our mother."

She burst out laughing.

"Why do you laugh?" I asked.

"Never mind," she said. Then she stared out to sea

and said: "You never know what is going to happen, do you? Right across the sea, that's France over there."

"Of course," I said, a little nettled by her laughter. "What's odd about that? It's always been there, hasn't it?"

"Imagine it over there," she said. "There'll be a lot of excitement. The old King dying and now the new one."

"There isn't a new one. It's a Queen we have."

"They don't think so over there."

She hugged her knees, smiling secretly.

I was about to remark that she was in a strange mood. But then Carlotta was often in a strange mood.

A few days later when I was riding I passed the same spot and there she was seated by the rock staring out to France.

Night in the Forbidden Wood

A year had gone by. I had passed my fourteenth birthday and was now rising fifteen. The war was still going on. My uncles Edwin and Carl were abroad serving with Marlborough, who had now become a duke. But for the fact that they were engaged in the fighting we should have thought little of it for the war itself did not intrude on our lives.

It was Maytime, a lovely time of the year. After I had finished lessons with my governess, Mistress Leveret, I would exercise my horse, Tomtit; sometimes I would take him to the sea and ride along close to the water. He loved that and it was exhilarating to take deep breaths of air, which we all said was fresher on our coast than anywhere else. There was always a sharp tang in it which, having been brought up with it, we all loved.

Sometimes I rode deeper into the country. I liked to leave Tomtit to drink by a stream while I lay in the grass very quietly watching the rabbits come out to gambol and sometimes voles and baby field mice. I could watch the frogs and toads and the water beetles for hours. I loved the country sounds and the melodious song of the birds.

One day Tomtit cast a shoe and I took him along to the blacksmith. While he was being shod I went for a walk and that led me near Enderby Hall.

The place had a fascination for me as it had for most people. I rarely went in it. My mother was always complaining that nothing was done about it; it was absurd to keep the place cleaned and aired for nobody she said. Carlotta must be made to see reason and get rid of it.

Close by the house was that land which my father had acquired when he bought the Dower House. He had never put it to use and was always going to do something about it but somehow never did. It was fenced in and he made it quite clear that he did not want it used as common ground. I guessed he must have had some plan for it.

I leaned against the fence and looked at the house. Dark and forbidding it seemed; but that was because of its reputation. And then suddenly I heard a sound. I listened. I looked towards the house. But no, it was not coming from the house. It was somewhere behind me. It was beyond the fence. I listened again. There it was. A piteous whine. Some animal in distress. I thought it sounded like a dog.

I was going to see. My father had put up such a strong fence around this land that it was not easy to scale it. There was a gate, though heavily padlocked, but it was possible to climb over this and I did so.

I stood there for a moment listening. The place was overgrown. I called it the Forbidden Wood because my father had stressed often that it was very private. I wondered afresh why he should have taken such pains to prevent people getting in and then do nothing about it.

Then I heard the sound again. It was definitely some animal in distress.

I went in the direction of the sound. Yes, I was getting nearer. Then I saw it. I had been right. It was a dog, a beautiful mastiff bitch—buff coloured with slightly darker ears and muzzle. I saw at once what had happened; one of her hind legs was caught in a trap.

She was looking at me with piteous eyes and I could see she was in considerable pain.

I had always had a way with animals. I think it was because I always talked to them and I had a special love for and understanding of them which they were quick to sense.

I knelt down. I saw exactly what had happened. Someone had set a trap to snare a hare or rabbit I guessed, and this beautiful dog had been caught in it.

I was running considerable risk, I knew. She might have bitten me, for the pain must have been intense, but I soothed her as I got to work, and as I had never been afraid of animals somehow they never seemed afraid of me.

In a few minutes I had seen how to release the trap. I did so and the dog was free.

I patted her head.

"Poor old lady," I murmured. "It's bad, I know."

It was indeed bad. She could not stand up without intense pain.

I coaxed her along, murmuring still. I sensed that she trusted me. I knew something about broken limbs. I had set them before for other animals with some success. I promised myself I would have a try with this one.

The animal was in excellent condition and was obviously well cared for. Later I would have to set about finding the owner. In the meantime I would tend the wounded leg.

I took her back to the Dower House and to my room, and Miss Leveret, who passed me on the stairs, cried: "Oh, Damaris, not another of your sick animals!"

"This lovely creature has hurt her leg. She was caught in a trap. People should not be allowed to use such traps. They're dangerous."

"Well I've no doubt you will put it right."

Mistress Leveret sighed. Like the rest of them, she thought I should be growing out of my absorption with animals.

I sent for hot water and bathed the leg. I found a very big basket which I had used for one of the bitches when she had puppies and I put the mastiff in it. I had a special ointment which was soothing and nonpoisonous. I had had it from one of the farmers who made it himself and swore by its healing properties.

The mastiff had ceased to whimper and was looking at me with her liquid eyes as though she was thanking me for easing her pain.

I gave her a bone which I found in the kitchens and there was quite a bit of good meat on it, and some water in one of my dogs' dishes. She seemed contented and I left her sleeping in the basket and went down to supper.

Mistress Leveret, who took her meals with us, was telling my parents that I had brought another wounded stray into the household.

My mother smiled. "There is nothing unusual about that," she said. We sat down at the table, and my father was talking about some of the cottages on his estate and the repairs which would have to be done, and we had almost finished when the talk came back to the dog I had saved.

"What had happened to this one?" asked my father smiling at me.

"His leg had been caught in a trap," I explained.

"I don't like traps," said my mother. "They're cruel."

"They're meant to kill at a stroke," my father explained. "It's unfortunate for an animal if he just gets trapped by a leg. The men like to get a hare or a rabbit for the pot, you know. They consider that a part of their wages. By the way, where was the trap?"

"It was on the closed-in land by Enderby," I said.

I was astonished by the change in my father. His face turned red and then white.

"Where?" he cried.

"You know ... the fenced-in land which you're always going to do something about and never do."

"Who put a trap in there?" he demanded.

I shrugged my shoulders. "Someone who thought he'd trap a hare or a rabbit for the pot, I suppose."

My father was a man who was rarely roused to anger but when he was angry he could be violently so.

He said: "I want to know who put that trap there."

He spoke quietly but it was the quiet before the storm.

"Well, you said that they used traps as part of their wages."

"Not on that land," he said. "I gave express orders that no one was to go there."

My mother looked frightened.

"I don't suppose he's done any harm, Leigh," she said.

My father brought his fist down on the table. "Who ever put that trap there disobeyed my orders. I am going to find out who did it."

He stood up.

My mother said: "Not now, surely."

But he had gone out. I heard him riding out of the stables.

I said: "He is in a great rage."

My mother was silent.

"I hate those traps," I said. "I'd like to stop them. But why is he so angry?"

She did not answer. But I could see she was very shaken.

The next day there was terrible trouble. The owner of the trap was found. He was Jacob Rook. My father dismissed him. He was to take everything and go. My father would not have his orders ignored.

It was most distressing, for when the people on the land were dismissed they not only lost their work but their homes. Jacob and Mary Rook had lived fifteen years on the Eversleigh estate in one of the small cottages which now belonged to my father.

They had a month to get out.

We were all very upset. Jacob was a good worker; Mary often helped in the house, and I hated to think my father could be so cruel.

It was terrible when Mary came to the house and cried; she kept clinging to my mother and begging her to let them stay. My mother was very unhappy; she said she would speak to my father.

I had never seen him like this before. I had not realised he could be so hard.

"Please," I begged, "overlook it this once. He'll never do it again."

"I will be obeyed," said my father. "I gave special orders and Jacob Rook deliberately disobeyed them."

He was adamant and there was nothing we could do.

I blamed myself for saying where I had found the mastiff. I had not thought it would be so important.

In a day or so the bitch was healed enough for her to limp about. I fed her on the best I could get and it was clear that she had taken a fancy to me, but my joy in the adventure had gone because of the Rooks.

Two days after I had found the dog I was riding past Grasslands Manor when I saw Elizabeth Pilkington in the garden. She called to me. "I have been meaning to send a messenger over to you. I wanted you to come and visit me. I have someone who very much wants to see you."

As she spoke Matthew Pilkington came out of the house.

He hurried over to me, took my hand and kissed it.

He looked very elegant but not so fancifully dressed as he had been in London. He wore high leather boots and knee-length jacket of dark blue frogged with black braid. I thought he was even more handsome than when I had last seen him.

"How delightful to see you again," he said. "You must come in, must she not, mother?"

Elizabeth Pilkington said that I must indeed do so.

I dismounted and went into the house.

I was tingling with pleasure at the sight of him. He seemed different from the young men of the neighbourhood whom I met from time to time. It was that air of immense sophistication which hung about him and which I had never noticed in other people. I suppose it was due to his living so much of his life in London.

He had been with the army overseas for a spell, he said, and then he had gone back to his estates in Dorset for a while. "One cannot neglect them for too long," he added.

"You've grown up since we last met," he commented.

Then his mother said: "Matthew has had one great unhappiness since he arrived here. He has lost a favourite dog."

I stood up in my excitement and cried: "A mastiff bitch?"

"Yes," said Matthew. "How did you know?"

I started to laugh. "Because I found her."

"You found her? Where is she?"

"Reclining in a basket in my bedroom at the moment. She was caught in a trap. I found her, took her home and dressed her wound. She is recovering very nicely."

Matt's eyes were beaming with delight.

"Well, that is wonderful. I am so grateful to you. Belle is my favourite dog."

"She is a beautiful dog," I said. "Poor dear, she has been very sorry for herself."

"And grateful to you . . . as I am." He had taken my hand and kissed it.

"Oh," I said blushing, "it was nothing. I would never pass by an animal in distress."

Elizabeth Pilkington was smiling at us benignly. "This is the most wonderful news," she said. "You've been our good angel, Damaris."

"I am doubly glad for Belle's sake. I could see that she was no stray. She is used to the very best."

"She's a good faithful creature. Not so young now but you couldn't find a braver and more devoted guard."

"I know well her qualities. I am so glad to have restored her to you."

"If you hadn't discovered her . . ."

"Who knows what would have happened? People hardly ever go to that land. In fact . . . there is great trouble because Jacob Rook set a trap there."

"Which land is it?" asked Elizabeth.

"It's close to Enderby. It was Enderby land at one time. My father bought it. He has some plans for it but at the moment it is strictly out of bounds. I call it the Forbidden Wood." I turned to Matt. "Your dog will be able to walk tomorrow, I think. I'll bring her back to you then."

"That's wonderful. How can we ever thank her?" he asked his mother.

"Damaris doesn't need to be told how much we appreciate what she has done. She knows it. She would have done the same for any little hedgerow sparrow."

I rode home in an exalted mood which I realised was not only due to the fact that I had found the dog's owner and that he should be Matthew Pilkington; it was largely because Matt had come back.

My pleasure was dampened as I went in by the sight

of Mary Rook in the kitchen, her eyes swollen with crying. She gave me a reproachful look. I was the one who had discovered the trap and reported where it was found. Had I known what my father's reaction would have been I should have kept quiet, but it was no use telling Mary that now.

I did not mention the fact that I had found the dog's owner and who he was at the supper table, for the dog was a subject we did not now discuss in front of my father; he was still in an angry and unrelenting mood; and I believe suffering because of it.

I did say to my mother as we were going upstairs for the night, "By the way, Matthew Pilkington is paying a visit to his mother, and, do you know, the dog is his."

"How strange," she said quietly.

She did not seem overjoyed.

The next day I took the dog over to Grasslands. There was no mistaking her joy to see her master again. She barked in ecstasy; nuzzled up to him while he knelt and fondled her. I stood watching them. I think I fell in love with him at that moment.

One can fall in love quite deeply at fourteen—and I should soon be fifteen. Mistress Leveret had said to my mother that in some ways I was old for my years. I was serious; and I believe I had an intense desire to be loved. All people have, of course, but I had been so overshadowed by Carlotta, so much aware of her superiority, that I supposed I needed it more than most.

To have someone's attention directed on me was rare. I revelled in it.

Matthew and I had so much in common. He loved his horses and his dogs even as I did mine. We could talk about them for hours. We loved to ride; I felt I could even take an interest in clothes, which he seemed to care so much about. I had never bothered with them much before. I had always known that however grand my gown, Carlotta would look so much more attractive in the simplest garment.

All that was changed since Carlotta went away. I missed her; I longed sometimes to be with her. And yet

I could not have this sense of being a person in my own right, capable of living excitingly, if she were here. Matt made me feel that I was interesting. He was delighted that I had saved his dog. He was sure the beautiful creature would have died if she had been left in the trap. It had been wonderful for me to have saved her for him, he kept telling me.

Elizabeth joined us and Belle settled down leaning against Matt's knees and looking at me with an expression of affection in her soulful eyes.

It came out in conversation that my father had discovered who had set the trap and that he was very angry about it. He had forbidden any of them to go to that particular spot.

"It's very wild and overgrown, is it not?" said Elizabeth. "Why does he shut it off like that?"

"It's some plan he has for it, I think. He is very annoyed that Jacob Rook should have disobeyed him. In fact he has dismissed the man."

"Wherever will he go?" asked Elizabeth.

I looked wretched and she said: "Oh, poor man... I know he did wrong to disobey his master... and I hate the thought of traps—they're cruel—but for such a small offence..."

"It isn't like my father," I said. "He has always been so kind to all the people who work for him. He has a reputation for being just and good to them. Even more so than my grandfather, who could often be harsh, but father... Anyway he is firm about this."

"Poor Jacob!" said Elizabeth.

A few days later I saw Mary Rook at the pump in the garden. She had changed completely. She was smiling almost truculently.

I felt very happy, believing that my father had relented. He only wanted to give them a warning, I told myself. He let them think that they were dismissed for a day or two and then had taken them back. He felt so strongly about complete obedience that he had considered it necessary.

"You look pleased with life, Mary," I said. "Is everything all right now?"

"You might say that, mistress," she replied.

161

"I knew my father would forgive you."

"Master be a hard man," she said through tight lips. "But it's all right now, you say?"

"We'm off. There's other places in the world besides this 'ere Dower House, mistress."

I was amazed. "What . . . what do you mean?"

"There be Grasslands, mistress, that where we be going. Mistress there have places for us both."

Mary tossed her head. A smirk of triumph was on her face.

I turned away and went into the house.

Well, I thought, it was good of Elizabeth. But it would make an awkward situation between our families—living so close together as they did.

Through the June and July that followed I saw a great deal of Matt. They were enchanted months for me. We discovered so much that we had in common. He knew a great deal about birds and we used to lie in the fields quietly watching for hours at a stretch. The birds had ceased to sing so joyously because they were busy with the young, though the wren and the chiffchaff now and then made themselves heard and the cuckoo was still announcing his presence. Matt taught me a good deal and I loved to learn from him. We took Belle for long walks and sometimes when we rode out she would follow us; she liked to trot beside the horses and run with us when we cantered and galloped, until she tired. He was always reminding her that she was no longer a puppy. Sometimes we rode down to the sea and walked along the shingle. We explored the pools for sea anemones and sometimes we took off our shoes and paddled, looking for all the curious little creatures which inhabited the shallow water. We had to be watchful and look out for dragonets and weevers. Matt showed me what looked like a three-bladed knife on either side of the dragonet's head, and the weever was even more deadly, with spines on its back which could be poisonous.

They were such happy days for me.

Once I overheard my grandmother say to my mother:

"He looks upon her just as a child. He must be at least seven or eight years older than she is."

My mother replied: "She *is* such a child, but I think she may be seeing too much of him."

I was very much afraid that they were going to try to stop our meetings, but I suppose they thought he would go away in due course, and as I was so young they could let our friendship come to a natural conclusion.

One day we passed by Enderby Hall and, as usual, paused to look at it. There was something impelling about the house which made most people do that.

"It's a delightful house," said Matt. "I was sorry my mother didn't take it."

"Are you still sorry?" I asked.

"No, not now she has Grasslands. That's as near to Eversleigh Dower House as Enderby."

I glowed with pride when he said things like that.

"I'd like to have a look at it again," he said. "I saw it once when my mother was considering taking it."

"That's easily done. The keys are at Eversleigh. I'll get them tomorrow and take you over the house."

"I should enjoy that."

"We will go in the afternoon—not too late. We want to see it before dusk."

"Ah, you mean when the ghosts come out. Are you scared of ghosts, Damaris?"

"I shouldn't be if you were there."

He turned to me and lightly kissed my brow. "That's the spirit," he said. "I'd protect you from all the perils and dangers of the day and night."

He did little things like that. He had great charm. But he did them lightly and naturally and I sometimes wondered how deeply he meant them.

The outcome was that I took the key from the desk where it was kept at Eversleigh and met him the next afternoon at the gates of Enderby Hall.

Belle was with him.

"She so wanted to come," he said, "I hadn't the heart to refuse her. She must have known I was meeting you."

She leapt round me showing her pleasure. I patted her and told her how glad I was that she had come.

I took out the keys and we went through the gardens to the front porch. The garden had been kept in some order. Jacob Rook had been one of the men who had looked after it. I thought, it will have to be someone else now. The house was of red Tudor brick built like so many of its era with its central hall and a wing on either side. The creeper covered large portions of the wall. It looked lovely with the red bricks showing through the green glistening leaves—but not really as beautiful as it would look later in the autumn when the leaves were in the full glory of their russety colours.

"If we cut back the creeper it would be much lighter inside," I commented.

"You would detract from the ghostly atmosphere," said Matt.

"Well, that might be a good idea."

"No. You'd take away its aura of mystery."

We stepped into the hall. Matt looked up at the magnificent vaulted ceiling.

"It's lovely," he said.

"Look. There's the haunted gallery."

"That's where the minstrels used to play."

"It's the scene of the tragedy. One owner hanged herself there . . . or tried to. The rope was too long and she injured herself and was an invalid and suffered a great deal before she died."

"Is she the ghost?"

"I believe there are others. But that's the story which is always told."

Belle was running about the hall, sniffing in corners. She found the place as exciting as Matt obviously did.

"Let's go upstairs," I said.

"It has a lived-in look," said Matt.

"That's because it is furnished. Carlotta wouldn't have the furniture taken away."

"Carlotta seems to be a very determined young lady."

"Oh, she is."

"I should like to meet her. I daresay I shall one day."

164

"If you stay here long enough, yes. We visit them and they come here. I'm longing to see Clarissa."

"I thought her name was Carlotta."

"That's my sister. Clarissa is her baby. The dearest little girl in the whole world."

"All baby girls are that, Damaris."

"I know, but this one really is," I sighed. "Carlotta is so lucky."

"To have this incomparable little girl, you mean?"

"Yes, that and to be Carlotta."

"Is she so very fortunate?"

"Carlotta has everything that anyone could want. Beauty, a fortune, a husband who loves her . . ."

"And . . ."

I interrupted. "You were going to say, 'And Clarissa.'"

"No, I was going to say and a charming sister who admires her enormously."

"Everyone admires her."

We had come up to the minstrels' gallery and Matt went inside.

"It is rather dark," he called out. "It's chilly too. It's those curtains. They're beautiful but a bit sombre."

Belle followed him into the gallery . . . and was sniffing around.

I said: "Come and see the rooms upstairs."

He followed me. We went through the bedrooms and came to the one with the big four-poster bed hung with red velvet curtains. I immediately remembered that I had seen Carlotta there one day—lying there talking to herself. I had never forgotten it.

"An interesting room," said Matt.

"Yes, it's the biggest of the bedrooms."

At that moment we heard Belle barking furiously somewhere below.

We found her in the gallery. She was in a state of some excitement. She was staring at the floor and barking as she scratched at the floorboards as though she would tear them up. There was a gap between the boards at that point and she seemed as though she was trying to get at something down there.

Matt knelt and put his eye to the crack.

"It looks as though there is something bright down there. It must have caught her eye."

He put his hand on Belle's head and shook it gently. "Come on, you silly old girl. It's nothing down there."

She responded to his caress but would not be put off. She was trying to lift the board with her paw.

Matt stood up.

"Well, it's an interesting place," he said. "I'll agree it has something which Grasslands lacks. But I would say Grasslands is more cosy. Come on, Belle."

We started down the stairs, Belle following us with some reluctance. We stood in the hall and paused for a while to look up at the roof and as we paused Belle was off.

"She's gone back to the gallery," said Matt. "She's very singleminded, is Belle. She was my father's dog once. He used to say that when she gets a notion in her head she doesn't let go lightly."

Belle was barking so wildly that we could scarcely hear ourselves speak. We retraced our steps to the gallery.

She was still staring at the crack in the boards and doing her best to lift them.

Matt said: "In a moment she'll rip that board up."

He knelt down: "What's the matter, old girl? What is it you want down there?"

Now she was barking with wild enthusiasm. She had captured his interest and she was not going to let it go until she had whatever it was she wanted down there.

Matt looked at me.

"I could lift up the board," he said. "There shouldn't really be this gap. It does need repairing."

I said: "Lift it up. We can get one of the men to come and put it right. I don't think the girls come to this gallery very much. They are all terrified of it."

"Oh, it is the haunted room, isn't it? Strange that Belle has selected it for her attention. They do say that dogs have an extra sense."

"Matt," I said, "do you think we are about to stumble on some great discovery?"

"No," he said, "this is just Belle's obsession. She can

166

see something down there and she is not going to be satisfied until she gets it. And I'll tell you something, Damaris, I'm getting rather curious myself."

"So am I."

"Well, shall I see what I can do with that floorboard?"

I nodded.

"Right. With your permission I will lift it up. It does need repairing in any case."

Belle was growing wildly excited when Matt began to lift the board.

It creaked; there was a shower of wood dust at that part where it touched the wainscot.

"Oh, yes," said Matt. "It needs replacing. Well, here goes."

The board came up and we were looking down onto the dust of ages; and there, lying in it, was the object which had attracted Belle. It was a buckle which looked as though it might have come from a man's shoe.

Belle was making strange sounds of excitement—half whimpering, half whining, punctuated with sharp barks.

"Nothing much to get so excited about, old girl," said Matt.

"It could be silver," I said. "Must have been lying here for years."

"It could have slipped through the gap in the boards, I suppose. There's room."

"It must have done."

Matt was holding it in the palm of his hand and Belle was watching it intently, her tail wagging, and every now and then she would make that strange sound which I imagined was meant to convey ecstasy. She had got what she wanted.

"I daresay it came off a shoe," Matt said, "and the owner of the shoe wondered where on earth he had lost it. He wouldn't have thought of looking under the floorboards. Now what about this board? I'll put it back. You'll have to get it done, someone could catch a foot in it and fall."

"I'll tell them."

Matt put the buckle on the floor. Belle immediately seized it.

I patted her head. "Don't swallow it, Belle," I said.

"She's too smart for that. She'll take care of it, won't you, Belle?"

I watched while Matt replaced the board.

"There," he said. "That doesn't look too bad."

He stood up and we surveyed it.

"But don't forget to tell them about it," he said.

Belle was still holding the buckle in her mouth. She stood there watching us, wagging her tail.

"You're a spoilt girl," said Matt. "You only have to cry for something and it is yours. Even if it means pulling up the floorboards to get it."

We came out of the house and locked it up.

Matt said: "Come and see my mother. She loves to see you."

So we went to Grasslands. Belle was still holding the buckle. She wouldn't let it go.

Elizabeth greeted me warmly as she always did.

"What's Belle got?"

As though in answer, Belle put down the buckle and sat looking at it, head on one side, with what I can only call immense satisfaction and gratification.

"What is it?" asked Elizabeth.

We explained.

"It must be filthy," she said. She picked it up. Belle looked anxious.

"A man's shoe buckle," she said. "Rather a fine one."

Belle began to whine.

"All right, all right," she went on. "I'm not going to take it from you."

She gave it back to the dog, who immediately seized it and moved away to the corner of the room.

We all laughed.

Then Elizabeth said: "It would be interesting to know to whom it belonged."

It was soon after that that we began to have one of those periods of hauntings which happened now and then about Enderby Hall.

It was usually started by some silly little incident. Someone would see, or fancy they saw, a light in Enderby Hall. They would mention it and then everyone would be seeing lights.

My mother said it was the way the light of the setting sun caught one of the windows, and it could, to anyone who was looking for strange sights, appear to be a light.

However, the rumours grew.

I had mentioned the faulty floorboard and it had been repaired, but I did not say anything about the buckle because it involved Belle and I thought it would remind my parents of the unfortunate incident which had led to the dismissal of the Rooks.

I saw them now and then, and their attitude towards me was always a little truculent. When I asked Mary if she had settled in at Grasslands she replied with relish: "Oh, yes, Mistress Damaris, me and Jacob has never been so well served. We'm in clover." Which was her way of telling me that it had been a change for the better and a good day for them when my father had sent them packing.

Elizabeth said they seemed over anxious to please and were really very good servants. I noticed that the servants at Grasslands always regarded me with a special interest and I wondered what stories the Rooks told of our household.

Carlotta had always said that servants were like spies for they knew too much about the private lives of their masters and mistresses. She said: "One should never forget them; they are there watching and chattering together, seeing much and making up what they don't see."

I wished more than ever that I had not told them where I had found Belle.

Belle herself had become obsessed by some sort of treasure hunt since she had found the buckle. She kept it with her. Once we thought she had lost it; then we discovered she had buried it in the garden with a bone.

She had suddenly become interested in the land where she had been caught in the trap. Up till now she had refused to go near it. Whenever we had come near the fence she would cringe away from it and keep very close to us. We knew she was remembering her experiences in the trap.

Then suddenly, when we were passing that way, we

169

missed her. We called and called and she did not appear.

We knew that the house fascinated her because she was always trying to get into it. And when we passed it she would sometimes sit down at the gate and look at us appealingly.

"Oh, come, Belle," Matt would say, "there aren't any more buckles."

She would put her head on one side and give that little murmuring whine which was meant, I think, to plead with us.

But up to that time she had never wanted to go over the fence.

On this particular day when we lost her and called and called, Matt said: "I wonder if she has got into the house? Someone may have left something open."

And just at that moment she was squeezing under the gate looking rather shamefaced.

We were astounded. It was the last place we expected her to be in view of her previous reluctance.

She leapt up at Matt, wagging her tail.

"What have you been doing?" he asked. "You're covered in mud."

It was the next day when we could not find her at all. We were in the same spot. It was surprising how often we walked that way. I think it was because Belle led us there and we just followed her without thinking very much where we were going.

It might seem that we, like everyone else, were obsessed by Enderby.

On this day we could not find Belle. We called and called but she did not come.

I turned pale suddenly. "You don't think Jacob Rook has defied my father and set another trap?"

Matt stared at me.

"And Belle caught in it! Oh, no! Once caught never again. She's intelligent enough to recognise that sort of trap when she sees it. And Jacob wouldn't set a trap. He's no need to. He lives in the house now and wouldn't want a hare or a rabbit for his pot."

"No. But I have a feeling that Belle might be in there. She has been acting rather strangely lately."

With Matt's help I clambered over the gate. He joined me on the other side.

"Belle!" we called. "Belle."

In the distance I heard the answering bark but she did not come bounding towards us as she would normally have done.

"This way," said Matt and we penetrated farther into the undergrowth.

"I can't think why your father doesn't use this land," he added.

"He has a great deal to do at the moment. He'll come round to it."

Then we came across Belle. She was digging and had made a considerable hole in the ground.

"What are you doing, Belle?" cried Matt.

"We must get her out of here," I said. "My father gets really angry if anyone comes here."

"Yes, come on, Belle."

She paused and looked at us with sorrowing eyes. "What is the matter with you?" asked Matt.

She then picked up a ragged object from the ground and laid it at Matt's feet.

"What is it?" I asked.

It was very dirty, covered in mud and there was a green lichenlike patch on it.

"It was a shoe at one time, I think," said Matt.

"Yes . . . so it was."

"Another find, Belle!" said Matt. "But you can't bring this one into the house, I promise you."

He threw it from him into the bushes. Belle immediately leapt forward and retrieved it.

"You're a strange collector, Belle," I said. "Matt, do let's get out of here. If anyone saw us and reported it to my father he'd be angry. He hates people to come here. He's made it strictly private."

"You heard that, Belle," said Matt. "Come on. Drop that dirty object."

Belle dropped the shoe immediately.

"Home," said Matt.

As we came to the gate, Belle, who had lingered behind, caught up with us.

Matt said: "Look what she's brought."

It was the old shoe.

Matt took it from her and threw it back into the undergrowth. Belle gave a little protesting whine and then, realising that it was her master's will that we went, gave in with resignation and we went into Grasslands.

Elizabeth said: "I am going to give a little party. We'll have charades and a lot of fun. I shall invite your family of course and a few others. I feel it is time I did a little entertaining. You must help me, Damaris."

I said I would with pleasure but I was not much good at that sort of thing. Parties had never been very enjoyable occasions to me. I had always been too shy, and when there was dancing I had often been one of those who was without a partner. However I had changed lately. It was due to my friendship with Matt. He had made it so clear that he enjoyed my company and we were together a great deal. We were always discovering interests in common. In town, where he looked so much the dandy, I found him a little formidable but here in the country he seemed like a different person. Of course I knew all this was transient. He would go away soon. He was always saying he would have to return to his estates in Dorsetshire and also he had commitments with the army. I was not sure what, and he never seemed to want to talk about them. I was very much in harmony with him. I think it was because I could understand his moods and respected them.

I was brought face to face with the change in myself when Elizabeth's suggestion of this party excited me instead of filling me with apprehension.

My grandmother was very interested in the proposed charades. She said it took her back to the days when she and Harriet were young.

"Harriet was very clever at that sort of thing," she told me. "It was due to her being an actress. I expect Elizabeth Pilkington will be too. That's why she wants to do it I suppose. We always want to do what we do well."

However, I was at Grasslands frequently and we

172

worked out our charades and went through trunks of clothes which she had had for the theatre.

It was great fun dressing up and trying on the various wigs and things she had brought with her from her acting days.

Once when she had dressed me up, she put her hands on my shoulders and kissed me. "Do you know, Damaris, I am growing very fond of you," she said. "I know Matt is too."

I flushed a little. There was an implication in her words. I thought: Can she really mean what I think?

It seemed possible. I was indeed in love, and like all people in love I lived between ecstasy and apprehension.

I could not believe he could love me. He was so splendid, so worldly, so much older than I. I forgot Carlotta's mockery. I was beginning to have a different opinion of myself and believe in myself. So when Elizabeth Pilkington said that I was so happy.

I knew my mother did not like Matt. She had a strange antipathy which I could not fathom. But my grandparents liked him—even my grandfather did, and he did not easily like people.

So we planned our charades.

My grandmother came over to Grasslands one day. She said all this talk about charades had revived memories. She remembered Harriet Main years ago acting in a château where they were all staying just before the Restoration. "You remember Harriet, Mistress Pilkington?" she asked.

"Not very well. I did a child's part just at the time when she was thinking of leaving the stage. That was when she was going to be married."

"Yes, she married into our family. Of course, you're years younger than she is. It is wonderful how Harriet deceives us all into thinking she is still a young woman."

"Is she still very beautiful?"

"Yes, she is," said my grandmother. "She has that rare beauty which now and then appears. It is as though all the good fairies were at her christening. Your sister, Carlotta, has the same, Damaris."

173

"Yes," I agreed.

"We played Romeo and Juliet," went on my grandmother, her eyes vague as she looked back into the past.

"We'll content ourselves with charades," said Elizabeth.

So we planned. And I was at Grasslands every day rehearsing under Elizabeth's instructions. Matt was no good as a performer and I loved him all the more for that. It put him in the same category as myself.

One day I was a little upset. I was in Elizabeth's sewing room and as it was a warm day the window was wide open. I was on the window seat and Elizabeth was examining a dress which she was holding up.

The sound of voices floated up from below. I recognised that of Mary Rook.

"Well, it struck us as really strange like. He were so mad. Now why should he want to keep everyone away so . . . if it weren't for what was there and what he do *know* to be there."

My heart had begun to beat faster. I knew that Elizabeth was listening, although she was stroking the silk of the dress as though completely absorbed by it.

"Mark my words, there's something there."

"What do you think it be, Mary?"

"Well, I don't rightly know. Jacob he thought it might be some sort of treasure, he did."

I was very still. The impulse to move away came to me but I felt I had to listen to what they were saying.

"You see, them that used to live there . . . they was took away suddenly. It were some plot. Well, Jacob says mayhap they hid something in that patch . . . some treasure like and he do know it and wants it for himself."

"Treasure, Mary . . . !"

"Well, 'tis something there, ain't it? Must be. Why should he get so raving mad just because Jacob sets a trap. They be setting traps all through the woods . . . *they* don't matter there. Is just a trap."

"But there be this ghost up at the house . . . ."

"You're asking me. I tell you there's something in that patch he don't want people to know about . . . ."

174

They had moved away from the window.

Elizabeth laughed.

"Servants' gossip," she said. "I think this dress would do for you, my dear. I wore it in one of my young girl roles."

We were all excited about the charades. It was to be a sort of tableau to describe words. We should do it in a most elaborate fashion and there were to be two teams competing against each other.

Elizabeth would be in charge of the teams, and when she selected them she put Matt and me together. Our words were "cloak and dagger" and we were to illustrate these historically. The cloak was to be represented by the scene from Queen Elizabeth's reign when Raleigh spread his cloak for Elizabeth to walk on and I was to be Elizabeth, Matt, Raleigh. I was to be dressed in a most elaborate Elizabethan costume and Matt's would be equally authentic.

"I have to choose parts according to what I had in my trunk," Elizabeth explained.

After the scene with the cloak I was to make a few changes to my costume and become Mary Queen of Scots. Matt was Rizzio and we would then enact the scene by mime of that supper in Holyrood House when Rizzio was murdered. That would represent the dagger.

The other team were to do theirs first. We should watch that and guess. But first there was to be a buffet supper.

It had been one of the lovely September days— golden days. I think all days were golden to me at that time for I was becoming more and more certain that Matt loved me. He could not have stayed here all this time, been with me so often and *pretended* to enjoy my company. Oh no, there was something in this. I had an idea that if I had not been so young he would have spoken of his intentions by now.

That Elizabeth liked me, I was sure. She had taken to treating me as a daughter, so surely that was significant.

When I had arisen that morning the first thing I thought of was the party and the dress I would wear, which was most becoming. Elizabeth's sewing woman had altered it to fit me and I could scarcely wait to play the part.

My mother said: "You've changed lately, Damaris. You're growing up."

"Well, it's time I did," I said. "You sound as though you don't want me to."

"Most mothers want to keep their children babies as long as possible."

"And that," I said, "is quite impossible."

"A sad fact we all have to realise." She put her arms about me and said: "Oh, Damaris, I do want you to be happy."

"I am," I said ecstatically. "I am."

"I know," she answered.

Then I started to tell her about my dress, which I must have described to her twenty times before, and she listened as though she was hearing it for the first time. She seemed reconciled. I hoped she was getting over that first unreasonable dislike of Matt.

It was warm when the sun rose and chased away the morning mists. The summer was nearly over. "In the autumn I shall have to go," Matt had said.

The only sadness at that time was the thought that it could not last.

But before he goes he will speak to me, I thought. He must.

I was not quite fifteen. It was young but obviously not too young to be in love.

In the afternoon I went to Grasslands. I was going to wear the Elizabethan costume for the whole evening.

"We can't get you all dressed up like that in five minutes," said Elizabeth. "Besides, all those in the charades will wear their costumes."

"It makes it like a fancy dress ball," I said.

"Well, let us call it that," she said.

She took great pleasure in dressing me, and how we laughed as she helped me to get into what was called the under propper, the purpose of which was to make my skirt stand out all round me. Then I put on—with Elizabeth's help—the dress, which was magnificent in a way, though perhaps it would seem a little tawdry by daylight.

"It has been lying in a trunk for a long time," said Elizabeth, "but it will look really fine in the light of the candles. No one will see where the velvet is scuffed and the jewels bits of glass. How slender you are. That is good. It makes it easier to wear."

The skirt was rouched and festooned with bows of ribbon; it was lavishly sprinkled with brilliants which might look like diamonds in candlelight.

"You make a good queen," said Elizabeth.

Then she frizzed my hair and made it stand up and stuffed false pieces into it to make it look abundant. "A pity you aren't red haired," she said. "Then everyone would recognise you at once as the Queen. Never mind, I believe she wore wigs of all colours, so this is one of her nights for brown."

She put a circlet of brilliants in my hair and then when she added the lace ruff about my neck and stood back to admire her handiwork, she clasped her hands together.

"Why, I wouldn't recognise you, Damaris," she said.

It was true. I gasped as I looked at my reflection.

"Who would believe anyone could be so changed?"

"It's a few deft touches here and there, my dear. We learn that in the theatre."

When I saw Matt we stared at each other and burst into laughter. He too had become a different person.

He stood there before me in his yellow ruff and his bombasted breeches, which were so wide that it was impossible for him to walk easily. His doublet was embroidered; his hose gartered at the knee, displaying his well-shaped calves, and he wore a little velvet hat with a fine feather curling over the brim. Most important of all was the cloak—an elaborate affair to fit the occasion. It was velvet and decorated with shining red stones and massive glass imitation diamonds.

He looked different. I was glad to see him without his periwig and I thought it a pity that the fashion of wearing wigs prevailed in our times. He looked younger in spite of the elaborate costume and the fact that the

177

cut of the breeches made him walk with a very stately gait.

He bowed to me solemnly.

"I do declare," he said, "Your Majesty looks most forbidding."

"It will be for the first time in my life," I replied.

There was dancing before the supper. Elizabeth Pilkington was a great organiser and she knew how to arrange these affairs. She had asked exactly the right number of guests. Besides members of my family there were several who had come in from the neighbouring countryside.

Matt and I were together throughout the evening.

"No one else could dance with us," he said. "I feel more than a little cumbersome. How do you feel?"

"The same," I said.

Everyone admired our costumes and said how they were looking forward to seeing the charades, which were to be the highlight of the evening.

I had never enjoyed a party so much before. This one I wanted to go on and on forever, although I was a little apprehensive about my performance in the charades.

"You'll be wonderfull," said Matt. "In any case it's only a game."

During the evening he said to me: "I'm getting very fond of you, Damaris."

I was silent. My heart was beating fast. I had had a feeling that he would speak to me about our future on an occasion like this.

"Oh, Damaris," he said, "it's a pity you're so young."

"I don't feel young. It's only a matter of years . . . ."

He laughed. "Well, that's what it's all about, isn't it?"

He patted my hand and then changed the subject.

"Thank heaven," he said, "that we don't have to speak lines. I should never remember them. I'm afraid I have not inherited my mother's talent."

"Your mother should have been Elizabeth. She would have done it beautifully."

"No, she was anxious for you to do it. Besides, she's busy being the hostess."

178

I was sure that he had been on the point of making some proposal. Oh, how I wished he had!

We should have to wait awhile, of course. Everyone would say I was too young for marriage. I would have to wait until I was nearly sixteen. That was more than a year. Well, that did not seem so bad. I would be Matt's betrothed. If I only knew that we were to be married in a given time I could wait and be happy.

He took me into supper and I did not notice what I ate. I was too excited. The wine was cool and refreshing and I was nervously awaiting my appearance as the Queen.

Then the moment came.

Elizabeth announced that the guests were now going to see the charades and the audience must guess the words we were acting.

We had taken supper in two of the rooms which led from the hall and it was in the hall itself that the performances would take place.

There was a dais at one end, which was very useful, and a curtain had been drawn across it.

The first of the charades went off very well. Then it was our turn. Behind the curtain Matt and I waited. It would be drawn back and I would be standing at one side of the dais in all my finery and Matt would be at the other. We had two attendants each—all dressed in Elizabethan costume.

There was a round of applause and we went into action. I tried to assume a Queen's regal manners and Matt was most courtly as the gallant Walter Raleigh.

This was a short scene. The next one would be longer. I looked across at Matt. He smiled at me. He took off his hat and made a deep bow. Then I stepped forward and looked down at the ground and tried to assume an expression of distaste as Elizabeth had taught me. I shrank back and Matt took off his cloak, spread it on the floor and I walked over it.

I looked at him fondly. He bowed. Left the cloak where it was. I put my arm through his and the curtain fell.

There was loud applause.

The curtain was drawn back.

"Take a bow . . . together," said Elizabeth from the side of the stage.

So we just stood there, rather embarrassed, while they applauded.

The curtain was dropped and a small table was put on the dais. I had donned a headdress of black trimmed with pearls which came to a peak in the centre of my forehead. I had put a black cloak over my finery and was seated at the table. Matt had discarded his hat and wore a wig of dark curls. It was amazing how that transformed him.

He was seated at my feet and the others who had been our attendants in the spreading of the cloak incident were seated beside me at the table.

Matt had a lute on which he was strumming and he was looking up at me with an adoration which I found most affecting.

We remained thus for some time. Then those who had been Raleigh's attendants and were now transformed into Rizzio's enemies came onto the dais from the other side. They dashed at Matt. One of them held high a dagger, which he pretended to plunge into Matt's heart.

He looked so fierce that for a moment I was really frightened.

Then Matt rolled over realistically and the curtain fell.

The audience applauded wildly. The curtain was drawn back and Matt stood up.

"Take a bow," whispered Elizabeth.

So we stood in front of the dais hand in hand and then there was a sudden bark. Everyone turned round. Belle had come into the hall.

She bounded up to the dais, evidently highly pleased with herself. Then we saw that she carried something in her mouth. She laid it almost reverently at Matt's feet.

"Whatever is it?" cried Elizabeth coming forward. She was about to pick it up when she drew back.

My father had come forward. He knelt. Belle watched, head on one side, tail wagging with delight.

"It looks like an old shoe," said my father, and I noticed that he had grown rather pale.

"It *is* an old shoe," said Elizabeth. "Where did you find that, Belle?"

I lay in my bed thinking about the evening. It had been such fun. I was sure Matt had been going to say something to me...something about our future. But he didn't, and from the moment when Belle had come in the atmosphere had changed.

Elizabeth had sent for one of the servants to take the shoe away. It was too filthy for us to touch. It was unfortunate that it should be Mary Rook who came. She brought an ash pan and a little broom. Then she curtsied and went out with it, Belle following her.

The charades were over. Our words, "cloak and dagger," had been guessed and we guessed our opposing team, which was "Gunpowder Plot."

There was to be more dancing but as I stepped from the stage with Matt, my father had come up to me and said: "Your mother is not feeling well. We're going home now. You'd better get those things off and come with us."

So the evening had ended. I took off the clothes in Elizabeth's bedroom and resumed my own and went back with my parents.

Dear Belle, she had been so happy with her find, so eager to show Matt so that he could join in her pleasure.

And somehow that incident had seemed as dramatic as our amateur acting in charades.

We had been so happy together, Matt and I. I had looked forward to dancing with him again. He danced beautifully when he was not encumbered by those heavy clothes, which did not fit too well. I could not match him but somehow when we had danced together I had felt I danced better than ever before. That was how it was with Matt. I felt different in his company. I felt I had changed my character, become more interesting, more attractive.

That was what Matt had done for me and I wanted him to go on doing it.

It had been a wonderful evening, but I felt faintly

181

frustrated. But I went to sleep assuring myself that Matt did love me.

During the next week a change seemed to have come over everything. My mother was in bed for a few days. She looked very wan when I went in to see her. She was very tired, she said. She certainly looked pale and ill. I suggested she should see the doctor but she refused to do this.

My father was clearly worried about her. It changed the household. Things did not improve when a rumour started that will-o'-the-wisps had been seen in the woods and in that patch of fenced-off land. Will-o'-the-wisps were said to be the souls of departed spirits who could not find rest and came back to earth to try to wreak vengeance on those who had wronged them in life.

My father said that it was a lot of nonsense and he was going to put a stop to it, but when I asked him how he had no solution to offer.

"It was all due to that dog getting in a trap there. You know it's the Rooks who are spreading these rumours." He was so vehement that I couldn't help remonstrating with him.

"It's all a lot of fuss about nothing," I said. "Father, you must do something with that land. If you turned it into pasture or grew something there or even took down the fences it would be like the rest of the land."

"All in good time," he said.

But he was very uneasy. He was worried about my mother, I was sure. She did not seem to want anyone to be with her except him, and when I had gone in to her room once I found him sitting by her bed holding her hand and saying over and over again: "It will be all right, Priscilla. I'll see that it's all right."

After a few days my mother was about again but she still looked strained and ill.

I found it very difficult to settle. Matt did not call for a day or so. I had an idea that he was not sure about his feelings for me and I believed that it was all because of my extreme youth. How I wished I were a few years older!

Oddly enough my footsteps always seemed to lead me in the direction of Enderby. I was becoming obsessed by the place and the patch of fenced-in land. It was because of all the talk about it; the will-o'-the-wisps and the gossip that was circulating about something's being hidden there. I was sure the Rooks had started that.

Oh, Belle, I thought, why did you want to get caught in that trap!

Then I thought of my father, and I really did wonder why he became so angry about his rights over a piece of land which was no good to anyone.

I came close to it. I leaned against the fence and looked towards the house, and it occurred to me that if some nice ordinary family went to live at Enderby it would stop all this gossip. Carlotta must see sense and either let or sell the place.

Then as I sat there I heard the bark of a dog. My heart sank. I thought, oh, Belle, you're in there again. You're like everyone else, you are obsessed by the place. What is the attraction?

If my father discovered Belle in there he would be angry, I was sure. There was only one thing to do. That was climb over the gate. Find Belle and get her out.

There was certainly something eerie about the place. I found myself looking about nervously. Had people really seen mysterious lights about the place? Were there such things as spirits which could not rest—people who had sinned on earth and perhaps died by violent means before they had been able to repent? Will-o'-the-wisps . . . lights shining through the trees. I shivered.

I heard the bark again. I called: "Belle. Belle. Where are you?"

I listened. But there was only silence.

I went on through the undergrowth. The fenced-in land was not very large—I imagined about half an acre. My father had behaved really very oddly about it.

"Belle," I called. "Belle."

I heard the bark again. She was answering me. Not caught in another trap. No, no one would dare put a trap here after what had happened to Rook.

I saw Belle. She was not alone. I gasped with astonishment for she was on a lead and Elizabeth was with her.

"Oh, Damaris," she said, "I heard you calling."

"I was on the other side of the fence and I heard Belle. I was afraid she might be in another trap."

"She has a fancy for this place." Elizabeth laughed but her manner was different from usual. She seemed nervous and her hair was untidy as I had never seen it before. She was wearing a dark dress and thick woollen gloves. I noticed that there was mud on her skirt.

She went on speaking rather quickly. "I heard her in this place and I didn't want any more trouble so I came after her."

"You brought the lead. Belle's not used to that."

She said: "I saw her leave the house and I guessed where she had come. I was determined to bring her away so I brought the lead . . . ."

I supposed that she had put on the gloves because she thought holding the lead with a rather boisterous dog at the other end of it might have bruised her hands.

"I was doing a little gardening . . ." she said, as though she had to make excuses to me.

I said: "Poor Belle. She doesn't like being on the lead."

"Perhaps I should let her off. Are you going back past Grasslands?"

"I might as well," I said, "I was just out for a walk."

So we walked and we talked mostly about the success of the party. We laughed over the charades, and by the time we reached Grasslands Elizabeth was her old relaxed self. But she did not invite me in.

My uneasiness persisted. After my morning lessons the next day I went out again, and once again almost involuntarily I went in the direction of Enderby Hall.

And when I came to the fence I felt an irresistible urge to go into the forbidden territory and look again at the spot where Belle had found the old shoe. I had become adept at scrambling over the gate.

The place was less eerie in the early morning. The sunlight filtered through the trees almost denuded of their leaves by now. I saw two magpies black and white against the sky and a cheeky little robin strutted a few paces ahead of me flicking his tail and his head. I thought sadly that many of the birds would already have left for warmer climes. The swallows, the house martins and my beloved sandpipers.

The oaks were bronze now—the leaves dry and ready to drop.

I came to the spot almost before I was aware of it. There it was. The ground was rough. I went closer. It looked as though it had been recently dug up. Surely Belle had not done all that with her scratching?

I knelt down and touched the earth. It was so still all around me. I suddenly felt an irresistible desire to get away from this spot.

There is something evil here, I thought. Get away. Forget it. Don't come here again.

I stood up and stumbled away. I did not want to search in those bushes. I felt I might find something there which I would rather not see, that I might discover something which would add to my uneasiness.

My father had been so angry. Why? And why had Elizabeth Pilkington brought Belle out on a lead? Why had she been so nervous, so full of excuses, so anxious to make me feel that what she had been doing was perfectly normal?

That afternoon Elizabeth came over to see us.

"I have to go to London," she said. "I may be away for a week or so."

"Is Matt going with you?" I asked quickly. I had spoken before I could stop myself.

"No," she said. "He will stay here. Of course, he will have to go away soon."

We talked awhile of the successful party she had given and how well staged the charades had been; but I sensed some tension even in Elizabeth. My mother's nerves were certainly on edge.

Elizabeth left the next day.

I often think how strange it is that we have no warning of events which are going to shatter our illusions and change our lives. I had been so happy after the party.

185

I was so sure that Matt loved me—perhaps not so intensely as I did him, but I did not expect that. Carlotta's opinion of me, so often expressed, had so influenced me that I still saw myself as a very ordinary, rather dull and not very attractive creature who must be grateful for every crumb of affection which fell from the tables of the irresistible such as herself.

It was true that I was aware of a heightening of tension, a certain uneasiness about me which had been caused by the discovery of Belle in the trap and the dismissal of the Rooks. But unfortunate as these incidents were, they did not seem to concern me personally.

The day after Elizabeth Pilkington had left, my mother and I were in the stillroom. She had always taught me her skills in that direction and I had been a good pupil, which pleased her. She had often said: "At least I will make a housewife out of one of my daughters." Which indicated that she had long despaired of doing so with Carlotta.

There were sounds of arrival in the courtyard. We looked at each other. We were always excited by visitors. Sometimes they came from Westminster and we loved to hear the news; but mostly they went to Eversleigh, where my grandparents and Jane could entertain them more easily, having so much more room.

But this sounded like visitors for us.

We went hastily down to the hall and my mother gave a cry of joy, for there was Carlotta herself.

Whenever I saw Carlotta after an absence I was always overwhelmed by her loveliness. She looked so beautiful in a dove-grey riding habit and a dark blue hat with a feather of a paler shade. Her eyes were sparkling blue, the colour of bluebells; there was a faint colour in her cheeks and startlingly thick black brows and lashes made such an entrancing contrast to her blue eyes. Her dark curls escaped from under the hat and she looked as young as ever. Having a child had certainly not detracted from her beauty.

"My darling child!" cried my mother.

Carlotta embraced her.

"Is Benjie with you?"

186

"No," she said.

My mother looked astonished. It was unthinkable that Benjie should not travel with his young wife.

"I just wanted a few days to be with my family," said Carlotta. "I insisted on coming alone."

"Alone," said my mother.

"There were of course the attendant grooms. Ah, sister Damaris." She put her cheek against mine. "Still the same young Damaris," she said and I immediately felt stripped of the confidence I had been acquiring over the last weeks.

"And Harriet and Gregory?" said my mother.

"All well. They send their love and greetings."

"So you've come alone, Carlotta." My mother looked worried. "What of Clarissa?"

"Clarissa is being well cared for. Have no fear of that. She is rapidly becoming a spoilt child."

"Well, you have come and I'm delighted to see you."

Carlotta laughed. She had a lovely laugh. Everything about her was more beautiful than I remembered. I was beginning to experience the old feeling of being plain and awkward.

"Come up to your room. Leigh will be so pleased to see you and so will they be at Eversleigh."

"What of little Damaris? Is she pleased to see me too?"

"Of course," I said.

"Well, I could do with a wash and I should like to change. I've told them to bring the bags up to my room. They will be taking them up now."

My mother slipped her arm through Carlotta's.

"It is wonderful to see you, darling," she said.

I stayed with my sister to unpack.

She had some beautiful dresses. She had always understood what became her most. I remember the scenes we had had with Sally Nullens and old Emily Philpots over clothes. Once Carlotta took off a red sash and threw it out of the window because she insisted on having a blue one. One body's work, they said Carlotta was. "Give me a good child like little Damaris."

I hung up her dresses for her while she stretched on the bed watching me.

"Do you know," she said, "you've changed. Has anything happened?"

"N-no."

"You don't sound very sure whether anything has happened or not."

"Well, nothing very much. Elizabeth Pilkington gave a lovely party a little while ago. We did charades. I was Queen Elizabeth."

Carlotta burst out laughing.

"My dear Damaris. You! Oh, how I should have loved to see you."

"They said I did very well," I replied somewhat nettled.

"What were you doing?"

"Raleigh and the cloak."

"Oh, I see, and you most regally walked on it."

"Elizabeth did my dress and my hair. She's been an actress you know . . . like Harriet. They can do such wonderful things with ordinary people."

"She must be a miracle worker if she could turn you into Queen Elizabeth. Who was Raleigh? I'm trying to think of someone round here. I suppose they were all from these parts."

"Oh, yes. It was Elizabeth's son—Matt."

"What fun!" she said languidly. "I should have come earlier."

"Is everything all right?" I asked.

"All right? What do you mean?"

"With you . . . and Benjie."

"Of course it's all right. He's my husband. I'm his wife."

"That doesn't necessarily mean. . . ."

"Benjie is an indulgent husband . . . which is what all husbands should be."

"I'm sure he's very happy, Carlotta. Now he has you and dear little Clarissa. How can you bear to leave her?"

"I bear it with amazing fortitude," she said, her lips curling. "You're still the same sentimental Damaris. Not grown up yet. Things are not always what they seem, dear sister. I just wanted to get away for a while.

188

That's how it is at times. I couldn't think of anywhere else to go."

"It doesn't sound as if you are very happy, Carlotta."

"You're such a babe, Damaris. What's happiness? An hour or so . . . a day if you're lucky. Sometimes you can say to yourself, 'I'm happy now . . . *now*.' And you want to cling to *now* and make it forever. But *now* becomes *then* in a very short time. That's happiness. You can't have it all the time and when you think back to when you did you're just thinking of it, so that happiness has really deserted you."

"What a strange way to talk."

"I'd forgotten. You, dear Damaris, wouldn't see it my way. You don't ask for much. I hope you get what you want. Sometimes I think people like you are the lucky ones. It's easy for you to get what you want because you don't ask for the impossible. And when you've got it you just go on believing it's happiness. Lucky Damaris."

She was in a strange mood. I thought of her sitting on the cliff looking out to sea as though she were dreaming of the past and longing for it to come back.

My mother had said that Matt must come over to us whenever he wished while his mother was away. She would not issue formal invitations. He was to consider himself one of the family.

"That's easy," he said. "I think I already do."

Words to set my spirits soaring.

That day my mother had been busy in the kitchens preparing everything that she knew Carlotta liked to eat. She looked better than she had for some time and I knew it was due to the pleasures of having Carlotta home.

About half an hour before we were about to sit down to dinner, Matt arrived.

I was in the hall alone when he came. He took my hands and kissed them. Then he bowed low, which he had done since we had played Elizabeth and Raleigh. It was a little joke between us.

"It is so pleasant to come here," he said. "Grasslands seems empty without my mother."

"You are well looked after there, I hope."

He touched my cheeks caressingly. "I am absolutely cosseted. But I assure you I do appreciate being allowed to come here."

At that moment Carlotta appeared at the top of the stairs.

Matt looked up at her and kept looking. I heard his quick intake of breath. I wasn't altogether surprised that he should be overwhelmed by Carlotta's beauty. Most people were, and I felt that pride in her which I had always felt when people met her for the first time and were startled by her outstanding looks.

She was wearing a simple blue gown with a long-waisted bodice and elbow-length sleeves with frills of lace at the edge of them. It was cut rather low and was close fitting and accentuated her tiny trim waist. It was laced in the front to show her undergown of a lighter shade of blue. The skirt was long with side panniers. Not an elaborate gown but I had often thought that the more simply Carlotta was dressed the greater impact her beauty had. I was wearing green— a colour I think which suited me as well as any. It gave more colour to my eyes; and I had taken more pains with my appearance since the coming of Matt. Mine was a pretty dress with a laced bodice showing a pale pink undergown, and my sleeves had matching pink frills at the edges. But I had always had the feeling that anything I wore would look homely beside Carlotta's simplest gown.

It seemed to me that there was a long silence while they looked at each other and that Carlotta was as taken aback as Matt was. Then she came slowly down the stairs.

"This is my sister, Carlotta," I said.

Her eyes seemed enormous and brilliant. She was looking at him as though she could not believe he was real.

She walked towards us—it seemed to me very slowly but perhaps that was my imagination, because everything seemed to have slowed down. Even the clock in the hall seemed to pause between its ticks.

190

Carlotta was smiling. She held out a hand. Matt took it and kissed it.

She gave a little laugh. "Damaris," she said. "You haven't introduced me."

"Oh," I stammered. "This is Matt . . . Matt Pilkington, whose mother has taken Grasslands Manor."

"Matt Pilkington," she said, keeping her eyes on him. "Oh, yes, of course, I have heard of you. Tell me, what do you think of Grasslands?"

He began to talk rather fast about Grasslands and how his mother had fallen in love with it the moment she had seen it. She had gone to London. He did not know how long she would be. He hoped Carlotta would have a long stay here. He had heard so much about her from Damaris.

"I believe you have seen a lot of my family . . . and my little sister," said Carlotta, and I immediately stepped back into that niche from which my friendship with Matt had helped me emerge.

"They have been so good to me," he said.

My mother came into the hall. "Oh, Matt," she said, "how nice to see you."

"I have taken advantage of your invitation to call in when I'm lonely," he said.

"And right glad I am that you have. You see, I have my other daughter with me now." She went to Carlotta and slipped her arm through hers. Then she reached for my hand to show me that I must not feel that I was left out. But I did feel it. And I went on feeling it through the days that followed.

I had become accustomed to seeing the effect Carlotta had on men. It had always been the same from the time when I was first aware of her; it did not matter who they were. I had often heard the story of how she had charmed Robert Frinton, who had left her his fortune; and even my grandfather was not immune to her charm.

What was so amazing about it was that she did it effortlessly. She said what she pleased and she never went out of her way to impress or attract. It was some charm, some magnetism, which flowed from her.

Emily Philpots had hinted that she was a witch. There had been times when I could believe it.

During that first meal she dominated the table. She had been to London recently and had all the Court news. She was aware of what the Duke of Marlborough was doing on the Continent and how the war was progressing; she talked of the new book Daniel Defoe had written: *The Shortest Way with Dissenters, or Proposals for the Establishment of the Church.* "Such a brilliant satire on the intolerance of the Church party," she commented. She talked blithely of the Whigs and the Tories and was apparently on terms of friendship with some of the leading men of affairs.

This made her conversation racy and amusing. She sparkled and became even more beautiful every minute.

My mother said: "But how can you do all this? You have your household now you are married. What of Benjie and Clarissa?"

"Oh, Eyot Abbass was never like it is here, you know," said Carlotta, somehow relegating our household to the category of boring dullness. "Harriet was never one to concern herself with domestic affairs and the men of the family were brought up to understand and like it that way. Benjie goes to London when I want to. As for Clarissa, we have an excellent nurse and a very good little nursery maid. Clarissa doesn't need more than that."

"Why on earth didn't Benjie come with you?"

"I wanted to come alone. I was longing to have a glimpse of you all. You have been telling me in your letters how Damaris has grown up, emerging from her shell like a baby chicken. I wanted to see my little sister on the brink of womanhood."

So the conversation went on, dominated all the time by Carlotta.

I was glad when the evening was over. Matt left to ride over to Grasslands and I retired to my room.

I was brushing my hair when there was a rap on the door. It was Carlotta.

She came in smiling.

"It's nice to be home, Damaris," she said.

"Don't you find it rather dull?" I asked.

"Quiet . . . but it's what I wanted . . . for a while."

I went on brushing. I said slowly: "You get tired of things quickly, Carlotta."

"I don't think I would if . . ."

"If what?"

"Never mind. He's an interesting young man, this Matt Pilkington, do you think?"

"Oh, yes, I do."

"The son of that actress. I can't remember what she looks like now. I saw her when I showed her round the house. Has she got a lot of red hair?"

"Yes."

"Rather elegant?"

"Yes."

"You're not very talkative tonight, Damaris."

"You always pointed out to me and others that I had little to say for myself."

She laughed. "You were always such a meek child. But you're supposed to have grown up now. Are you sixteen yet?"

"No, I'm not."

"Still you will be in the not too distant future. When I think of how I had lived at your age, Damaris, I realise how different we are."

She came over suddenly and kissed me.

"You're good, Damaris. You know, I could never be good like you."

"You make it sound as though there was something rather disgraceful about being good."

"I didn't mean it. Sometimes I wish I were like you."

"Never!" I cried.

"Yes, I do. I wish I could settle down and be good and happy. After all, I have so much, as you are all so anxious to keep telling me."

"Oh, Carlotta, you're pretending. Of course you're happy. Look how merry you were tonight."

"Merriment and happiness do not necessarily go hand in hand. Still, Damaris, I rather like your Matt."

"Yes," I said, "so do we all."

She bent swiftly and kissed me again.

"Good night," she said and went out.

I sat looking at my reflection in the mirror and seeing not my own face but her beautiful one. What had she been meaning to say? Why had she come to my room in this way? I thought she had been going to tell me something. But if she was she had changed her mind.

The next day Matt came over to go riding. I was in the garden when he arrived.

He called to me.

"It's a lovely morning. There won't be many more like this. Winter is advancing on us."

Carlotta came out then and when I saw that she was dressed for riding in her dove-grey habit and little blue feathered hat and had evidently expected him, I realised with a twinge of dismay that they must have arranged this the previous evening.

I looked from one to the other and flattered myself that I hid my disappointment admirably.

"Oh . . . so you plan to take a ride?" I said.

Matt said: "Are you coming with us, Damaris?"

I hesitated. Obviously they had arranged this on their own and he had only asked me to join them because I was here.

I said: "Well, I'm supposed to be doing lessons, and then I was going to deal with the herbs I've been drying in the stillroom."

Was it my fancy or was he relieved?

He said with some alacrity—or perhaps I imagined that—"Well, let's get going, shall we? Days are getting very short."

They went off and I went back into the house feeling depressed.

The morning seemed endless. I kept wondering whether they had returned. I went to the stables twice. The horse Carlotta was riding was not there.

It was about four o'clock and they had not returned. I was too restless to remain in the house. I decided to go for a ride. I loved Tomtit and he always seemed to understand my moods. I thought irrationally I might not be as attractive as Carlotta but animals loved me

194

far more than they ever had her. She rode with grace and ease but there was no rapport between her and her horses. She would have laughed me to scorn if she heard me say that. Matt had understood. There was that feeling between him and his horses and with Belle, of course.

As we rode along I thought I heard the sound of a shot. I stopped and listened. Someone potting a hare or rabbit in the woods, I thought. The workers on the land did it often.

Without thinking I allowed Tomtit to lead to where he would and took the familiar road to Enderby.

I stopped in a clumb of trees and looked at the house. I tried to think of practical things and I thought while Carlotta is here we must talk to her about doing something about the house.

My gaze wandered over the creeper-covered walls, now so beautiful, gleaming reddish in the pale sunshine of an autumn day. I looked towards the fenced-in land close by. It was very silent. The summer was over, there were few flowers left—just a sprinkling of campion and shepherd's purse, a clump of gorse here and there, and woolly seed heads of thistles and a little roundwort.

So many of the birds had gone now. I saw a sparrow hawk hovering, looking for prey, and heard the sudden cry of a gull.

That meant stormy weather. They flew inland when gales and wind and rain were threatening. I marvelled how they could sense these conditions long before we could. We were about three miles from the sea and whenever we heard the gulls we always said: "Bad weather on the way."

It was warm for November. What was the old saying: "A cold November, a warm Christmas." Perhaps it worked the other way too.

As I sat there taking comfort from the contemplation of nature, which I had been able to do from the time I was aware of anything at all, I saw a movement in the fenced-off land. I was not far from the gate and could see through the bars. I remained still and silent, wondering who it was who had ventured there.

It was a man. He came to the gate and unlocked it. I saw that it was my father and that he carried a gun under his arm.

My impulse was to call to him; then I decided not to. Ever since Belle had been trapped there he had shown a disinclination to talk about the land. I decided therefore that I would not let him know I was here. He might wonder why I came. I hid myself among the trees. It would not be easy to explain the impulse which prompted me. So I thought: Let well alone.

I watched him walk away in the direction of the Dower House. Then I continued my ride.

When I returned Carlotta was back from hers. Matt had returned to Grasslands and we did not see him again that night.

The next morning he came over in some consternation.

"Belle has not been home all night," he said.

I was very concerned.

"It is so unlike her," he said. "I know she likes to roam about on her own, but she always returns at night."

"You don't think she is caught in a trap, do you?"

"Oh, no. Your father has shown his disapproval of them. I don't think anyone would use them after what happened to the Rooks."

"Let's go out and look for her," I said.

We went everywhere we could think of. We even went into the fenced land and I got the key of the house and we explored that.

They had been Belle's favourite haunts but there was no sign of her.

It started to rain while we were looking.

"That will bring her in," said Matt. "She hates the rain."

We went back to Grasslands. Matt went all over the house and grounds calling to Belle, but there was no sign of her.

That brings me to that day when my whole world was turned upside down—a day I cannot bear to think of even now.

The sky was overcast and it was dark when I awoke. It had been raining heavily during the night, and although it had let up for a while, by the appearance of the clouds it would start again at any moment.

Matt came over in the morning.

I saw him coming and called: "Any news of her?"

He shook his head blankly.

Carlotta came down in her riding habit. "Let's go out and look for the dog," she said to Matt.

They went off together. I could have gone with them but I declined as I had the previous morning and they made no effort to persuade me.

I could not concentrate on my lessons, and Miss Leveret said: "I think we'd better abandon lessons until that dog is found."

The day seemed endless again. What had happened to time? The clouds were still heavy but the rain had kept off. I decided that Tomtit could comfort me and, who knew, I might come across Belle. Hurt perhaps, shut up somewhere. It was possible; she had a passion for exploring, she might have crept into some hut and the owner could have come along and locked her in not knowing she was there.

As usual I went past Enderby and suddenly a thought hit me. It was about here that I had heard the sound of a shot. I had seen my father emerge from the land with a gun under his arm.

No. It was impossible. I marshalled my thoughts. The shot which I had heard could reasonably be supposed to have been made by my father. Had I not seen him with the gun under his arm?

Belle had been fascinated by the land and by Enderby generally.

It seemed possible that he had found the dog there, been so angry—his temper was fierce when aroused— and shot her.

To kill Belle—that lovely, happy, friendly, creature whom I had loved so much! And to think it had been done by my father, whom I also loved.

I would not believe it.

But the more I thought of it the more likely it seemed.

I slipped off from Tomtit's back and tethered him to a tree.

"I won't be long," I said. "Wait for me. There's a good boy. But I must go in there. I must see what I can discover."

Tomtit pawed the ground twice. An answer to my pat. He understood. He was to wait for me.

I climbed over the gate and was inside the enclosure. I suppose it was because of the rumours attached to the place that I felt a sense of evil. It was as though eyes watched me, as though trees would take on the shape of monsters if I turned my back on them. Little girl fears. Relics of my childhood days when I had plagued Emily Philpots to tell me gruesome stories by day and then when darkness fell wished I hadn't.

I was wishing I hadn't come now. What did I hope to find? If he had shot Belle . . . No, I would not believe it. I could not bear to think of that dear creature lying stiff and silent with a shot through her head.

I was being foolish. My father often went out with his gun. He had just decided to look at the land. Perhaps he had been contemplating what he would do with it. There had been so much talk about that lately.

Nevertheless I went walking on. The leaves were wet and slushy. The wind had brought the last of the leaves off the trees and bushes. My feet made a swishing noise which broke the silence of the air.

"Belle," I called softly. "You're not hiding here, are you?"

I kept thinking of her as she had looked at the charades, when she had bounded in and laid the dirty old shoe at Matt's feet—a tribute of love and loyalty. I could see her at this moment, her head on one side, her tail thumping the floor as she had sat down revelling in the old shoe as though it were the Golden Fleece or the Holy Grail.

"Belle, oh, Belle, where are you? Come home, Belle."

I had come to that spot where she had found the shoe. And then I noticed . . . The ground had been disturbed recently. It had been dug up and carefully replaced. A terrible understanding came to me. I knew that Belle was underneath that soil.

I stood staring at the patch for some time. I was so overcome by emotion that I could not move.

Two dreadful realities struck me. Belle had been shot and my father had killed her and buried her.

"Oh, father, how could you?" I murmured. "What harm had she done? She came in here and she found the shoe. It was natural to her; she was delighted with her find. Why were you so angry when she was caught in the trap? Why is it so important?"

That was the question. Why?

It had grown dark in the wood. A heavy raindrop fell on my upturned face. The threatened rain was starting again.

The gloom in the wood had increased. It was overpowering. It was evil . . . evil . . . all around me. I sensed it. It was true about the will-o'-the-wisps. They were here in this evil land which turned good kind men like my father into murderers. For Belle had been murdered. I called it so because Belle was very dear to me. And my father, who was also dear to me, had done it. What was it about this evil spot which changed people?

I had to get away from it. I wanted to be alone to think. I wanted to see Matt and tell him what I had discovered. Or did I? I would not tell anyone that I had seen my father with a gun.

Then the most fearful thought of all struck me. What was hidden in this place which could have this effect on my father?

I was seized with a sudden fear. I must get away. I was caught up in something evil and I must escape from it as soon as I could.

I started to run and as I did so it seemed that the trees reached out to catch me. I found progress difficult through the sodden leaves. I caught my foot and for a horrible moment thought I was going to fall. The prospect of spending a night in this place appalled me.

I caught at a tree trunk. My hand was grazed from the contact but it saved me from a fall. I rushed on. I was caught and held and felt faint with horror but it was only a bramble which had caught my sleeve. At last I came panting to the gate.

The rain was now pelting down. I was going to be

199

saturated if I went back in this. Moreover, it was falling in such sheets that one could hardly see where one was going.

Then I thought of the house. How I was to wish later that I had not done so. But then perhaps it was inevitable and best for me to know.

I untethered Tomtit, who whinnied with pleasure at the sight of me.

"It can't last long like this," I said to him. "We'll wait a bit. There's an outhouse close to the house."

I took him over and it was difficult to find our way in the blinding rain. There was just room for him in the shed. I patted him and he nuzzled against me.

I decided to wait in the house porch because I could get more shelter there.

Murmuring that I would not be long and that we would go as soon as the rain abated a little, I stumbled towards the house.

I reached the porch and leaned against the door. To my amazement it opened. It had evidently not been properly shut.

I went inside. It was a relief to get out of the wind and rain. I stood in the great hall and looked towards the minstrels' gallery.

How gloomy it was. There was an atmosphere of menace, I always thought, in this house even when the sun was shining. But in the gloom it really was forbidding.

Even so it offered comfort after the conditions outside.

I don't know why it is one can sense human presence but one often does, and as I stood there the firm conviction came to me that I was not alone in the house.

"Is anyone there?" I said. My voice seemed lost in the sound of the rain outside. A sudden flash of lightning illuminated the hall. It startled me so much that I gasped. A few seconds later came the roar of thunder.

A great desire came to me. "Get out." It was as though a voice was warning me. I stood uncertainly.

The darkness outside had deepened. It was like the dead of night.

Then suddenly the hall was lit up by another flash of lightning. I was staring at the minstrels' gallery expecting to see something up there. There was nothing. I braced myself for the tremendous clap of thunder. The storm was right overhead.

I stood leaning against the wall. My heart was beating so fiercely that it seemed as though it would choke me. I waited for the next burst of thunder. It did not come. As I stood there, the darkness lifted. I could see the curtains at the gallery. I could have fancied they moved, but that was only fancy.

And yet I had the conviction that someone was in this house.

"Go away," said the voice of common sense.

But I could not go. Something was impelling me to stay.

I was in a state of shock, I believe. I was obsessed by the certainty that my father had killed Belle and buried her in the forbidden wood and that there was some dark secret there which I dared not discover. I felt that it would wrench the whole structure of my life if I found out.

It was as though I could hear voices, whispering voices, voices of the Rooks fabricating tales about my father, gossip, rumour. But there was something there. Normally I should be afraid to stay in this house. Now, although I sensed more than I ever had before that atmosphere of doom which hung over it, it did not frighten me. Or perhaps I was so afraid of reality—of what might lie under the soil of the forbidden wood— that I could not feel this fear of the supernatural. There was so much that could be explained to the human mind going on around me—that was if one could piece the evidence together.

There was another flash of lightning, less brilliant than those which had gone before, and some seconds passed before I heard the thunder. The storm was moving away. It had become lighter.

I wondered why the door was not shut. We always locked the doors when we left. It was not as though it

201

was empty of furniture. All Robert Frinton's furniture had been left here when he died and had remained since. Carlotta had wished it that way and it had been her house and her furniture—left to her by the adoring Robert Frinton, uncle of the father she had never known.

I looked up the staircase and it was as though some force impelled me to mount it.

I did so slowly. I could still hear the rain pelting down outside. I looked into the gallery. There was no one there.

Someone must have forgotten to lock the door, I told myself. Why not go out? Go to comfort poor Tomtit, who would be waiting patiently for me in the out-house.

But I went up the stairs. I was going to look through the house to see if anyone was there.

I had a fantastic idea that the house was beckoning me on; I could almost fancy it mocked me.

"Silly little Damaris, always such a child."

That was like Carlotta's voice.

"When I, as a child, went and explored the haunted house I hid in a cupboard. It was called Carlotta's cupboard after that. Robert Frinton said he was reminded of me every time he used it."

Carlotta had loved to tell me tales like that when she was younger but so very much my senior—seeming to be more so then than now.

Oddly enough my fear had left me, although never had the house seemed more sinister. It was simply because I was not really here. I was in the wood looking down at that patch of land which I believed to be Belle's grave.

Now I had reached the first-floor landing. I thought I heard whispering voices. I stood still listening. Silence . . . deep silence.

I imagined it, I thought. It was easy to imagine voices with the rain pelting against the window and the wind sighing through the branches of the trees which would be completely leafless after this violent storm.

I opened the door of the bedroom which Carlotta had

liked best of all. The room with the four-poster bed with the red velvet curtains, the bed where I had come across her lying and talking to herself.

I stepped into the room. I took a few paces forward and almost tripped over something lying on the floor. I looked down. There was enough light to show me a riding habit . . . dove grey with a hat with a little blue feather.

I gave a little gasp. At that moment a flash of lightning illuminated the room and I saw them clearly. Carlotta and Matt. They were lying on the bed . . . naked . . . They were entwined about each other.

I took one look and turned. I felt sick. I did not know what to do, what to think. My mind was a blank. As I shut the door the clap of thunder burst out.

I ran. I did not know where I was running. All I wanted to do was to get away. I could not bear to think of what I had seen, of what it implied. It revolted me, nauseated me.

I did not know where I was running. I was unaware of the rain beating down on me. I came to the gate of the forbidden land. Where to hide? Where to be alone with my jumbled thoughts? In there . . . there at the side of Belle's grave.

I climbed the gate and went stumbling through the leaves. I flung myself down beside the disturbed earth. I lay there trying hard not to think of that scene in the bedroom.

It was dark. It was still raining but it was a softer rain now. I felt dazed and lost to the world. I was not sure where I was. Then I remembered. I was in the wood and Belle was murdered and I had seen something in the bedroom at Enderby which I could never forget. It had shattered my own personal dream; but it had done more than that. I did not want to know anymore. I wanted to forget. My father . . . my mother . . . my sister . . . I could not bear to be with them. I wanted to be alone . . . by myself . . . here in the forbidden wood.

My mind started to wander, I think, because I fancied I saw the will-o'-the-wisps dancing around me as though to claim me as one of their band. I was not

203

afraid of them. I understood something of human un-happiness now. I just wanted to be wrapped round in nothingness. "Nothing, nothing," I whispered. "Let it stay like this for ever."

It was long after that night before I wrote again in my journal. They found me in the morning. It was my father who came into the wood looking for me and car-ried me home. Tomtit, sensing that something was wrong, had late that night left the hut and gone back to the Dower House. They were at that time very anx-ious about me and when he came back alone they were frantic with anxiety.

Then they searched . . . all through that night of rain and storm.

I had a raging fever and I came near to death. For a whole year I was in my bed. My mother nursed me with all the love and tenderness of which she was ca-pable.

They didn't question me. I was too ill for that, It was more than three months before I discovered that the Pilkingtons had left. Elizabeth had grown tired of the country, they said, and had left for London and put Grasslands up for sale. Matt had left a week or so after that terrible night.

My limbs were stiff even when I was recovered, and for a long time it was agony to move my hands. How devoted my mother was to me, how tender was my father. I found that I loved him just as much as I ever had, and we never spoke of Belle. I think he knew that I had gone to look for Belle and what I feared, for he had found me at that spot.

Carlotta did not come to see me. "She was here for a long time in the beginning," said my mother. "She was so anxious about you. She wouldn't go until she knew you were going to recover. I have never seen Carlotta so put about. Then she had to go home of course. She had been away so long. When you are well enough we will go to Eyot Abbass."

Sometimes I thought I would never be well again. The pains in my limbs were excruciating at times and they were stiff when I tried to walk so that I tired easily.

My mother would read to me, my father played chess with me. They were anxious to show me I was their precious child.

So the time began to pass.

CARLOTTA

A Willing Abduction

For months I believed I should never forget that moment when on the night of the great storm my sister, Damaris, opened the door of the red room and saw me with Matt Pilkington. It was a bizarre scene with that sudden flash of lightning showing us there... caught flagrantly, blatantly, so that the truth could not be hidden.

To her I must have seemed the ultimate sinner. The adultress taken in adultery. I could never begin to explain everything to Damaris. She is so good; I am so wicked. Though I do not believe any living person is entirely good nor any entirely bad. Even I must have some good points, for I did suffer terrible remorse on that night when she was missing. When her horse came home without her I was frantic with anxiety and all through that night I suffered such fear and there was born in me a repugnance of myself which I had never experienced before. I even prayed: "Anything... anything I will do," I murmured, "but bring her home." Then she was found. I shall never forget the overwhelming relief when my father carried her into the house.

We fell on her—my mother and I; we stripped off her sodden clothes; she was limp and raving with fever. We got her to bed; the doctors came. She was very ill and for weeks we were not sure whether she would live. I wouldn't leave the Dower House until I was sure that she was going to recover.

I had lots of time for thought when I used to sit by her bed while my mother rested, for my mother would not allow her to be left for one hour of the day or night. While I longed for her to get better I used to dread the moment when she would open her eyes, look at me and remember.

For the first time in my life I despised myself. Always before I had been able to make excuses for my conduct. I found that difficult now. I knew how she had felt about Matt Pilkington. Dear Little Damaris, she was so innocent and obvious. Damaris is in love, I thought. I could just imagine her romantic fantasies— so far removed from reality.

When I sat by her bed I used to imagine myself explaining to her, trying to make her see how events had led up to that scene in the bedroom.

I would never make her understand my nature, which was different from hers as two natures could be.

"Damaris," I imagined myself saying to her, "I am a passionate woman. There are instincts in my nature which demand to be satisfied. An impulse comes to me at certain times in certain company and when it comes it is beyond my control. I am not alone in this. You are fortunate, Damaris, because you will always be able to control your emotions; in any case you would never have these intense desires—animal desires, perhaps you would call them. They are like that. It is like a fire that suddenly is there and it has to be quenched. No, you would not understand. I am learning more and more about myself, Damaris. There will always be lovers for me. Marriage doesn't alter that. I have met men who are as I am . . . Beau was one; there was a Jacobite who kidnapped me, he was another. And Matt, yes, Matt too, but there was another reason with Matt."

I should never explain to Damaris and if I tried she would never understand.

I thought back to the moment when I had arrived at the Dower House. I was coming down to the hall and there was Damaris with him. For the moment I thought he was Beau. . . . It was the clothes, I suppose, really, and there was that faint musk scent he used. He told me later that he kept his linen in musk-scented trunks.

So for that moment I thought he was Beau.

We stared at each other. He said afterwards: "I couldn't stop staring. I didn't think you were real. I had never seen anyone so beautiful."

I had received many compliments, but I never tired of them.

I realised as I came closer to him that it was a fleeting resemblance, something about the style of the dress and scent of musk. There is nothing like scent to bring back memories. At any rate from the first moment we were interested in each other.

It became clear to me during the first evening that he was becoming infatuated. There was something innocent about him which made him different from the men I had known. Beau and Hessenfield were adventurers, buccaneers, the sort of men who roused me more than any others. Benjie was the good dependable type, the perfect husband for a good woman. Alas, I was not that. But Matt Pilkington was different. He was capable of passion, no doubt about that, but as yet he was innocent—inexperienced. I could never outwit Beau or Hessenfield; and the game of trying to was completely fascinating to me. That was why I missed them so bitterly. I could guide Matt Pilkington; I could command him; he was completely mine, I knew, whenever I wished it.

I enjoyed his admiration—adoration, more likely. I would never tire of homage to my beauty. So we went riding. Damaris came out when we were about to leave. Matt asked her to join us and I couldn't help laughing at his relief when she declined. Poor Damaris, I thought, she imagines herself in love with him. She's a child really. It is calf love. A good experience for her, though.

We rode out together; we stopped at an inn for a tankard of ale and some hot fresh baked rye bread and a piece of cold bacon.

All the time his feeling for me was growing. When he helped me mount he was loathe to let me go and I

211

leaned forward and kissed him lightly on the brow. That seemed to fire both of us. Memories of Beau came sweeping over me. I had thought I had forgotten them with Hessenfield. He had taught me so much about myself. But it seemed I had not forgotten Beau, for whenever I went to Enderby I remembered our meetings there.

I had firmly fixed in my mind the idea that there was a resemblance between Matt and Beau and I wanted to prove to myself that I had forgotten Beau even if I could not forget Hessenfield.

We rode on for a while and then I suggested we tether the horses and sit by the stream. We did.

I wanted him to hold me, but I was not sure how far I wanted this go to. I did love Benjie in a way but my feeling for him was different from that I had had for Beau and Hessenfield. Benjie was gentle, tender and a good husband. But he did not satisfy my craving for that wild adventurous passion which men like Beau and Hessenfield could give me.

I had not been unfaithful to Benjie... yet. I now realised that was because there had been no incentive to be. Suddenly, desperately, I wanted Matt Pilkington to be my lover. My reasons were mixed. I needed the wild illicit adventure which I had had from Beau and Hessenfield. I wanted to be dominated, I suppose. Beau had laughed at my innocence and been determined to deflower it; Hessenfield had made it clear that I had no choice. Situations, I suppose, which would have horrified a person like my good little sister, Damaris, but which titillated me.

We sat side by side on the grass. I put my hand over his and said to him: "It's strange, but when I first saw you I thought I had met you before ... just for a moment when you stood in the hall."

"I could not believe you were real," he said.

"I saw your mother once ... some time ago. I can't remember much about her now ... except that she was beautiful and elegant and she had masses of red hair."

"She's very proud of her hair. I'll tell her you thought her beautiful and elegant. That will please her."

212

"I hope she wasn't upset because I decided not to sell Enderby."

"I think she understood. She has Grasslands now and is very satisfied with that. It's a brighter house than Enderby."

"Did you ever see Enderby?"

"I came to look at it when my mother thought she might buy it. She had the key and took me over."

A flash of understanding came to me. Of course. I had smelt the musk perfume there. It was strong stuff and lingered on after whoever was wearing it had gone. And the button which I had thought was Beau's . . . it was Matt's of course. I had been certain that button was Beau's. But of course buttons were obviously duplicated, even when they were as valuable as the one which I had found.

It was a mystery cleared up. I almost told him that it was because he had been to Enderby and I had thought he was someone else—a ghost from the past— that I had decided not to sell the house.

But there was time for that later.

I was exerting myself to draw him to me. Although he did not really look so much like Beau, and his character was very different, I kept having flashes of memory when I was with him, and Beau seemed nearer to me than he had for a long time.

And as I sat there beside him I knew that I could let myself believe that Beau had come back. I wanted to test myself, to ask myself whether I still wanted Beau. During those few wildly exciting days I had spent in Hessenfield's company I had forgotten Beau. I wanted to forget him; I wanted to forget Hessenfield. It sounds hypocritical, really, to say I wanted to be a good wife to Benjie while I was at the same time contemplating breaking my marriage vows.

Harriet had once said: "There are people who disregard the laws laid down for good and honourable behaviour, people who, because of something they possess, think they are above the rules which others obey. You are one of those, Carlotta. . . . So was I. We used other people perhaps. It's unfair because we invariably

213

win in the end." Then she smiled and added cryptically, "But who can say what is victory?"

I could have seduced him there and then, but the idea had come to me that it would be more effective if it were in the four-poster bed in Enderby Hall where Beau and I had made love so many times.

I was excited by the prospect. I was aware of the desire in him which could not be quenched by the efforts he was making to suppress it. He did not know that the obstacles to it make it the more enticing. I was a married woman; he was contemplating betrothal to my sister; he had only known me for a day or so. I knew exactly what he was thinking—he was a good man, or he wanted to be, which is perhaps the same thing.

I was neither good nor bad when passion took possession of me; and I was allowing Matt Pilkington to have this effect on me. I wanted to lie on the bed with Matt Pilkington and delude myself briefly into thinking that Beau had returned.

It was so easy to arrange. The gloomy afternoon with threatening rain, the damp leaves which seemed to cling to everything.

"Let's go and look at Enderby. I have the key here with me. I meant to go in this afternoon."

I opened the door and forgot to shut it. We went round the house and in the bedroom we stood for a moment looking at the four-poster bed.

Then I put my arms round him and kissed him. It was the spark to the flames.

We lay on the bed listening to the rain. The lightning and the thunder seemed to add something to this adventure. The two of us alone in an empty house, a haunted house where ghosts could look on.... The ghost of Beau perhaps....

And then we were not alone. She was there and that revealing flash of lightning betrayed us to her before, a few seconds later, she ran from the room.

That was how it happened. How could I explain that to Damaris?

It was an abrupt ending to our passion. Matt was
214

horrified. I realized then that his feelings for Damaris had been strong and tender.

He could only repeat: "But she saw us. Damaris saw us."

"It's very unfortunate," I agreed.

"Unfortunate!" he cried. "It's disastrous."

We dressed in silence. We found our horses and rode back to the house. I told him to go back to Grasslands. I kept rehearsing what I would say to Damaris when she came home.

Then she did not come. And when my father brought her home we thought she would die.

It may sound hypocritical when I say I suffered great remorse. I did. We had shocked the child so completely. She could not understand what had happened; she would never understand.

I rode over to Grasslands late the next day to tell Matt how ill Damaris was. He was terribly sad. He regarded me as though I were some evil witch. Good people are always like that. When they misbehave they look for scapegoats. "It was not my fault, oh, Lord, the evil one tempted me." Whereas people like myself and Harriet at least see ourselves as we really are. We say, "I wanted that and I took it. No, I did not think of the consequences of my act. It is only now that it has gone wrong that I think of it."

At least we have a certain self-honesty. Oh, yes, there is a little good in the worst of us .... and sometimes it is not all good in the best.

Matt kept calling, and when he knew that she would in time recover he went away. I don't think he could ever bring himself to face her.

It was going to be made easy for him because his mother stayed in London and at that time decided that the town was more suited to her and she was going to sell Grasslands.

She did not come back while I was there. Indeed I saw very little of Matt. Our brief idyll, which had had such disastrous effects, was over.

I said I must go back too. I had been too long away from my husband and child.

So I travelled back to Eyot Abbass and tried to forget the havoc I had wrought.

A year had passed. I had not seen Damaris or my mother since I left the Dower House when I knew Damaris would recover. The days had slipped by. I had said that I found it difficult to leave my little daughter and my mother said Damaris, although improving, was unfit to travel.

We must content ourselves with letters.

I was relieved. Even after all the time which had elapsed I could not imagine what meeting Damaris would be like. It would certainly be embarrassing.

Moreover, in view of what had happened I felt penitent. I had been unfaithful to the best of husbands and all because of a momentary whim. I had not had the excuse that I had been overwhelmed by a great love. I had deliberately taken the man who was more or less betrothed to my sister and betrayed my husband at the same time. There was no excuse I could offer for my conduct. But at least I could try to compensate my husband in some way.

Benjie was delighted. He had never known me in this mood. I was loving, I was docile, I was thoughtful for his comfort. It did not take much to make him happy.

Then there was Clarissa. I am not a maternal woman by any means but in spite of myself the child began to charm me. She was two years old, talked a little, had passed the crawling stage, was, as her nurse said, "into everything, a proper bundle of mischief, that one."

There was a look of Hessenfield about her. She had fair hair with a faint wave in it and her eyes were light brown—there were golden lights in them and in her hair; she was sturdy and healthy; a child to be proud of. Benjie treated her as though she were his. He never mentioned the event which had led to Clarissa's brith and our marriage.

Harriet was aware of the change in me. She watched me with alert blue eyes. I don't know how old Harriet was now—she had never told us how old she was and, according to my grandmother, even when she was in

216

her twenties she had pretended to be much younger. But she must have been in her late twenties at the time of the Restoration and that was over forty years ago. Her hair was still dark; her eyes still violet blue; she was rather plump, but her laughter was still like a young woman's and frequently heard and she was interested in the young people about her—in particular me, for she said I was like her and she had posed as my mother for the first years of my life, which made a great bond between us.

She wanted to know what had happened. I told her that Damaris had been out in the rain and had some virulent fever because of it.

"Whatever made her do that?" she asked.

I shook my head, but Harriet was perceptive.

"It may have had something to do with Matt Pilkington. I think she had a romantic feeling for him."

"And it went wrong when you were there?"

"It couldn't have been right before, could it?"

"But the climax came after your arrival?"

"She was out in the storm. That was how it happened."

"What is he like, this Matt Pilkington?"

"Very . . . young."

"Suitable for Damaris?"

"Oh, Damaris is too young yet."

"I'll swear," said Harriet, "that he took a fancy to Damaris's sister."

I shrugged my shoulders.

"Well, if he is easily diverted perhaps it is just as well."

"Damaris is only a child really," I insisted.

"I seem to remember when you were her age you were planning an elopement."

"Damaris is young for her years."

"Something has happened," said Harriet. "I have always found that the best way to discover a secret is not to probe."

"It's a good rule," I said.

She knew of course that my visit had had something to do with Damaris's illness. She would, as she had implied, discover the secret in due course.

And when I showed no inclination to visit the Dower House and she was aware of my determination to be a good wife to Benjie, she guessed.

It amused her somewhat. It was the sort of adventure she would have had in her youth.

She always smiled when she found some similarity between us. She said: "It was a joke of the gods because at your entry into the world—which, my dear Carlotta, was not the most discreet—I pretended to be your mother."

I knew the day would have to come when Damaris and I would meet. It was over a year since we had seen each other, but in the summer of 1704 Harriet said we must go to visit my mother and Damaris.

Gregory had bought a coach, which made travelling far more comfortable. We had not taken it so far as yet but we had made one or two journeys in it which had been very much more convenient than travelling on horseback.

It was a magnificent vehicle on four wheels with a door on either side and drawn by four horses. We could travel a little more slowly so as not to tire the horses, and although our baggage could go by saddle horses as before, we could take refreshments with us in the coach.

Clarissa could travel with us and there would be myself, Harriet and Gregory in the coach. Benjie would have to stay behind to take care of the estate. Then we should have two grooms with us, one to drive the team and the other to ride behind and take his turn with the driving.

For protection we should have with us a blunderbuss and a bag full of bullets besides a sword; so we need have no fear of highwaymen. Many of them made off at the first sign that passengers could defend themselves.

Clarissa was very excited at the prospect of the trip. I was growing very fond of her. She was so full of vitality and she did remind me of Hessenfield. She was a little disobedient; one would not have expected his to be a docile child; but she had that charm which never failed to ingratiate her with those who had been ready to scold her for some misdeed, and as her nurse said, she wound us round her little finger.

She looked delightful in her red woollen cloak and her red shoes and mittens—the colour matched that in her cheeks and her golden eyes sparkled in anticipation. She was very intelligent for her age and seemed a good deal older than she actually was. She asked endless questions about the journey, about her grandmother, her aunt Damaris and grandfather Leigh. Then there was Great Grandfather Carleton and Great Grandmother Arabella to be visited at Eversleigh Court with Aunt Jane and Carl, her boy, and Uncle Edwin and Uncle Carl, if they were home, as they might well be for they had been away for a very long time.

It was a day in July when we set out. Benjie stood in the courtyard as we settled ourselves in the coach. At our feet was a hamper containing cheese and bread, cold beef and mutton, plum cake and Dutch gingerbread as well as various kinds of liquid—wine, cherry brandy and ale.

Clarissa, seeing the hamper, declared that she was hungry already.

"You have to wait awhile," I told her.

"Why?" Everything one said to Clarissa at this stage produced a why, when or where.

I said: "They are for during the journey, not before it starts."

"Not for when you're hungry then."

"Yes, of course when you're hungry."

"I'm hungry now."

Her attention was diverted by the horses being harnessed and she forgot about the hamper.

Then we were settled in, and after waving farewell to Benjie, Clarissa's nurse, nursery maid and some of the other servants who had come to see us off, we were rattling along the road.

Our road took us along by the coast and we passed that house where I stayed with Hessenfield and his conspirators. It was inhabited and looked just like an ordinary house.

Harriet glanced at me as we passed it but I pretended not to be aware of it and, putting an arm round Clarissa, I pointed out the gulls to her who were wheeling round and round diving down to the sea every now and then in search for food.

At last we came to the Black Boar—that inn of many memories—and there we were greeted effusively by the landlord, who remembered us, and now that we came with our coach we were treated with very special respect.

It was a strange feeling to be in that inn again. I found I was reliving every minute of that other visit. I really believed that Hessenfield had sent Beau right back into the recesses of my mind only to be brought out very rarely when something reminded me of him. The climax of my experience with Matt Pilkington had been so like a nightmare that I did not want to think of it anymore.

I had to, though, because I would soon come face to face with Damaris.

The landlord apologised again for once long ago having to put me into a room which was so unworthy of me.

"The gentleman were back here not so long ago, my lady."

"The gentleman?" I said.

"Yes, one of they who took the whole floor just before you arrived on that day. Do you remember?"

"Oh . . . he came back did he?"

"You know the one, my lady, that's if you remember. The tall one . . . the leader of them all, you might say."

I felt a wave of excitement sweep over me. "He was back?" I repeated.

"Yes . . . he remembered you, my lady. Asked if you'd been this way since. I told him I hadn't had a sight of you . . . bar once. There was the time you and my lady came and stayed here, you remember, with the gentlemen. I said: 'Only once, sir, and I ain't seen nothing of her since.'"

"How long ago was it?" I asked.

"Matter of weeks . . . no more."

I changed the subject by saying we should like the partridge pie for our supper.

Harriet and I shared a room in which the General had rested. Clarissa slept in a little pallet beside the bed; but in the middle of the night I was awakened by her creeping in beside me. I had been dreaming of her father.

I held her tightly. I had never thought I could feel the disinterested love I felt for this child.

I was not sorry to leave the Black Boar, and early the next morning we set out on our journey. There is something very exciting about the clop-clop of horses hooves on the road and exhilarating in the early morning air. Clarissa and I watched through the window exclaiming to each other when we saw something which interested us.

She called out for me to look at the lovely butterflies and directed my attention to the beautiful red admiral she had discovered. I wished that I knew the countryside as Damaris did, for I should have loved to instruct Clarissa.

I was growing more and more apprehensive as we approached the Dower House. The desire kept coming over me to turn back. But of course that was impossible. I had to face my sister sometime. I could not imagine what her reaction would be. Perhaps she would refuse to speak to me. Perhaps she would reproach me bitterly. At least she would be prepared for our meeting—as I was.

I wondered if she had told of what she had seen to my mother perhaps.

I should have to wait and see.

When we arrived at the Dower House they had already heard the sound of the carriage wheels, and there, waiting to greet us, were my mother and Leigh.

I opened the door and I was in her arms. She was always emotional when we met.

"Dearest Carlotta. It is so wonderful to see you." There were tears in her eyes and she smiled brightly.

"Hello, Priscilla," said Harriet, "and here is your granddaughter. Clarissa, come and kiss your grandmother."

My mother knelt while Clarissa put her arms about her neck; she gave her a hearty kiss and my mother's eyes beamed with happiness to look at her.

"We had Dutch gingerbread in the hamper," said Clarissa as though that was a most important piece of news.

"Did you indeed?" said my mother.

"Yes, and cake with fruit in it and cheese... and mutton and... and..."

"Carlotta, you are as lovely as ever," said Leigh. "You too, Harriet."

"Well, what do you think of our coach?" asked Harriet. "It has caused a lot of interest on the road so spare a thought for it, please."

"We are so happy to see *you*," said my mother, "that we have no thoughts to spare just yet for anything else. But it is a magnificent vehicle. I must say that."

"The pride of Benjie's life," commented Harriet. "Next to Carlotta and, of course, Clarissa."

"They can take the coach to the stables. There's room there," said Leigh. "I'll go with them to make sure."

"And you'll come in," said my mother. "You must be tired from the journey even in such a luxurious coach."

I said: "Where is Damaris?"

My mother's face was a little sad. "She is in her room. She did not feel well enough to get up today. I said I knew you would understand."

"Oh, yes," I said, "I understand. Is she often... unwell still?"

My mother nodded and a worried expression appeared on her face.

"She is better than she was, of course. But this terrible fever did something to her. Her limbs are often stiff... and they are painful. Sometimes she cannot lift her hands to brush her hair."

"Poor Damaris," I said. "How is she... in spirits?"

"In good spirits... sometimes. At others a little quiet. You know Damaris. She tries to hide the fact that she is in pain. She is always thinking of what is best for us... her father and me... and always puts on a bright face. Your coming should cheer her. She has been excited about it. I think she longs to see Clarissa."

"Shall I take the child up to her now?"

"Yes, go up now. Go immediately. Then she'll know that you went to her as soon as you came. Harriet, come with me and I'll show you your room."

I took Clarissa by the hand.

"We are going to see your aunt Damaris," I said.

"Why?"

"Because she'd like to see you. She's your aunt."

"Why is she my aunt?"

"Because she's my sister. Now don't say why is she my sister. She is, and that's it."

Clarissa hunched her shoulders with glee and we went upstairs. I clung to her hand. I felt she was going to ease an embarrassing encounter.

I knocked on the door. Damaris said: "Who is it?"

"Carlotta," I said.

A brief hesitation then: "Come in."

I opened the door. Clarissa ran forward. She stood by the couch looking at Damaris.

"Oh, Damaris," I said, "how . . . are you?"

Her gaze met mine blankly. "Oh, I'm all right, Carlotta. Some days I am better than others."

She had changed, grown up. I hardly recognized her. She was thinner—but she had been too plump before. She was pale and there was a blank expression on her face as though she were lost and couldn't find her way. I knew at once that the old admiration—almost amounting to adoration—which I had once inspired in her was gone.

"Have you had a good journey?"

"Yes, we came in the new coach."

"We had Dutch gingerbread," Clarissa began.

I said: "Oh, please, Clarissa, not again. Nobody wants to hear about food."

Damaris looked at the child's bright face.

"I'd like to," she said, and her face was illuminated suddenly. It was as though life had returned to it.

Clarissa then began to recite the items of the hamper and Damaris listened as though she was relating the most exciting adventure.

"You're my aunt," she said suddenly.

"Yes, I know," said Damaris.

"It's because you're my mother's sister. Can I come up on your couch?"

She climbed up and lay stretched out beside Damaris. She kept laughing as though it was a great joke.

"Are you ill?" asked Clarissa.

"In a way," said Damaris. "Some days I have to rest."

"Why . . . ?"

Somehow they had managed to exclude me. They had formed an instant friendship. I remembered how Damaris used to be with all stray cats and dogs and birds with broken wings. It seemed she was the same with children.

I was glad. Clarissa had saved me from an awkward situation. We had come through the first vital moments. I knew now that we were going to behave as though she had never come to Enderby Hall and seen me there with Matt Pilkington.

I was immensely relieved. I was sure she was hating me, but being Damaris, brought up to a strict code of of behaviour which insisted that good manners were paramount and must never be forgotten even in the most trying moments, we should behave as though our relationship was a normal one and had not changed in the least.

Clarissa and she had struck up a very firm friendship and the child would spend hours in Damaris's room. Damaris read to her and told her stories and sometimes they just talked.

"I am so pleased," said my mother, "that Clarissa is fond of Damaris. It is so good for Damaris to have her here. I am sure she has changed since she came."

I wanted to talk to my mother about Damaris. She was very much on my conscience.

"What is wrong with Damaris?" I asked.

"We've had several doctors. . . . Your father even had one of the court physicians here. It started with a fever which was brought about by her being out all night in that fearful rain, lying there on that sodden ground in her wet clothes. All those hours she was there."

"Does she say...why she went into those woods while the storm was on...?"

My mother was silent and my heart started to hammer against my side.

I stammered: "She left Tomtit....That was not like her. You know how she always felt about horses and dogs. She always thought of them first."

"She had not been well for some days...." My mother frowned. "I suppose this fever suddenly overcame her and she wasn't sure where she was....Then she went into the wood and collapsed, I suppose. Whatever it was...it happened and it has left her with this...I don't know what."

"Is she in pain?"

"Not so much now. But sometimes she finds it difficult to walk. She must rest. The doctors all say that. We are with her a great deal. Leigh plays chess with her and reads to her. She loves to be read to. I sit with her; we sew a little together. She seems happiest with us...and now Clarissa has come there is a change in her. Your little girl is doing Damaris a great deal of good. What a darling she is. Benjie must be proud of her."

Sometimes the secrets in my life weighed me down.

I said: "What about...the Pilkingtons?"

A look of scorn came into my mother's eyes.

"Oh, they've gone...completely."

"It's odd..." I began.

"Elizabeth Pilkington found the country too dull apparently."

"And...the son...? Wasn't he interested in Damaris?"

"Not when she became ill, apparently. He came to ask once or twice when she was very ill. Then he went away. Duty, he said. Something to do with the army. It was rather mysterious, really. We heard about estates in Dorsetshire and some career in the army. Yet he was here all that time during the summer. Then he went. And his mother left too. I understood her reasons for going. But I should have thought he..."

"Do you think he had...upset Damaris?"

"I think it's likely. I think she may have had some-

225

thing on her mind that worried her and brought on this fever. Then unfortunately she had this collapse when she was out. That made it so dreadful."

"She will recover. . . ."

My mother said: "It has been a long time. She seems to have no life in her. It seems as though she wants to be shut away . . . by herself . . . with just me and Leigh. So it is wonderful to see her so happy with Clarissa. Oh, I am so glad you came, Carlotta. It has been so long . . . so dreadfully long."

"We must not let these absences happen again," I said.

"No. Whether Damaris would be fit to travel I don't know. Perhaps we'll have one of the new coaches. Leigh was talking about it. That must make travel easier."

"I don't think we could have brought Clarissa without the coach. She's going to have her first pony soon. Benjie thinks she can't begin too early."

She took my hands in hers. "I am so glad to see you happy with Benjie. He is such a good man, Carlotta. I shall never forget that terrible time when you and . . ."

"Beaumont Granville," I said.

She shivered as though the mention of his very name had its effect on her.

"We came through it," she said, and there was a strange note to her voice. "It is all behind us now. . . . *All* behind us."

I was silent. I was not so sure. But I would not say so to her. She had enough to worry her with Damaris in this state.

She said brightly, "I wonder if you have changed your mind about Enderby. It just stands there year after year . . . that can't be sensible, Carlotta."

"No," I said, "it isn't sensible."

I knew then that I never wanted to go into that house again. The memory of Damaris's coming into that bedroom had suppressed all others.

"Mother," I said, "I've made up my mind. I am going to sell Enderby Hall."

Naturally we went to Eversleigh within a few days of our arrival. The grandparents were eager to see us.

226

There was a big family party—the biggest for a long time. My uncle Edwin was there, the present Lord Eversleigh home from the war for a brief while. My other uncle, Carl, was also there. Besides them there was Jane and her son. Then there was my grandfather Carleton and grandmother Arabella, besides myself and Harriet with my mother, Leigh and Clarissa. Damaris was with us. It was the first time she had left the house and Harriet had said that she should go the short distance in the coach and if it was one of her bad days someone could carry her into the house.

"I will,". declared Clarissa which made everyone laugh.

Damaris was about to protest, and Clarissa said: "So you'll have to come now, Aunt Damaris, or I'll think you're laughing at me like all these other people."

That seemed to decide Damaris.

"Well, I could try," she said.

My mother was delighted. "I have thought all along," she said, "that if we could get rid of this listlessness..."

"If she made an effort, you mean," said Harriet. "Well, Clarissa has made it impossible for her to refuse on this occasion."

So Damaris came with us and Clarissa sat beside her and told her all about the coach once more, to which Damaris listened as though enthralled.

My grandmother was delighted to see us and was really excited because Damaris had come.

"It's a step forward," she said.

I was pleased to be at that table again. I had always enjoyed the conversation there, which was usually dominated by my grandfather, who always stated his opinions with vigour. He cared for nobody, did my grandfather. He and I were kindred spirits in a way. He had taken more notice of me when I was a child than he ever had of any one of the others.

He insisted that I sit beside him.

"Never could resist a pretty woman," he said. "And ods bodikins [using an oath from King Charles's days] you're one of the prettiest I ever clapped eyes on."

"Hush," I said. "Grandmother will hear."

That amused him and put him in a good mood.

They were talking about the war—and Marlborough's successes.

"A good leader, that is what is wanted, and we've got it in Churchill," said Edwin.

He had always been a keen supporter of the Duke of Marlborough and so had Uncle Carl. They should know, for they had both served under him.

My grandfather started to complain about the influence Marlborough's wife had on the Queen.

"They say Duchess Sarah rules this country. Women should keep out of these things."

"The hope of this country," countered my grandmother, "is that women will stay in them . . . aye, and have more and more influence. That's what we want. I can tell you there would be an end to senseless wars."

This was an old argument which was brought up from time to time. My grandfather enjoyed pointing out what disasters women had created in the world and my grandmother would defend her sex and decry his with fierce vehemence.

My mother, I knew, agreed with my grandmother and so did I. It was a war of the sexes and there was no doubt that my grandfather enjoyed it.

I said: "What amazes me is that those men who take such pleasure in feminine society are the first to denigrate us and try to keep us in what they consider our places."

My grandfather said: "It is because we like you so well when you behave as you are meant to behave."

"There are times," said my mother quietly, "when it is the lot of the woman to act in such a way as only she can."

My grandfather was subdued for a moment and the subject was quickly changed by my grandmother.

It was not long, however, before it was back to the war.

"A senseless war," said my grandmother. "Fighting about who shall sit on the throne of Spain."

"A question," retorted my grandfather, "which concerns this country."

"It's to be hoped," said Uncle Carl, "that we are not going to have trouble from the Jacobites."

"They haven't a chance now," I said. "Anne is firmly on the throne."

"We thought James was at one time," put in Edwin. "He and we learned that this was not the case."

"Do you think they are working overseas?" I asked and I hoped no one detected the excited note in my voice ... no one but Harriet, that was. She was aware of it and why I was interested. Harriet could be uncomfortable sometimes. She understood too much about me.

"I know they are," cried Edwin.

"Louis encourages them," added Carl.

"Naturally, " said my grandfather. "The more disruption he can bring to us the better for him."

"I should have thought with the death of James ..." said my mother.

"You forget, my dear," said Leigh, "that there is a new James."

"A boy," snorted my grandfather.

"About your age, Damaris," said Edwin.

"Who might not even be the true Prince," grumbled my grandfather. "There was a bit of a mystery about his birth."

"Surely you're not thinking of that warming pan scandal," said my grandmother.

"What was it?" asked Damaris.

"Oh," said my mother, "before the boy was born they had had other children, none of whom had survived. There was a rumor that the Queen had given birth to another stillborn child and the boy James was smuggled into the bedchamber in a warming pan. It was such utter nonsense."

"It was an indication even at the time of the unpopularity of James," said my grandfather. "He should have seen what was coming and given up his adherence to the Catholic faith. Then he would have kept his crown."

"The trouble," said my mother, "is that we rarely see what is coming. It would be so easy to avoid it if we did. And to ask a man to give up his faith is asking a good deal."

"We've got a warming pan," Clarissa told Damaris. "I wonder if we've got any babies in it."

"Now," I said, "you have started something."

"I'd like a little baby in a warming pan," mused Clarissa.

"Clarissa," I said sternly, "warming pans are for warming beds. They are not meant for babies."

Clarissa opened her mouth to protest, but my mother laid a hand on hers and with the other put a finger to her lips.

Clarissa was not to be so easily subdued. She opened her mouth to speak, but my grandfather startled her by banging on the table. "Little children are here to be seen but not heard."

She looked at him fearlessly in much the same way as I imagine I did at her age.

"Why?" she asked.

"Because," he said, "what they have to say is of no interest to their elders and betters."

Although Clarissa was not surprised to hear that there were people in the world older than herself she was momentarily taken aback to think that they could be better.

Uncle Carl said: "There's going to be trouble from the Jacobites at some time, I'm sure. They're not going to give up easily, you know."

"They'll never succeed. We're never going to have the Catholics back here, depend on it," said my grandfather. He brought his brows together; they had grown very bushy in the last years and had fascinated Clarissa from the moment she had seen them. Now she was absorbed by them and forgot to ask why.

My grandfather had always been staunchly Protestant. He had supported Monmouth because he represented the Protestants against Catholic James. I vaguely remembered the terrible time that had been when he had come before Judge Jeffreys and been miraculously saved at the eleventh hour.

"Some of them," said Carl, "are fighting with Louis."

"Disgraceful!" said my grandfather. "Englishmen against Englishmen."

"Fighting in a stupid war about Spain!" put in my grandmother.

"Of course the King of France offered hospitality to James and his Queen and his son," said Carl. "I daresay they feel they wish to repay him."

"Oh, yes," added Edwin. "A herald was at the gates of St. Germain-en-Laye when the King died, and in Latin, French and English proclaimed the Prince as James the Third of England and the Eighth of Scotland."

"I wish I were young enough to take up arms against him," said my grandfather. "How many of these Jacobites are there, do you think, Carl?"

"Many in France. They come over here quite often I believe . . . spying out the land."

"And we allow that?"

"They come in secret, of course. It's so easy, isn't it? A ship brings them over . . . a little boat is let down . . . near some lonely stretch of coast and they're here."

"What are they doing?" I asked.

"Assessing the possibilities of victory. Finding out how many supporters they have. Believe me, there are a considerable number. They decide where a landing would be possible if they came with an army. They need to know where they are most likely to get a footing."

"And," said Harriet, "do we do nothing about this?"

"We have our spies as they have. They must be many . . . even at the Court of St. Germain. What we need to do is to get the ringleaders. There are a handful of men who are the very core of it. Men like Lord Hessenfield."

"That fellow!" said my grandfather. "The Hessenfields of the north. They were always Catholics. They plotted in the reign of Elizabeth and tried to get Mary of Scotland on the throne."

"Well, it is not surprising that he is one of the Jacobite leaders, I suppose," I said, and hoped my voice sounded normal.

"It's not so much a religious conflict now," said Edwin. "True, it was religion which drove James from the throne. Now it is a question of right and wrong. Many

231

would say that James is the true King and his son James is the Third of that name. It's a reasonable assumption. And if William and Mary had not deposed her father and taken the throne, this young man who calls himself James the Third would indeed be our King."

"You talk like a Jacobite," growled my grandfather.

"No, indeed I do not," said Edwin. "I merely put forward the facts. I can see reason in the actions of Hessenfield and his kind. They believe they are fighting for the right and it is going to take a great deal to stop them."

"Hessenfield got General Langdon out of the Tower and away to France," commented my grandfather.

I felt so emotional that I dared not attempt to speak again. I was aware of Harriet, watching me.

"A daring thing to do," said Carl. "We have to be wary of a fellow like that. Clearly he's a man to reckon with."

"There are others like him," added Edwin. "They are all dedicated men. Otherwise they would not have given up so much to serve what might be a lost cause."

"Ah," put in Harriet, "but they do not see it as a lost cause."

"It must be. With Anne on the throne and men like Marlborough to fight for her."

There was a brief silence and the conversation turned to local matters.

I told them I had decided to sell Enderby Hall. They applauded, every one of them.

"So you have seen sense at least," commented my grandfather.

"I wonder who'll buy it?" said my mother.

"It's not the best proposition," added by grandmother. "It's a gloomy old place and standing empty so long . . ."

I looked at Damaris, who was smiling at Clarissa.

"What's gloomy?" she was asking.

I turned to my mother. "Will you show people round if they want to see it?" I asked.

"Someone from the house will," she said.

"We'll have some keys here," said my grandmother. "Prospective buyers are almost certain to come here."

Then we talked of other matters and I was glad. Enderby Hall was almost as affecting as talk of Hessenfield and his Jacobites, but in a different way.

The weeks passed and we were still at the Dower House. Damaris's attitude toward me had not changed. It was blank, as though she was scarcely aware of me. When I remembered what she had been like in the past I felt I was with a different person. Not that I was ever with her alone. I wondered what would happen if I were, but I did not want to test it.

August came and there was news of Marlborough's victory at Blenheim.

There was great excitement at Eversleigh and Carl and Edwin fought out the battle on the dinner table using dishes and salters for the troops and the guns.

Apparently it was a resounding victory. Louis had hoped thorugh the battle to menace Vienna and strike at the very heart of Austria, but Marlborough had once more thwarted him, and the French troops in Blenheim were surrounded and at length forced to surrender. The French were no match for Marlborough's cavalry and had been forced to retreat beyond the Rhine.

I wondered how the news had affected Hessenfield as I listened to the rejoicing at Eversleigh.

I went once to look at Enderby Hall with my mother and Leigh.

I stood in that Hall with its strange brooding atmosphere. I could see that it had an effect on my mother and Leigh.

"Come on," said my mother briskly. "Let's go through the house and get it over with."

So we went through. I went into that bedroom of many memories.

"That's a very fine bed," said my mother. "I daresay anyone who brought the house would want the furniture too."

I was glad to get out of the room. I never wanted to see it again. Once I had loved it. Beau used to call it Our Sanctuary with that half-amused smile which indicated that anything with a trace of sentiment in it was something of a joke.

We came out of the house and I saw that that part of the land which had been fenced in was so no longer.

Leigh saw my surprise and said: "It was a waste of land."

"I could never understand why you fenced it in in the first place."

"Oh, I had ideas for it, but I never did anything about them. There never seemed to be the time. Now we are growing flowers there as you see."

"I have my rose garden in there—my very own," said my mother. "I planted it myself and I have given orders that it is completely mine."

"Woe betide anyone who tramples on her flowers," said Leigh.

"So it is still for forbidden territory?"

"Forbidden territory?" said my mother sharply. "What a strange way of putting it."

"Well, it makes a beautiful garden," I said. "And not too far from the house."

"And my own," said my mother. "My very own."

We went in and looked around.

She had left a good deal of it wild, which was very attractive, and here and there she had her flowers growing. And there was her rose garden, which was full of lovely roses of all kinds including a goodly array of damask roses, which were especially favoured in the family because an ancestress had been named after it when Thomas Linacre first brought the flower to England.

It would soon be September, time we returned if we were to do so before the bad weather set in.

On the last of August we set out for Eyot Abbass.

There was a faint mist in the air when we left—a sign that the autumn would soon be with us. Some of the leaves were already turning to bronze and Harriet remarked that we were wise to depart while there was a little summer left to us.

Clarissa had taken a tearful farewell of Damaris.

234

"Come with us," she kept saying. "Why can't you? Why? Why?"

"You must come again, darling ... soon," said my mother.

And Clarissa put her arms round Damaris's neck and refused to let go.

It had to be Damaris who gently unclasped them.

"We shall see each other soon," she promised.

As we rode away Clarissa was quiet and could not be comforted even by a sugar mouse which my mother had put into her hands at the last moment.

But after an hour or so she was looking out of the windows and calling our notice to a goat tethered to a stave and telling us that a goat would tell you what the weather was going to be like.

I said, thinking to bring back her spirits and mocking her a little: "Why?"

"Because he knows. If he eats with his head to the wind it'll be a fine day; if he eats with his tail to the wind it'll rain."

"Who told you that?"

"My aunt Damaris." She was at once sad. "When are we going to see her again?"

"Oh, my dear child, we have just left. But soon."

She was thoughtful. She took the sugar mouse from her pocket and regarded him sadly. "If I bit off his head how would he see?" she said.

She was silent for a while and then she leaned against me and slept.

It was afternoon. We had picnicked by the roadside. My mother had put a hamper of food in the coach ... enough for several alfresco meals. "For," she said, "you don't want to have to make for an inn during the day. You can eat by the roadside whenever you have the fancy to."

It proved a good idea and Clarissa was so intrigued with the idea that she ceased to fret about leaving Damaris. It gave the horses a good rest too. We found a pleasant spot on the road and under a great oak tree we had our feast.

The two grooms joined us and Clarissa plied them with questions about the horses and told them a story

235

about a pig and a hedgehog which Aunt Damaris had told her.

It ended with: "And they all lived happy ever after." Then she went to sleep.

It was a beautiful day and the sun was warm. We dozed a little, which meant that we stayed later than we had intended to.

Finally we were back in the coach and rumbling on our way.

As we were passing a wood through which a path had been made, a man on horseback stepped out of the shadows.

I vaguely saw him as he flashed the window. Then the coach drew up with such a jolt that we were thrown forward in our seats.

"What's wrong?" cried Harriet.

A face appeared at the window. It was a man and he wore a mask over his face.

"Good day, ladies," he said. "I fear I am going to inconvenience you somewhat."

Then I saw that he held a blunderbuss in his hands and I realised that we were facing the situation we had heard so much about and until now had had the good fortune to avoid.

"What do you want?" I cried.

"I want you to step out into the road."

"No," I said.

His answer was to lift the blunderbuss and point it towards me. Then he wrenched open the door.

"Pray step out, ladies," he said.

There was nothing we could do but alight. I held Clarissa's hand tightly in mine. I did not want her to be frightened. I saw at once that she was not but she was regarding the highwayman with intense interest.

As I stepped out into the road I saw the two grooms. There was a second highwayman, who was covering them with his blunderbuss, and I prayed that someone might come along at this moment and rescue us.

Then the highwayman said: "What great good fortune. My lady." He bowed to Harriet, repeated "My lady" and bowed to me. "It is rarely that one meets such beauties on the road."

236

"Why are you stopping us?" asked Clarissa in an excited voice.

His attention was on her. I made a step forward. I had had a sudden impulse to try to snatch the gun. That would have been madness. Besides, there was the other one.

Aware of my intention, his lips curled mockingly. "Unwise," he said. "You would never do it." Then he looked at Clarissa. "It is all in the way of business," he told her.

"Why?"

"Just the way of the world," he said. "Your child is of an enquiring mind," he added, and then suddenly I knew that what had seemed a vague possibility had become a certainty. He was no ordinary highwayman. Could I be mistaken in one with whom I had lived so closely?

The man behind the mask was Hessenfield.

"What do you want?" I asked.

"Your purse, of course. Or have you anything more to offer me?" I took my purse from my pocket and threw it on the ground.

"Is that all you have to offer? And you too, my lady?"

"My purse is in the coach," said Harriet.

"Get it," he said.

She obeyed. Then he came close to me.

"How dare you!" I said.

"Men such as I am dare much, my lady. 'Tis a pretty locket you are wearing." His hands were on it, caressing my throat.

"My father gave it to her," said Clarissa.

He snatched it suddenly. The clasp broke. He put it into his pocket.

Clarissa said: "Oh!"

I picked her up. "It's all right, darling," I said.

"Put the child down," he commanded.

"I intend to protect her," I replied.

He took her from my arms, still holding the blunderbuss. Clarissa did not know fear. I suppose it had never occurred to her that anyone would ever hurt her. She was petted and loved by all who saw her. Why should anyone in the world want to hurt charming Clarissa.

She studied him intently.

"You look funny," she said. She touched the mask. "Can I have it?" she asked.

"Not now," he said.

"When?"

Harriet had stepped out of the coach.

She said: "I can't find my purse." She gasped. "What is he doing with Clarissa?"

"Will you please put the child down?" I said. "You're frightening her."

"Are you frightened?" he asked.

"No," said Clarissa.

He laughed and put her down.

"My dear ladies, cease to fret. I will call off my man and you shall go on your way in peace. Of course I have the lady's purse and I have her locket. Have you some little token for me to remember you by, my lady?"

He had his eyes on a bracelet Harriet was wearing.

She took it off and handed it to him. He smiled and put it into his pocket.

"You're a robber," said Clarissa. "Are you hungry?"

Her face wrinkled in pity. One of the greatest calamities she could visualize was to be hungry. "I'll give you the tail of my sugar mouse."

"Will you?"

She felt in her pocket, produced the mouse and broke off the tail.

"Don't eat it all at once or you'll be sick," she told him, repeating my mother.

"Thank you. I won't. Perhaps I won't eat it at all. I might keep it in memory of you."

"It'll get sticky in your pocket."

He touched her head gently and she smiled up at him.

Then he bowed.

"I will detain you no longer, ladies, but bid you farewell."

He picked up Clarissa and kissed her. Then he took Hariet's hand in a very courtly manner, bowed, kissed it then kissed her lips.

238

It was my turn. He drew me to him; he held me fast. Then his lips were on mine.

"How dare you!" I cried.

He whispered: "I'd dare much for you, sweetheart."

Then he laughed. "Into the coach," he cried, "all of you."

He gave one fleeting look through the window and was gone.

Harriet sat back in her seat and stared at me.

"What a strange adventure! I didn't think being held up on the road was like that."

"I doubt it ever was before and ever will be again."

She looked at me oddly.

"A most gallant highwayman."

"One who has taken my purse, my locket and your bracelet?"

"And the sugar mouse's tail," piped up Clarissa. "Though I gave him that. Do you think he'll remember not to eat it all at once?"

The grooms were at the door, white and shaken.

"God help us, ladies," said the driver. "They were on me before I had a chance."

"The blunderbuss in the coach didn't prove much use," I said. "Have they taken anything of yours?"

"Not a thing, my lady. It was you passengers they were after robbing."

"They didn't take much," I said.

"It could have been worse," agreed Harriet. "Get back and drive on as fast as you can. We want to get to an inn before it's dark."

We rattled on in silence for a while. Harriet was looking at me very intently.

I shut my eyes and thought about him. He was back. How like him to have chosen this way to let me know. For I was sure he had known whose the coach was. He had meant to surprise me. I should see him again soon, I was sure of it.

I pretended to be asleep. I had to escape Harriet's searching gaze. She had known. We had betrayed something. Or she had guessed.

Clarissa was soon fast asleep and once again I marvelled at the way in which children could accept the most extraordinary happenings as the natural course of life.

The first thing she said was: "He was nice. I liked him. Will he come again?"

"Do you mean the highwayman?" said Harriet. "Good heavens, no."

"Why won't he?" asked Clarissa.

Neither of us replied and Clarissa did not press for an answer.

Benjie was delighted to see us back. He said it seemed like years that we had been away. I had been thinking so much about Hessenfield since our adventures with the highwayman that my conscience worried me; and when that was the case I always tried to make up for my deficiencies by being especially affectionate to Benjie, which always delighted him. At such times I often thought what a happy lot could have been mine if I had only been of a different nature.

Benjie was horrified to hear of our adventure with the highwayman. "It's the coach," he said. "These people think those who ride in coaches are very rich."

Gregory reproached himself because he had not come with us, but Harriet said perhaps it was better that he had not been there.

"He was one of those gentleman highwaymen we hear of," she said. "He took pity on two women travelling with a child. He really dealt with us very gently. Do you agree, Carlotta?"

I said I thought she was probably right.

We had been back two nights and were in the winter parlour, a small cosy room at the back of the east wing with windows which overlooked the shrubberies.

It was dark and the candles had been lighted. Gregory remarked, as he did frequently, that the evenings were drawing in and he could notice the difference every day.

A fire burning in the grate, throwing flickering shadows over the panelled walls, and four candles guttered in their brackets on the wall. Harriet was playing the spinet and occasionally breaking into song. Gregory was sprawling contentedly in a chair watching her, and Benjie and I were playing a game of chess. It was a typical evening scene at Eyot Abbass and one I had shared many a time.

And as I sat there looking at the chessboard and deciding on my next moves, I was aware of a shadow, or it might have been some instinct which made me look up—but I did so.

Someone was outside looking in. Someone tall, wrapped in a dark cloak . . . and I knew who it was.

My impulse was to shout: "Someone is outside." But I restrained myself.

What if he were caught in the grounds? If they released the dogs he might well be. He would be captured and I knew what that would mean. I had heard enough at my grandfather's table to understand that it would be a feather in the cap of anyone who brought about his capture. We should be applauded for giving up one of the Queen's enemies.

You fool, I thought. Why do you play with danger? Why do you have to risk your life?

I looked away from the window and back to the chessboard.

"Your move, Carlotta," said Benjie.

I moved a piece without thinking.

"Ha!" said Benjie triumphantly. And a few moves later: "Checkmate."

Benjie always liked to analyse a game.

"It was that bishop's move of yours. Till three or four moves back you were on the offensive. You lost your concentration, Carlotta."

I thought angrily: Of course I did. How could I help it? Hessenfield has come back.

It was an hour later when I was able to slip out. I would not be missed for a little while. I had wrapped a cloak over my dress and told myself that if I were seen I would say I heard one of the dogs or something like that.

In any case I had no intention of being missed if I could help it.

He had come to see me. He might have gone by now. Even he must realise how dangerous it was to hang about here. I would tell him so if I found him.

I examined the flower bed under the window. It had quite clearly been disturbed.

I looked towards the shrubbery and as I did so I heard what could have been the call of an owl.

I stepped towards the bushes and said softly: "Is anyone there?"

"Carlotta ... ?"

It was his voice. I ran forward, glancing over my shoulder as I did so to assure myself that no one was about.

I was caught in his arms and held tightly. He kissed me again and again and so fiercely that I gasped for breath.

"You fool!" I cried. "To come here. Don't you know they will be after you?"

"Dearest, everyone is always after me ... just everyone."

"Do you want to end up with your head on a block?"

"No, on a pillow side by side with yours."

"Will you please listen to me."

"I will talk," I said. "I have heard your name mentioned. You have only to be recognised and it will be the end of you."

"Therefore we should leave as soon as possible."

"You should indeed."

"We. I have come back for you, Carlotta."

"You are mad," I said.

"Yes," he agreed, "for you."

"It has been years ..."

"Four," he said. "It is too long to be without you. No one else will do for me. I have learned that."

"You did not come for me alone."

"I mix business and pleasure."

"You waited a long time," I said.

"I did not know then how important you are to me."

"I suppose you imagine that you only have to come and beckon and I shall drop everything and follow you. Do you think of yourself as some divinity and I your humble disciple?"

"What gave you such an idea? Was it because you felt that fitted the case?"

"This is nonsense. I must go. I saw you at the win-

242

dow. It was foolish to come here. Someone might have seen you. The dogs could have been released. I came out to warn you—that was all."

"Carlotta, you are more beautiful than ever and you lie just as glibly. Did you enjoy our adventure on the road? You did not recognise me immediately, did you? I know just when the moment came. Then I knew . . . and you knew . . . that it was just as it had been. . . ."

"You play such foolish jokes. You could have been caught on the road there and hanged as a thief."

"Dear Carlotta, I live dangerously. Death is prowling round the corner all the time. He may catch up with me at some time. It is a great game I play with him. I am on such familiar terms with him that he has ceased to frighten me."

"It would be a different matter if you were in some noisome dungeon in the Tower, I'll swear."

"But I am not. And I don't intend to be. By the way, who won the chess?"

"My husband."

"So you have been unfaithful to me, Carlotta."

"I married him because of you," I said.

He gripped my arm.

"I was going to have a child. It seemed the easiest way out."

I heard him gasp. Then he said: "That enchanting creature . . ."

"Clarissa. Yes, you are her father."

"Carlotta." He almost shouted and I said: "Be quiet. Do you want to bring someone out here?"

He held me against him and put his lips to my ear. "Our child, Carlotta. My daughter. She took to me. She gave me the tail of her sugar mouse. I shall tell her that I shall keep it forever."

"It will probably melt," I said. "And I shall certainly not tell her. I want her to forget the incident as soon as possible."

"My daughter Clarissa, you say. I loved her on sight."

"You love very easily, I daresay."

"You are coming with me . . . both of you. I shall not rest until we are all together."

243

"Do you really believe that you can uproot us like that after all this time?"

"I invariably do what I set out to," he said.

"Not with me."

"I did once. Ah, but you were willing, were you not? What a time that was. Do you remember when we were down there by the sea and the horseman came riding by?"

I said: "I am going in. I shall be missed."

"Get the child and come with me."

"You really are crazy. The child is in bed and fast asleep. Do you really think I can get her up and walk out of my husband's house just like that?"

"It is not an impossible feat."

"It is. It is. Go away. Go back and play with your conspirators. Go and plan your Jacobite plans. But don't involve me in this. I am for the Queen."

He laughed aloud. "You care nothing who is on the throne, my darling. But you do care a little, I think, who shares your life. I am going to do that. I shall not leave this country without you."

"Good night and take my advice. Go away quickly and don't come here again."

I pulled myself away from him but he held me fast.

"One moment," he said. "How can I reach you? How can I get in touch with you?"

"You cannot."

"We must have a trysting place."

I thought of Benjie then I said firmly: "It is over. I want to forget we ever met. It was unfortunate. You forced me to become your mistress."

"It was the happiest time I ever knew and I did not force you."

"That is how I see it."

"And the result was that child. I want her, Carlotta. I want you both."

"You did not know of her existence a few days ago."

"I wish I had. You are coming away with me."

"No, no, no," I said. "I have a good husband. I intend never to deceive him again. . . ." The word slipped out but he did not notice. I kept thinking of Benjie's face when I had returned and how tender he had been, how

244

unsuspecting, endowing me with qualities I did not possess and shaming me so that I felt I wanted to be as he thought me.

But I kept remembering Hessenfield and those magic moments with him; and I wanted to be taken up and carried off as I was on that other occasion.

"I might have to communicate with you suddenly," he said. "How?"

"You can scarcely come to the house and call."

"Is there somewhere where I can leave word?"

I said: "There is an old tree trunk at the edge of the shrubbery. We used to leave notes in it when I was a child. Come, I'll show you."

He followed me swiftly through the shrubbery.

"If you approach from the back," I said, "you would stand less chance of being seen, but do not attempt to come here in daylight."

I showed him the tree. It was an oak which had been struck by lightning years ago. It should have been cut down, people were always saying that it should be done, but it never was. I used to call it the post box, because there was a hole in the trunk and if one put a hand in there was quite a little cavity there.

"Now go," I begged.

"Carlotta." He held me against him and kissed me. I felt myself weakening. It must not be. I hated myself. But my feelings would not be suppressed.

I tore myself away.

"I shall come back for you," he whispered.

"You waste your time. Go away...quickly, and please do not come back."

I ran through the shrubbery and back to the house. I slipped off my cloak relieved that no one had noticed my absence.

I went up to Clarissa's room and opened the door and looked in.

I tiptoed to the bed; she was sleeping peacefully. She looked serene and beautiful.

"Is anything wrong?" It was Jane Farmer, her nursery governess, a good and efficient woman who was devoted to Clarissa without spoiling her.

"No. I just looked in to see if she was all right."

If Jane was surprised she did not show it.

"She's fast asleep," she whispered. "She drops off almost immediately she's in bed. It is because she has so much energy. She tires herself out but she'll be full of life when she wakes up. Well, that is as it should be. She is more full of life than any child I ever knew."

I nodded. "I won't disturb her."

I went quietly out. His child! I fancied she had more than a slight look of him. I was not surprised—and a little proud—that he had been so taken with her.

I was deeply disturbed. I wanted to be alone to think. But it was impossible to be alone.

I went up to our bedroom. I had only been there a few minutes when Benjie came in.

I was at the dressing table brushing my hair and he came and stood behind me looking at it.

"Sometimes I wonder what I did to deserve you," he said.

I felt sick with shame.

"You are so beautiful," he went on. "I never saw anyone as lovely. My mother was a great beauty in her day. . . . But you . . . you are the most lovely creature that ever was."

I put up a hand and touched his. "Oh, Benjie," I said. "I wish I were . . . better. I wish I were good enough for you."

That made him laugh. He knelt down and buried his face in my lap.

I caressed his hair.

"I know what you're thinking," he said. "It's that devil . . . Clarissa's father. I understand it, Carlotta. I understand it perfectly. You mustn't blame yourself for that. You could do nothing else. . . . You had to save yourself. Don't think I should ever reproach you for that. Besides, there is Clarissa."

"I do love you, Benjie," I said. "I do. I do."

Another shock awaited me next day.

It was morning. Clarissa was having a riding lesson. She was very young of course, but Benjie had bought her a tiny Shetland pony and she was allowed to ride round the paddock on a leading rein. She loved it and

246

talked endlessly of "Shets," her pony, with wild accounts of how he talked to her and what fun they had together, creating the most impossible adventures in which they were supposed to have shared.

I came down to the hall and Harriet appeared at the door of the winter parlour.

"We have a visitor, Carlotta," she said.

My heart began to pound. For a moment I feared that Hessenfield had been foolhardy enough to call on us.

I went into the parlour.

Matt Pilkington rose from his chair and came forward to take my hand.

I felt the blood rush to my face.

"Why..." I stammered. "I... I had not expected..."

"I am staying at the Fiddlers Rest for a few nights," he said.

The Fiddlers Rest was an old inn about a mile from Eyot Abbass.

"I felt," he went on, "that I could not be so close and not call to see how you were."

I heard myself say: "It... it is a long time."

Harriet said: "I am just going to the kitchens to tell them to bring some wine. You can talk to our guest while I am gone, Carlotta."

And she left us.

He said: "I had to come, Carlotta. I almost have many times but..."

"Perhaps it would have been better not to," I replied.

"Have you seen Damaris?" he asked.

"Yes, I have recently returned from a visit to Eversleigh. It is the first time since..."

"How was she?"

"She was very ill, you know. Some mysterious fever which has changed her. She is more or less an invalid."

He was silent and stared for a moment at the floor.

"I have told myself so often that I could never forgive myself. Nor can I," he said at length. "And yet... and yet... I know that if I could go back it would be the same. I have thought of you constantly. I can never be happy again without you...."

247

"Please," I interrupted, "I do not want to listen. You see me here. I have a husband . . . I have a child."

He said: "You had a husband . . . you had a child when . . ."

"I know. There is something wicked about me. I am selfish. I am impulsive. . . . I do things which hurt others and myself and I do them recklessly. I am trying now to live a better life. You must go away, Matt. You should never have come."

"I had to, Carlotta. I was afraid to call here . . . but I had to talk to you again. I saw you yesterday. . . ."

"Where?" I cried.

"It was . . . near the house and I saw you ride in. It was in the late afternoon . . . and once I had seen you again that was enough."

"Listen to me, Matt," I said, "that which was between us is over now. It was a momentary madness on both sides. It was wrong . . . it was wicked. I blame myself. Damaris loved you . . . and to find us as she did . . . She was out all that night, you know, in that dreadful storm. They were frantic . . . searching for her. She would have died if her father had not found her when he did, and it was our fault, Matt. We could have killed her. That is enough. We must never meet again. I am selling Enderby Hall. I can never bear to go into the place again. Nor could Damaris I am sure . . . although she is unable to. We visited Eversleigh and she had to be helped in. Imagine that! Damaris, who used to ride everywhere on old Tomtit. It is unbearable. The only way we can endure it is to try to forget."

Harriet came back.

"They are bringing the wine," she said. "Now tell us what you have been doing since you left Grasslands. I suppose you are on leave from the army. I remember that you were a soldier. I suppose everyone is being pressed into service now with all these glorious battles on the Continent."

"Yes," he said. "I am on leave."

"And you will soon be rejoining your regiment, I suppose. I hope Marlborough will soon be bringing this silly old war to its conclusion."

"Let us hope so," said Matt.

"And how is your mother?"

"She is well, thank you."

"And happily settled in London, I hope, after her brief taste of the country."

"Yes, I think the town suits her best."

Harriet sighed. "The town has so much to offer. Does she go to the theatre often?" She turned to me, for she seemed to have realised that I was unusually silent. "Do you know, the theatres are not flourishing in France. Madame de Maintenon is making poor old Louis quite pious. He is repenting in his old age. He has closed most of the theatres. As if that will ensure him a place in heaven! He will not win this war, I promise you. The best way to court defeat is to close the theatres."

"Oh, Harriet," I said with a forced laugh, "what extraordinary reasoning!"

"Oh, yes, my dear, it is so. People need cheering— especially in wartime—and the best way to depress them is to take away their divertissements. Do you agree?" She smiled at Matt.

"I am sure you are right," he said.

"Of course I am," she cried. "The people were delighted to welcome back King Charles because they were so tired of Puritan rule. I remember well the rejoicing when the good old days came back. Mind you, I was very young at the time...."

"Of course you were, Harriet," I soothed.

"I wonder if your mother remembers when we played together. It was in *The Country Wife,* I believe."

"Yes," said Matt, "she has mentioned it."

"I left the theatre soon after that. But once an actress, always an actress. I confess the sight of the footlights can never fail to thrill me."

So the talk went on and I believe neither Matt nor I listened.

When he took his leave Harriet asked him when he expected to arrive in London.

He replied that he might stay at the Fiddlers Rest for a day or so. He liked the inn, and the surrounding country was very attractive. He had a few days to spare. He liked to walk and ride in the country.

"Call and see us again if you wish to," said Harriet.

"Oh, thank you," he said.

We were not alone again but I knew by the fervent look in his eyes that he would return to Eyot Abbass.

It was later that day when Jane Farmer came to me with considerable apprehension. She wanted to know if Clarissa was with me.

I was surprised. Clarissa was usually in the garden at this time. She rested in the afternoon. It was something Jane had insisted on, although Clarissa was inclined to rebel. However, Jane was always firm and Clarissa had come to the conclusion that it was wiser to obey her.

"I was sitting in the summer house," said Jane, "with my sewing, as I always do, and she was playing nearby with her shuttlecock. She was batting it up and down and was calling out now and then as she always does; and then suddenly I realised there was no sound. I immediately put down my sewing and went to look. I couldn't see her anywhere. I presumed she had come in to see you."

"But, no," I said. "She has not been to me."

"She was talking about you and how she was going to show you the new bat she had . . . so I thought . . ."

Alarm was beginning to stir within me.

"She is a wilful child," I said. "She has been told not to stray away but to keep you within sight."

"We were only in the garden. I think she must have come in to see you."

I refused to face the idea which was beginning to come to me.

"We must find her at once," I said.

Harriet came in and when I told her, she said she would search the house. I said I would do the same in the garden.

She must be somewhere there, I thought. I remembered the occasion when she had hidden somewhere to tease us and another when she had gone to sleep in the shrubbery.

Jane was growing more and more worried. She was blaming herself, but I knew how mercurial Clarissa could be and that it was impossible to watch her all the time.

We searched everywhere and in an hour's time we had not found her. Now we were beginning to get very frightened.

Benjie and Gregory, who had been out on estate matters, came in and joined in the search. It was Benjie who found a green feather in the shrubbery. We recognised it as coming from her shuttlecock.

Then I feared the worst.

Harriet said: "She will be safe somewhere. It reminds me of the time you were lost and found in Enderby Hall."

I didn't want to think of Enderby Hall ever again and I was terrified for Clarissa.

My fears were now beginning to take a definite form. I thought: He couldn't. He wouldn't do such a thing. But I knew he was capable of anything.

I went to the tree I had mentioned—the old oak where we had put our notes and of which I had spoken to Hessenfield. I put in my hand.

Inside was a note and with trembling hands I opened it and read:

My darling, do not be distressed. The child is well and happy. You must join us. Meet me in this spot tonight. I will be ready for you.

H.

I stood there crunching the paper in my hand. I could not describe my feelings. Relief that she was safe; pride, I think, because he had wanted her so much that he risked his life to take her; excitement at the thought of being with him again; and a certain desperate determination to be true from now on to Benjie. My feelings were all so jumbled. I was wildly happy and desperately sad all in the matter of seconds. My mind kept wandering on to the night, to seeing him again, to flying with him . . . where? . . . to the coast of course. I knew that a boat would be waiting there. I knew that this night I could begin a life of excitement and exhilaration. I could be reunited with my child, who was

251

meaning more to me every day. The child and her father.

That was what I wanted. What was the use of denying it? This sober life in the country was something I was not meant for. Damaris would have enjoyed it. And Damaris had been denied it. How happy she would have been married to Matt and having children. But I had spoilt that for her. I could so easily spoil Benjie's life ... but I must not. There was enough on my conscience already.

What should I do?

There were two alternatives. No, three. One would lose me my child, and I was determined that should not be. It was that I should say nothing of this, do nothing ... not go to meet him. Refuse to see him until he went away taking Clarissa with him. Another way was to show the note to Benjie and Gregory and Harriet. To let them know that he had Clarissa, who he was, and to have soldiers surround the shrubbery and take him at the time when I was to meet him. He would have to give up Clarissa then and that would be the end of him. That would be the loyal course of action— to Benjie and to my country. The last alternative was to go to the meeting place in secret to see him....

I knew what would happen. He would carry me off, by force if need be. Knowing him, I realised what was in his mind.

I could not return to the house yet. My thoughts were in a turmoil.

How could I let them go on searching frantically for Clarissa when I knew where she was? Yet how could I let them know that she was in the keeping of the Jacobite leader who was a wanted man.

Finally I went back to the house. Benjie put an arm about me. His face was white and strained.

"Where have you been? I was beginning to get anxious about *you*."

That was the moment to show him the paper which I had screwed up and put inside the bodice of my gown. My hand went to it. It was the sight of Benjie, who loved me so much, who was such a good man. But the
252

moment passed and I did not mention it. I went on letting them believe that Clarissa was still lost.

So the search went on. I shut myself in my bedroom and wrestled with myself.

How could he have done this? He had no right to take her. But what would be the use of talking to Hessenfield about rights? He knew only one law and that was his own. What was right would always be what he considered best for him.

An hour passed and still I was undecided.

They were all out searching the district. Jane Farmer was frantic and I almost told her to put her out of her misery.

What folly! How could I?

I had come to a decision. I would go and see him. I would insist on his bringing back the child.

I put on a cloak and went down to the shrubbery. I waited there in the shadow of the trees.

I did not wait long. I was caught from behind and held against him. I heard his low laughter as he pressed his lips against my ear.

"You are mad," I said. "This could cost you your life. Where is the child?"

"Safe. We are going to France tonight. My mission here is done. I have everything I came for . . . and more. My daughter. I adore her already."

"Where is she?" I insisted.

"Safe," he repeated. "Come on. The sooner we're away the better. I have a notion they are on my trail. We have to get to the coast. I have a horse here to take us. There is a boat a little way along the coast . . . at a nice secluded spot."

"You really are mad. Do you think I am coming with you?"

"Of course you are coming. Don't waste time."

I pulled myself away from him. "I came to tell you that . . ."

He caught me to him laughing and began kissing me.

"That you love me," he said between kisses.

"Do you think I am as cruel and callous as you are?

253

Do you think I can just walk out on my husband because you have come back?"

"I am more to you than he can ever be. I am the father of our child, remember."

"I wish I had never met you, Hessenfield," I said.

"You lie, dear Carlotta. Admit it. That was love, was it not? Do you remember how you refused to betray me? You could have done so now."

"Yes, I could, and how do you know that I have not? Perhaps a troop of soldiers is waiting to take you now."

"I was ready to risk that," he said. "And I'll tell you why. I didn't believe it possible. Come, sweetheart, we don't want to tempt the fates, do we?"

"Where is my daughter? Give her back to me and go and I will tell no one that you have been here."

He laughed at me. "Your daughter is very happy. We get on very well. She was delighted to come with me."

"Where is she?"

"At sea," he said. "Where you and I will be this night. This night, dear Carlotta. Think of it. There are so many memories. No one can ever be to me what you have been. Never shall I forget that brief period when we were together, you and I."

"I cannot go," I said. "You must understand that."

He took my arm suddenly; then I was lifted from the ground. My cloak dropped from my shoulders. He was carrying me out of the shrubbery. There at its edge was a horse.

He put me on the saddle and leapt up beside me.

I am not sure how much I struggled. I did not entirely want to. Hessenfield's adventurous spirit called to mine but I kept seeing Benjie's face and I pictured him stricken as he would be if he knew that I had willingly gone away.

It was only a mile or so to the coast. There was a crescent moon which gave out a faint light and I could see the Eyot lying out there on a sea that was as calm as a lake.

He gave a low whistle and I saw a figure appear from the beach. It was a man who had evidently been lurking there.

"All well, sir," said the man.

"Good," replied Hessenfield.

He dismounted and lifted me down. The man took the horse and as Hessenfield dragged me over the shingle I heard the horse being ridden away at a gallop.

A small boat was bobbing about on the sea. A man was holding the oars, waiting.

We waded out to it the water up to our waists before reaching it. Hessenfield lifted me in.

"Lose no time," said Hessenfield.

The man started to row out towards the Eyot. There was silence. Then Hessenfield said: "Faster. They're on the beach. By God, we were just in time."

I could see vague figures on the beach. A shot was fired. It narrowly missed the boat.

"We'll soon be out of range," said Hessenfield.

"We should have been well away but for your romantic adventures," said the man.

"I know. But we're going to be well away in any case. We're nearly there." We had rounded the island and I saw the ship.

"Safe!" said Hessenfield.

We came to rest by the side of the ship, a rope ladder was put down, I was sent up first. Hands reached out to drag me in.

Then in a few seconds Hessenfield was standing beside me.

He put his arm about me and laughed.

"Mission accomplished!" he said. "The most successful I ever carried out. We'd better leave at once. Come," he went on, "you want to see our daughter."

She was lying there asleep clutching her shuttlecock. I stooped over her and held her close to me.

She awoke.

"Mamma," she said.

"Yes, darling..."

She opened her eyes wide.

"I'm on a big ship," she said. "I've got a new father."

Hessenfield knelt beside us.

"And you're quite pleased with him, are you not? Tell your mother so."

"He's going to give me a new shuttlecock," she said.

"You haven't told her you're pleased with me," persisted Hessenfield.

She sat up and put her arms about his neck.

"This is his ship," she said. "He's going to show me how it sails."

Crime Passionnel

I was thrust into an entirely new scene. At the beginning it was so bewildering that I was more or less bemused by it. In the first place I had renewed that extremely demanding, satisfying, exhilarating and incomparable life with Hessenfield. We resumed it as though it had never been interrupted; and although at first I pretended to be outraged. Hessenfield quickly put an end to that and made me admit, if not in actual words, that I was as enchanted with his company as he was with mine.

It was not unalloyed joy, of course, for it could not be quite as it had been on that first occasion. Although I cannot make any great excuses for myself and have to admit that I was secretly delighted to have been abducted, seduced, raped or whatever name I could put to it when I was trying to make a case for myself, I can honestly say that I felt a deep remorse for what I had done to Benjie and I was glad that I had left my cloak in the shrubbery, which would indicate that I had been taken by force. At least he would not believe that I had gone willingly; and although his grief would not be assuaged, at least he would not think that I had betrayed him.

Poor Benjie, he had lost both me and Clarissa, and I could not be happy because I must think of him.

The crossing was smooth and in a short time we had reached the coast of France.

Clarissa was excited by everything that was happening and, childlike, accepted this extraordinary adventure as a matter of course. She did ask once when her father and grandfather were coming with Harriet. I said evasively that we should have to wait and see.

"I want to show them my new father," she said, and the pride in her voice both thrilled and pained me.

We had journeyed across France staying at various inns and it surprised me how well known Hessenfield was. The best rooms were always at his service and now he was travelling, as he said, *en famille* he was especially determined on comfort.

The man who had rowed us to the boat travelled with us. He was Sir Henry Campion, a firm and trusted friend, Hessenfield told me. "A loyal Jacobite as you must be now, my darling, since you have joined us."

I was silent. I wished that I could forget Benjie and the unhappiness I knew he must be feeling. I thought if it was not for Benjie I would be wildly excited now. I wished that I had not married Benjie. If I had been bold and given birth to my child and waited ...

But that was absurd, of course. I had had to act as I did. I think even Hessenfield realised that.

Once he said: "I should never have let you stay. I should have taken you to France with me from the first."

But Hessenfield was not one to look back. He had a joyous way of living each day as it came along. I doubt he ever felt remorse. There was an enchanting gaiety about him, a devil-may-care attitude. He would be laughing when he died, I was sure.

He was completely captivated by Clarissa. I was surprised that he should care so deeply for a child. But I suppose it was because she was his; she was so charming and she was beautiful. There was a love of adventure in her already, an immense curiosity in everything around her. I could see why any ordinary father should have been proud of her but that Hessenfield should have spared the time from all his activities to talk to her gave me infinite pleasure.

We went first to Paris. He had prepared me for what I should find and how we should live. "The Court is at St. Germain-en-Laye. The King inhabits the castle there; and it is conducted just as it would be in England. I am there a good deal but I have a house—called an *hôtel*—in Paris, for much of my work is done there. That is where you and the child will live, but of course as my wife you will be presented to the King and we will go to Court often."

"As your wife!" I said.

"You are my wife, dear Carlotta. Oh, I know you were unfortunately married to someone else... but that was in England. We are in France at this time. And you are my lady now. You will have to grow accustomed to being called Lady Hessenfield."

He took my face in his hands and kissed me.

"I love you, Carlotta. There is that in you which matches something in me. I feel closer to you than I ever have to anyone else. We have our adorable daughter. Thank God, I have you with me."

I looked into his face. He was serious, not joking now. He really meant what he said and it made me happy. If I could have forgotten Benjie I think I could have been perfectly so.

On another occasion he said: "You are an exile now. You are one of us. Although you have come to us not exactly through your own convictions, you and I belong and my cause must be yours. Our motive is to get back to England. Who wants to be an exile forever? Whenever I go home I have to do so in secret... skulking into my own country like a thief. There is a price on my head. I who have estates in the north of England, where my family have lived like kings. Yes, we are going back one day but not until we have reinstated the rightful King. I would not return to live under the present reign."

"Indeed," I reminded him, "you could not. You are branded now as a traitor to the Queen. You would not be allowed to remain."

"You are right," he said. "Every time I go... as you see, it is as a conspirator who becomes a fugitive."

"It is a pity," I said. "Why must you be involved in such matters? Life is good under Anne."

"Feminine logic," he mocked. "Never mind the righteous cause if we're comfortable. No. That won't do for me, Carlotta. And don't forget you are one of us."

"Only because you have forced me to it."

"Spoken like a good Jacobite," he mocked. But I could see clearly that he was right. Whether I liked it or not I should be considered one of them.

I told him I did not care a pennyworth of candy for his Jacobite cause.

"No, but you care for me," he said. "And I shall have to trust you with many a secret which I shall do without fear because I know that your love for me is as strong as any belief in a cause. We belong together, Carlotta. And so shall it be until death divides us."

In those rare moments when he was serious—and he was then—he could move me deeply. I loved him. Yes, I did. His daring, his strength, his essential male qualities struck a chord within me. He was a leader; I could see now that in comparison Beau would have failed to hold me. I had been dazzled by Beau; but I was caught and held firmly by Hessenfield.

If only we had met differently . . . if only I could have gone to him as his wife in very truth . . . if only I could wipe out the past . . . not Beau, that did not matter. It was Benjie, who haunted me and threw the shadow of deep remorse over my happiness, and it was only in rare moments that I could forget him.

Paris excited me. As soon as we arrived in that fascinating city we went at once to the *hôtel* in the quarter of the Marais which I learned later was one of the most fashionable areas of the city. The King of France had been hospitable to the English nobility who were the enemies of England's reigning sovereign; and with good reason, for he was at this time at war with that country.

At Eversleigh we had always been brought up to regard loyalty to the crown as one of our chief duties but I reminded myself that my grandfather Carleton had been involved in the Monmouth Rebellion. James would have called him disloyal just as Anne would Hessenfield. It was not as much a matter of lack of loyalty as it was adherence to a principle. I was becoming more and more of a Jacobite every day.

It was a fine house and there were several servants. Hessenfield introduced me formally as Lady Hessenfield and I held a wide-eyed Clarissa by the hand and he added: "This is our daughter."

There was no question from anyone in France. Hessenfield had returned to England on a Jacobite mission and had brought his wife and child back with him. It was reasonable enough. I slipped easily into the new role. So did Clarissa.

I felt like a young bride in those early days. Hessenfield delighted in showing us a little of Paris. And how excited we were—Clarissa and I—to walk through those streets with him beside us. For, he said, that was the best way to see it.

We strolled through the discreet streets of the Marais—that part of the city which had once been the home of the Valois kings. Hessenfield explained to Clarissa that the rue Beautreillis was where the vineyards once were, the rue de la Cerisaie where the orchards were and the rue des Lions was the site of the royal menagerie.

We were excited by the quaint houses which overhung the river; the water lapped at their walls, and Clarissa wanted to know whether it ever came in through the windows. She kept shrieking with excitement and sometimes was so overawed that she forgot to ask why.

Hessenfield was anxious to show us the centre of the city. We crossed the Pont Marie and reached the Ile de la Cité, where we looked up at the great towers of Notre Dame and he bought magnificent blooms for us on the Quai des Fleurs. Clarissa wanted to go down among the little streets near the cloisters of Notre Dame but Hessenfield would not allow us more than a peep. These were the homes of the poor and the streets were narrow lanes with houses built close together and almost meeting over the narrow streets so that they completely shut out the sunlight. I saw a gutter running down the middle of the street. It was full of slimy rubbish.

"Come away," said Hessenfield. "You must never venture down streets like that. They abound in Paris

261

and you can come across them quite suddenly. You must never wander out alone."

I said: "It is the same in any big city. There are always slums."

"What are slums?" asked Clarissa.

"These are," said Hessenfield.

She was overcome with curiosity and tried to wriggle free but I held her hand firmly and Hessenfield picked her up and said: "You are tired, little one. Shall I be your carriage for a while?"

I was moved to see the way she smiled and put her arms about his neck. She had not forgotten Benjie and Gregory but she did mention them less than she had at first.

Not far from the *hôtel* in the rue Saint Antoine we passed an apothecary's shop. Sweet scents emerged from it and I was reminded briefly of Beau, who had dabbled in the making of perfumes and was himself always redolent of that strange musklike scent. It was what had attracted me to Matt. He had used a similar scent.

Hessenfield saw my glance and said: "Ah, there are not so many apothecaries in Paris as there once were. Years ago they abounded and there were quacks selling medicines and elixirs, potions and draughts in every carrefour in the city. Then it changed. That must have been some forty years ago but they still talk of it. There was a notorious poisoner called La Voison and another, Madame de Brinvilliers. They suffered hideous deaths but their names will never be forgotten and all apothecaries have had to tread very warily ever since. They are still suspect."

"You mean people buy poisons from the apothecaries?"

"They did. It is more difficult now, but I reckon it is done for a price. They were mostly Italians. The Italians have the reputation for being adept at poisoning. They can produce poisons which are tasteless, colourless, and without smell, and even work through the clothing—they can kill gradually or instantly. This Brinvilliers woman wanted to poison her husband and used to try out her poisons on people in hospitals, where

262

she became known as a very pious lady who cared deeply about the sick."

"She sounds like a fiend."

"She was. Imagine her taking some delicacy impregnated with a new experiment and going along to visit the victim later to see how it had worked."

"I am glad Clarissa is asleep. We should be plagued by whys, whens and hows if she were not. What an exciting city this is! I never saw so much mud nor heard so much noise."

"Be careful not to get splashed. It's pernicious mud and would burn a hole in your clothes if it touches them. The Romans called it La Lutetia when they came here, which means the City of Mud. It's improved since then of course, but still take care. As for the noise—this is a vociferous nation. We are quiet in comparison."

How I enjoyed those days—discovering Paris, discovering Hessenfield and loving both of them more each day.

Before I had been a week in Paris, Hessenfield said that I must go to the Court of King James to be presented.

St. Germain-en-Laye was some thirteen miles from Paris, and we rode there in a carriage for I must be suitably dressed for the presentation. Hessenfield had sent for one of the Paris dressmakers the day after we arrived, for I was without any garments other than those I had been wearing when I had been, as I put it, "snatched from the shrubbery," but as Hessenfield said, "So willingly left England to follow my own true love."

A simple gown was quickly made for me and then there was concentration on my Court dress. It was most elegant yet at the same time discreet. It was in a shade of blue that was almost lavender.

"Milord has said it must be the exact colour of milady's eyes," said the couturiere, who puffed and sighed over the garment as though it was to be compared with the finest work of art.

It was an exquisite colour and such as I had never seen before. The Parisian dyers were masters of the art and the colours they produced delighted me again and again. I was put in a canvas petticoat with whalebone hoops. The panniers of blue silk were ruched and gathered and the tight-fitted bodice was made of the same lavender blue silk. Beneath it was an underskirt of green so delicate in color that one was not absolutely sure it was green.

I had never seen such a dress.

"Of course you haven't," said Hessenfield, surveying me. "When it comes to fashion we're years behind the French."

My hair was dressed by a hairdresser selected by Hessenfield. She cooed over it as she combed and back combed it until it stood out round my head in a frizz; then she started to set it and I had to admit that when she was finished I was amazed by the effect. It was piled high on my head and brought up into a coil about which she placed a diamond circlet like a coronet.

When Hessenfield saw me he was overcome with delight.

"No one ever did justice to you before, my love," he said.

He took me into see Clarissa, who stared at me in amazement.

"Is it really you?" she asked.

I knelt down and kissed her.

Hessenfield cried out in dismay. "You'll wreck your skirts."

I laughed at him and he laughed with me.

"Are you proud of her, Clarissa?" he asked.

Clarissa nodded. "But I like the other way too."

"You like me however I am, don't you, Clarissa?"

She nodded.

"And do I come into this magic circle?" asked Hessenfield.

"What's circle?"

"Later we'll talk," said Hessenfield. "Come on, my dear, the carriage awaits us."

So I went to St. Germain-en-Laye and to the château there.

I was presented to the man they called James the Third as Lady Hessenfield. James was younger than I. I think he must have been about seventeen at this time. He greeted me warmly. Although he had a regal manner, he seemed to wish to show his gratitude to those exiles who had gathered round him and particularly those who, like Hessenfield, had sacrificed a good deal to serve him.

"You have a beautiful lady, Hessenfield," he said.

"With that I am completely in agreement, Sire."

"She must come often to our court. We need all the grace and beauty we can get during this period of waiting."

I said how glad I was to be here and he replied that he would have said he hoped I would stay a long time, but none of us wished to stay as the guests of the King of France a moment longer than we need.

"Let us say, Lady Hessenfield, that you and I will be good friends in Westminster and Windsor."

I said: "I trust it may be soon, Sire."

I was presented to his mother—poor sad Mary Beatrice of Modena. I was drawn to her more than to her son. She was by no means young and must have been about thirty when James was born. And she had suffered a great deal when as a very young girl she had come to England most reluctantly to marry James—the Duke of York—already a widower with an established mistress. I was sorry for her. She had been a beauty once but now she was so thin as though worn out with the sorrows of life. Her complexion was pale but with those fine dark eyes she must have been very beautiful in her youth.

She was as welcoming as her son and told me how glad she was to see me and I should be welcome at court whenever I wished to come. She had heard I had brought my daughter with me and she talked of children for a while.

"Lord Hessenfield gave such support to my husband and now gives it to my son," she said. "I am happy for him to have his beautiful wife with him, and having seen you, my dear Lady Hessenfield, I understand his pride in you. You are a very beautiful woman and a joy to our court."

Hessenfield was delighted that I had been such a success.

"I knew you would," he said. "Beauty like yours is a rare gift, sweet wife. It is for me alone but I am glad to let others have a glimpse of it—a glimpse, nothing more."

"I am not your wife, you know," I said. "But everyone here seems to think I am."

"You are . . . you are mine. We are bound together for ever. . . . I have told you only death shall part us. I swear it, Carlotta. I love you. You must love me too. We have our child. I would marry you tomorrow if it were possible. But here we *are* married. Everyone believes it to be so . . . and after all, what people believe to be is true for them. So let the strength of their belief be ours. My love . . . I am happier than I have ever been in my life. . . . You and the child . . . I ask for nothing more."

I realised that this was a strange speech for a man like Hessenfield to utter. There had been little sentimentality in his life until now. I could see that what was there had been born out of the strength of his feeling for me.

I was tremendously happy riding back in the carriage to our *hôtel* in Paris.

Yes, Hessenfield had changed. He had become the family man. He was still the passionate and demanding lover by night, and I was amused that during the day he became absorbed by arranging his household.

The dressmaker who served the French court was often at our house. I was to be the centre of her attention. I recognized her skill and I had always been proud of my good looks so it pleased me, therefore, to discover that there were so many ways of enhancing them.

I heard that I was referred to as the Beautiful Lady Hessenfield and when I rode out people stood about to watch me.

I was vain enough to enjoy it.

Clarissa commanded a good deal of Hessenfield's attention and one day he said to me: "We shall have to stay at St. Germains at times. There is work for me to do and it can only be done there. We can't take Clarissa. We should have a good nursery governess for her. Someone who can teach her and look after her at the same time."

"I should not want her to speak French entirely. It would change her somehow."

"She shall speak both languages."

"But a French nurse would not speak English to her."

"We should do that. It is hardly likely that you would find an English nursery governess here. We must look round. I have already let it be known that we are searching for someone suitable."

"It must be someone of whom I approve."

He kissed me. "It must be someone of whom we both approve."

It seemed the greatest good fortune when Mary Marton arrived.

I was with Clarissa when she was announced. I left the child and received her in the *salon*. She was of middle height, very slender, with pale yellow hair and light blue eyes. She had an extremely deprecating manner. She had heard that I needed a nursery governess for a young child and had come to offer her services.

She told me that she had been brought to France by her mother, who had followed her father, who had been in the service of the late King. Her father had died almost immediately and she and her mother had gone to another part of France—near Angoulême. Her mother was now dead and she had come to Paris to see if she could earn a little money as she had become very poor.

She had a family in England and hoped eventually to return to them, but as her father had been a Jacobite it would not be easy for her to return. In the meantime she had to earn a living.

She was well educated, was fond of children and qualified to take on the care of a child. In any case she would be most grateful for the chance.

I was delighted because I wanted Clarissa to retain her English characteristics. I was always hoping that we should return to England. I wanted to see my mother, and Damaris was on my conscience a great deal. She and Benjie were like two reproachful shadows

267

who would appear at any moment to cloud my happiness.

I believed, and so did a good many other people, that when Anne died James would be invited to come back. That was the time we were all looking forward to. Anne was a sick woman; surely she could not live very long. She had that fearful dropsy which made it difficult for her to walk; and she had long given up hope of producing an heir.

So when we did go I wanted my daughter to be English. She could already chatter a little in French, which she did with the servants. That was good but her main tongue must be English.

Therefore I was delighted to engage Mary Marton, and when Clarissa seemed to take to her that settled it. Clarissa of course took to everyone; she had the beautiful notion that everybody in the world loved her and therefore she must love them. I would have liked to have taken that up with some of those who had declared she was spoilt. Spoiling perhaps had its point. It had certainly turned my child into an extremely affectionate one.

Hessenfield was delighted that we had found our nursery governess so quickly. He was beginning to talk to me about his plans and how members of his society were constantly going back and forth to England and that when the day came for the great invasion it would be known where they could most safely land and how many people they could rely on.

There was a tremendous project in progress at that time. Several men were going over to land arms and ammunition. They knew where it could safely be deposited. It would be left in the possession of trusted Jacobites who lived in England posing as loyal subjects of the Queen.

"There will be these strongholds throughout the country," he explained to me. "We already have one or two but the one we are now planning will be the most important so far."

"You are not going . . . ?" I said fearfully.

"Not this time. I have work to do here."

I was thankful for that.

It was two weeks or so after Mary Marton joined us when Jeanne, one of the maids, came in to tell me that a gentleman was asking to see me.

"Who?" I asked.

"Madame, he would give no name. He is an English gentleman."

"A . . . a stranger?" I asked.

"I have not seen him before, Madame."

I said he should be shown in.

My amazement was great when Matt Pilkington entered.

"Matt!" I cried.

He looked at me helplessly.

"Carlotta," he said, and coming forward seized both my hands. "I know I shouldn't have come . . . but I couldn't help it. I had to see you again. . . ."

"Matt!" I cried. "How could you? How did you get here . . . ?"

"It was not too difficult," he said. "I came on a boat . . . landing along the coast, and made my way to Paris."

"You are mad. England is at war . . . and you are a soldier. You're in enemy territory."

"Yes, I know. I know all that . . . but I had to see you. I heard, you see."

"What did you hear?"

"That you had been forcibly taken away."

I felt an immense relief. So that was what they believed.

"I called at the house . . . at Eyot Abbass. You remember I was not very far off . . . at the Fiddlers Rest. . . . And they were all talking about it. About you and the child . . . I had to come here and see if it was true . . . to see you again. . . ."

"You are in great danger."

He shook his head. "I have long had Jacobite sympathies," he said. "They know it. I am welcome here. They want everyone they can get. I am in no danger, Carlotta. I came to see you. . . ."

"You must not come here, you know."

"You are with him. They say you are Lady Hessenfield."

"It is easier that way."

"But your husband...?"

"Did you see him?"

"Yes. He was very sad. He was talking of coming over here. But that is impossible ... only Jacobites are welcome."

"Did you tell them you were coming?"

"No. They would know where my sympathies lie. I had to be secret about it. I slipped away. But I have friends over here so ... I am all right."

I sighed. Then I said: "You mustn't come here again, Matt. That ... incident ... it is all over. It was a momentary madness ... do you understand?"

"On your part, yes," he said. "For me it is my most precious memory."

"Oh, no, Matt."

"It is no use, Carlotta. I don't want to hurt you, or embarrass you in any way. I just want to see you sometimes ... to be near you. I promise you ... I swear it ... that I will never mention that time. If I could just be here ... see you sometimes ... it's all I ask. I just want to know that you are here. You are so beautiful. More than that. You are an enchantress. Carlotta, you owe me this. Let me come here sometimes. Let me see you. Please."

I said: "Well, I suppose if you are one of them and are working for them you will see Lord Hessenfield from time to time."

"It is you I wish to see. And the child. She is so like you, Carlotta. I should like to see her too."

"Where are you staying?"

"In the rue Saint Jacques. It was the best lodging I could get just now. I shall move later, I daresay. Carlotta, let me be your friend. Let me see you sometimes."

"Matt, if you will promise me to forget all that ..."

"I can't promise to forget," he said fervently, "but I will promise never to mention it to you nor to anyone. If I can come here now and then ... see you from time to time ... that is all I ask."

I said he might. I was shaken. He was gentle and adoring as ever, but there was so much of which I did not want to be reminded.

During the next few weeks Matt was a frequent caller at the house. He made a point of seeing Clarissa and they got on very well together. I thought he did it just to have an excuse for calling at the house; but it occurred to me that Mary Marton might believe that he was attracted by her.

It would be quite a likely assumption. He talked to her a good deal and they often took the child walking in the streets; the servants were beginning to smile about them and whisper of romance.

I was delighted but I did not believe he was really attracted by Mary. Whenever I was near him I was aware of the effect I had on him.

Hessenfield said that he was an enthusiastic worker and had brought some valuable information about the position of the Jacobites in England.

"He has been working well for us in England," he said. "He was just waiting for the right moment to come over here."

I was not so sure of his fervent views. I was vain enough to think that he had come to see me.

He kept to his bargain, though. He never mentioned that time we had spent together and I was glad that everyone thought he was interested in Mary Marton, although I did hope that Mary, who was a sweet and rather innocent girl, was not going to be hurt. Sometimes, though, I thought he really was fond of her. It was not necessary for them to spend quite so much time together.

Hessenfield was often at court. I knew there was some very big project afoot.

At night when we lay in bed together he would be less discreet than he was by day. I knew that he was tense and uneasy.

He did tell me that this was going to be the most important venture so far.

"I know you are taking arms over to England," I said.

"Did I tell you that? Then forget it, my dear."

"You didn't tell me where."

"Nor shall I. The fewer who know the better. I know

and two others—one of them the King. Even the men who are going do not know where yet. It is imperative that the secret is kept. It would be disastrous if it were betrayed."

"Then I will ask you no more. Only this: *You* are not going ... really not going?"

"No. I shall send them off and then start preparing for the next."

A few days later there were visitors at the *hôtel*. They came ostensibly to pay a social call, but I knew it was not the case.

Hessenfield entertained them in his private study, which was on the first floor. I did not disturb them and gave orders that the servants should not do so.

On the floor there were three rooms leading from one another. The study was in the centre and the other rooms were never used. There were some books in one of them and they were really an extension of the study.

A rather disturbing thing happened while Hessenfield was entertaining his visitors. I had been playing with Clarissa in the nursery and she had suddenly become rather drowsy, so I carried her to her bed, covered her up and left her.

I came downstairs intending to go out, for I often wandered round alone. It was safe to do so if one did not stray from the Marais and I was quite fascinated by the little boutiques which abounded in the nearby streets. I liked to buy ribbons and fans, buttons and such trifles which seemed to have an extra charm when compared with those I had bought at home.

It was a tall house and the nursery and our bedroom were right at the top, and as I was about to descend I thought I heard a sound on the lower landing. I stopped. If Hessenfield's visitors were just leaving it would be well for me not to run in to them. I knew that he'd not want them seen if that were possible, although he did not wish to labour the point. It was a very important matter and he wanted everything to seem as natural as possible. People called to see him at all times, and he wished this to appear as nothing out of the ordinary.

So I paused. Distinctly I heard the quiet shutting of

272

a door. Then the sound of footsteps, obviously meant to be stealthy, going down the stairs.

I went down. As I came into the street I saw Mary Marton hurrying away.

Then it must have been Mary who had come out of the room next to the study. I wondered what she was doing there. Oh, of course, she would have gone to return a book. She was always trying to get books from the study. Then, having returned, she must have heard voices in the next room, realised she should not be there and tiptoed out.

I wondered whether I would catch up with her and was in the process of doing when she rounded a corner. As I turned the corner in her wake I saw that she had met Matt.

I drew back. Then it must be true that he was attracted by her and had arranged to meet her. They went into an inn called L'Ananas. A large pineapple was depicted on the sign which creaked over the door. It was a place of good repute, where people could drink a glass of wine and talk in pleasant seclusion during the day, although perhaps at night it became more noisy.

I smiled. I was rather pleased. If Matt and Mary were falling in love my conscience would be relieved on one score. I always felt I had used Matt and abused his innocence.

I bought my buttons and went back to the house. Hessenfield was still in conference in his study.

It was late that night when he came to our bedroom. There was a certain increased tension in his manner.

"Did you complete your business?" I asked.

"Complete!" He laughed. "It has only just begun."

Hessenfield took me to Court again. This time I stayed there with him for a few nights. It was exciting. I had never been to the English Court, for although in the old days my grandfather had been an intimate friend of Charles the Second's, he had been an enemy of that King's brother James; and he had never been on the same terms with William and Mary as he had with Charles. So it was a new experience for me. I soon began to prefer the life in Paris. The city had enchanted me. Every morning I would lie in bed and listen to the sound of Paris waking up. The quietness of the night would gradually be broken. Just a sound here and there and then by nine o'clock it would be completely awake again. I loved the smell of baking bread which seemed to permeate the streets; I loved to listen to the street cries of the various vendors. As I wakened I knew that the peasants who came in from the neighbouring country villages would already have arrived at the barriers with their vegetables and flowers, with their chickens and their rabbits and fish of all kinds. They would make their way to various parts of the town which they had come to regard as their territory; so that if one wanted a certain produce one knew where to go to get it.

It had been a great joy to me to go out with the cook and one of her assistants and watch her do the marketing. She would pretend to refer to me but of course I knew that I was completely incompetent either to choose or to bargain, which seemed to be an important part of the transaction.

I began to learn a good deal about the life of Paris and I loved it. All through the morning the hubbub continued; I enjoyed mingling with those shouting, gesticulating people. I was delighted by the apothecary's shop, where I could try a variety of perfumes and choose which I liked best, always taking account of the apothecary's advice, which he gave as though we were deciding a matter of life and death.

Sometimes I went riding with Hessenfield right out to the barriers which marked the boundary of the city. They were made of pine wood and iron and there were sixty of them enclosing Paris and there were customhouses at the river's edge.

The days began to pass and all that time I was aware of Hessenfield's eagerness to learn that his business was satisfactorily completed. He was not generally one to doubt success so I gathered that this was an operation of paramount importance. I did not mention that I noticed his preoccupation. I was determined that we should share that immense joy which I found in his company and which did not decrease as the weeks passed.

One day we had been with Clarissa in the carriage and had been out beyond the city into the countryside. It had been a very happy day. Clarissa scarcely mentioned Benjie now. She was as entranced by the new life as I was.

We arrived at the *hôtel* in the late afternoon. One of the servants met us in some agitation.

There was a gentleman from the Court who urgently desired to see milord.

Hessenfield pressed my hand. "Take Clarissa up to the nursery," he said.

I went.

In a few minutes he was up there. He said: "I have to go to St. Germains at once."

I nodded.

"I don't know how long I shall be. Back tomorrow, I expect."

He was back the next day.

It was late afternoon. I heard him arrive and went down to meet him. I saw at once that something was wrong.

We went straight up to our bedroom. He shut the door and looked at me.

"Disaster!" he said.

"What?" I stammered.

"Our men went right into a trap. They were waiting for them when they landed. Everything is lost . . . men, arms, ammunition . . . all."

I stared at him in disbelief.

"How . . . ?" I began.

"Yes," he said fiercely. "How! How did they know the exact spot where they were to land? Somebody betrayed them."

"Who could?"

"That's what I have to find out."

"Was it someone in England . . . someone pretending to be with you while working against you?"

"It was a spy, all right. But not over there, I think."

"Then where?"

"Here."

275

"Here! But nobody knew. Who could possibly? You did not even tell me. It must have been someone over there."

"I think it was someone here."

"But *who?*"

"That is what I am going to find out."

The following day Hessenfield went back to St. Germain-en-Laye. I tried to behave as though nothing had happened but I could not stop thinking of those men who had walked into a trap and were now probably in the Tower or some prison awaiting sentence, which would certainly be death. I was concerned for Hessenfield, who had cared so passionately that the arms which he had been given by the King of France should have been lost, but what was most disturbing was that some of their most gallant men had been taken.

I had never seen him so sad before. It was a new side to this character.

I went to the nursery.

"Where is my father?" asked Clarissa. She always called him *my* father. I think it implied that she had only recently acquired him.

I said, "He has gone to see the King."

"He left in rather a hurry," said Mary Marton.

"Oh, yes," I answered. "Important business."

"He looked a little *distrait,* I thought," said Mary.

I lifted my shoulders.

Clarissa said: "Where are we going today?"

"I want to buy some lace," I said. "Mademoiselle Panton"—she was my couturiere—"wishes to trim a dress with it and for once she is most anxious that I should choose the colors."

"I expect it is unobtainable," said Mary with a laugh, "and she will want to blame you because you will have to take a substitute. 'It was of Madame's choosing,'" she said, imitating Mademoiselle Panton to perfection.

"Mary can be Mademoiselle Panton and Jeanne and me . . ." said Clarissa looking with admiration at Mary.

We all went to choose the lace. We came back to dinner, and then in the afternoon Clarissa slept and I rested in my bedroom, reading. It was the quiet hour
276

when everyone was either eating or digesting what they had eaten. By five o'clock the streets would be noisy again.

I wondered what Hessenfield was doing and what measures he would take to find out who had betrayed them. It was disconcerting to discover that there were spies in our midst.

It was a lonely evening. It was at times like this that I realised how much I missed him.

I was now deeply in love with him. Our union seemed to be perfect; he was what I had always wanted; I believed I was the same to him.

We were adventurous spirits, both of us. This life suited him and it suited me. I wondered what it would be like if they brought James back to the throne and we returned to England where we would lead the lives of an ordinary nobleman and his wife . . . except that I should not be his wife. I could not imagine it. Hessenfield would always have to have some plot to be involved in. In the old days he would have gone to sea and plundered the Spanish galleons. In the Civil War he would have behaved in much the same way as he did now, I suppose. He was a man who had to have a cause. Danger was a fillip to his existence. There were men such as that.

But what happened to them when they grew old?

I thought of my grandfather then. He had been such another. What a life he must have led when he was holding Eversleigh during the Protectorate—an ardent Royalist posing as a Roundhead. That would have suited Hessenfield well.

The evening passed slowly without him. I was with Clarissa until it was her bedtime. Mary Marton put her to bed and I stayed with her telling her stories until she went to sleep.

Then I returned to my lonely bedchamber and slept.

I awoke early, took the usual bread and coffee and then went along to Clarissa's room.

She was sitting up in bed playing with a doll I had bought for her the day before.

"Mary's gone out," she said.

"Gone out! At this hour? She can't have."

Clarissa nodded.

"Yvette's got blue eyes," she said, holding the doll out to me. "Look."

"I am sure Mary is in her room," I said. "I'm going to see."

Clarissa shook her head, but I went through to Mary's room.

The bed was made. Could it be that she had not slept in it last night? Unless she had made it before she left, but one of the servants usually did that . . . later in the morning.

I looked round the room. I opened a cupboard. Her clothes had gone.

Then I saw the note. It was lying on the table and it was addressed to me.

Dear Lady Hessenfield, [I read]
I have had to leave quickly. I had a message from my aunt who is dangerously ill in Lyons. The messenger came after you retired and as you have had an anxious day I did not want to disturb you. There was just time to catch the coach to Lyons. So I left at once. I will come back and see you when I can leave my aunt.

Thank you for all your goodness to me,
Mary Marton.

The paper dropped from my hand. Something strange was going on. I knew it.

Why had she gone like that? When had the messenger arrived? Surely I would have heard him come? She had never mentioned an aunt in Lyons. I had understood she had had no family but the parents of whom she had spoken.

My thoughts immediately went to Matt.

That is it, I thought. She was in love with him and he must have made her understand that he did not love her. Mary had always seemed a strange girl to me; she was aloof and although she had got along comfortably with Clarissa, I fancied she had never felt completely at ease with me. I had been delighted by her friendship for Matt and had immediately presumed that it was
278

serious. The answer to the question of her hurried departure seemed to be that because her love affair with Matt was at an end she wanted to cut herself adrift completely; she did not want probing questions asked. A quiet, controlled person, such as I had imagined her to be, could act in this way.

Hessenfield returned the next day. He had been away two nights.

He looked exuberant now, his old self.

He could scarcely wait to embrace me.

He said: "I want to see that governess woman at once."

"Oh, the strangest thing has happened. She has gone."

"Gone!"

He looked at me blankly and I said quickly: "Yesterday morning I went to her room. Her bed had not been slept in. There was a note. She had gone to a sick aunt in Lyons."

"A sick aunt in Lyons! Oh my God, she's got away. She was the one. The leak . . . it came through her."

"Do you mean that . . . she was a spy?"

"That's exactly what I mean. I told you I was going to find out how it happened. She was one of the first I checked and got right to the heart of the matter. It must have been someone in the house. That was the only time it was mentioned. That day they came to me and I had them in my study . . . we worked out the route. It was only then that the name of the place was given away. I didn't even put it on paper—it was so secret. Everything has been passed by word of mouth. I guessed it was someone in the house . . . who overheard and immediately passed on the information. I decided to check on the backgrounds of everyone. It was an easy task because I started with her . . . the latest comer. Her parents are in England. She has been working as a spy for the Queen's government. They are determined to wipe us out. They knew these shipments were getting in, that they were being landed at quiet spots on the coast and that the arms were being hidden until the great day when we should use them. Thank God, she

279

was one of the first suspects and I hit the mark right away."

"I can't believe it of Mary," I said.

"One never can of the good spy. She was that, I grant you, and now we have lost her . . . unless we catch up with her somewhere, which is hardly likely. At least she won't dare come out to France again. It would be too dangerous for her."

"I should have seen it," I said. "I remember the day you were here with those men. I heard Mary on the landing. I thought I heard a door open. I went down and she was going out as I came down the stairs. I didn't think anything of it. I thought she was only creeping out for a rendezvous with her lover."

"With her lover?" said Hessenfield sharply.

"Oh, with Matt Pilkington. You know we thought there was something between them. I thought at first that she had left because something had happened with him . . . that he had told her he didn't want her. That's what the servants think. They talk about it all the time. They love anything that has a hint of romance in it."

"Let them go on thinking it," he said thoughtfully.

The incident had had a sobering effect on me, but Hessenfield quickly recovered his optimism. "It is the fortunes of war," he said. "Sometimes success, sometimes failure. We can only go on in hope."

He was gay and lively and we resumed the old way of life; but I could not help those moments of reflection which kept intruding. I kept remembering details about Mary. I should have seen that she was no ordinary nursery governess. I should have checked her story more thoroughly. That she had been a spy in our household and that I was the one who had brought her in, distressed me. Moreover, Clarissa was continually asking questions. I had told her that Mary had gone to her sick aunt in Lyons, which seemed the easiest way of dealing with the matter. And, as Hessenfield had suggested, that was the story which was circulated through the household. The servants thought it a little odd that she should have gone away without telling anyone, but she was English, and, as I overheard Jeanne say, the English often did odd things.

It was a week after Mary had left when I was out with Clarissa and Jeanne. We had shopped in the market for vegetables and were returning home along by the river when we noticed a crowd and a commotion.

Naturally we were curious and went over.

Jeanne turned to me and whispered: "Not for *La Petite*, madame."

La Petite was immediately all ears.

"What is it? What have they found?" cried Clarissa.

"Oh, it is something they have dragged out of the river," said Jeanne.

"What? What?"

"I don't suppose they know yet. And I have the dinner to see to."

"Maman." She had already taken the French form and used it all the time. "Let us stay."

Jeanne was throwing anxious glances at me.

I said firmly: "No, we must go home. It is nothing much."

"Just a bundle of old clothes someone has fished out of the river," said Jeanne.

"Who threw them in?"

"Well, that is what we don't know," said Jeanne.

"Who does know?"

"Whoever threw them in."

"Who did?"

"Oh, Clarissa," I cried, "we know no more than that. We are going home now so that Jeanne can cook the dinner. You want some dinner, don't you?"

Clarissa considered. "I want to know who threw his clothes in the river first," she said.

"You won't say that when we are having dinner and you're waiting to hear about river-sodden clothes," I said.

"What's river sodden?"

It was the opportunity. I took her hand firmly and more or less dragged her away.

Later that day Jeanne sought me out.

"I thought madame would want to know. It was a man they pulled out of the river this morning."

"Oh, dear, some poor unfortunate man. He must have been unhappy to take his life."

"They're saying that he didn't, madame. They're saying he was murdered."

"That's even worse. I am glad we didn't let the child see or hear. Don't tell her, Jeanne, or let any of the others."

"No, madame, I will not."

I knew that something had happened even before they told me. There seemed to be a perpetual buzz of conversation in the household—but more subdued than usual and it stopped at my approach.

Finally Jeanne could restrain herself no more.

"Madame," she told me, "they know whose was the body in the Seine. . . . They know who the man is."

"Oh," I said, "who was it?"

There was a short pause then Jeanne said quickly: "It was the gentleman who used to come here so much."

"What!" I cried.

"Monsieur Pilkington."

"No," I whispered. "It can't be."

"It is, madame. And he was murdered. Shot, they say."

I was terribly shaken. I stammered: "I don't believe it. Why should anyone shoot him?"

Jeanne looked sly.

"Someone who was jealous, madame?"

"Jealous. Who would be jealous of him?"

Jeanne lifted her shoulder.

"I thought you should know, madame."

"Yes . . . yes . . . thank you for telling me. Please see that none of this reaches my daughter's ears."

"Oh, no, madame. Certainly not. It would not be good for *La Petite*."

I shut myself in my room. It was hard to believe it. I felt sure there must be some mistake. Matt . . . dead . . . murdered. His body thrown into the Seine.

I went out. They were talking about it in the streets, in the shops. Those who knew me looked at me oddly as though they were speculating about me.

Good heavens, I thought, they cannot think I had anything to do with it!

I came back to the house. That same hush, that whispering. As I went up the stairs I heard two of the servants talking together in one of the rooms.

"*Crime passionel*," I heard. "That is it. . . . It is love."

"Fancy having someone killed for love of you."

"Well, that's what a *crime passionnel* is all about, silly."

I fled up to my room.

What were they saying? What were they hinting?

Hessenfield came in late that night. I was waiting for him.

He looked unruffled. I wondered if he had heard of the body which had been brought out of the Seine and the rumour that it was Matt Pilkington's.

"What's wrong?" he demanded.

I told him.

"Matt Pilkington," I cried. "Murdered! There must be some mistake."

"There is no mistake," he said.

I cried: "You . . . you did it."

"Not personally," he said. "It was decided on and carried out. The man was a spy."

"I don't believe it."

"My dear Carlotta, you are new to all this. I blame myself for not seeing it earlier."

I stared at him. Matt a spy. I thought back quickly. He had stayed at Grasslands for a long time when he was courting Damaris. He had talked of estates in Dorset and a post in the army. He was in the army in a way, I supposed, and was available when he was needed. He must have been having a long leave of absence when he was at Grasslands. Then I remembered. . . . On the night when I had left England he had been near Eyot Abbass. Then events seemed to fall into place. He had known that Hessenfield was there. He was looking for him when he came to Eyot Abbass; and I had been vain enough to think he came for me! I was the excuse . . . and a good one. It was because of him that we had narrowly escaped being taken. They must

283

have been close to have shot at us as we rowed out to the boat.

"Matt was a spy. Suppose he and Mary Marton had been working together."

Hessenfield nodded. "She got the information. She must have been hiding in the next room when we discussed it."

"And," I said, "she passed it on to Matt Pilkington. That was why she went out to meet him."

"So I believe. It was fortunate that you saw them meet after she left. That put me on to him. He was caught . . . red-handed, one might say. There were letters on him which exposed him absolutely."

"And you killed him."

"We could not afford to let him live. He was shot and his body dumped in the river."

"And now he has been found."

"And people are looking towards me," said Hessenfield. "Do you know why? They suspect that Pilkington either was or was attempting to be your lover. They think I killed him out of jealousy."

"That must be stopped."

"On the contrary, no. That is what I wish to be generally believed."

"But they will brand you as a murderer."

"That does not worry me."

"What of the law?"

"It is inclined to turn a blind eye here on crimes of passion. Besides, I can prove he was a spy. His was the fate spies must expect."

"So they are saying that . . ."

"Yes, and I want them to go on saying it. They know my devotion to you. They know Pilkington called often at the house. You are an outstandingly attractive woman. It is for our enemies to believe that he was killed through jealousy, not because we know that he was one of their spies."

I shivered.

Hessenfield put his arms about me.

"Dearest Carlotta," he said, "this is not an amusing game, you know. This is a matter of life and death. We are facing death all the time, all of us. Pilkington knew it. Mary Marton knew it. We live dangerously, Carlotta. And you're one of us now. We die for the cause. We accept all that fortune throws at us if it is all for the cause. I don't forget that, ever. Death is always there ... leering round the corners waiting to catch me unawares. He is often at my heels. If you are afraid I could send you home. It would not be very difficult."

"You would send me away? Then you are tired of me."

"You are a fool if you think that. Don't you know that it because I love you that I would send you back ... away from our plots ... away from danger."

I threw myself into his arms and clung to him. "I will never leave you," I said.

He stroked my hair. "Somehow I knew you would say that." He laughed. "That was why I offered to send you back."

We were wildly passionate that night; but I could not feel lighthearted. I wondered if I ever could again. There was so much to come between me and peace of mind. There was Damaris, there was Benjie, and now I could not get out of my mind the thought of Matt's murdered body lying on the banks of the Seine.

Two Pairs of Gloves

It was not my good fortune to meet Louis XIV, the Sun King, until he had passed into the last phase of his life. He was an old man then and had been married for some twenty years to the pious Madame de Maintenon and was more concerned with the glories of heaven than of earth. He must have been about sixty-seven years old then and in that case he could have been on the throne for sixty-two years. He was indeed the Grand Monarque.

He was all that one would expect of a king and a King of France at that. Protocol was far more rigid at the court of France than ever it was in England. One little slip and a man could lose all hope of favour. I remarked that the life of the courtier must be a very hazardous one.

Hessenfield had primed me again and again on what I must do. He was perfectly at ease and like all friends of James received graciously by the King of France, for there was no doubt that at this time Louis must have been growing very anxious on account of Marlborough's persistent victories.

I was to be presented at the most magnificent palace in Europe—Louis's own creation, equalling him in splendour: Versailles.

I had a special gown for the occasion. Madame Panton had been beside herself with excitement. She had fussed and chattered, gesticulated, despaired and rejoiced, and once or twice came near to fainting because she thought the cut or flare in my voluminous skirt was not what she called quite true.

But at last I was ready—splendid in diaphanous blue and discreetly scintillating with jewels, for as Hessenfield said, Louis's susceptibilities must not be offended and he had been influenced by Madame de Maintenon for twenty years and she had subdued his tastes considerably.

"At one time," said Hessenfield, "I should have been afraid to show you to him. He will admire your beauty. He is a lover of beauty in all things but now of course Madame de Maintenon has persuaded him that beauty lies in heaven not on earth. In any case he is an old man now. I wonder if I shall be pious when I grow old?"

"Many people become so," I reminded him. "And the more sinful they have been the more vigorously they must wash away their sins. You will need to be very pious."

"You too?" he asked.

"As vigorous as you, I fear."

"We will scrub together, sweetheart," he said. "In the meantime let us think of your presentation to the Setting Sun."

Versailles! How beautiful it was. How impressive! I had never seen anything like it, nor have I since. We rode out in the carriage. It was some eleven miles or so from Paris. There was little that was memorable about the town itself. Perhaps that was why Louis had decided to build this most magnificent of all palaces there so that the contrast might be more striking. We drove past the cathedral of St. Louis and the church of Notre Dame in the quarter of Satory and swept round to the west where a gilded iron gate and stone balustrade shut off the main palace from the Place D'Armes.

I gazed at the allegorical groups on either side and the statues of France's great statesmen and the enormous one of Louis himself on horseback. It was a most overwhelming sight. To the right and the left were the long wings of the palace, and as breathtaking as the palace itself were those magnificent gardens which had been laid out by Le Nôtre—the flowers, the ornamental basins, the groups and statues, the great avenue, the mighty trees and the green grass of the Tapis Vert.

Hessenfield said: "Come on. Don't gape like a country woman. The best view is from one of the windows of the Galerie des Glaces."

Faced with so many glories it is difficult to remember them all. I came away from Versailles with a jumbled memory of wide staircases, of rooms each more elaborate than the last, of pictures, sculptures, tapestries—a storehouse of treasure, a setting suited to the King who believed himself far above ordinary mortals, a god. The king of the sun.

It was not to be expected that we should be received here as we had been at St. Germain-en-Laye. This was a very different court from that of the exile who was perhaps tolerated here largely because the Queen he wished to replace was the greatest enemy of the Sun King himself. It was the English and the Duke of Marlborough who were giving Louis cause for concern such as he had rarely known before. It was unthinkable that he should be forced to sue for peace and it seemed that was what Marlborough was attempting to force him to do. Therefore any who could cause the smallest trouble to the enemy was welcome and to be helped. So Jacobites were most graciously received at Versailles.

It was not to be imagined however that the great King of France would concern himself with those who were eager to be presented to him. It was necessary for the supplicants to present themselves in an anteroom close to the royal lodging through which he would have to pass on his way to other parts of the palace. There patiently every day those who hoped to catch his eye waited. Of course he might not come, in which case they would have waited in vain. They would come again the next day.

It was a great achievement, however, to get to this antechamber. "The first step," said Hessenfield. "But until the King has *acknowledged* you, you cannot go to Court."

So we made our way to that part of the palace behind the Galerie des Glaces to that side of the court where Louis's rooms were situated and found ourselves in the antechamber which was known as the Oeil de Boeuf—so called from the shape of its window.

Here were assembled a group of people, all elaborately dressed, all, like ourselves, waiting to catch the eyes of the King should he pass through that morning.

It was a long wait. I looked around the room at these people, all very serious, all intent on one thing, and some spirit of mischief within me wanted to laugh outright. I wanted to say, Why should we all stand here so humble, so servile and await the pleasure of one man? I don't care if he is the Sun King; I don't care if his wealth has built this palace. Why should I? For what purpose? I thought: I will take the matter up with Hessenfield tonight.

I knew what his answer would be. "We have to keep Louis's goodwill. We could get nowhere without his help. We have to keep him willing to help put James on the throne."

Yes, that was a good enough reason. And these others, what did they want? Promotion of some sort. So it was after all ambition which prompted them to stand there, ready at any moment to kneel in adoration when the scintillating presence was before them.

I was aware of a woman watching me. She was an extremely handsome woman with masses of dark hair elaborately dressed. She wore a silver grey gown and pearls in her ears and about her neck. She was very elegant. I thought something about her face was familiar and wondered if I could possibly have met her somewhere before.

She half smiled at me. I returned the smile.

A few minutes later she had edged a little nearer to me. "It is weary waiting," she said in a low voice speaking in English with a marked French accent.

"Yes," I said.

"I have waited yesterday. He did not come. Let us hope he comes today."

I said: "You speak English well."

She lifted her shoulders. "My grandmother was English."

Conversation was not considered to be in the best of taste. One spoke in whispers while one kept one's eyes on that spot where the King might at any moment make his entry.

"You are Lady Hessenfield?" she murmured.

I nodded.

"You are doing such good work...such excellent work."

"Thank you. I am afraid I do very little."

"You support your husband. That is good."

"May I ask your name?"

"Elisse de Partière. My husband was killed at Blenheim."

"Oh...I am so sorry...."

Silence fell between us. All eyes were on the door, for at that moment there was a stir of excitement.

The great moment had come. The presence was about to shine upon us.

With what dignity he walked! Of course he was an old man now, but the splendour of his garments dazzled the eyes so that one did not notice the lined and wrinkled face beneath the luxuriant wig. The dark eyes were shrewd and alert. There was something about him which set him apart. Was it assurance? He was so confident that he was above all other men that he convinced them that he was.

He stopped here and there to exchange a brief word with one or two of the elect and so briefly covered them with the glory of the reflected sun.

Hessenfield stepped forward, holding my hand.

"Sire, may I present my wife."

The dark eyes, alive among the wrinkles, were regarding me steadily. I flushed slightly and sank to the floor in the required obeisance. The eyes brightened. He smiled faintly. His eyes travelled from my face to my neck and bosom.

"Very pretty," he said. "Congratulations, my lord."

Then he passed on. It was triumph.

He had gone. The morning in the Oeil de Boeuf was at an end.

"What an honour," said Hessenfield. "I might have known you would make your mark. It's not often he sees a woman as pretty as you."

"What of all the mistresses he has had?"

290

"Hush. He likes discretion. None of them had half your beauty. Praise the gods that he is an old man now working a quick passage to heaven."

"Be careful. You may jeopardize your position."

"You are right," he whispered, pressing my arm. "Now you may go to court. The King has acknowledged you."

There was a press of people walking in the gardens and Hessenfield said to me: "Let us go now. Our mission is accomplished. I want to get back to Paris as soon as possible."

As we were about to step into our carriage a woman came up to us. I recognised her at once as the elegant Madame de Partière who had spoken to me in the Oeil de Boeuf. She was clearly in some distress.

"Madame . . . I wonder if you would help me. I must get to Paris without delay. Are you going back there now?"

"Yes," I answered.

She said: "It is most unfortunate. The wheel of my carriage is broken. . . ." She lifted her shoulders. "I do not understand. . . . But my coachman tells me that it will take some hours to put right . . . even if he can get it done this day. I *must* return to Paris." She looked very apologetic. "I was wondering if . . . if you would take me there with you."

Hessenfield had come up. She explained to him. "I saw you in the Oeil de Boeuf. I noticed Madame . . . who would not notice Madame? I spoke to her . . . I could not restrain myself. Now . . . I am asking this favour of you. If you could let me travel with you to Paris."

Madame de Partière's eyes filled with tears. "It is such a relief to me," she said.

So we travelled back to Paris with our new acquaintance. She had a house in the rue St. Antoine, and she was very unhappy at the moment.

I said to Hessenfield: "Her husband was killed at Blenheim."

"Madame, my condolences," said Hessenfield.

"You are too kind." She turned away and wiped her eyes.

After a while she went on: "So kind . . . and so brave.

I know that you came over here...exiles from your country...fighting for a cause. That is noble."

"Madame," said Hessenfield, "you speak such good English."

"Oh, but there is the accent, eh...the intonation....It is amazing how the French can never truly master the English tongue."

"Nor the English the French," said I.

"There is always something to betray it," said Hessenfield.

"My mother was English. Her people had been over here during the days of Cromwell. She was a little girl then but her family met my grandfather's family. The two young people fell in love and married and after the Restoration she stayed in France. Their daughter, my mother, was taught English...by her mother and I was taught by my mother....That is why I have knowledge of your English. But I am afraid it is not always as good as it should be."

"Are you living in Paris?"

"For the time. The death of my husband has...how do you say it?...stunned me. I am at this time a little uncertain."

"Have you any children?"

She was silent and turned her head away.

"I have a son," she said.

"And shall you live with him?"

"He is dead," she said.

I said I was sorry and realised that we had been asking too many questions.

We talked then about Versailles and the wonders of the palace and the gardens, the groves and the waterfalls and the bronze statues.

Had we seen the basin of Apollo, she wanted to know, with the god represented in his chariot drawn by four horses and the water spouting from the fountains?

We had, we told her.

"How I should love to see one of the displays on water," she said. "I have heard that that is like a visit to another world."

"I have seen it," said Hessenfield. "With the Venetian gondolas all decked out with flowers, it is quite

292

fantastic, particularly at night, when there is a display of fireworks."

Then Hessenfield discussed the merits of the Orangery, the Rockery and the waterfall. He was much more knowledgeable about Versailles than we were.

"I feel," said Madame de Partière, "that I have been given not only a ride home but a tour of the palace."

She turned to me and picked up one of my gloves which was lying on the seat beside me.

"I cannot but admire it," she said. "What exquisite embroidery and this delicate tracing of tiny pearls. It is so beautiful. Tell me, where do you get your gloves?"

"I have an excellent couturiere," I said. "She scarcely allows me to choose anything myself. She brought these gloves in the other day and said that she thought they would be suitable for this occasion."

"How right she was. I am interested because I congratulate myself that I have one of the best glove makers in Paris. It is true it is a small shop. It is in the carrefour near the Châtelet. A very small shop, but the owner is an artist. He has four or five girls stitching and embroidering for him but the design is his. It is that which counts, of course, and he is a master. This, though, equals what I have had from him."

She smoothed the glove and replaced it on the seat. So passed the time until we reached Paris.

Hessenfield said that we should take Madame de Partière to her house and then we should go home. When we reached the rue St. Antoine, Hessenfield alighted from the coach to help her out and as she was about to step down she gave a cry of dismay. She stooped and picked up something. It was my glove which had been lying on the seat. She had swept it to the floor as she rose and had stepped on it.

I thought she was going to burst into tears as she picked it up and gazed at it.

There was a dirty mark on the embroidery and some of the pearls had broken away.

"Oh, what have I done!" she cried.

I took the glove. "No matter," I said. "Madame Panton will probably repair it."

"But I have spoilt it! You have been so kind to me and this is how I repay you."

Hessenfield said: "Madame, I beg of you. It is nothing . . . a bagatelle."

"I shall never forgive myself. After all your kindness."

The concierge had come out to bow to Madame de Partière.

"Please," I said, "do not distress yourself. It has been a most enlivening journey and we have enjoyed your company."

"Indeed yes," said Hessenfield, "and we have done nothing. We were coming back to Paris in any case."

"How kind you are." She lapsed into French. *"Vous êtes très aimable. . . ."*

Hessenfield took her arm and led her towards the house. She turned and gave me a woeful smile.

I laughed. "Good-bye, Madame de Partière," I said. "It has been a pleasure."

"Au revoir," she said.

And that was my visit to Versailles.

I missed Mary Marton. She may have been a spy but at the same time she had been an excellent nursery governess. Clarissa asked after her a great deal.

It was hard to put off a child who had such an enquiring mind with explanations which could not sound plausible, for I could not tell her the truth. I wondered what her child's mind would make of this account of spies and plots.

Jeanne emerged as a great help to me. She had more or less taken on the duties of looking after the child. Clarissa loved her and she had a way of dealing with the numerous questions, which were constantly plied, with answers which satisfied.

She spoke French constantly to Clarissa, who was now speaking both English and French with perfect accents so that she could have been taken for either nationality.

"It will stand her in good stead," said Hessenfield. "And the only way to speak French is to learn it as near the cradle as possible. You never get round those vowels otherwise."

Since she had slipped so naturally into the nursery I spent a certain amount of my time with Jeanne too, which was good for my French as it was for Clarissa's, for Jeanne had scarcely a word of English.

She was an interesting girl in her early twenties. She had been delighted, she told me, to find a post in a fine house like this. She had been very poor before. She had been a flower seller. The cook used to buy flowers from her to decorate the tables.

"Ah, Madame," she said, "it was my lucky day when Madame Boulanger came to buy my flowers. She was a hard one ... and paid me very little. She was one for a bargain. I lived with my family ... there were many of us. A sad part of Paris that. You do not know it, Madame. It is not for such as you. It is not far from Notre Dame ... behind the Hôtel Dieu before you get to the Palace de Justice. The streets there ... they are terrible, Madame ... dangerous. We had a room in the rue de Marmousets.... The gutters were pretty, though. I used to stand and look into the gutters. The dyers were there, and their colours flowed through the gutters. Such colours, Madame, green, blue, red ... the colours of my flowers. We used to beg from the great lords and ladies. But I never stole ... never, Madame. My mother said 'Never steal, for though you have money for a while they will catch up with you. You will end up in the Châtelet or the Fort L'Evêque. Then your fate will be too terrible to speak of.'"

"Poor Jeanne," I said, "you have had a sad life."

"But now it is a good one, Madame. I have a good position and I like so much to care for the little one."

And care she did. She used to tell her stories of old Paris, and Clarissa was enchanted with them. She would sit entranced, eyes round with wonder; there was nothing she loved more than to walk through those streets and listen to Jeanne describing everything to her.

Jeanne was extremely knowledgeable and I felt I could trust Clarissa with her. That was what I liked

295

most. If I had to go to Versailles or St. Germain-en-Laye with Hessenfield I could safely leave her.

I sometimes sat with her after Clarissa was in bed and we would talk together. She knew so much about the stories of the past which had passed down through her family.

She was most interested in the great poison scandal which had rocked Paris some thirty years ago and had brought Madame la Voison and Madame de Brinvilliers to justice. It was so notorious because many well-known people had become involved and suspicion had been cast even on the King's mistress, Madame de Montespan.

Her grandmother remembered the day Madame de Brinvilliers had been taken from the prison of the Conciergerie, where she had been submitted to cruel torture, to the Place de Grève and there lost her head.

"It was a terrible time, Madame, there was not an apothecary in Paris who did not tremble in his shoes. There was fear in high places. Husbands had removed wives and wives husbands, sons and daughters, fathers and mothers who had lived too long and by whose death there could be profit. Paris was in a turmoil. It was the Italians, Madame. . . . They had their strange poisons. We had had arsenic and antimony . . . but it was the Italians who produced the finest poisons. Poisons which were tasteless, colourless, poisons which could be breathed in the air. It was an art with them. People were talking about the Borgias and a Queen of France too . . . an Italian woman, Catherine de Medici. They knew better poisons."

"Jeanne," I said, "you have a morbid mind to dwell on these things."

"Yes, Madame, but they say there is an Italian near the Châtelet who has a beautiful shop and many noble customers . . . and behind his shop he works with strange substances. He is very rich."

"Rumours, Jeanne."

"Maybe, Madame. But I make the sign of the cross every time I pass the shop of Antonio Manzini."

It was interesting talk; and I was grateful to Jeanne.

When Clarissa grew older we should have to have an English governess for her, I thought. Then I paused.

When she was older should we still be here? Should we still be trying to bring a conclusion to this adventure?

Somehow I could not imagine it. I could not think ahead.

The future was perhaps too fraught with difficulties. How could I return to England? I had made everything too complicated there. At Eyot Abbass there was Benjie, the husband I had used and wronged. At Eversleigh there was Damaris, whose lover I had taken for a whim and ruined her life.

You do not deserve to be happy, I told myself.

Yet I was. For I loved Hessenfield so completely; and that intense burning passion which had flared up between us was becoming a deep and abiding love . . . an enduring love, I told myself.

So though I could be happy in the present, I could not look ahead.

Well, wasn't it a good plan to live in the present? Not to look ahead; not to look back. That was what I must train myself to do.

One day one of the servants brought two parcels to me. One was addressed to me, the other to Hessenfield.

I opened mine and found inside an exquisite pair of gloves.

They were beautiful—in grey leather so soft that it looked like silk. They were embroidered with pearls and were something like the ones I had to discard because Madame de Partière had trodden on one of them. I guessed who had sent them. And I was right.

There was a note with them.

My dear Lady Hessenfield,

I have been some time in sending you an acknowledgement of my gratitude. Forgive me but this was no fault of mine. It has taken so long to get the leather I particularly wanted. Now I trust these will please you. I have sent a similar pair to your husband.

I want to say thank you for being so kind to me

297

in bringing me back when I had that mishap with my own carriage. I was so grateful to you and how ashamed I was when to repay you I ruined your beautiful gloves.

I trust we may renew our acquaintance when I return to Paris. I am called away to the country just now and may be away for more than a month.

Dear Lady Hessenfield, in the meantime please accept these gloves and wear them so that I may have some satisfaction in doing something for all you have done for me.

I shall have the temerity to call when I return from the country. Many thanks once more.

Elisse de Partière.

What a charming gesture! I thought. The gloves are charming.

I tried them on. Then carefully wrapped them up to be used on a suitable occasion.

There was a great deal of activity throughout the court at St. Germain-en-Laye. It was not likely that they were going to let one disaster deter them.

The loss of all the arms and ammunition which had been brought about through Matt Pilkington and Mary Marton had been a great setback. None would deny it. Hessenfield told me that the French were impatient over the matter and blamed us for being so careless as to let spies into our household.

"I bore the brunt of that," said Hessenfield with a grim laugh. "Now I want to show them that that sort of thing can never happen again."

The days passed too quickly. I savoured each one. It seemed later that I must have had some premonition.

I think always at the back of my mind was the thought . . . the fear . . . that it could not last.

We lived passionately, fervently. I think Hessenfield felt similarly. I remembered he had said once that death was always waiting round the corner. It was a dangerous life he lived; and I was with him, clinging all the time to the present.

He had been to Versailles to speak with one of Louis's ministers who was more favourable than most to the English cause; and from there he had gone to St. Germains.

When he came back he looked unlike himself. He was distinctly pale; and I had never seen him before without his healthy colour. Moreover, there was now lacklustre in his eyes.

I looked at him anxiously.

"It has gone badly," I said. "Something worries you."

He shook his head. "The French are eager to help. They are all in good spirits at St. Germains."

I took his hand. It was clammy.

"You are not well," I cried in dismay.

Hessenfield was a man who had always known perfect health and could not understand sickness. I had always been under the impression that he would believe it was some deficiency in the sufferer, some quirk of the imagination ... unless of course it was a leg or arm or some visible disability.

I understood perfectly because I was rather like that myself. So I was very alarmed when he said: "I think I must lie down."

I helped him undress and got him to bed. I sat beside him and said I would get him a tasty meal. He shook his head. The last thing he wanted was to eat. It was nothing, he assured me. It would pass.

He did not speak. He just lay still and seemed to want nothing but that.

I was very worried and passed an anxious night. In the morning he was delirious. I sent for a physician who came and examined Hessenfield. He shook his head and murmured something about a fever. Perhaps two dead pigeons laid on the soles of his feet might help. He would send a lotion round which might also be of use.

I gripped the man's hand. "What ails him?" I asked.

"A fever. He'll recover," he said.

But by the afternoon he was no better.

I walked about the house in a daze. This was something I had never thought of. I put his clothes away— those which he had been wearing. The fringed coat, the

299

breeches, and the fine hose and the gloves which Madame de Partière had sent for him.

I would not leave him. I just sat by his bed. He looked different from the man I had known. He was pale; his eyes were closed; there was already a sunken look in his cheeks.

Jeanne said to me: "Madame, I know an apothecary who has the finest remedies. He is the Italian Antonio Manzini. They say he has cured many."

"I will go to him. You must come with me, Jeanne," I said.

We went to my room. "You will need your heavy cloak, madame. There is a chill in the air." She opened a drawer and took out the gloves which Madame de Partière had given me.

I put them on and we went out together.

Jeanne led me through the streets to the carrefour near the Châtelet.

We went into the shop together.

Jeanne said: "Madame is very anxious. Her husband is sick."

"Sick," said the man; he had dark bushy eyebrows and almost black, very penetrating eyes. "What ails him?"

"It is a fever which makes him listless and so unlike himself," I explained. "Till now he was a very healthy man."

I laid my hand on his arm. He looked down at it and drew away.

"I have a lotion," he said, "which cures fever. It is costly."

"I will pay," I assured him. "If it cures my husband I will pay anything . . . anything you ask."

Jeanne laid a restraining hand on my arm and Antonio Manzini retired behind his shop.

"Madame will forgive me," said Jeanne. "But it is not necessary to promise so much. Pay his price and that is good enough."

I paid the price and he brought out the bottle. We hurried back and I went straight to Hessenfield's bedside. I could see at once that he had grown worse.

300

I hastily poured out some of the liquid, forced him to take it and sat down waiting for the miracle.

There was none.

By nightfall Hessenfield's condition was unchanged.

I sat up beside him all night. Just before dawn I rose and as I stood up a terrible dizziness overcame me.

I touched my skin. It was cold and clammy yet I felt very hot.

I knew then that I had caught the fever or whatever it was, and that I too was going to be ill.

No, that must not be, I told myself. I had to keep well. I had to nurse Hessenfield. I would not trust him to anyone but myself.

I tried to fight off my lassitude. But I was becoming very worried.

I had a great desire to go to bed, but I would not. With all my might I would fight this terrible feeling which was coming over me.

During the morning Hessenfield took a turn for the worse. He was now raving in delirium. He was talking about General Langdon, about spies... about me ... about Clarissa. It was jumbled together and made no sense.

Meanwhile I was feeling more and more ill.

Jeanne came to my room. Her eyes widened with horror at the sight of me.

She said: "There is a lady downstairs who asks to see you most urgently. She says it is very important and she wants to speak privately with you."

I went to a small room which led from the salon and said I would receive her there.

She came in. It was Madame de Partière. But she looked different from when I had last seen her. I touched my eyes wearily for I had the most alarming headache. I wondered if I was seeing clearly.

"Madame de Partière..." I stammered.

She nodded.

"Ah, I see you are unwell, Carlotta."

I stared at her in amazement. Her French accent had disappeared. She spoke English like an English-woman.

Her face I noticed was very pale. She said: "Lord

301

Hessenfield is very sick. He will die. There is no antidote . . ."

I said angrily: "Have you come here to tell me this?"

She replied: "How many times have you worn the gloves? I see you have worn them."

I shook my head impatiently.

"It is important," she said. "They are deadly."

I stared at her. I thought: She is mad. I must get away from her quickly. I have not the strength to deal with her now. I stepped towards the door.

"You have worn them," she said. "It shows. All those good looks, they will be gone in a day or so. . . . We are tainted; your husband . . . you, and I . . . too. That is why I have come here. I want you to understand how . . . and why . . . before we die."

"Madame," I said, "this is a very unfortunate time to call. My husband is very ill."

"I know. Who better? You too are very ill—more than you know. I have not escaped. They are deadly. I have handled them too much."

I caught at a chair. I should have fallen otherwise.

"Madame, please go. I am going to call the servants. I have too much to concern me . . ."

"This concerns you," she said. "This concerns you deeply. You must start at once to repent of your sins."

"Sins . . . ?"

"You have committed many . . . so has my lord Hessenfield. . . . You have committed sins against me and mine . . . and I determined to have my revenge."

"Please explain then if you must."

"For a moment at Versailles I thought you knew me. We have met once before."

I said: "In the Oeil de Boeuf. . . ."

"No, not there. In Enderby Hall. Do you remember Beth Pilkington?"

"Beth Pilkington! You . . . ?"

Then I remembered. She had had amazing red hair then. It was easy to change that. I saw her face fall into the lines I remembered. She was a good actress. She had looked and acted the part of a woman of French nobility to perfection.

"I came to see Enderby Hall. You showed me round.

I was coming down to find out what had become of Beaumont Granville. I did find out in time."

"Beau? What was he to you?"

"My lover . . . for years. I was his favourite mistress. He said he would marry me if I could give him a son. He wanted children . . . he wanted a son."

I stared at her unbelievingly.

"Yes," she went on. "You put an end to that. Oh, do not think I blame you for that. It was not your fault. You came along. You had everything to offer him. Good looks, your own kind of fascination, youth . . . and a fortune. Most important of all, a fortune. But for that fortune Beau would have married me. I already had my beautiful son . . . his son."

"Matt, you mean."

"Yes, Matt!"

I understood then why I had been attracted by him. I had thought he reminded me of Beau because of a faint resemblance which I had believed was merely that of one dandy for another. I thought of the button I had found in Enderby Hall; the lingering odour of musk. Beau's son, of course, who perhaps had been wearing a coat with gold buttons which had belonged to his father—who had been brought up with a taste for the musk scent.

"I came to that place to find out what had happened to Beaumont," she went on. "I was sure that if he had fled abroad—which seemed plausible enough—he would have let me know at some time. Our association had lasted from the day we met. I was always there in the background, whatever other women there were. He looked on me as a wife and but for you . . . when my child was born . . . But that is of no importance now. I want you to understand how it happened. I came down to find out where Beau had gone . . . and I did. The dog had been his dog. Matt took her when Beau went. The dog found his shoe. That was why she died."

"Where . . . ?" I murmured.

"Under the soil in that patch of land where people were forbidden to go. He was buried there by your mother's husband."

I gasped. "I don't believe it."

"He killed the dog but he did not kill Beau. That was Christabel Willerby. Beau was blackmailing her and she shot him; your father buried the body thinking that your mother had done it. If you knew all the details it falls naturally into place, but that is not why I am here. You are innocent of Beau's death."

"I think, Mistress Pilkington, that you are imagining these things. You are suffering from hallucinations. You are ill."

She shrugged her shoulders. "It is the end for us all—for me no less than you. I want you to know but I want you to understand. I wanted my son to be happy. He would have been with your sister. She is a good girl. It made me happy to see how gradually they began to love each other. She was the girl I wanted for him. She was different from anyone he was likely to meet in London. He realised her virtues. She would have provided him with a steadying background...the sort I had never been able to give him. I wanted that for him."

She looked at me malevolently and put her hand to her heart. She was growing breathless.

"But you spoilt it," she went on. "He followed you here...and he was murdered. But for you he would be alive to this day. My only son. He was everything to me. All my life was centered round him. But you lured him here and then Lord Hessenfield killed him...had him murdered and his body thrown in the Seine."

"You are wrong," I cried. "That was not how it happened. He was a spy. He did not come here for me. He came to spy against the Jacobites."

"He came because of you. That was his excuse for coming. He came for you."

"It is not true. He worked here with a nursery governess in this household. He was caught.... There were papers on him that proved him to be a spy."

She shook her head. "I know my son. He was like his father. He would pursue what he wanted until it was his. He wanted you and he came here to get you and Hessenfield was jealous. He is hard and a ruthless man. He killed him. I heard about it. I was told that it was a *crime passionnel*."

"You are wrong . . . wrong. . . ."

She shrugged her shoulders. "It is the end," she said. "Soon for me and for you. You must die. I knew that there was something fatalistic about you when I met you in that house. Beauty such as yours has something evil in it. It is not a gift from God but from the devil."

She was looking at me strangely, her eyes glittering. She is mad, I thought. The death of Matt has unhinged her mind.

"You are like the legendary mermaid who sits on the rock singing and luring mariners to come to her, and to go to her is certain death. It is . . . the song of the siren. Come to me and I will be all to you that you most desire. That is the song. But it is not so. You are luring them to death."

"This is nonsense, Mistress Pilkington."

She shook her head. "Beau died because of you. But for you he would not have gone down to Eversleigh. He would not have found that woman he was blackmailing. He would have been alive today. I might have been married to him. Matt would be here. But you came with your strange wild beauty. It was more than your fortune he wanted. So he pursued you and found not a beautiful bride and a fortune, but death. Then Matt, he heard your song too. He was lured into the rocks of destiny. And where did it lead? To death in the Seine. My son . . . my darling son . . . And your husband— what unhappiness have you brought to him? Even your present lover, Hessenfield, has not escaped. He thought he was clever. He thought he was in command . . . but Death is waiting for him now. . . ."

"I must ask you to go," I said. "I have much to do."

"Yes, make a shroud for your lover. Make one for yourself . . . and for me. . . ."

I felt sick with horror, for I knew that she was telling the truth.

She went on: "I planned to destroy you. It is better that no others should suffer through you. Three men all dead . . . and all because of you—although I do not blame you for Beau. You see, you are disaster. You are the siren. Even involuntarily you deal death. You have to go. There is no way for it. I contrived the meeting.

305

I disguised myself for fear you should remember me. But we met only once and I was one of the best actresses on the London stage. I listened to all I could of those long ago poison trials. I talked to people who remembered . . . and I decided what I should do. I did not believe that there could be poisons which could be transmitted through the skin. But there are . . . there are. . . . And if you know where to go for them and if you are prepared to pay . . . So I went and I paid and I had the gloves made. Lord Hessenfield has been more virulently attacked. He must have worn the gloves I sent him for a long time. You are less so. And I even less. But we are all doomed. I no less than you, although mine will be a more lingering death. I have the poison in my blood just as you have. . . . You see, I have destroyed the siren and my son's murderers, but in doing so I have destroyed myself."

I stood up uncertainly. These were the ravings of a mad woman.

I must get rid of her. I must get back to Hessenfield. I must call the doctors and tell them what this woman had told me.

I left her. I heard her walk out unsteadily behind me.

I went up to the bedroom.

Hessenfield was lying white and still on his bed . . . unnaturally still.

I knew that he was dead.

Till then I had not believed her. I had told myself that she was lying about the poison. Such things might have happened thirty years ago but they could not happen now. But I had heard such strange stories of those long ago poisonings and the subtleties of the Italian art of producing deadly substances which could attack in many different ways. There were still Italian poisoners in Paris, still men who worked out their secrets in dark places and grew rich on them.

I was bewildered. It was too much to grasp. All that time Beau had been lying under the soil near Enderby. And Leigh, whom I had looked on as my father, had buried him; my mother was involved too, and Matt was Beau's son.

I could not believe it. And yet everything that had happened clothed it with reasonable truth.

Beau . . . dead all those years. Matt and I together. No wonder I was drawn to him. There was a grain of comfort in that. It had not been such a wild whim.

But there was one terrible fact which threw a dark pall over everything, and I was thinking of the past now so that I might not look to the present.

Hessenfield dead. I would not accept it. He who had been so full of life . . . dead . . . and all because of a pair of gloves. He would get up from the bed soon. He would laugh at me.

It was a trick. It was a joke . . . to prove to me through my desolation how much he loved me.

How much I loved him! "Oh, Hessenfield," I murmured, "infinitely!"

I covered my face with my hands. How clammy they were. . . . My face was burning and yet I was shivering.

Then a sudden wild joy possessed me. "I am coming to you, Hessenfield. We always said only death could part us . . . but even death can't do that."

I sat there by his bed watching him and an exultation came over me.

"I am coming with you, Hessenfield. I shall not be long."

Death! It was very close. I could almost hear the flap of his wings as he hovered over me. Odd to think of death with wings.

An old illusion, I thought. Why . . . Why?

I stopped. I stared before me. I had been rejoicing that Hessenfield and I would not be parted. And now the thought had come to me: Clarissa. My daughter . . . our daughter . . . when we were both dead what would become of her?

I clasped my hands together to stop their shaking.

"My child . . . my little girl. What will become of you? You will be left alone here and who will care for you?"

I must do something. I must act quickly.

I stood up. The room was swaying round me.

"Hurry," I said aloud. "Who knows how much time there is left to you."

I prayed then. I could not remember praying before. I supposed people such as I only prayed when they wanted something; and I had had so much.

It was only when things were denied me that I thought of prayer.

Then suddenly, as though there was an answer to my earnest supplication, I saw what I must do.

I went to my bureau and took out paper. In this terrible hour of bewilderment, anxiety and tragedy I thought of my sister.

I remembered how she and Clarissa had been together during that time when I had gone with her to Eversleigh. Clarissa and Damaris had loved each other then. There had been some special relationship between them.

Damaris, I said to myself. It must be Damaris.

Dear Damaris [I wrote hurriedly]

I am dying. By the time you receive this I will be dead. Lord Hessenfield, who is Clarissa's father, is also dead. I am desperately anxious about my Clarissa. She is here in a strange country and I do not know who will care for her when I am no longer here.

I have been wicked but that is no fault of my daughter's. Damaris, I want you to take her. You must send over here at once. You must take her and bring her up as your daughter. There is no one I should rather see her with than you. I am known over here as Lady Hessenfield and Clarissa is acknowledged as our daughter, which she is. I cannot tell you now how all this came about. It is of no importance. All that matters is Clarissa.

There is a good woman here, named Jeanne. I shall leave her in this woman's care until you come. She is a good woman who has been looking after Clarissa and is fond of her. She was once a flower seller and lived in great poverty, but I trust her more than anyone else.

Damaris, I have been wicked. I have brought

trouble and disaster wherever I have been. I ruined your life, but Matt was not really good enough for you otherwise he would not have behaved as he did. You need someone specially good.

Do this for me, please.... No. For Clarissa's sake. Send for her as soon as you receive this.

Your sister Carlotta.

I sealed the letter. I sent for the courier who had taken Hessenfield's urgent messages back and forth from England.

"Take this," I said, "with all speed."

Then I prayed that he would reach Damaris, for naturally traffic between the two countries was difficult and such missions had to be taken with the utmost care. Often couriers did not reach their destination; and I suppose that after that disastrous mission which had cost Matt his life there would be more checks than ever on people coming into the country.

But I prayed that Damaris would receive the letter, and that she would come and take Clarissa away.

I sent for Jeanne.

"Jeanne," I said, "I am dying."

"Madame ... it is not possible."

"You know Lord Hessenfield is dead."

"Oh Madame, what will become of us all?"

"There is the child. Jeanne, I trust her to you."

"My lady?"

"Care for her. I have a sister in England. I have written to her. She will send someone to take Clarissa away."

"When will they come, my lady?"

"Soon ... soon. They will come. I know they will come."

"From England, Madame...."

"They will come, Jeanne. I promise you they will come. Wait for them, and care for the child until they come. Jeanne ..." I caught her hands and looked pleadingly into her eyes. "Jeanne, this is the wish and the command of a dying woman."

Jeanne looked frightened.

But I knew she would keep her word.

I burned the gloves—both mine and Hessenfield's. They gave off a strange light as they flared up. I thought there would be a conflagration, but after blazing for a few moments they subsided into a black powder.

I took up my pen and wrote in my journal of what had happened to me. I set it out and thought there might be some comfort in the writing of it.

I had told Jeanne that I wanted her to keep my journal and when messengers from my sister came to give it to them to take to her.

I wanted her to understand how it had happened. To understand is often to forgive.

I put down my pen. Then I called Jeanne again and I told her where she would find the journal.

She looked bewildered. But she listened to my instructions and after she had gone I could not resist taking my pen again.

Then I wrote right at the beginning of my journal: "This is the Song of the Siren who did not ask to be as she was. But she was so and it happened that one who accused her was right. Those who came near her were lured to their deaths. It seems right and fitting that death should overtake her in the midst of her singing."

DAMARIS

The Tenant of Enderby Hall

I am lonely. The days seem endless. Hour after hour I lie here on my couch and I tell myself that my life is over. It never began really.

I was happy. I was on the threshold of what had seemed a great adventure. Then suddenly it was over. I saw everything I had dreamed of shattered in one revealing instant. And then it was that this further blow was delivered.

It sometimes seems that life is not content with taking happiness from one, then decides that there is something else that can be done to make life more intolerable. I lost the man I loved on one dark November day—and that night was stricken with a terrible illness which has made an invalid of me ever since.

Oh, I am surrounded by love. No girl could have parents who loved and cherished her more than mine do. I have been shown in a thousand ways that I am the centre of their lives. They blame themselves for what happened to me; and they are not to blame, but how can I tell them without involving Carlotta?

I do not want to think of Carlotta. I cannot bear to think of Carlotta. Sometimes her image creeps into my mind and I tell myself that I hate her. But I see her there in my mind—that almost unbelievable beauty. I used to think: No one has any right to be as beautiful as Carlotta. Everything was given to her. It was as though the powers above who decide how we shall be had been in a very happy mood when they planned for Carlotta. She shall have everything ... everything ... they said.

And so she had. I had often seen the way in which men looked at her when she came into a room; she had only to look at them and they were at her side. I admired her so much. I was so proud that she should be my sister.

Now I understand more than I did. My mother has shown me her journal. I know about Carlotta's romantic birth in Venice and the terrible thing that happened to my mother. I know about that wicked man who died and who killed him and the terrible suspicions my parents had of each other. It explains everything. I understand why my father had to shoot Belle and bury her. If only I had known of what my parents had suffered I should not have gone to Belle's grave when I saw Matt and Carlotta together.

I had been shocked, it was true, for I thought that it was not only Matt who had deceived me. It was also my kind father, who had secrets to preserve because of which he had killed an innocent animal. So I thought but it was not quite like that.

And because of my ignorance I had suffered with them.

Had I been more knowledgeable in worldly matters I might have suspected the attraction between Matt and Carlotta. It would have hurt me deeply of course but I would not have suffered that fearful shock. I would have been prepared for my discovery.

But what was the use of going over it. It was over. It was done, Matt had gone out of my life. I saw little of Carlotta—nor did I want to see her, for that was too painful. But I had loved her dear little daughter and I should have liked to know her better.

It was strange, but when that child came I felt new interest in life. Since that terrible night I had not been interested in anything at all, but the child came and when we were together I forgot my grievances against her mother. I loved the way in which she demanded to know the answers to every question that occurred to her, I loved to play games with her. "I Spy" was the favourite. I would hint at what I was looking at and she had to guess. She would ponder seriously until she found the answer and shriek with delight when she was right.

It was love at first sight between us.

One day when I was lying on my couch I heard her playing in the garden; she was shouting and chanting as she bounced a ball; then suddenly there was silence. I listened and the silence went on. I suppose it was only a minute or two but it seemed like five. I had the terrible suspicion that something might be wrong. She had fallen and hurt herself. She had wandered too far away.

I got up from my couch and ran to the window. She was lying on the grass watching something there . . . some insect. I saw her stretch out a wary finger and touch something. It was probably an ant.

I went back to my couch; and then I remembered that I had run to the window. I had not run anywhere since that terrible night. I had walked only with the utmost difficulty.

It was a revelation. I found after that that I could walk about my room a little.

I knew that visiting us was embarrassing to Carlotta because she found it difficult to face me; so we saw little of her and that meant not seeing the child.

But I thought a great deal about her. I often thought of little things that used to happen when I was well and roaming about the countryside. My special love of plants and birds and animals had made that a delight for me. There were so many stories of living things that I had known and now I wanted to tell them to Clarissa.

Then I heard the news which shattered my family. Carlotta had been abducted and taken to France; Clarissa was with her.

There was terrible consternation. Harriet came over to see and tell us what she knew.

My mother told me afterwards because since I had been ill she told me things. I think she felt that had I not been in ignorance of what had happened I would not have gone into the forbidden wood that night but

315

would have come straight home, in which case I could probably have been nursed back to health.

What she told me was this: "Harriet says that Carlotta has been taken away by a man called Lord Hessenfield who is an important Jacobite. He was known to be in the neighbourhood. He made his escape to France. And has taken Clarissa with him. What is not generally known is that Lord Hessenfield is Clarissa's father."

Then Harriet told us how Carlotta had been captured by these Jacobites when she was at the Black Boar Inn on her way to Eyot Abbass and that Lord Hessenfield had raped her. The result was that she was pregnant and Benjie had married her to help, as Harriet said, "straighten matters out." Benjie had long been in love with her and eagerly grasped the opportunity to marry her. So Clarissa is the daughter of Hessenfield. He must have cared something for Carlotta to risk his life to take her back with him. That she had been taken by force was clear because her cloak came off in the struggle and was found in the shrubbery. It seemed likely that Clarissa had been taken before, because she was missing some hours before Carlotta was forced to go.

It all seemed wildly incredible. But Carlotta was born to be the centre of storm. Moreover, when I considered what had happened to my parents I wondered whether almost all of us did not at some time have to face unusual and stormy episodes in our lives. Even I had once had a frightening adventure with Good Mrs. Brown. For a long time after that I used to let my imagination run on as I pictured all sorts of horrible consequences which could have ensued. I had never really grown away from it and occasionally had a nightmare.

We have a tenant at Enderby Hall. It amazed me that anyone should take the place. It was so gloomy and had this reputation of being haunted. One or two people came to see it. My mother or my father and sometimes my grandmother from Eversleigh Court showed them over it. In fact people were more inclined to go to Eversleigh Court than to the Dower House.

I remember the day my grandmother came to tell us about this man who had come.

We were all sitting in my room because my mother always brought visitors to me. She had some notion that it cheered me.

My grandmother said: "I cannot think why he came to see it. He seemed determined to dislike everything even before he saw it and heaven knows it is easy enough to find fault with Enderby."

"I always think," said my mother, "that if one set out to change all that, one could."

"How, Priscilla dear?" asked my grandmother.

"Cut away some of the undergrowth, for one thing. It's terribly overgrown. Get a little light into the place. Bring in the sunshine. I visualise a happy man and his wife with a horde of children. It's light and laughter that place lacks."

"Dear Priscilla!" was all my grandmother said.

Of course, I thought, there had been a murder in it. Beaumont Granville was murdered there and lay buried nearby. Then there was the original ghost who had tried to hang herself from the minstrels' gallery.

"Tell us about this man," said my mother.

"He fitted the place, I will say that. He was lame, and of a morbid countenance. He looked as if it would really hurt him to smile. He was not by any means old. I said to him: 'And if you took the house would you live here alone?' He said he would, and I must have looked surprised for he added: 'I prefer it that way,' as though warning me to keep my thoughts to myself, which I certainly decided to do. He said the place was dark and gloomy. I said exactly what you have been saying, Priscilla. Cut things down and let the light in."

"What about the furniture?" said my mother, and I immediately thought of the bedroom and the four-poster bed with the red curtains.

"He said that it would suit him to have the place furnished."

"Well, that would solve a problem," said my mother.

"It will solve nothing. I think he just revelled in looking at the place for the purpose of showing us how unsalable it was."

"Well, it looks as though he succeeded."

"I think we should get rid of the furniture, clear it out . . . repair the place from top to bottom and then see what happens. In any case we need give no more thought to Jeremy Granthorn. We shall not be hearing from him again."

But there she was wrong.

The new owner of Enderby Hall was Jeremy Granthorn.

He did nothing to improve the reputation of Enderby Hall.

Abby, one of the maids whose duty it was to attend to my special needs and who had been given the task of doing this by my mother because not only was she a good worker but, as I had heard my mother say, a cheerful one, which I think meant that she was rather garrulous.

I did not talk much. I was always shut in with my own thoughts but Abby was one of those people who did not need a very attentive audience.

As she dusted and polished my room, and I lay idly watching or reading or sewing, she would give out a stream of conversation about what was going on. I would nod and murmur occasionally because I did not like to spoil the pleasure she took, although I was rarely very interested.

That was my trouble. Nothing nowadays was of any interest to me.

She chattered about the affairs of the neighbourhood and gradually I found that the name of Jeremy Granthorn was creeping more and more into her conversation.

"He's got a man there, mistress, his only servant. They say he don't like women." She giggled. "Funny sort of man I'd say, mistress. And this man . . . Smith 'is name is . . . is just like him. Emmy Camp was walking by one day and she thought she'd look round a bit. This Smith was in the garden . . . and Emmy asks him the way to Eversleigh village. As if she don't know. Born and bred there. Emmy says: 'Which path do I take?' And he points it out to her without a word, and she says, 'Are you dumb, sir?' And then he tells her to mind her tongue and not be insolent. Emmy says all she was doing was asking the way. Emmy says he didn't believe her. 'You've come prying,' he said. 'We don't like pryers here. Be careful. There's a big dog here and he don't like pryers either.' Emmy was all taken aback. She's got an eye for the men and they for her in the general way. Not this Smith, though. She reckons he's just like his master."

I said: "Emmy should not have pried. It's none of her business."

"Oh, no, mistress, but you know how it is. We all likes to know what's going on. . . ."

Another day she told me: "Nobody's ever been there. Biddy Lang says she reckons they're only ghosts themselves. Two men . . . in that big house . . . it don't seem natural, that's what Biddy says."

It was no concern of mine what happened to the house. I had promised myself that I would never go in it again.

Since Clarissa's visit I had walked a little. My mother was delighted. She said it was a sign I was getting better and in time I would be quite well.

I did not tell her that the only thing that had changed was that I could use my legs . . . but only a little. I was soon tired. And it was not so much the physical nature of my illness but the terrible lassitude, the listlessness, the not caring about anything which was the hardest to bear.

When my mother read to me I had little interest in what she was reading. I pretended to but it was a poor pretence. When my father played chess with me I played the game joylessly without excitement. Perhaps that was why I won more than he did; I was calm, dispassionate, unmoved by victory or defeat.

That was what was so hard to bear, this lack of interest in life.

But I did find that I was listening more to Abby. I rarely commented and never asked questions but when she mentioned the strange pair at Enderby I did feel a slight quickening of interest.

I had taken to riding a little. I never went far because

I became so tired. But when I went to the stables and Tomtit nuzzled against me and whinnied and showed so clearly how happy he was to see me I felt I would like to ride again. And how he tossed back his head and expressed delight in every quiver of his body when I mounted, so I thought I must ride now and then . . . because of Tomtit.

I had behaved so badly to him on that night. I had left him shivering in the outhouse while I had gone into the forbidden wood. I had forgotten him. That was the worst way to treat an animal.

He bore me no malice. When I first approached him, full of remorse wondering what reception I should get from him, he had shown me so clearly that he had forgotten my carelessness towards me. Malice? There was nothing of that. There was only that fond devotion and the bond between us was as strong as ever.

So I rode out now and then and I used to let Tomtit take me where he would. He never galloped; he rarely cantered; he would walk with me gently and when I was tired I'd bend forward and say to him: "Take me home, Tomtit." And he would turn from where we were going and we'd take the shortest cut home.

I think my parents would have been anxious if I had gone out with any other horse. They used to say: "She's safe with Tomtit. He'll look after her."

He was a wonderful horse, my dear friend Tomtit.

On that morning as usual I gave him his head and he led me to Enderby Hall, and when we reached there a desire came to me to visit Belle's grave.

I dismounted, which was an unusual procedure because I did not usually do that until I was back in the stables.

I tethered Tomtit to a stake and I whispered to him: "I won't forget you this time. I'll soon be back."

So I went into what I used to think of as the forbidden wood. How different it was now. The gloom had vanished. Over what must have been Belle's grave the roses bloomed in the summer.

It was my mother's private garden now.

Much of the undergrowth had been cut away. It was
320

beautiful—an oasis in the heart of the country. A garden of roses where once there had been gloom.

I stood for a moment thinking of Belle, whose curiosity had brought about her death; dear Belle, she had been beautiful and friendly and good. Her death would have been quick, though, and now I knew why it had happened I could not blame my father.

I turned away and started back to Tomtit, but the temptation to take one look at the house was too much for me. The wind had risen and was taking the last of the leaves off the trees. I liked the wind. It blew away the mists which were so prevalent at this time of the year.

There was the house—gloomier than ever. I thought of the misanthrope who lived in it now. It must be a house which suited his mood.

Then suddenly I was seeing it all again so vividly— Matt there with Carlotta. I felt a wave of pity for myself and I realized my eyes were wet. I took out a handkerchief to wipe my eyes. The wind caught it and carried it along the drive to the house. I ran to retrieve it, and, like a mischievous child playing tricks, just as I was about to pick it up the wind lifted it and carried it along the drive.

Thus I penetrated farther than I should and as at last I picked it up, I heard a growl and a dog came bounding toward me.

He was a large black Newfoundland and he was coming straight for me.

I was trespassing. I remembered, as one does on such occasions, that Abby had said something about a dog who did not like people who pried . . . and I might be suspected of that. But I knew dogs . . . all animals in fact. There was a special camaraderie between us which was recognised on both sides.

I murmured: "Good dog . . . good dog . . . I'm your friend. . . ."

He hesitated. He looked very fierce. Then he saw the handkerchief in my hand and it seemed as though he thought I might have stolen it for he caught and held it; and as he did so he nipped my hand.

There was blood on the handkerchief.

I did not let go of it. I stood there holding it while he held the other end in his teeth.

"We should be good friends," I murmured. "You're a good dog to protect your master's house."

I put out a hand to pat him.

A voice close by cried: "Don't touch him." Then: "Here, Daemon. Come here."

The dog dropped the handkerchief and immediately walked towards the man who appeared.

Smith? I thought. Then I saw that he walked with a limp and I realised that I was in the presence of Jeremy Granthorn himself.

He looked at me with distaste.

"He would have bitten you...severely," he said. "What are you doing here?"

"I was passing only and my handkerchief fluttered away in the wind. I was trying to get it."

"Well, you have it now."

"Yes, thank you."

I thought: What a disagreeable man. This was not how we behaved in the country. My mother would have called on him; he would have been invited to Eversleigh Court; but it was clear that he wished to be a hermit.

I said: "I am sorry to have intruded. But, you see, it was the wind. Good day."

He said: "The dog nipped your hand."

"It is nothing. My own fault, you will say, for coming where I shouldn't."

"It should be attended to at once."

"I have a horse here. I live a very short distance away. At the Dower House. I shall be home very soon."

"Nevertheless it should be attended to now."

"Where?"

He waved his hand toward the house.

This was too much to miss. I was being given the opportunity of entering the house, to which, according to Abby and my parents, no one had yet been invited.

"Thank you," I said.

It was a strange feeling to go into that Hall again.

I said: "You haven't changed it at all."

"Why should I?" he said.

"Most people like to imprint their own personalities on their houses."

"This is just a place where I can live in peace and quiet," he said.

"You certainly make sure of that. I feel I should not intrude."

He did not say that I was not intruding as I expected him to. He just said: "Come. Sit down."

So there I sat in that hall and I looked up to the haunted minstrels' gallery and I thought it more dreary than it had ever been.

I heard a noise above. "Smith," called Jeremy Granthorn. "Come here, Smith."

Smith came and stared at me incredulously. He was as grim as his master and a few years older.

"The young lady has been bitten."

"Trespassing," said Smith.

My less than gracious host said, "Get some hot water ... and a bandage or something."

"Bandage?" said Smith.

"Find something."

I rose. I said with hauteur: "I can see I am giving a great deal of trouble. It was only a nip. It was entirely my own fault, as you imply. I will go home. I shall then do what is necessary."

"Sit down please," said Jeremy Granthorn.

I obeyed.

I looked round the Hall and tried to make conversation. "My sister was the owner of this place. It was from her you bought it."

He did not answer.

"And are you liking the house ... the neighbourhood?"

"It's quiet ... peaceful ... almost always," he said.

A reproach for my inquisitiveness? Heaven knew I was only asking polite questions.

Smith returned with a bowl of hot water, a cloth and some sort of liniment. There was also a strip of linen which looked as though it had been torn from something.

I put my finger in the bowl. I washed it and he dabbed some of the lotion on the wound.

"This has been tested," he said. "It's good for sprains and light cuts."

He himself bandaged the wound and while he was doing so the dog came up and sniffed at my skirts.

"You haven't done much harm," I said to the dog. He put his head on one side and wagged his tail.

I could see that for the first time I had aroused the interest of my host.

"That's odd," he said. "He's quite friendly."

He realises that you accept me and that makes me acceptable to him."

"Good Daemon," he said in a voice very different from that with which he addressed me.

He patted the dog, who moved nearer.

I reached out a hand and patted it too.

I had clearly impressed Jeremy Granthorn.

"You like dogs. . . ."

"Dogs, all animals . . . and birds too. I am especially fond of birds."

"I have never known Daemon to make friends so quickly."

"I knew that we would be friends. After all it was only a token nip. Very slight . . . more like a caress."

He looked at me incredulously.

"He had to do it, didn't he?" I went on. "He had to show me that it was his duty to protect the place. I was trespassing. I couldn't explain that I had no wish whatever to call. I was only retrieving my property. But he knew that I meant no harm."

He was silent for a while.

"There," he said at length, "I think that will be all right. You'll have no trouble with it."

"Thank you." I rose.

He looked dubious. I think he was wondering whether he should offer me some refreshment. But I was going to let him see that I had no intention of intruding further on such an ungracious host.

"Good-bye," I extended my hand. He took it and bowed. Then I walked towards the door. He followed, the dog at his heels.

He stood at the door watching me.

I walked slowly and rather painfully to where Tomtit was tethered.

Strangely enough I felt different from the way I had since I had entered that house in the storm.

I felt a wild resentment against this hermit of a man whose manner bordered on rudeness. Certainly he had no social graces.

And yet I felt I had regained something which I had lost when I had come across Carlotta and Matt Pilkington in the red room.

I was very tired when I reached home. My mother was anxious. She was glad to see me ride out and take an interest in Tomtit but I know she fidgeted until I returned. She was afraid I would do too much and have a relapse. The next day I was too tired to got out; but the different feeling persisted. I was interested in the man and his manservant and the dog at Enderby Hall.

It was a week later when I saw him again.

I was riding past the house on my way home when I came upon him walking, the dog at his heels.

I was feeling very tired and I had just whispered "Take me home" to Tomtit and he had set his resolute steps in that direction.

I was about to ride past Jeremy Granthorn when he called, "Good day."

I pulled up.

I was so tired, I felt near fainting. Tomtit pawed the ground impatiently. I had said "Take me home" and he always knew by a certain note in my voice when I wanted to get there urgently.

"Are you feeling ill?" he asked.

I was about to speak but he had taken the reins from my hands.

"I think you should rest awhile," he said.

He led the horse towards the house. Tomtit seemed to sense that he was a friend, for gruff as Granthorn was towards his own kind I had recognised in him that great bond between himself and the animals because I had it myself.

He tethered Tomtit to the post by the mounting block

at the side of the house and lifted me down. I was surprised at his gentleness.

"I do not want to intrude," I said. "You hate intruders."

He did not answer but led me into the hall.

"Smith," he shouted. "Smith."

Smith came running.

"The lady is ill," he said. "I'm taking her into the parlour. Help me."

They were one on either side of me.

"Thanks," I said, "but I feel better now . . . I could go home."

"Not yet," said Jeremy Granthorn. "You must take something which will revive you. I have a special wine." He turned to Smith and whispered something. Smith nodded and disappeared.

I was seated in a chair in the small winter parlour, which I knew from the past. It was one of the pleasantest rooms at Enderby and seemed to have escaped some of the general gloom.

I said: "I should have been all right, you know. My horse would have taken me home. He does it when I'm tired."

"You are often . . . like that?" he asked.

"Now and then. But it's all right. If I'm with Tomtit. He knows. He takes me home."

"You should not be riding alone."

"I prefer it," I said.

Smith had come in with a tray and glasses. He poured out something from a bottle. It was a rich ruby colour.

"A very special wine," said Jeremy Granthorn. "I think you will like it. And I promise you it will revive you. It is noted for its beneficial qualities."

Smith went out and left us together.

I sipped the wine. He was right. It was reviving.

"I have been very ill," I told him. I explained the nature of my illness. "The doctors think I shall always be an invalid. It is only recently that I have taken to going out."

He listened intently.

"It is depressing to be incapacitated. I am myself to

a certain extent. I was wounded at Venloo. I shall never be able to walk properly again."

I told him that I had been taken ill during a storm and had spent the night out of doors in a state of unconsciousness and that this had brought about a fever which had affected my limbs.

He listened attentively and suddenly I laughed, for it had occurred to me that this morbid subject had given us a certain interest in each other which nothing else could have done.

He asked why I laughed. And I replied that I was suddenly struck with the thought that it was rather funny that illness could be such an absorbing subject.

"Of course it is, to those who suffer it. It is their life."

"There are other things in the lives of us all, surely?" I said.

I found that I could talk easily. Daemon came in and I was certain that he was pleased that I had become friendly with his master.

I asked how he managed here in this big house with one servant.

He replied that he did not use the whole house. Part of it was shut up.

The question trembled on my lips: Then why choose a house of this size? I did not ask it but he answered it all the same.

"There was something about this house which appealed to me."

"Enderby appealed to you! We always thought it was a gloomy, miserable place."

"I am gloomy and miserable—so it fitted my moods."

"Oh," I said suddenly, "please don't say that."

The wine or whatever it was was making me bold. I went on: "I have felt lost ... listless. ... Do you know what I mean?"

He nodded.

"When I found I could not move my limbs without pain ... when I knew that I must spend the greater part of the day on a couch ... I just felt there was nothing left. I was lying on a couch waiting for time to pass and that was all there was for me ... I still feel it often."

"I know," he said. "I know it well."

"And then little things happen...when Daemon nipped me...it was funny in a way. A little thing like that...it's out of routine, I suppose...and one starts being interested again."

"I know," he said, and there seemed to be a lifting of his voice.

He asked about the nip.

I held out my hand. "The stuff you put on it must have been very good. It healed very quickly."

"It was stuff I had in the army."

I wanted to know about him but I never asked questions. I always waited for him to tell. I think he appreciated that.

I was rapidly feeling better and when I rose to go he did not try to detain me, but he did insist on riding back to the Dower House with me.

I said he should meet my parents but he said no, he would go straight back.

I did not press him but I felt better than I had for a long time, and although I was too tired to ride the next day, I could lie on my couch and remember the details of our meeting.

It was the beginning of a friendship. I never called. I would ride by and he would often be walking and we would meet as if by accident. Then I would go in and sit with him and drink a glass of wine. He was knowledgeable about wines and produced several for me to try.

Daemon would come out when I rode by and bark joyously and that always brought either Jeremy Granthorn or Smith out to see who was there. When they learned who it was I would find myself being entertained in Enderby Hall.

My mother was interested when she knew. She was rather pleased.

"I must ask him to dine with us," she said.

"Oh, no, don't," I said quickly. "He never accepts invitations."

"He must be a very strange man."

"He is," I said. "A kind of recluse."

She did not try to prevent our friendship. She

thought it was good for me to meet people, and if this was a rather unconventional relationship, she accepted it.

So our friendship grew.

I told him quite a bit about myself. I mentioned my beautiful sister, Carlotta. I hinted that I had been in love with someone but that he had preferred Carlotta.

He did not ask questions. It was an unwritten code between us, so that I could talk of the past without having to face any probing which might have been distressing.

It was the same with him. I let him talk. He too had had a love affair. After he was wounded at Venloo and came back crippled he found she preferred someone else.

I could see there was a great deal left unsaid and that it had made him very bitter.

I think, too, that he suffered a certain amount of pain from his wounded leg.

There were some days when he was very miserable. I liked to see him on those days for I was sure I had a way of making him happier.

We talked of dogs we had had, and Daemon would sit at our feet watching us with limpid eyes, every now and then beating his tail on the floor to express his approval.

Jeremy—I called him that in my private thoughts, though I never addressed him by his name—looked forward to my visits, though he never asked me to come again. I wondered what would happen if I ceased calling. Ours was a strange relationship. Yet I knew that we were both profiting by it.

Little by little he volunteered bits of information about himself. He had travelled widely before the war. He had lived awhile in France. He knew that country well.

"I should like to go back," he said, "but of course I'm no use to anyone now. A crippled soldier . . . what could be more of an encumbrance?"

"At least you served well while you could."

"A soldier is a pretty useless creature when he is unable to serve in the army. England does not want him. What is he fit for? There is nothing for him but to go to the country...get out of sight, out of the way. He's an embarrassment because it has to be remembered he came to this state in the service of his country."

When those moods came on him I used to laugh at him and often I succeeded in making him laugh at himself.

Thus my friendship with the new owner of Enderby Hall began and progressed.

And one day a courier came to the house.

My parents were not at home and I was rather glad of this because the letter he brought was for me and it was the strangest letter I had ever received in my life. It was from France...from my sister Carlotta.

My fingers trembled as I held the paper. I read it through scarcely believing what I read.

Carlotta...dying. Clarissa...needing me.

"You must come. You must take my child."

I just lay there with the letter in my hand.

From far away I seemed to see Clarissa alone ...frightened...stretching out her arms to me.

Discovery in Paris

Some instinct made me hide the letter from my parents. They would have tried to send a secret messenger to France with instructions to bring the child to us. It was the only reasonable thing to do, but something told me that it might very easily fail. For one thing we were at war with France. There was no normal communication between the two countries. No one could land except secretly; only Jacobites were welcomed in France from England.

My parents would do what they thought best to bring Clarissa to England, but it might not be possible. My father, once a soldier in the army, would be suspect. A man of his kind riding through an enemy country would not get far.

I read the letter through again and again. Carlotta dying.... What could have happened? Lord Hessenfield was dead. It must be some sort of plague.

And Clarissa ... an orphan.... alone ... No, not entirely alone, there was a servant Jeanne, a one-time flower seller.

I was bewildered. I had to do something, but what?

I was white and strained. My mother noticed and scolded me for doing too much. I must rest, she kept saying.

So I pretended to rest, and all the time I was thinking of Carlotta's letter and Clarissa in France ... needing me.

It was in the middle of the night that the wild idea

331

came to me. I woke up in a state of great excitement. In fact I was trembling. I was sure at that moment that I could have got out of bed, ridden to the coast and crossed the sea to Paris.

I could feel strength flowing in to me so that when common sense said: *It is impossible,* I cried: "No, it is not impossible. I could do it."

I lay in bed waiting for morning, and I must admit that with the coming of daylight all sorts of truths raised their heads and common sense said: *It's madness. It's a dream—a fantasy of night.*

My idea was that I should go to France myself and bring Clarissa home.

It was as though voices mocked me—my own voices! *You . . . an invalid . . . who tires quickly . . . who has never been in the least adventurous . . . who has always taken the quite conventional path . . . plan such an adventure? It's incongruous. It's worse than that. It's madness.*

All the same I could not dismiss it.

It excited me, and what was so odd was that, almost like a miracle, I could feel new strength growing in me.

Before the morning was out I was not saying to myself: *It is impossible.* But: *How can I bring it about?*

A woman travelling through France would not attract much attention, would she? I could hire horses, grooms. Paris was a big city. It was easier in big cities to hide oneself than anywhere else.

I would go to the house in Paris. I had the address. What joy it would be to see the child again!

It was after I had been with her that I had first begun to improve. She had made me want to live again. That was it, and now that there was this tremendous project lying before me I was growing more and more alive with every minute.

But how . . . how . . . ?

I knew if I broached the subject to my father he would think he must act. My mother would be frantic with anxiety. "We must see what we can do to bring her home," she would say. And there would be lengthy deliberations and that would be too late. Something told me that I alone could bring Clarissa out of France.

All through the day and the following night the plan was with me. There were questions which kept coming into my mind. How? How?

The next morning I awoke fresh in spite of a restless night. I had made up my mind. There was one person who might just understand. He had a knowledge of France. I would put my plan to him. He would laugh it to scorn . . . at first. And yet if he would listen, I believed he would understand. And one thing I was certain of. If he could he would help me.

I rode over to see Jeremy Granthorn.

It was just as I had imagined. He was scornful.

"It's madness," he said. "You . . . go to France? Even if you were in full possession of your health it would be impossible. How will you start on this venture . . . tell me that?"

I said: "I will get someone to take me to France."

"How?"

"I will hire a boat."

"From whom?"

"That I must find out."

"Do you realise that there is a state of war between this country and France?"

"France is not a battlefield."

"I grant you that. But how do you think the English will be received in France?"

"I do not intend to be received. I shall make my way to Paris . . . and go to this address."

"You are talking like a child. What you suggest is wildly impossible. You betray absolute ignorance."

He was regarding me with a certain contempt.

I said: "I had thought you might give me some advice. You know France. You have lived there. . . ."

"I am giving you advice and it is: Leave this alone. Show the letter to your father. You should have done that as soon as you received it. What happened to the man who brought you the letter?"

"He went away."

"You should have detained him. You might have gone back with him. It would have been madness of

333

course, but I can see you are not using your common sense in this matter."

I said: "And I can see that you have no advice to offer me."

"I am offering you advice. Show your parents the letter. They will say the same as I do. There is nothing to be done but wait until the war is over. Then you can send for the child."

"How long do you think it will be before the war is over?"

He was silent.

"And," I went on, "you would advise me to leave the child. How do I know what is happening to her?"

"She had a father of standing, did she not? He will have friends."

"I can see you don't understand. This is so mysterious. It must be some plague or something. My sister, who was young and strong and should have had years left to her, wrote me this letter . . . the letter of a dying woman. She begs me to care for the child. You suggest I ignore that."

"I suggest that you wait, behave reasonably, consider all the difficulties."

"Nothing has ever been achieved by considering all the difficulties."

"Nothing was ever achieved by rushing madly over a precipice."

I stood up. I was quivering with rage.

I walked out of the house to where Tomtit was waiting. I felt wretched and I had relied on him more than I had realised.

As I was mounting he came out of the house.

"Wait a minute," he called. "Come back."

I said: "There is nothing more to be said."

"You are too hasty. Come back, I want to talk."

So I went back. A great relief had come over me. I looked at him; and I knew my eyes were bright with unshed tears.

He turned away as though embarrassed.

He took me into the parlour and we sat facing each other.

"It is possible," he said.

I clasped my hands in delight.

"It's mad and it's dangerous," he went on, "but it is just possible. Now please remain calm. How do you propose to get someone to take you over? That is the first hurdle."

"I don't know. Make enquiries.... There are people who have boats."

"My dear Damaris, one does not go round to people who own boats and ask to be taken into enemy territory. After the recent Jacobite scares, how do you imagine that would be regarded? It would have to be done in secret."

"Yes," I said breathlessly.

"I know a man. . . ."

"Oh, thank you ... thank you . . ."

"Mind you, I do not know whether he would agree.... He would have to be approached very cautiously."

"And you could approach him?"

He hesitated. "Perhaps."

I said: "It would be costly. I am ready to pay. I have lots of things of value. I could sell them."

"There would be delay."

I felt sick with disappointment.

He said: "You could pay me back later."

I was so happy. I couldn't help it. I leaned forward, took his hand and kissed it. It was a foolish thing to have done. He drew back at once frowning.

"Oh, I'm sorry," I said. "But it is good of you. Please ... go on. You see, I love this child and I imagine what could be happening to her."

"It's all right," he said gruffly. "I could see it is just possible. I could give you letters to friends of mine who would receive you in their houses as you cross France. Do you speak the language?"

"A little," I said.

"A little is not much good. You will be betrayed as English as soon as you set foot on the soil." He shrugged his shoulders.

I said: "I know you think it is madness. I daresay it is. But this is a child in need of me ... my own niece.

335

I love the child...but one would have to do the same for any child."

"You are running into danger, you know that."

"I realise it. But I *will* do it. I must find Clarissa. I must get to the house and take her from Jeanne."

"I will do what I can."

"Oh, thank you, thank you. I don't know how to thank you."

"Wait until you are safely back on English soil with the child before you do that. I tell you this: You are running your head into a noose."

"I am going to succeed, I promise you."

"If I can find someone to take you, if it can all be arranged, you must tell your parents what you are doing."

"They would do everything in their power to stop me."

"That is what I hope they will do."

"I thought you were helping me."

"The more I think of it the more crazy it seems. You are not fit for such travel. It will be hazardous and exhausting. You are tired out after a short ride on some days."

"I feel different. Can you understand that? I felt as I did...before this thing happened to me. I can stay in the saddle all day if I have to. I know it. It is different when you have a purpose, a determination...."

"It's a help," he said, "but it doesn't remove a sickness."

"I feel well again. I am going to do this, whether you help me or not."

"Then let me say this: If I can arrange it, you must leave an explanation for your parents. Leave the letter your sister wrote and tell them that I have arranged for you to go and am doing my utmost to make your journey safe."

"I will," I said. "I will." I stood before him. I felt a great inclination to hug him.

I called next morning. He was not at home, Smith told me.

Later in the afternoon I went again to Enderby Hall. He was back.

"I have arranged it," he said. "You are going tomorrow evening. At dusk you will leave England. Let us hope for a fair wind."

"Oh ... Jeremy ..." I cried, and I realised that I had used his name for the first time.

The old embarrassment was between us. I must remember not to be demonstrative, not to show my gratitude.

"Go back," he said. "Make your preparations. I have found someone to accompany you. Come here tomorrow, late afternoon. I will take you to the spot where the boat will be waiting. It is a small boat and even in calm weather crossing is dangerous. But once you are on French soil it should not be too difficult. You will be taken to the safest places on the way to Paris. And if you are discreet, you should come through. Do what your companion asks. And do not forget to write to your parents before you leave and explain. It is better for them to know what you are doing—even though your folly will cause them great anxiety—rather than that they should think you have just disappeared."

I promised to do exactly as he said and I was ready long before the time to depart.

I went to Enderby, where he was waiting. We discussed our plans and how I was to act. The man who would accompany me would bring me back. I could trust him.

We set out just before dusk and in due course reached the coast.

When we reached a lonely spot a man came riding after us.

I thought this was my companion for the journey.

It was Smith.

We tethered the horses to iron spikes and walked over the shingle.

There waiting was a boat with a man in it.

"Now," said Jeremy to Smith, "is all clear?"

"Yes, sir," answered Smith promptly.

"You know exactly what to do?"

"Yes, sir."

"Very well. Thank God for a calm sea. We should be off."

I stepped into the boat.

Jeremy was beside me.

I turned to say good-bye. "I shall bless you all my life," I said.

"Let us hope that I continue to enjoy those blessings for a very long time," he answered.

Smith was standing on the shingle.

Jeremy said: "Well, let us be off."

I looked at him wondering: "You . . ."

He said: "Smith will take the horses back. Of course I'm coming with you."

I felt a great singing in my heart, an excitement such as I had never known before.

I wanted to turn to him, to tell him what this meant to me.

I looked at his face, stern, taciturn, expressing nothing but his disapproval of my folly in wanting to attempt this desperate adventure.

I quickly realised that I could never have done it without him.

He spoke fluent French, and that forbidding manner of his, with the suggestion of good breeding which accompanied it, forbade questions.

Sometimes we spent the night at inns where he demanded comfortable accommodation for himself and his niece and servant, and invariably we got it. If there was only one room I had it, and he and the man he called Jacques would spend the night in the inn parlour. We had to make various stops because in spite of my determination and my renewed strength I could not travel too far—or at least he would not allow me to. If I wanted to go on he would remind me of my promise of obedience, and he was not the sort of man it was easy to disobey.

That journey did something for us both. He smiled now and then; as for myself I was amazed at what I could do. I did not tire half as easily as Jeremy insisted that I did. I did not need all the care he was giving me.

I could not understand myself. The listlessness had dropped from me. Every morning when I awoke I was aware of an excitement.

338

"How many miles to Paris?" I would ask.

And it was wonderful to know the distance was diminishing.

I began to wonder about myself. How ill had I been since I could make this recovery? Perhaps it had not really been that I was not well enough to go about meeting people and live a normal healthy life so much as that I did not want to.

And at last we saw the city of Paris in the distance.

I was overcome with exhilaration and impatience. The most exciting city in the world, I thought it. But that was because it contained Clarissa.

It was late afternoon when we arrived. I looked ahead to where the fading sunlight touched the turrets and spires. I saw the outline of the Palais de Justice and the belfreys, towers and gargoyles of Notre Dame.

We crossed a bridge and I felt the magical aura of the city embrace me.

I looked at Jeremy. A grim satisfaction showed on his face.

We had got so far. He had said many times that he was surprised how well we were going; and I told him that he was not really surprised at all. He knew as well as I did that if one was determined to succeed, one would; and we were going to bring Clarissa to England.

"We'll find an inn for the night and we'll go to the Marais district."

Jacques said: "It should be Les Paons, Monsieur. It is the best for us."

"Les Paons it shall be."

I said: "First let us go to the house."

"First to the inn," said Jeremy. "We cannot go to the house . . . travel-stained as we are. Look at the mud on your skirts. The horses are tired out. They hate this Paris mud. It's the worst mud in the world."

I wanted to protest even though I realised he was right.

"We *must* go to the house," I said.

Jacques shook his head.

"Better not to go out at night, Mademoiselle."

I felt desperately frustrated, but I knew they were right.

The inn was decorated with the peacocks from which it took its name. It was comfortable and a room was found for me which looked down on the street. I stood at the window for a moment, watching the people pass by. It was almost impossible to conceal my impatience, but I knew I must wait.

We must present ourselves at the house as decorously as possible tomorrow morning.

This time tomorrow, I promised myself, I shall have Clarissa.

What an age that seemed! I wondered how I should get through the night. I was here . . . in Paris . . . I was on the threshold of success. And I had to get through these hours of darkness somehow before the morning.

We took supper in the inn parlour but I was too excited to eat. Jeremy was calm and tried to steady me, but I could concentrate on nothing. I was just looking for the time to pass.

I could not sleep that night. I sat at my window and looked down on the street. It was strange how its character changed as darkness fell. The well-dressed people were replaced by those of a different kind. I realised that Jeremy had been right when he had said that we should wait till morning.

I saw the beggars waiting there holding out their hands piteously to those who passed by. I saw a woman get out of a carriage with a young girl and take the girl into a house. The woman came out alone and drove away. Something about this reminded me of my own adventures as a simpleton in London. I knew that the girl had been taken to the house on an assignation and that the woman in the carriage had arranged it.

The incident brought back vividly to my mind that time when I had gone out to buy violets for my mother and had fallen in with Good Mrs. Brown.

Then I noticed a woman standing outside the house into which the girl had gone. A man came out; he was well dressed. The woman caught at his arm. He threw her off.

I saw a great deal that night, for there was no sleep for me. I did lie down for an hour or so but as sleep was impossible I rose and sat at the window.

It was evidently a house of ill fame opposite.

Then I saw a terrible thing. A child ran out of the house suddenly. She was half naked—without shoes and stockings; she just wore a short spangled shift. She ran as though terrified and as she reached the street a woman came out, seized her kicking and struggling and bore her back.

I saw the woman's face briefly in the moonlight. It struck me as the most evil face I had ever seen.

I felt sick, for a terrible thought had come to me. Clarissa was in this city, this wicked city. I knew something of the wickedness of cities since I had come face to face with it in the cellar of Good Mrs. Brown.

I had been fortunate. Worse things could have happened to me.

I would take Clarissa home; I would care for her; I would love her.

I must get well and strong, for Clarissa needed me.

I would do it. I must. Clarissa needed me.

It was morning. I was dressed and ready. Excitement set the colour burning in my cheeks and none would guess I had had a sleepless night.

I was impatient for Jeremy to come. He was exactly on time but I could not keep still.

He smiled at me as we stepped into the street.

We came to the house where Carlotta had lived with Lord Hessenfield and Clarissa. It was a grand house— tall and imposing.

We walked up the steps to the front porch. The concierge appeared.

Jeremy said: "This is Lady Hessenfield's sister."

The concierge surveyed me. She said: "Lady Hessenfield is dead."

"Her daughter..." I began.

The next words terrified me.

"She is not here any more."

"Perhaps there is a servant...Jeanne."

"Madame Deligne would see you perhaps," said the concierge.

"Oh, yes, please," I cried fervently.

We were taken into a salon where the lady of the house received us.

Jeremy stated our reasons for being here and she answered in French, which I was able to follow.

Both Lord and Lady Hessenfield had died of some mysterious illness. It was a sort of plague, for a lady who had visited them, a Madame de Partière, had also died of the same disease. There had been quite a scare at the time.

Jeremy said: "Lady Hessenfield had a daughter and it is this child whom we have come for. We want to take her back to her family."

"Ah, yes," said Madame Deligne. "There had been a young child."

She wrinkled her brows. She had not heard what became of the child.

"What of Jeanne, the servant?"

"Monsieur, when we came here we brought our own servants."

"And what happened to those who were already here?"

Madame Deligne lifted her shoulders. "They went to other houses, perhaps. We could not take them, we had our own."

"Do you remember this Jeanne?"

Again she thought back. "A young woman...oh, yes...I remember her faintly. I think she went back to what she was doing before she came to the house."

"And what of the child? Did you hear about the child?"

"No, I never heard about the child."

Madame Deligne was friendly and apologetic, eager to help but it was clear that she had no more information to offer.

I shall never forget coming out of that house. Despair and misery enveloped me. We had come so far and not found her.

What should we do now?

Jeremy, who was a pessimist when we were getting on well, was now full of optimism.

"We have to find this Jeanne," he said. "That's all."

"Where...where...?"

"What do we know of her?"

"That she comes of a poor family and used to sell flowers."

"Then we must question every flower seller in Paris."

I was fearful; and yet Jeremy inspired me with hope.

"We must begin without delay," I said.

He took my hand and pressed it. It was the first sign of endearment I had ever had from him.

"We'll find her," he said.

The days that followed were like a nightmare. At the end of them I was completely exhausted and would sink on my bed and fall into a deep sleep until I was awakened by dreams of horror. In these I was always searching for Clarissa; I would be running through the streets and I would find myself in a cellar and people with dreadful leering faces would be closing in on me. Good Mrs. Brown was invariably there.

My dreams came from what I had seen during the days, for I did see terrible things. I suppose I could have found life like this in any big city; but I had had little experience of big cities. Only once had I fallen into the clutches of Good Mrs. Brown of London and I had never completely forgotten it. It was an incident which had remained in my mind to be brought out now and then, and because of what I saw in this city it had been brought right into the forefront of my mind. I imagined Clarissa with Good Mrs. Brown; I imagined her running out of a house in a spangled shift and caught and taken back ... to what?

These were the dreams which followed the frustrating, exhausting days, and in those dreams Clarissa and I were one and the same person.

What could we do? Even Jeremy had nothing to suggest. He had discovered people who had known the Hessenfields. Yes, they had died; the household had been broken up. No, they had no idea what had become of the child. The servants? Oh, they had dispersed ... as servants do.

We had one clue. Jeanne had been a flower seller. It was a business she would know. It seemed logical to

343

presume that she would go back to it. Therefore we must question the flower sellers of Paris.

What a task! We walked about the streets. It was spring now.

"A good time," said Jeremy in his new wave of optimism. "People buy flowers in the spring. They are so glad to see them, they remind them that the winter is over. There will be plenty of flower sellers about."

It was a frustrating task. We bought flowers and engaged the sellers in conversation. Did they know of someone called Jeanne, who used to be a servant in one of the big houses in the Marais?

Often we encountered blank stares; sometimes the flower seller would chatter volubly leading us on so that we thought we were on the trail. We even followed up one Jeanne who knew nothing of a child and was certainly not the sort of person with whom Carlotta would have left the child.

It was not only the fact that we found no success that depressed and frightened me. It was what I saw and the realisation of what could happen to someone alone in such a city.

I saw the beggars, the drunkards, the pickpockets; I saw little children scantily clad with a lifetime's misery written on their little faces. And in everyone I saw Clarissa.

We wandered through the markets; we saw barefooted children creeping between the stalls to snatch a bit of fruit; we saw them struggling with baskets as big as they were. We saw them beaten and abused; it broke my heart. Good Mrs. Brown seemed very close to me. It was as though she walked beside me chuckling at my naïveté. I was being rudely awakened now.

I wanted to run away from all this, to go back to my couch, to be petted and pampered and shut out the world.

Of course it is so easy, I thought, to shut out the world if you are surrounded by people who love you. You can forget all this; you pretend it does not exist. You can shut yourself into a little cocoon and never, never think of Good Mrs. Brown and two people writhing on a four-poster bed.

But you cannot forget. You must know of these things. Because the more you know the more readily you will understand the trials of others... and your own. Ignorance, shutting your eyes to evil, will not find Clarissa.

As the days passed my anxieties grew. I thought of what could be happening to my darling child in this wicked city.

Those days were like watching a show of pictures... as soon as one faded another took its place. There was the bustle, the laughter, the excitement of the streets—the patched and perfumed ladies, the exquisite gentlemen in their coaches... eyeing each other. I saw meetings arranged between languishing ladies and lanquid gentlemen; I saw the beggars, the market sellers and always those with the baskets of flowers.

It was the children who moved me most. I could not bear to look at them with their poor pinched faces already marked with shrewd cunning, already showing the signs of depravity. My impulse was to turn away to save myself the pain of looking. But how could I be sure that one of these was not Clarissa?

What really upset me were the women whom they called the Marcheuses. They were the poorest, saddest creatures I had ever seen. Jeremy told me that they had been prostitutes in their youth, and God knew they were not old now—in their twenties perhaps, though they looked fifty or sixty. They had become diseased and worn out in their profession and their only hope of earning a sou or two now was to run errands for their more wealthy kind. Hence their name, the Marcheuses. Worn out, weary, finished with life—keeping themselves alive until a merciful death came and took them.

I saw the milliners and sewing girls—young and innocent—coming out into the streets laughing and eyeing the apprentices... and looking out for a milord who would give them a good supper in return for services rendered.

I knew I would never be the same after this experience.

It had taught me a great deal about myself. It had

shown me that I had been hiding beneath my illness because I was afraid of what I would meet in the world.

If I were going to live, I must come out and face life. I must recognise the fact that there was evil in the world and it would still be there if I shut my eyes and refused to look at it. That was what I had seen in my frustrating rambling through the streets of Paris. But there were other things too. There was Clarissa to be found; there was the love of my parents; there was the goodness of Jeremy, who had given up his sheltered life to help me in my need.

We were two of a kind, for had he not come down to Enderby to hide from the world?

We were out in it now. We were living at last.

We had come in after an exhausting day. We had gone to our rooms. Jeremy had said: "We'll rest before supper."

It was seven days since we had arrived in Paris and it seemed to me in a moment of despair that we were no nearer the end of our quest than we had been when we began it.

I lay on the bed for a while but I could not sleep. Images of what I had seen during the day kept intruding on my mind. I saw the stalls in the great market...the women with their live chickens and their vegetables, the flower sellers who knew no Jeanne...the child stealing a purse from a fat woman who had come to market, being caught in the act and severely beaten. I could hear voices screeching out the merits of what they had to sell and the low but incessant chatter of two women who had sat on a low wall to set down their baskets and rest their feet awhile.

Sleep was impossible.

I got out of bed and went to the window.

It would be dark in half an hour. How tired I was. Jeremy had been right to say we should rest. He needed to rest, I know. His leg was painful at times.

I sat by the window watching the people. The street fascinated me. It had not yet changed its daytime face. That would come in half an hour. Now, respectable people walked by without fear. Dusk would fall and they would be no longer here...I looked at the house opposite. Now it was presenting its almost smug face to the world. I shuddered to think of what went on behind those windows. I had looked for the little girl in the shift but I had not seen her again.

Then as I watched a woman came hurrying along the street. She had black hair tied back and she was carrying a basket of violets.

Wild excitement filled me. It was almost like a command. A flower seller. Perhaps she would be the one. She was coming up towards the *hôtel* but on the other side of the street. She was walking hurriedly ... going home, I guessed, with her unsold flowers.

There was no time to lose. I must run if I was going to catch her before she disappeared.

I snatched up my cloak and ran out of the inn.

I caught a glimpse of her as she was turning the corner. I ran as fast as I could. She was halfway up the next street.

"Mademoiselle," I called. "Mademoiselle ..."

She turned and looked at me.

"Violettes," she cried, a smile illuminating her face. She held a bunch to me.

I shook my head. I said: "Jeanne ... Jeanne ... You are called Jeanne. *Vous appelez* Jeanne ..." I stumbled.

"Jeanne ... *moi*," she cried.

She repeated: "A little girl...."

"Clarissa ..."

She smiled. "Clarissa," she repeated.

I struggled to find the words I needed. My heart was beating so fiercely that I could not get my breath. It was due to the exertion of running and the fact that she was smiling and nodding, which might mean ... anything.

She started to walk away beckoning me.... I followed. She looked over her shoulders and quickened her pace.

I said: "I am looking for a little girl...."

"Oui, oui," she said. Then slowly and in laborious English: "A little girl."

"I must find her.... I must...."

She continued to smile and I followed.

We had come to narrow streets. It would be dark soon. A terrible fear came over me. What was I doing? How did I know who this woman was? So had I been lured by Good Mrs. Brown.

So many thoughts crowded into my head. You were lucky then. What could await you if you act foolishly again? I thought of the house opposite . . . of the little girl in the shift . . . of the painted women and the smug matrons who guarded them. And a terrible fear overcame me.

I should have waited for Jeremy. If I had, this woman would have passed on. Something had impelled me to follow her. The violets she carried had seemed symbolic. I had gone out to buy violets when I was met by Good Mrs. Brown.

Go back now. You could find her way. Tell the girl to come to the inn. She will if she is honest.

But suppose she does not, suppose she is Jeanne. Suppose I have not made myself clear. Suppose she could lead me to Clarissa.

And all the time I was going on.

We were in narrow alleyways now. But I could still run.

It was a battle with myself. I had time now. I could find my way back. I could get to the inn before darkness fell. And yet I went on. Because I kept seeing Clarissa. Clarissa like the little girl in the spangled shift. I must find her. I must. I must. I dare not leave any avenue unexplored. We have had days of failure. Can this be the end of the road?

The girl had smiled implying her name was Jeanne. She had nodded when I mentioned Clarissa's name. She had even repeated it.

Don't be a fool, of course she would. She is well versed in the art of villainy.

Go. Go while there is time. Talk to Jeremy. Tell him. Bring him with you.

But still I went on.

The girl had stopped. We were before one of the small houses all huddled together and almost touching the one opposite.

She pushed open a door and beckoned to me to follow.

I hesitated. I could come back here tomorrow with Jeremy. I should go now. It was unsafe to enter.

But I had to go on. "She is here," something inside me said. The girl has violets . . . and it was violets before. There is something significant in that.

I followed her down a flight of stairs.

I was right back to the days when I was a child in London . . . following in the wake of Good Mrs. Brown.

A door was pushed open. It was the scene all over again. I might have stepped back over the years. I thought, they are going to take my clothes and send me naked into the streets.

There was an old woman there. She said: "That you, Jeanne?"

I cried out: "The child. The child. Where is the child?"

Something moved on the floor. It looked like a bundle of old clothes.

Then I heard a voice cry: "Aunt Damaris."

And the bundle of rags was in my arms.

I knelt on the floor, holding her.

I had found Clarissa. And more . . . I had found myself.

Jeanne took us back to the inn and I was deliriously happy.

I shrieked for Jeremy. He stood there looking at us, his eyes shining. They went from the child to me and they lingered on me.

It was a wonderful moment.

Jeanne was talking volubly to Jeremy. She had been dismissed from the house; there was no work; she had gone back to flower selling. It was a poor living. She had kept the child because Lady Hessenfield had said: "My sister will certainly come for her."

"She was so sure, monsieur," said Jeanne, "that I believed her. How happy I am. It is no life for the child."

"We must do something for them. They are very poor. She must be compensated."

Jeremy told Jeanne that we were going to look after her and her mother.

We would find some means of doing so.

I had one or two pieces of jewelry which I gave her.

I said she could come to England with us and be Clarissa's nurse.

Her mother was ill, she said, and she could not leave her, but perhaps one day ...

One thing I was determined on was that Jeanne was going to be taken out of that squalid room.

It was necessary to clean Clarissa and provide her with clothes, which I did most joyously. And how happy she was to be with me. Jeanne had been kind to her and never allowed her to go selling flowers alone, though she had been out with Jeanne once or twice. She chattered about her beautiful mother and her wonderful father as though they were a god and goddess, and since they had not been quite of this earth she did not seem surprised that they had departed for celestial regions.

Oh, they were happy days with Clarissa! The love which had sprung up between us on our first meeting was growing stronger every day. We were necessary to each other—she to me no less than I to her.

The journey over to England could not be delayed. On the day before we left, Jeremy told me that he had found a place for Jeanne with one of his friends and she could take her mother with her.

I said: "That's wonderful. Life is good, is it not?"

"I am glad you find it so," he said.

I was bold enough to touch his hand.

"I shall never forget what I owe you," I told him.

He turned away.

Clarissa was delighted with everything that happened, though she was a little sad to leave Jeanne but I told her one day I intended Jeanne to come to England to be with us and that satisfied her.

She was full of questions as she had ever been, but her adventures had sobered her and brought her out of childhood in spite of her youth.

She asked why and how as often as ever but she asked thoughtfully now, and listened carefully to the answers.

How different it was going back! I was so joyous I sang a great deal to myself. Clarissa joined in when she knew the songs and so we rode along. She sat with me sometimes . . . sometimes with Jeremy. The journey was a great delight to her.

We reached the coast. Again we were lucky and blessed with a smooth sea.

I felt I had come a long way since I had set out on this journey, as though I had lived years in a few weeks. I no longer wished to shut myself away from life. I was going to face it whatever it brought. That moment when I had hesitated outside the house in the alley had taught me that. If I was going to be happy I had to grasp happiness with both hands and not be afraid to for fear I might be hurt. I would no longer lie on my couch sheltering under my invalidism. I was no longer an invalid. I was a woman who had made a dangerous journey and achieved the impossible.

What a thrilling moment when we stepped on English soil.

Clarissa was laughing as Jeremy carried her over the shingle. I stood beside them inhaling the fresh sea air . . . looking towards the land and my home.

Clarissa said: "Are you going to be my mother now?"

My voice was choked with emotion as I said: "Yes, Clarissa, I'm going to be your mother."

Then she looked up at Jeremy. "You are going to be my father?" She took his hand and held it against her cheek.

He stood there without response and she looked at him.

"Are you? Are you?"

A moment's silence, with the gulls swooping over the water, screeching their mocking cries.

"Are you?" repeated Clarissa impatiently.

He said slowly: "It will depend on what Damaris says."

"Then," said Clarissa triumphantly, "it's all right. I know."

He put out his arms suddenly and held us. The three of us stood there.

Clarissa broke the silence. "It's nice coming home," she said.

NEW FROM FAWCETT CREST